Praise for the novels of Lee Tobin McClain

"Lee Tobin McClain dazzles with unforgettable characters, fabulous small-town settings and a big dose of heart. Her complex and satisfying stories never disappoint."
    —Susan Mallery, *New York Times* bestselling author

"Fans of Debbie Macomber will appreciate this start to a new series by McClain that blends sweet, small-town romance with such serious issues as domestic abuse.... Readers craving a feel-good romance with a bit of suspense will be satisfied."
    —*Booklist* on *Low Country Hero*

"[An] enthralling tale of learning to trust.... This enjoyable contemporary romance will appeal to readers looking for twinges of suspense before happily ever after."
    —*Publishers Weekly* on *Low Country Hero*

"*Low Country Hero* has everything I look for in a book— it's emotional, tender, and an all-around wonderful story."
    —RaeAnne Thayne, *New York Times* bestselling author

Also by Lee Tobin McClain

The Off Season

Cottage at the Beach
Reunion at the Shore
Christmas on the Coast

Safe Haven

Low Country Hero
Low Country Dreams
Low Country Christmas

For additional books by Lee Tobin McClain,
visit her website, www.leetobinmcclain.com.

LEE TOBIN McCLAIN

home
to the
harbor

HQN

HQN®

Recycling programs
for this product may
not exist in your area.

ISBN-13: 978-1-335-91159-9

Home to the Harbor
Copyright © 2021 by Lee Tobin McClain

Second Chance on the Chesapeake
Copyright © 2021 by Lee Tobin McClain

This edition published by arrangement with Harlequin Books S.A.

For questions and comments about the quality of this book,
please contact us at CustomerService@Harlequin.com.

HQN
22 Adelaide St. West, 40th Floor
Toronto, Ontario M5H 4E3, Canada
www.Harlequin.com

Printed in Lithuania

MIX
Paper from
responsible sources
FSC® C021394

CONTENTS

To my readers

HOME TO THE HARBOR

CHAPTER ONE

"THAT'S A WRAP on oyster season." Bisky Castleman tied her skiff to the dock, fingers numb in the March morning chill, then turned toward the wooden shed that connected the dock to the land. She hung up her coverall on the outside hook, tossed her gloves in the bin and sat down on the bench to tug off her boots. "You coming?" she asked her sixteen-year-old daughter, Sunny.

"I'm coming, I'm just dragging." Sunny hung her coverall beside Bisky's and then flopped down on the bench beside her, letting her head sink into her hands. "*Some* kids get to chill out during teacher work days."

"I appreciate your coming out dredging and culling when most of your friends were sleeping in." Bisky slung an arm around her daughter and tugged her close for a quick side-hug. "Come on, I'll make pancakes and then you can take a nap."

Sunny frowned. "No pancakes, thanks."

"You sure? You've been working hard. Too hard." Bisky paused, thought about it. "Maybe I'll see if we can hire some of the teenagers from around here to work the traps with us, come crab season. Heard Tanner Dylan dropped out of school."

"He's not going to want to work with us, Mom." Sunny's face flushed a deep red. "Please don't ask him."

If Tanner was one of the boys who'd been teasing Sunny about her height and size, Bisky would tan him herself. She lifted her hands. "I said maybe. We need to find some help. If you have better ideas, tell me, because I'm not keeping you out of school."

She paused to look out over the Chesapeake Bay and a feeling of peace settled over her heart. The bay was the love of her life. Which was fortunate, since no man had ever stuck around long enough to fit that bill. Not that she minded. Bisky was too independent, she'd been told, but it had always served her well.

Usually. Not always.

She shook off a stab of melancholy. Now that they were done oystering, the second half of March would give them a rare break. Mostly, they'd spend the next couple of weeks scraping down and repainting the hull of their boat and trading out the dredging rig for the simpler setup they'd use for crabbing season.

It was increasingly hard to find a crew to work the water, and Bisky worried about her family business. Worried about a lot of things.

At the outdoor sink, she and Sunny washed their hands, and then they both pulled their hair out of ponytails, shook it out. Bisky ran a hand over Sunny's brunette strands, removing a piece of oyster shell. "Don't worry, I won't ask Tanner if it embarrasses you. But if you think of anybody else who needs a job, send 'em my way."

If she could help out a needy teen in the process of hiring, she would. The community of Pleasant Shores had taken care of her and helped her out since she was a kid, and she tried to pay it forward.

"I'd know you as mother and daughter if I'd never met the pair of you before." The voice behind them came from Mary Rhoades, the energetic seventy-year-old philanthropist and bookstore owner who was one of Bisky's closest friends. She approached with her dog, Coco, a young chocolate-colored goldendoodle who was as tall as Mary's waist, but lanky. Coco let out a bark, but remained at Mary's side. Clearly, her training was coming along.

"Hey, Mary." Sunny turned and smiled at the older woman. "No, don't hug me, I need a shower. And Mom needs one too," she added, wrinkling her nose at Bisky. Then she knelt down to pet Coco. The big dog promptly rolled on to her back, offering her belly for Sunny to rub.

Bisky pulled a plastic lawn chair forward for Mary and then flopped back down on the bench. "Have a seat. I'm too tired to stand up talking."

"I will, just for a few minutes," Mary said. "I'm supposed to meet the new Victory Cottage resident this morning. Hoping he'll take on the therapy dog program. If not, I'll have to advertise for someone." As one of Pleasant Shores' major benefactors, Mary had started many useful programs in town, including her latest, a respite cottage for victims of violent crimes and their families. Victory Cottage was a place for them to heal, volunteer in the community and find new hope.

"Don't advertise for someone," Sunny said with more energy than she'd shown all day. "I can do it. I can start the therapy dog program."

Mary raised her eyebrows, frowned and then patted Sunny's hand. "You're good with dogs, for sure. Just look how Coco loves you. But I need an adult for this."

"But—"

Mary cut off Sunny's protest. "There are legal requirements and regulations. And anyway, you need to be a kid, not take on more work."

"She's never had the chance to be a kid," Bisky said, sighing. "And it's my fault." Money had always been tight, and Bisky had the business to look after. Sunny had started early with cooking, cleaning, doing laundry and serving as Bisky's assistant on the boat. No wonder she was strong and assertive, just like Bisky was.

"It's not like you have people pounding down your door to work in Pleasant Shores," Sunny argued now.

"I have connections, if the Victory Cottage resident doesn't work out," Mary said.

"When he doesn't, and you can't get an adult to take the job, you know where to find me," Sunny said, just on the edge of disrespect. She gave Mary's dog a final ear rub and then headed across the street and toward the house.

"Sorry she's sassy," Bisky said. "Getting up at the crack of dawn puts her in a mood."

"*Aaanddd* the apple doesn't fall far from the tree," Mary observed, watching Sunny depart. "She got her sassiness from you, and it's a useful trait in a woman."

"It can be. I'm glad she's not afraid of her shadow like some kids."

Mary nodded. "You've raised her well. No doubt she *could* start a therapy dog program. She could probably run the high school or Salty's Seafood Company if she wanted to."

"You're right, she could." Bisky watched Sunny walk toward the house, holding her phone to her ear as she jabbered with one of her friends, and a wave of mother-love nearly overwhelmed her. "Raising her is the best thing I ever did."

"Of course it is." Mary's voice was a little pensive, and it made Bisky remember that Mary had had a daughter and lost her.

"So tell me about this new guy who's coming to Victory Cottage," Bisky said, trying to change the subject.

Mary ran a hand over Coco's furry head, and the dog sat down, leaning against Mary. "He's from here, actually. And he has a sad story, but that's his to tell." She frowned. "I just hope that the support system we've put into place will work. He's set up with counseling, and the cottage is a dream, but I'm still unsure about what volunteer gig he'll be best suited for." Volunteering was an integral part of the Victory Cottage program, just as it was in Mary's other program, the Healing Heroes project.

At the dock beside them, an old skiff putted in, and eighty-year-old Rooker Smits gave a nod as he threw a rope to his five-year-old great-grandson, who'd been waiting to tie up the boat. Rooker waved to the boy's mom, who was dressed in a waitress uniform, obviously headed for work now that Rooker was back to help with childcare.

Like many watermen from these parts, Rooker didn't talk much, but he'd give the coat off his back to her or Sunny or any neighbor. Now, he and his great-grandson tossed scraps from the oysters he'd culled into the bay. Gulls swooped and cawed around them, drawn by the remnants of a day's fishing.

The smell of brackish water and fish mingled with that of the newly fertile March soil. Spring was coming, Bisky's favorite season. Maybe she'd plant some flowers later today, if she could find the energy to get to the hardware store for seeds.

She stretched and yawned. "Boy, that change to daylight savings is a tough one," she said. "I'm like Sunny, probably going to need a nap today."

"You work too hard," Mary said. "And speaking of work, I should be on my way. Lots to do." She stood and hugged Bisky against her protests—Sunny had been right, Bisky needed a shower—and then she and Coco walked off toward town.

Bisky stood and stretched her back. At thirty-seven, she was starting to feel the aches and pains of a lifetime's physical work. She loved what she did, loved the water, but it took its toll.

She spent a few minutes wiping down her rig, did the minimum she could get away with and then called it a job done. Not well-done, but done. As she crossed the road, heading for her house, she glanced in the direction Mary had gone.

A tall figure walked slowly down the middle of the road. So tall and broad-shouldered that she had to look twice at him, because it wasn't anyone from around here.

Or rather...

She stared, then took an involuntary step toward the man, unable to believe what she was seeing. It looked like her beloved childhood friend William Gross, only that wasn't possible. After the sudden way he'd left, so many years ago, she'd never expected him to come back to Pleasant Shores.

As WILLIAM WALKED the familiar and yet strange road toward the home he'd successfully escaped almost twenty years ago, he heard a man's shout. "Look out, boy! I told you not to play by those..."

William cringed, an instant flashback to his childhood here: his father's yelling and the likely painful aftermath. He snapped back to the present and turned in time to see a huge pile of crab traps teetering near a boy of five or six, who was poking at a small crayfish on the dock. The child didn't even glance up.

William bolted toward the child and swept him up just as the big wire boxes crashed to the ground.

A couple of the traps bounced against William's back, and he tightened his hands on the boy's waist, holding him high and safe. As the clatter died away, William blinked, studied the startled-looking boy to ensure he wasn't injured, and then deposited the child in front of the old man who'd shouted. "Is he yours?"

"He's my great-grandson, and he's not to be playin' around this close to the docks or the water. And that's why." He gestured at the cluttered heap of crab traps. "Come on, boy, you can help me clean up the mess you made."

Fair enough. William was just glad the kid wasn't going to get a beating. "Need any help?"

The old man looked at him. "No, the boy needs to learn. Sure do appreciate your pulling him out of harm's way." He cocked his head, studying William. "You look like a kid used to live here, name of Gross."

William held out a hand. "That's me, William Gross." He tilted his head to one side. "And you're…Mr. Smits?"

"Guess you're old enough to call me Rooker." The old man shook hands and studied William, curiosity in his sharp blue eyes. "Been a while." He limped over to the cluttered traps, ushering the boy in front of him.

"You sure I can't help you straighten out these traps?"

"We got it. Get to work, boy," he told his great-grandson, and then turned back to William. "Heard you're living in the city."

"Uh-huh," William said. "Nice talking to you." He wove his way through the fallen crab traps before the man could ask any more questions.

When he got back to the street, he stood a minute, processing what had just happened. Three college degrees and twenty years had changed him a lot, but the local people would still think of him as the big, gawky kid from a bad family. He'd have to figure out how to deal with that.

The sun was at its peak now, casting a surprisingly warm light that made William slide out of his sports jacket and sling it over his shoulder. He shouldn't wear a sports jacket, anyway. He felt pretentious, dressed up, here on the docks.

He wasn't even sure why he'd come, except that the

docks were like a magnet, even though the memories they evoked were anything but pleasant.

"William?" came a soft voice behind him. A voice that brought him back to laughter on sparkling water, and catching crayfish, and good meals around the table of a family that actually liked each other.

He turned and studied the tall brunette who stood before him. She wore work clothes, and she was older than the last time he'd seen her, but he'd never forget the eyes and the smile of his childhood best friend. "Bisky Castleman?"

"It *is* you!" She flung herself at him and hugged him fiercely.

She was tall for a woman, and more muscular than she'd been in school. Still, she was the first woman he'd held in two years and the hug felt good. Having a friend felt good, and was something he needed to try to cultivate, now that he'd sworn off love.

They let each other go, finally, and stepped back.

"Where have you been, and what are you doing back?" Bisky asked. "I heard you were teaching in a college."

"I was." The casual way she asked the question told him she didn't know what had happened. "Life's dealt a few blows, and I'm here for an R&R break." He tried to keep the words light.

She didn't buy it. "Come over here and sit down," she said, taking his hand and drawing him toward the same old fishing shack her family had always had. There was the same bench outside it, a little more weathered than he remembered. "Tell me what's going on, because I know it would take a lot to bring you back to Pleasant Shores."

"I appreciated your note when Mama died," he said instead of starting up the story of where he'd been and what all he'd been doing, what had transpired.

"I'm glad my note found you. No one seemed to have a recent address."

"I've lost touch." He looked out over the bay, watched a pelican dip, snag a fish and carry it away.

"Heard you had a daughter. Couple of years older than my Sunny, so she must be, what, eighteen?"

She definitely didn't know. He glanced at her and then shook his head. "Not anymore," he said through a tight throat.

It had been two years, and he still couldn't talk about it. Still hadn't really processed it, and that was why his department head at the college had teamed up with someone from HR to find this program for him. It was his last chance to heal before he'd lose his job that he'd gotten worse and worse at.

He'd agreed to do the program despite its location, because Mama was gone and his father had moved away. He wanted to heal for the sake of his students, who'd come to be his whole world.

But those of his students who'd gotten too close had seen the ugly, damaged side of him, had scraped his emotions raw. He couldn't let that happen again. Couldn't let anyone get too close.

He had to make sure that these people who'd known him in younger days didn't worm their way into his heart.

"What happened to her?" Bisky asked quietly.

He'd dodged that question a million times, but for some reason, he couldn't dodge it when it came from Bisky. He cleared his throat, hard. "She was shot by an intruder who broke in to steal a TV. She was taking a nap and surprised him, from what the police could figure out."

Bisky's face contorted with horror she didn't try to hide. "You poor, poor man," she said, tears in her voice and eyes.

"Don't feel for me, feel for her." He didn't deserve the sympathy of Bisky or anyone.

She ignored that. "As a mother, I can only imagine…oh, William." She leaned close and hugged him again.

Maybe it was because of the familiar, salty smell of her, or the fact that she knew him from childhood, but something broke off inside William then, a tiny piece of his grief. His throat ached and tears rose to his eyes, even though he tensed all his muscles trying to hold them back.

"You can cry in front of me," she said, patting his back as if *he* were the child. "It wouldn't be the first time."

She was right about that. He remembered, then, the rabbit he'd kept as a pet, what his father had done to it, and how he'd beaten William for crying. William must have been seven or eight, and he'd run to his best friend for comfort. She'd hugged him and cried with him then, just like now.

He pulled out his bandana, wiped his eyes and blew his nose. Then he smiled at her, a real if watery smile. "Thanks. I guess I needed that," he said.

"You're here for the Victory Cottage program." It wasn't a question.

He nodded. "The woman who runs it wanted to seek out people who had a connection with this place. I'm the perfect candidate according to her." He quirked his mouth to show Bisky he didn't think he was perfect at anything.

"You are," she said thoughtfully. "There are plenty of people who'll be glad to see you."

"That I doubt," he said. "My family wasn't the most popular."

"No, but most folks knew you were cut from a different cloth. Come inside." She gestured toward the house across the road, where her family had always lived. "I'll make pancakes and coffee. Sunny could use a meal, and I could, too."

The thought of sitting around the table with Bisky and

her daughter—her alive and healthy daughter—tightened a vise around William's insides. "Thanks for the invitation," he said, "but I won't be able to. I need to get going." He ignored the puzzlement in Bisky's eyes as he turned and strode away.

He couldn't let himself get that close, feel that much.

CHAPTER TWO

SUNNY WALKED THROUGH the small downtown of Pleasant Shores and turned onto the road that led to Victory Cottage. She was thinking hard about her plan when she heard a shrill voice behind her.

She turned and pasted a smile on her face. "Hey, Mindy! Hey, guys."

Mindy Ford and her cronies sauntered up behind her. "I love your shirt!" Mindy said. "Where are you headed?"

Sunny looked down at the heavy fisherman's sweater she'd worn against the cold wind. Mindy didn't love it. She was a big fake, and no way was Sunny letting Mindy and her friends know her business. "Home," she said, glad she had a little shopping bag from the hardware store. "Errand for my mom."

"Sucks to do errands on your day off," Mindy said, and Sunny couldn't tell if she was being sympathetic or making fun of the fact that, unlike her, Sunny didn't have a house-keeper to take care of most of the errands.

"What are you guys doing here?" Sunny let her eyes skim over the other two girls, Veronica and Sam, and then refocused on Mindy. The other two would do whatever Mindy said, say whatever she wanted to hear.

"We're stalking," Mindy said in a low, conspiratorial voice. "I have the hots for Caden Reese, and someone said he's been hanging around this end of town."

"Why here?" Sunny knew Caden, vaguely. He was from

Mindy's neighborhood and would have no reason to be among the more modest dwellings here.

Mindy shrugged and lost interest. "If you see him, message me," she said airily.

"Sure," Sunny agreed, although she had no intention of making that kind of a connection with Mindy.

The trio headed on down the street toward Sunset Lane and the school, and Sunny kept up a slow pace until they'd gotten out of sight.

The air was chilly, the day dark and cloudy. But crocuses and daffodils poked out of the ground, promising that spring would come after all.

She looked toward Victory Cottage. Mom had said an old friend of hers was living there, which made Sunny mildly curious. Mom didn't have guy friends. She worked with men all the time, but for socializing, she'd started hanging out with a group of women from town, one of them the mom of Sunny's best friend, Kaitlyn.

Sunny breathed in the loamy, salty spring air and passed Victory Cottage. She had her sights set on the little blue house next to it, the place Mary had tagged for starting the therapy dog program.

Sunny wanted to scout the place, get it organized. Then she'd make a written plan for how to use it for the dogs. She'd overheard Mary saying she hadn't decided how to use the house: as somewhere for the dog trainer to live, or just as a central location for the therapy dog training sessions.

If she made good enough suggestions to Mary, maybe Mary would see that she was just as capable as any adult of setting up the therapy dog program. Better, because she knew the lay of the land here.

She wanted it more than anything. For one thing, working with therapy dogs might mean Mom would finally allow her to bring one home. But mostly, she just wanted to have *something.* Something for herself, because she wasn't fitting in as well with her friends these days. They were all focused on boys, even her best friend, Kaitlyn, and Sunny wasn't all that interested in boys.

Or rather, they weren't interested in her, the biggest, tallest girl in tenth grade and a dock kid to boot.

She approached the low-slung Blue House—that was what everyone on the street called it, since it was painted a bright, blueberry blue—and took a stroll around. The paint was fresh, and the flower beds in front were weed free, but a broken screen sagged down from one window. Mary had done some work on the place right after she'd bought it, but Sunny wasn't sure how far she'd gotten with it.

There was a fenced backyard from which you could see part of the Victory Cottage backyard, and beyond that, the Chesapeake. It was almost like the Blue House was part of the same property.

She tried the back door. Sometimes people left their doors unlocked in Pleasant Shores. But this house was empty so sure enough, it was locked.

She walked around to the front, glanced up and down the street to make sure no one was watching. At this late-afternoon time of day, the street was quiet. She tried the front door, but it was locked, too.

She stood, thinking. She should really talk to Mary about getting a key. Except she wanted to get started on her plan now, today.

She strolled back around the side of the house, studying the windows, and a memory came to her. Once, when they'd accidentally locked themselves out, Mom had boosted her up to an unlocked window so she could climb in and unlock the front door.

Could she break into the Blue House?

That one sagging screen would be an easy opening. She

was tall enough to reach it, and she was pretty sure she could fit through the window.

She reached up, pulled down enough of the screen to grab the window frame, and pushed at the window. Sure enough, that opened easily.

Now for some gymnastics. The window was chest high, but her legs were strong from a season's oystering. She jumped up and sort of dove into the open window. The first time, she fell back down onto the ground, whacking her leg.

The second time, she made it. Poised on her belly on the window sash—ouch!—she started wiggling and finally got in far enough to swing around and put her feet on the floor.

And then her heart gave a great thump. She was looking down the barrel of a gun.

She drew in a breath that was a half scream and scooted back, feeling for the window sash behind her.

"Don't move."

It was a kid's voice, not an adult's, and a familiar one at that. She peered through the dimness. "Caden Reese?"

"What are you doing here?" he asked.

"What are *you* doing here?" Her tense muscles relaxed, because she was pretty confident Caden wouldn't shoot a classmate. She crossed her arms over her chest. "Could you put that thing down? It's making me nervous."

He lowered the weapon and kept it at his side. "How'd you find out I was here?"

"I didn't! What are you doing, anyway, trying to set up a party spot? Because it's not going to work." She started walking around the room she'd landed in—looked like a little dining room—and then peeked into the kitchen. "Do the lights work in here?" she asked as she found the switch and flipped it, throwing brightness into the shadowy room.

"Turn that off." He flipped the light switch, but not before she took in the plate and silverware propped and drying beside the sink. Interesting.

She walked past him into the living room. There, she raised the shade a little to see what was what.

"Would you stop?" He yanked the shade down.

She found a lamp and flicked it on. There was a blanket half off the couch and a duffel bag beside it. "You're living here?"

"Not your business," he said.

"It *is* my business," she said, "because this place is gonna be used for a program I'm involved with." Or at least, she hoped to be. "That's why there's furniture here. The owner, Mary Rhoades, is probably going to move someone in soon."

"No way," he growled.

She faced him then, hands on hips. "I can call the cops on you. What you're doing is squatting, and it's illegal." She frowned at the gun he was still holding. "Put that ridiculous thing away."

"It's a gun, not a ridiculous thing. It could kill you! Show some respect."

That made her smile a little. "Okay, okay, I respect your big gun. I'll respect it more if it's out of sight."

He rolled his eyes and stuffed it into the duffel. "Better?"

"Better." She studied him more closely. He was from the rich part of town, and wore the clothes to show it—expensive Orvis-type outdoor gear, same as the tourists wore—but his hair was growing out from his usual short, stylish cut, and beard stubble made his cheeks and chin look scruffy. "Seriously, are you planning a party? Because you don't own this place, and it's going to be used for something else."

"Who would use this place? It's not tourist season."

Sunny didn't want to go into it. "It's going to be used for

something related to Victory Cottage," she said, gesturing vaguely toward the window. "A guy just moved in there. He'll report you if you get too loud."

"I'm not getting loud, I'm just staying here." He looked away. "I need to not stay at home right now."

"Are you serious?" She knew kids whose home lives were rough, but not from the fancy homes. Of course, you never knew what went on in those places.

He crossed his arms and glared at her. "Are you gonna rat me out?"

Decision time. Sunny wanted to present her plan to Mary right away, before Mary found someone else to start the program. But there was something in Caden's eyes that told her he was in trouble. Sunny was a sucker for anyone— animal or human—who was in trouble. "I don't know," she said honestly. "Not right away, at least."

Sunny didn't like changing her plans once she'd figured them out, but if Caden was in trouble, she might have to make an exception.

THE EVENING OF the day William had come into town, Bisky lounged in a comfortable easy chair in the Lighthouse Lit bookstore. Mary had recently created a circle of chairs for a sitting area, and their little book group benefited from it.

Their discussion had ended, and the shop was closed, but Bisky, Mary, Amber, Ria and Kayla sat around talking and drinking wine. It was a late night for Bisky. She rarely stayed up past ten. Fortunately, though, oyster season was over and since crab season hadn't started, she wouldn't have to get up early tomorrow.

The little bookstore was a town landmark, its neat rows of books drawing in crowds during the tourist season and a decent number of customers year-round. Mary sponsored story times and book discussions and author visits, and her clientele was growing all the time.

Bisky had always liked to read, but until a couple of years ago, she'd never have pegged herself as a book club lady. But here she was, talking about a trendy historical novel with a bunch of bookish women. Amber was a writer, and Mary, of course, owned the bookstore. Kayla, who taught preschool, and Ria, who owned a local motel, both had college degrees.

They weren't snobbish, though; instead, they were often fascinated by Bisky's experiences working the water. Tonight, they'd discussed a book about Harriet Tubman, who had been enslaved in nearby Dorchester County and had led many people through the Eastern Shore's woods and swamps to freedom. They'd grilled Bisky about how someone might have been able to survive on the water without funds, what impact the currents and seasons would have, what a raw oyster tasted like straight from the water.

"We ought to do a road trip to the Tubman museum," Kayla was saying now. "I haven't been yet, and I hear it's wonderful." She waved off Mary's offer of more wine. "One glass is my limit, thanks."

"I'd love to go to the museum," Amber said promptly. "We could make it an overnight, even. There are some great restaurants in Cambridge, and a couple of cute bed-and-breakfasts."

"Count me in, too," Ria said, standing, "but for now, I need to get home."

"Don't want to keep that handsome husband of yours waiting," Amber teased, and Ria's cheeks flushed pink. She'd remarried her husband, the father of her teenaged daughters, early last year. That was how Bisky had gotten acquainted with these ladies, actually; Ria's daughter Kaitlyn was a good friend of Sunny's.

"I have to go, as well, not that there's any romance in my life," Kayla said. "I just have to get up early and face twenty adorable four-year-olds."

"You're such a great teacher." Amber stood and hugged Kayla. "Davey loves being in your class."

Mary saw Kayla and Ria out the door and then came back in and sat down.

"Speaking of romance," Amber said.

Bisky raised her eyebrows. "Were we?" she asked, and Mary laughed.

"We are now. Someone saw you with that new guy this morning."

"What?" For a minute, Bisky was confused, and then she remembered. "William's an old friend," she said. "In town for Victory Cottage."

"Oooohhhh." Amber nodded. "Hope it helps him."

"Me, too." She'd been thinking about William all day. How heartbreaking that he'd lost his daughter to violence. It had broken him, she could see that, and she wasn't surprised. Beneath his brawn, William was a softhearted guy.

And losing a child would break anyone. Just thinking of it sent a shiver through her body. She pulled out her phone and sent a text to Sunny:

Checking in. You okay?

When will you be home?

Half an hour max.

Good, want to read you my history paper.

Amber nudged Bisky. "So, this old friend," she said. "Is it an old boyfriend? Were there vibes between you?"

"With William?" Bisky tipped her head and frowned. "No way."

"Is it that ridiculous of a notion?" Mary asked gently.

Even the idea of getting together with William made Bisky uncomfortable. She rubbed the back of her neck. "For one thing, you know I don't do relationships."

"Not for longer than a week," Amber teased.

"Fair enough." Bisky had the occasional date when Sunny was away on a mission trip or at camp. "But that's different. William's a friend, and he *needs* a friend, more than anything."

"He certainly does, based on his application to the program," Mary chimed in.

And even if there *were* vibes between her and William—which there weren't—Bisky didn't want to ruin that friendship with an attempt at a relationship that wouldn't last, given how men always felt about her as a woman.

Oh, sometimes they found her a challenge: her size, her profession, her ability to throw around insults like a sailor. But it never took long for them to realize she was too much for them in every way.

And that was fine. Bisky did well on her own. Raising Sunny kept her busy.

"There could be potential." Amber nudged her again. "Don't let your past keep you from getting involved. At some point, it's your own fault if you're lonely."

"I'm not lonely! I have a job and a daughter and annoying friends like you."

"Your daughter is growing up," Amber pressed. "And your work and friends don't take up all your time, or keep you warm at night."

Amber's words hit uncomfortably close to home. "Just because *you* found your special someone and got a ready-made family, that doesn't mean every single woman wants love. Think about Harriet Tubman," she added, picking up her book and waving it at Amber. "She was a strong single woman, and look at all she accomplished."

"She had love in her life," Mary reminded them. "She was married twice, even if the first time didn't work out real well. Everyone needs a little love."

"I gotta get home. To my daughter, who's not nearly as nosy as the two of you." Bisky pulled on her coat and left, waving and smiling to let her friends know she wasn't really mad at them.

But they'd pushed her on something that she worried about herself: the fact that Sunny was growing up and that Bisky was a little bit lonely, with a loneliness friends didn't always fill.

She had a good life, though. She couldn't complain.

And the idea of her getting involved with William Gross was just patently ridiculous.

CHAPTER THREE

TWO DAYS AFTER his arrival in Pleasant Shores, William strolled the bike path that ran along the beach and the bay, his new acquaintance Paul Thompson at his side. Paul was a volunteer for the Victory Cottage program; apparently, he'd helped to set it up and was now student teaching at the local high school. He was an interesting guy, and William peppered him with questions about his career change from police work.

It was a breezy morning, cold enough that William had traded out his baseball hat for a woolen fisherman's one. "Thanks for making the time to get together," he said to Paul. "Sounds like you're pretty busy." He needed to show the people in the Victory Cottage program that he appreciated their efforts.

"Glad to do it," Paul said, and they both looked out over the bay for a few more minutes as they walked, the blue-gray water choppy, the seabirds seeming to be blown around on the wind. "So tell me," Paul asked, "what's your goal for your time in the Victory Cottage program?"

"Get back to work," William said promptly. Which meant he needed to regain his equilibrium and his mental health. "I teach developmental math at a community college in Baltimore. Head up the Student Success program, from the faculty end." He paused, then added, "I'm on a leave, but I'm hoping to go back."

Paul nodded. "I'm sure the counselor Mary has in place

will be able to help with that, whatever you need." He'd made it clear that he wasn't a counselor himself; he was just assigned to help William get the lay of the land. "Pleasant Shores is a good place to heal."

William made a noncommittal grunt. He could see that, these days, Pleasant Shores could seem like a vacation spot. It wasn't exactly resort-like, especially during the off-season, but the bay views and the quaint buildings and boats and friendly people gave the place a lot of appeal.

At least, to someone who didn't have William's kind of history here.

"There's the hardware store," Paul said, gesturing toward a building across Beach Street.

"I'm familiar," William said. When Paul looked curious, he added, "I grew up in Pleasant Shores."

"Is that why you chose Victory Cottage?"

William shook his head. "Programs to help people like me are rare. My department head had a connection with Mary Rhoades, and when they..." He didn't want to say it, but he forced himself. "When they suggested a leave, this was strongly advised. I almost didn't come when I found out where it was located, but I knew I needed something." Only because continuing along the same path would have cost him the only remaining good thing in his life—his job.

"You didn't want to come back to your hometown?"

"Long story," William said. Paul seemed like a good guy, but William didn't want to get into the gory details of his childhood with a stranger.

They walked across the street, a pickup pulling lawn-care equipment and an SUV with a couple of car seats both stopping to let them cross.

Inside the hardware store, the smells took William back so hard that he had to stop.

Fertilizer, paint thinner, wood dust and more: the array

of goods provided here made it unlike any other store William had been inside since. The emotions it evoked weren't bad, but he felt like he'd shrunk to half his size and was coming in unsure of his welcome, as he'd been at age ten.

Paul must have mistaken his pause for confusion. "Home supplies are along the wall," he said, gesturing. "You can find those nails you were looking for over that way, aisle six or seven. And Mary wanted us to get a spare key made."

William nodded, still taking in the crammed shelves, the various aisles holding everything from auto supplies to pots and pans, from work clothes to candy. It had been the main place to shop in Pleasant Shores twenty years ago. "Glad this place hasn't been replaced by a big-box store," he said.

"It would take three or four of them to carry the variety that we have," said a voice behind him. A voice that sounded familiar, and he turned, amazed.

Mrs. Decker, the owner, had been old when he'd been a teenager.

She stood there now, grayer-haired, maybe a little more stoop-shouldered, arms crossed. "William Gross," she said, shaking her head. "So you finally decided to come home."

"Yes, ma'am," he said, not telling her that this town had never been a real home and never would be. Besides, that wasn't quite true. If there had been any place in Pleasant Shores that felt homelike, it was here.

Mrs. Decker nodded at Paul and then turned back to William. "You've aged," she said severely. "You don't look so good."

He grinned. Trust Mrs. Decker to tell it like it was.

She held up a hand. "Don't say it. I'm a little grayer myself, but I can still haul boxes and lift lumber with the best of them." She turned to Paul. "I taught this young man his work ethic."

"She did," William said. "With an iron fist, but it was good for me."

"Heard you got a doctor degree," she said, her eyes softening. "Didn't I always tell you you'd go far?"

He nodded. She had, when few others saw any potential in him.

She studied him curiously.

Please don't question what I'm doing now, whether I have kids. He didn't mind making mention of his ex-wife, who lived in Baltimore, he was pretty sure with a new guy…it was hard to keep track. But although he could speak of her without emotion, Jenna was another story. He was likely to burst out crying, which was why he avoided the subject.

She looked at him a moment longer and didn't ask. "Reckon you have a few friends to smooth things over with," she said. "Like Bisky Castleman. The two of you were thick as thieves."

"I ran into her the other day," he said.

"She's right over there." Mrs. Decker nodded toward a big rack of seed packets. "You go say hello. I need to get to the register."

"I'm going to get that key made," Paul said. "Catch up with you in a few."

William nodded and turned toward Bisky.

She stood in front of the seeds, talking to a tall young woman, and William was struck by how she looked in casual jeans and a T-shirt, her hair in a long, loose ponytail down her back. She'd turned into a pretty woman, and he was surprised to notice it, because he'd never thought of her that way before. She'd always been just Bisky.

He headed toward his friend. "Hey."

Both she and the woman next to her turned, and William's heart stopped.

He was looking at an older and a younger version of his best friend. Bisky's daughter looked just like her.

She was also about the age Jenna had been when she'd died. Tall and slender, long hair. Just like Jenna.

He must have stood gaping, because Bisky stepped forward and put a hand on his arm. "William, I'd like you to meet my daughter, Sunny. Sunny, this is Mr. Gross, that old friend of mine I was telling you about. He's living in Victory Cottage."

The younger version of Bisky held out a hand. "Pleased to meet you."

"You look just like your mom did at your age," he managed to say, and smiled at Bisky. "Thought I'd seen a ghost there, for a minute."

Bisky put a hand around Sunny's shoulders and gave her a quick squeeze. "I was never as pretty as she is, nor as poised, either. She's a real good girl."

"Mom," Sunny said, twisting away a little and laughing. "I'm *not* prettier than you were. I've seen pictures."

"You're just biased."

They joked easily with each other, and William could imagine that they were well liked in this town. Both attractive, fun, openly caring for each other. It was a good thing to see.

Almost too good, because it reminded William of who he'd been and what he'd lost. Despite the pain of his childhood, he'd left Pleasant Shores thinking things would look up for him, and they had. He'd embarked on a happy life, a family life.

Sunny was nudging her mother now, and William recognized it for what it was; *come on, Mom, time to go.* Jenna had often done the same thing.

Sure enough, they soon made their excuses and headed up to the register with their packets of seeds.

"Nice woman, Bisky," Paul said. William hadn't noticed that the man had joined them. Mrs. Decker was beside him.

William nodded. "Bisky's the best."

"Single, too," said Mrs. Decker. She raised her eyebrows at William. "You ought to ask her out."

"Me? No." William wouldn't even venture in that direction. "She's a great person, but I don't date."

"Never?" Paul asked.

William shook his head. "Never."

AFTER SHE'D PLANTED half of the seeds she'd bought, Bisky headed down to the dock, Sunny at her side. She'd told Sunny she could take the day off, that she'd look to hire day labor if she needed help scraping their boat's hull, but Sunny had said she had nothing better to do and had joined her.

They'd only been working a few minutes when Mary and William approached them.

"Look how hard you two are working," Mary said. "I used to think of fishing as relaxing. No more."

"Not this kind," William said, kneeling between Bisky and Sunny to study their work. "Man, I haven't scraped a hull in twenty years, but I remember it like yesterday. How my hands would break open and bleed."

Bisky knew William's family hadn't been much on taking care of their boat, but William had used to hire himself out to other dock families, and they'd usually found work for him to do. Everyone had known William's family and their struggles and wanted to help.

Sunny flexed her hands, showing them to Mary and William. Sure enough, several small wounds were open.

"I told you to wear gloves," Bisky scolded her daughter.

"I didn't feel like it. I can't get a good grip if I do that."

Sunny looked up at Mary. "Did you reconsider about the therapy dog program yet?"

"No, but when I do, you'll be the first to hear about it." Mary smiled. "I have a couple of applicants I'm looking into."

Sunny's face fell. Bisky was going to have to talk to her about her expectations. Mary had made it clear she wasn't going to hire an underage girl, and Sunny needed to get the message and stop making a pest of herself.

There was high-pitched laughter from the street, and Sunny got very busy scraping. When two teenagers came into view, Bisky understood why. Bisky had seen one of them around enough to know she was a certified mean girl, and the other was a dock kid who'd reportedly just dropped out of school.

The boy and Sunny were on good terms, as far as Bisky knew. The girl, not so much.

"Hey, hulk," the girl said.

Bisky blinked. It was a name she'd been called as a teenager, but rarely since. And this girl better have been referring to her, not to Sunny, or Bisky would knock her flat. She stood and took a step toward the pair. "What did you just call me?"

"Oh, nothing."

Mary walked over to Sunny and started asking questions about what she was doing, not coincidentally shielding her from the kids in the street.

"That's what I thought." Bisky levelled a glare at the kid and then knelt and went back to her scraping, but her face felt hot. She knew a few unkind people along the shore joked about her six-one, muscular frame.

The boy and girl stood across the street, just one house down from Bisky's, still looking in their direction occasionally and laughing.

William stood and took a step toward the teens. He didn't speak. He just lifted an eyebrow, crossed his arms over his chest, and stared them down.

The girl opened her mouth, a snide smile on her face.

"Don't mess with him, he's huge!" the boy said. He took a few steps away from her, moving to where he was in Sunny's line of sight. "I'm taking off. See you, Sunny."

"Later," Sunny said and quickly refocused on her work.

Bisky was glad that the boy had seemed to distance himself from the girl and that he had been friendly to Sunny.

Still, as soon as they were out of sight, Sunny threw down her scraper. "I'm too tired to do this, Mom. Maybe later." She walked off toward the house, shoulders slumped.

William stared after her, long enough that Bisky joked, "Take a picture."

"Sorry." He turned and looked from her to Mary. "She reminds me of my daughter half the time, and of Bisky the other half. I don't mean to be creepy."

"You're not creepy." Bisky's heart ached for him, and on impulse, she handed him Sunny's scraper. "Want to take a turn for old time's sake?"

He smiled and took the scraper in his hand, which dwarfed it. Then he got down on his back and started scraping the most difficult part of the hull to reach. That was William, she remembered. He'd always just assumed that he should take on the hardest job. He hadn't shirked from it.

Mary sat in a deck chair and watched them work. "I've been racking my brain to figure out this man's volunteer job," she said, "but maybe we should just put him to work doing manual labor."

From under the boat, they heard his laugh. "It comes right back to me," he said, "but I don't know that I'd last a whole shift at it." He held out his own hands, already scraped. "I'm soft now."

"And you should do something in line with your train-ing and talents," Mary said firmly. "I don't suppose those include an interest in working with therapy dogs?"

William frowned. "I'm not against it, exactly, but I also don't know anything about dogs. I doubt I'd be good at it."

"Or you could work with teenagers," Mary said. "You know, young people like those two that just walked by. They're not always very well prepared for the world they'll live in."

Bisky smiled at William. "You'd be terrific helping kids like that," she said. "They don't know what they're doing, any more than you did. You'd relate well to them. They need a male role model, in many cases. Need to understand the value of an education." She turned to Mary. "William was a dock kid and dropped out of school," she said. "You probably already knew that."

"It sounds like a possibility," Mary said to William. "Do you like teenagers?"

William looked at her, and his face tightened. "I do, but…sometimes, I have some trouble," he said.

"Your daughter?" Mary asked.

He nodded, then turned back to his scraping.

"We'll keep thinking about it," Mary said. "I need to get back to the bookstore."

"I'll stay here and finish what I started," William said, and Bisky was unaccountably glad of it.

She started sweeping up the paint scraps from where she and Sunny had been working. The morning had started out cool, but the afternoon sunshine had warmed things up, and the sky was still bright Chesapeake blue. She leaned on her broom a minute and looked out over the bay, watch-ing the gulls fight over a small fish one of them had found.

"So the teenagers around here are struggling?" William asked as he scraped.

"Some. You know how it is. They're attached, they love the place, but there's nothing for them here." She looked back out over the water. "The bay's in their blood, but it's a hard way to earn a living."

He slid out from under the boat and wiped his hands on a towel. "Got the center bottom done. Hardest part. I can give you a hand with the rest of it if you want."

"What do *you* want?" she asked impulsively. She finished her sweeping and leaned back against the dock railing, looking at him. "Remember when we'd ask each other that and dream about the future?"

He hoisted himself up to the bench in front of the shed and nodded. "I talked about becoming a merchant marine," he said.

"And I was going to be a teacher. Now you're the teacher, and I'm…running the business. I should have figured."

"Your folks are both gone?"

Bisky nodded. "Mom got cancer, and Dad…well, you know. He smoked too much, and ate too much, and then his heart went out when he was fifty-eight." She sat down beside him on the bench.

William scooted closer and put a big, gentle arm around her shoulders. "I'm sorry. You've had it hard."

She let herself lean in. That was something she rarely got the chance to do. Others leaned on her, but she was the rock, the strong one.

"Nice to have an old friend around," she said, looking up at him. "I'm glad you came back."

He looked down at her, his face only inches away from hers. He was smiling, his expression open and guileless, but then his eyes darkened and he tilted his head to the side, studying her.

Her breathing hitched. She couldn't look away.

And then he was standing up, brushing his hands together as if washing off the feel of her. "Well. Good to talk. See you around."

He turned and strode away without a backward glance.

Bisky leaned against the wall, shaken, her heart beating hard. What had just happened between her and her dear old friend?

CHAPTER FOUR

SUNNY HAD BEEN excited when Mary asked her to come to the bookstore after school. Maybe Mary had changed her mind and wanted to put her in charge of the program. Sunny had watched a ton of YouTube videos already and knew that it would take a lot to get herself up to speed. All the dogs would need to be tested by a registered therapy dog group before they could get their certification; maybe, they'd have to be tested with their owners, so Sunny would end up training people as well as dogs.

That was the part that worried her. Dogs she could handle, but figuring out how to tell adults they were doing things wrong...that would take some finesse.

She was up for it, though. It would be fun. She felt a restlessness inside that doing this work would quell.

When she tuned in to what Mary was saying, though, her excitement turned to disappointment.

"So while I can't put you in charge of the program," Mary said, "I want to explore all avenues, and I wondered if you'd work with William today. Show him the Blue House and talk about whether it's suitable for the program, and give me your perspective on whether he's completely unwilling to work with dogs, or if he might at least assist someone I hire."

"Sure," she said, trying not to show how she felt. Mom had drummed into her the value of being respectful to her elders. And as long as Mary wanted her involved on any level, there was hope that it would turn into a real job.

Mary gave her a few more details and sent her on her way.

The air felt chilly as she walked through town toward Victory Cottage and the Blue House, especially since she'd opted for looking cute rather than being warm. She had on an orange sleeveless sweater, ripped jeans and Vans, and she rubbed her hands up and down her goose-bumpy bare arms. Flowers were pushing up through the soil, some little purple ones already blooming, which would make Mom happy.

Sunny, of course, knew what Mary didn't know about the Blue House: there was a squatter living in the place. That was why she'd agreed to go talk to William and show him around. She'd figure out how to handle it when she got there.

She approached the little blue cottage slowly, scanning it for signs of life. She hadn't seen Caden at school today, but that wasn't unusual; they weren't in any of the same classes. Sunny had a mix of mostly standard classes, with an advanced science class she'd squeaked into, and upper level Spanish because she got so much practice speaking the language with the pickers at the seafood company. Caden, she'd heard, was good at English and history and took the honors version of those classes. Their paths didn't cross all that often.

Now that she knew he was hiding out from his family, though, she'd kept her eyes open for him. She was curious. How had his family not gotten suspicious that he was staying away from home way longer than a standard sleepover? They had to have noticed. Didn't they care?

Victory Cottage sat next door to the Blue House, their backyards separated by a shed and some bushes. Behind the houses, the bay extended, wide like an ocean at this point, a lone fishing boat visible close to shore.

"Is that you, Sunny?" The deep voice came from Victory Cottage. "Are we meeting now? I just happened to look out and see you." It was William, wearing an old T-shirt and untied sneakers. His sleepy eyes made it look like he'd been napping.

Sunny didn't much like him so far. His eyes lingered on Mom in a funny way that made Sunny feel protective. Mom didn't need the hassle of some giant man hanging around her.

Besides, William was all haunted and everything. She didn't know what his story was, but Victory Cottage was designed for crime victims, or else people who'd lost a family member to violent crime. Mom *really* didn't need some sad-sack wounded guy in her life.

She spotted a movement in the window of the Blue House: Caden was looking out. She turned to face William, not wanting him to notice Caden. "Actually, I was stopping by to let you know it's not a good time," she improvised. "I thought of something else I have to do, something I'd forgotten."

"That's fine," he said quickly.

Too quickly. That was strange.

From the corner of her eye, she caught another movement in the window and frowned.

William studied her, arms crossing over his chest. "Is anything wrong?"

So he was more perceptive than she'd thought. "No," she said. "Let's just reschedule. Next week, maybe?"

"That's fine. See you." He turned and walked back toward the house. His easy acquiescence surprised her; he seemed as relieved not to be meeting with her as she was not to be meeting with him. Paradoxically, that made her curious to find out more about him.

She ambled along the sidewalk, kicking stones and pretending to be occupied with her phone, until William had disappeared inside. When he'd closed the door behind him, she hurried to the back of the Blue House. Here, Victory Cottage and its inhabitants were blocked from view, and she from theirs. She opened the gate of the chain-link fence and made her way up to the back porch.

Caden was there and opening the door before she could fork her fingers through her messy hair. "What are you doing here?"

"Helping you out, so don't get cranky," she informed him. "They're going to start using this place to train dogs, so you'd better make other plans. That big guy next door is a part of it, or might be."

There was the sound of a car driving by, country music blaring. It squealed to a halt, and the door opened, then closed. Then the car sped off.

Caden looked nervous. "Go, before someone else finds out I'm here," he said, and slammed the door in her face.

Great. Sunny had started to think Caden might be a good guy, but obviously, she was wrong. She headed down the back steps and out of the yard.

As she walked toward the street, she heard a whine. Then a scrappy-looking medium-sized dog ran away from her and around the corner of the house, out of sight.

She hurried forward, curious about the dog, but it was already running past Victory Cottage and on to the next yard. Oh, well.

As she turned to head home, something on the ground caught her attention. Big reddish-brown circles were melting into the dirt where the dog had been. She knelt and looked at the circles more closely, then touched one. Her finger came away red.

Blood. Why was the dog bleeding? Had the car with the loud music dropped it off?

And if so, why had they done it right in front of Victory Cottage and the Blue House?

FRIDAY AFTERNOON, WILLIAM stood outside of Goody's ice cream and sandwich shop, waiting for Bisky to arrive.

The place was doing a decent business, considering that it was only March and there wasn't a tourist in sight. It wasn't the season for ice cream and milkshakes. Then again, there weren't a lot of choices in Pleasant Shores during the off-season. Goody's had been around when William was a kid, although the place had gotten a face-lift.

He felt strange standing outside here, waiting for a woman to come and meet him. It was a little bit date-like, which was *not* comfortable. Just like that weird moment a couple of days ago, when he'd put an arm around his old friend to comfort her and ended up noticing her pretty, full lips.

That had been a fluke, of course, as was this anticipatory feeling he was having right now. It was a function of the weather, the first really warm day of spring, complete with a clear blue sky. The bay was mirror-smooth. A few people were out, too, walking in twos and threes. A white-haired man jogged on the bike path that ran along the bay.

He remembered, then, that he'd actually thought of bringing Jenna and Ellie, his ex-wife, here. He never would have taken them to see the run-down trailer where he'd grown up, of course, but he'd have liked to show them the land, the water, the natural beauty of the place.

"William!" Bisky called to him from across the street,

and then strode over. She wore faded jeans and a tank top, appropriate for the surprisingly warm day.

Bisky was in great shape. No need for her to join a fitness center; her gym was a skiff on the bay, her weights, crab buckets and oyster bushels. It worked a lot better, from the looks of things.

He shouldn't think of how good Bisky looked, but after all, he was a guy. It didn't mean anything.

He held the door for her and they walked inside. Refreshing, chilly air came from the ice cream section, while a sweet aroma of doughnuts and cookies wafted over from the baked goods shelves. A lingering smell of fried food, probably crab cakes, made William's mouth water. "They serve lunch now, too?"

"Yep."

"I thought I was going to get a cone, but I'm getting a full meal," he said to the woman behind the counter, then turned to Bisky. "What about you?"

"Same," she said promptly. "I've been working all day, and that bowl of cereal I started with wore off a long time ago."

"The two of you aren't much different than when you were kids," the woman said, and then William recognized her as Goody. She'd been a young woman when they were growing up here, helping out her mother. Now, it looked like she ran the place.

They ordered the allegedly famous Crab Cake Sandwich baskets and went to a table by the window to wait. "I didn't know I'd be recognized so much when I came home," he said.

"At our height, you can't exactly be invisible," Bisky said.

"You're right." He gestured toward himself. "I'm mostly used to being the biggest guy in the room. I don't mind it, but sometimes, it would be nice to be able to walk through a place without being noticed."

"Or commented on," she said. "Try being the woman who's taller than most of the guys."

"What are you, five-eleven? Six feet?"

"Six-one, actually," she said.

"Well, you look good that way." Why had he said that?

She met his eyes, then looked away. "Thanks?"

There was an awkward silence, so he dove in. "Look, I was hoping you could help me manage Mary. If I tell her I can't work with therapy dogs, is she going to boot me out?"

"Why can't you?" Then recognition dawned in her eyes. "Is it Diablo?"

"Exactly." He pushed out a laugh. "I shouldn't let it affect me. I know all dogs aren't like him, and I know he was the way he was because of how Dad treated him."

"Honestly? He terrified all of us," Bisky said. "Sunny's been wanting a dog since she was a toddler, and I've always put her off. There were reasons I could say, logical ones, but behind them, there's that picture in my mind."

William remembered the huge German shepherd that had been tied to a tree in front of their trailer home. He'd fulfilled his job as a watchdog, barking ferociously at everyone who walked by. Dad had made sure of it by throwing him raw meat every few days, but otherwise, keeping him hungry.

William had tried to befriend the dog a few times, but he'd gotten nowhere. Diablo had ended up mauling a couple of neighborhood dogs, and the sound of those fights had never left William. It had been a mercy when Diablo had died, although the suspicion that someone in the neighborhood had poisoned him had put William's father into a rage for days.

Goody brought their food and they both dug in. After

he'd sated his initial hunger, William leaned back. "There aren't many people who would get it about Diablo," he said.

"He was terrifying!" Bisky shook her head. "Still, I was never one of those kids who'd tease an animal. That's just wrong. Plus, I was afraid Diablo would bite my hand off."

"I wish I would have set him free." Add it to the list of regrets William had about his childhood. "Someone should have called the SPCA."

Bisky put a hand over his. "Don't beat yourself up. You were a kid. You didn't know any better. None of us did."

He met her eyes and saw only compassion there.

"So you want to turn down the therapy dog gig," she said now, pulling her hand back from his and wrapping it around her water glass. "Mary will understand."

"But I need to do *something*. If I'm turning this down, it would be best if I could suggest something I *can* do. It's always better to go to the boss with the solution."

She propped her cheek on her hand. "What are you looking for here? I mean, what's your endgame?"

Trust Bisky to cut to the chase. "I want to get my mind healed—" He broke off, because he knew he'd never heal. "I want to get better, so I can go back to my job."

"And what's so great about your job? I mean, I know teaching at a college has prestige, and it's probably rewarding, but what makes you willing to do all this to get it back? To come back here, which can't have been easy?"

"I help kids like I was," he said. "The ones who come to college, somehow, but they're not prepared. I help give them a leg up in life."

"Hey!" Bisky snapped her fingers. "I know. I'm supposed to help start a new branch of this after-school program from the high school up the shore, where most of the kids around here go. It's going strong up there, but the dock kids don't participate because of the location. I'm supposed to figure out how to make an after-school gig work down here. You could help me get that up and running."

He crumpled a straw wrapper, then unfolded it, then crumpled it again. "I'd be awful doing something like that," he said. "Teenagers remind me of Jenna."

"College students don't?"

"Some, but they're older, different," he said. "When I met your girl Sunny, I almost lost it. No way could I work with kids of that age."

"What better way to heal, though?" she asked quietly. "You can't go through life avoiding young people. And if you were struggling in your job before, maybe the college students weren't so different after all. Maybe working with high-school-age kids will help you get back to where you're good with the college ones again."

He pictured a roomful of kids Jenna's age and started sweating. "Won't work."

"How do you know? Maybe it's like what they do when you have a fear of spiders, you know?" She frowned, then snapped her fingers. "Desensitizing, that's it."

"Dealing with the death of your child is different," he said, and pushed his plate away.

"Of course it is." She put her hand on his and squeezed briefly, then pulled back. "I'm sorry. I don't mean to minimize it, not at all. But being around kids her age might help you get over this hurdle. Make it so you could go back to your job."

He looked away, watched a mother hand french fries to her toddler while she studied her phone. Behind the counter, Goody seemed to be scolding her cook.

"Hey." Bisky patted his hand again. "If it'll really be too traumatic, then don't do it. Mary will find you something else. But…" She trailed off.

He looked at her then. "But what?"

"But I could use the help. You know how rowdy dock kids can be. Having you there would keep them in line, and it would let me split them up into smaller groups. Plus... I'm not a teacher or anything. Mary thought I'd be good at this, but I've been putting it off because I can't figure out how to get it started."

That made him realize that this wasn't just a make-work volunteer job. And the thought of spending more time with Bisky had a certain appeal. If she really needed his help... "Do you *want* to work with me, though?" he asked. "Even knowing what a mess I am?"

"Well..." She drew out the word, tilting her head to one side. "You *are* kind of a mess." She paused. "I'd want you to shave."

"You'd...oh." He saw the laughter in her eyes, grinned and ran a hand over his chin. "Yeah, guess I should."

"We're probably just going to pilot it for the rest of the school year, see how it works with our kids," she said. "Give it some thought. I'm going to get us some milkshakes."

She didn't ask his flavor preference, didn't have to: she already knew he liked chocolate.

She already knew a lot about him. It would be good to work with his old friend. She'd understand.

They'd been teenagers together, at least until William had left. They understood this life, its ups and downs. Its poverty, but also its beauty. There was so much to love about the marshlands, the bay, even the people here, certain notorious ones in his own family excepted.

When she came back to the table holding two tall white cups, he took one, sucked in chocolaty richness that took him back to childhood yet again, and smiled at her. "If you're sure you don't mind working with me, and if you think Mary will go for it, then I'll consider it," he said.

"That's great!" She smiled, broad and uncomplicated.

Something shifted in his heart then, and his body warmed.

And that *wasn't* a good thing. He was having a very strange reaction to his old friend. And it was one he had to quell, especially if it turned out he was going to work with her. For his own sake, but most of all, for hers.

CHAPTER FIVE

"Takes you back, doesn't it?" Bisky leaned back in the Jimmy Skiff, watching William row. She felt odd doing nothing on the water, so she added, "Don't forget we've got a motor back here for when you're tired."

"Good exercise," he said. He leaned forward and rowed, powerfully, and soon removed his lightweight jacket.

If he was going to work with her, they needed to begin planning the program for teens, and it had been Bisky's idea to do it while boating out to Two Acre Island, an uninhabited piece of land where they'd spent as much time as possible when they were kids.

She'd suggested she might want to bring the teens out here, to get them in touch with the bay's ecosystems beyond what they could see in Pleasant Shores. More than that, she wanted to hook William's interest in the area and remind him of what was great about Pleasant Shores and the surrounding land and water.

He'd left on such bad terms that she felt like all the good parts of his childhood had been pushed out of his memory. If he were to be positive with the teens, possibly even convince some of them to stay and make a life here, he needed to change his attitude himself.

It was four o'clock, late for a waterman to be out on the bay, but she'd wanted him to remember how spectacular sunset could look from the water. The sun hung low in the sky even now, but she figured they had a couple of hours of daylight left for exploring and a picnic, and the trip back.

"I'd forgotten what rowing felt like," he said now, pausing and resting his arms on the oars. "I don't even use the rowing machine at the gym."

She raised an eyebrow. "You got citified."

"Some." He took up the oars again and pulled steadily. "I live in a small suburb of Baltimore and take the train into the city. I still see some green and some water."

"Not like this, though."

"No," he said, looking around. "There's no place like this."

Gulls swooped and cawed, and the water lapped against the boat. The smell of the bay's mixed salt-fresh water was distinctive, she'd heard people from other places say. As for her, she'd never been away from it long enough to know anything else.

There was a shout from another boat, and Bisky lifted a hand.

"Who's that?" William asked, rowing.

"Elmer Gaines and his son. They'll spread the news all over town."

"What news?"

"That we're together," she said.

He didn't answer, and when she met his eyes she caught a strange expression in his. She reviewed what she'd said. They were together. Well, she hadn't meant that like it had sounded. She opened her mouth to say so, but he spoke first. "We were lumped together through our teen years," he said, "we might as well be lumped together now, I guess."

She smiled, remembering. "It was good when you were here," she said. "I never minded having it thought that you were my boyfriend. Kept people from bothering me."

"Did they bother you after I left?" he asked, his forehead wrinkling as he watched her.

"Just the usual." She thought about high school days and shook her head. It was a hard time for unconventional girls, even confident ones like herself.

"What's the usual?" He sounded like he really wanted to know.

She shrugged. "I mean…look at me."

He raised his eyebrows. "Boys were hitting on you?"

"More like teasing me," she said. "I'm too big and independent."

"Men don't like that?"

She shrugged, suddenly self-conscious, and looked away from his piercing gaze. "Well, they didn't in high school."

"And since then?" He'd stopped rowing, letting them drift. The boat rocked, gently.

Bisky rubbed the back of her neck. "There have been men. But mostly, I've focused on Sunny." She looked down. "I never wanted to have to explain why some guy was at the breakfast table in my bathrobe. So I've stayed away from sleepovers." Which was also a way to limit involvement; she knew it and even embraced it.

"You light up when you talk about Sunny." He was watching her, his head tilted to one side. "Being a mom suits you."

"She's been everything to me, a reason to get up in the morning, a reason to work hard, set a good example. She's pretty much been my goal."

He nodded, glanced behind him to set their course, and then started rowing again, slowly, his expression pensive.

She suddenly realized why.

"I'm so sorry to go on about her when you…" She cleared her throat. "When you lost your daughter."

He rowed once, hard, and then let the boat glide. "I don't

begrudge other people their children. I just hate it when people don't seem to appreciate what they have. You do."

"I do."

"Where's Sunny today?" He obviously wanted to change the subject.

"She's on a school trip to DC. They'll stay through Sunday night and then get home late." She sighed. "I'm realizing that there are going to be more and more days like this, going forward. She's growing up, and I'm going home to an empty house."

"There's no reason a beautiful, talented woman like you has to be alone." He glanced behind them and adjusted their course as the tip of the island came into view.

"Head down toward that hummock," she said, gesturing.

He swung the boat around and rowed toward the spot she'd indicated, his powerful strokes bringing them rapidly toward the shore. "I mean it," he said. "You don't have to be alone."

The sun was setting behind him, the water turning pink and gold, the seabirds swooping and rising. He wasn't looking at the scenery, though; he was looking at her.

She'd wanted to get him enthusiastic on this trip, but maybe he was getting enthusiastic about the wrong thing. "Come around and I'll tie us up," she said, avoiding his gaze. "And then we should really stop talking about ourselves and focus on the teen program."

It was cowardly, but she was afraid to probe at what he meant when he said she didn't have to be alone.

As he jumped ashore and then helped Bisky pull in the boat, William could tell she was uncomfortable. She'd been too quick to change the subject, and now she was chattering on about the program she wanted to start for teenagers, in a fast, scattered way that was uncharacteristic of her.

He knew her so well.

But in other ways, he didn't. He'd known her as a child and young teenager, but Bisky the woman had some new layers. Why had talking about her personal life made her so uncomfortable? Why *didn't* she have a man in her life?

Not because she couldn't find one, he knew that. Pleasant Shores wasn't exactly a singles' paradise, but the main industry was commercial fishing, so there were far more men than women. Bisky was kind, and good, and undeniably attractive. She didn't dress to accentuate her looks, but she didn't have to. Plenty of men would take notice of her just as she was. Her faded jeans fit like a glove, and her hair shone in its long, slightly mussed ponytail.

It struck him that he'd almost never seen her with her hair down. What would she look like, that way? What would she look like dressed up for a night on the town?

She glanced sideways at him, eyebrows raised in a question, and he realized he hadn't been paying attention to her words, even though he'd been staring at her. And he should have been listening. He should definitely focus on her words and not her appearance.

"Sorry," he said. "This place brings back memories." He looked around, seeking to add evidence to his assertion, and frowned. "It looks different."

She nodded. "It's eroding. The island's probably lost a quarter of its landmass in the past twenty years."

He'd read about that, but this was the first time he'd really seen it, really felt it. "It's sad. Coming out here with you was one of the highlights of my childhood. It would be a shame for the island to go away."

She nodded and beckoned him over to a tidewater creek that emptied out into the bay. She knelt down and pushed aside a rock. "Bingo," she said, pulling up a crab by one of its jointed arms. It opened and closed its claws, and she set it gently back down into the water, where it disappeared into a sandy swirl.

William kicked off his boots and socks and rolled up his jeans, then stuck his feet in the water. "Whoa, that's cold."

She snickered. "You notice I'm not taking my shoes off."

"You used to." He remembered following her around the island, his own bare feet stepping into the same spots hers stepped.

Later, as they'd gotten older, he'd tended to take the lead; he'd gotten faster and stronger in adolescence. But she'd still kept up with him just fine.

She beckoned to him now, in the lead again and rightly so; this was her territory now, not his. "I'd like to have the teenagers experience the kind of fun we did. Fall in love with the land. So many of them live on their phones when they're not working the water. They see the water as a chore they want to escape."

"We saw it that way, too." He paused to look back across the bay toward Pleasant Shores. He couldn't see it, but his eyes went unerringly in the direction of his own family's dock.

"We did," she admitted. "I used to say I wanted to escape the drudgery. But here I am."

"Does Sunny say the same thing?"

"Nope. She's a harder worker than I am." She perched on a log, looking over the water. "I want her to have a better life, easier. I don't know whether to wish she'd stay here, or wish she'd go."

"Makes sense." He studied her. "She has a lot of potential, it seems. But you want some of the kids to stay around? The teens in the program?"

"I want them to *want* to stay around. To catch the passion for the land and the water. Maybe some of the more academic ones would even want to study it. Marine biology, or ecology or whatever you'd call it. Figure out some way to help the bay stay healthy and keep the land from sinking into it."

"That's a tall order."

"It is. But the people running the program up the shore are all about community involvement. Get the kids to connect with business owners, learn the history of the area, understand the issues."

It was a worthy goal. "How do you...how do *we*...get teenagers interested in something like that?"

"Give 'em high school credits for it, maybe even college credit, for those who are headed that way, which isn't many." She looked off into the distance. "That's what the program up the shore does. Those that aren't headed for college, I'd like to see some of them stay around. Especially the ones whose families have businesses here. I'd like to see our population stay the same, and not just because there are tourists moving in." She looked at the sky. "We'd better have our supper."

He nodded, and they strolled back toward the boat. "Remember that day we stayed out here too late?"

"I'll never forget it." She glanced sideways at him. "I don't guess you will, either."

"You're right. I made a mistake, not getting home before Dad." He'd never forget that sinking feeling when he'd seen his father's truck already in front of their place. Dad generally sold the day's catch and then stopped at a bar up the peninsula. By the time he got home, William had tried to be in bed, normally.

That day, he hadn't made it, and his father had greeted him with an expression of rage. Not only had William gone somewhere without permission, but he'd taken his father's spare boat. "I never had a beating like that, before or since."

"I was so worried. I thought he'd killed you."

"I'm tougher than that." He remembered coming to in his front yard with Bisky and a couple other neighborhood kids leaning over him. Bisky had helped him to his feet and slung his arm around her neck so she could walk him back to her house. There, her mother had cleaned up his cuts and put ice on his bruises.

"Mom was bound and determined to call child protective services," she said, "but Dad talked her down. Said it would only make things worse for you."

"He was probably right." Like usual, William deliberately turned his mind away from thoughts of his father. "That's all in the past, fortunately."

Back at the boat, she made him sit down and opened the soft-side cooler she'd brought. Inside were seafood salad sandwiches, two for each of them, on thick slices of sourdough bread. They both dug in, and William finished an entire sandwich before he spoke. "Lord, I remember these sandwiches. Your mom's seafood salad was the best, and you've got the same talent."

"I wrote down her recipe before she passed," Bisky corrected. "I made her slow down, and I watched every step and wrote it down. It still says things like 'a pinch of salt' and 'a handful of celery with leaves' but I got enough detail that I can make it and teach Sunny how, too."

What would it be like to have family traditions to pass down that weren't ugly? William had kept his past a blank slate to his ex-wife and Jenna. He'd just tried to avoid being anything like his folks, having Jenna's childhood be anything like his own.

Bisky handed him a foil-wrapped package, and when he opened it, his eyes widened. "Your mom's coffee cake?"

"I remembered how much you always liked it," she said. "I make it for Sunny all the time."

He took a big bite and closed his eyes, relishing the explosion of cinnamon and sugar and butter, surrounded by light, moist cake. "Delicious."

She'd wrapped her second sandwich back up, but she took a piece of cake and was enjoying it, too.

"Did you teach Sunny how to make this, too?"

"Not yet. She's a typical teenager, doesn't want to get up early if she doesn't have to, and that's when I make this. She'll learn."

He nodded and finished the coffee cake and studied her. She'd managed a lot as a single mom.

"What?" she asked, her cheeks going a little pink.

"You. You've done well. Better than me, despite all the degrees."

She didn't argue. "I came from a good family. You had more to overcome."

They both sat for a few minutes. The bay was glasslike, with fog starting to rise, making wisps above the water and among the trees. The sinking sun blinked in and out, half-hidden by clouds. In the distance, loons wailed, a long, mournful call and response he hadn't heard in years.

"This is what our teenagers need," she said. "More simple pleasures. More pride."

For the first time, he started to understand what she wanted to do with the teen program. Besides Bisky's family, who'd given him a hand when they could, the land and the water had been what had saved him. He'd loved it. Maybe more kids *could* learn to love the bay, and to help it thrive, too.

He sucked in the salt air and a vision came to him: what if he just left the city behind, left all the grief behind, built a life here?

Had another family?

As soon as he had that thought, guilt slammed into him. Nice that *he* could think of starting over; Jenna never would. Jenna couldn't even grow up, and it was all due to his failure as a father and a protector.

Bisky nudged at him with her foot. "So you think you can get into it? Take this new program for teenagers seriously, make it a success?"

He looked at her steadily, knowing he had to manage her expectations, because fulfilling them felt like too much fun, more than he deserved. "No," he said. "I'll do my part, what's needed, but don't count on me to have a passion for it. This is just a means to an end."

CHAPTER SIX

SUNNY PAUSED IN the middle of the road and sucked in breaths of fresh, rich-smelling air. "What better way to spend Saturday morning than hiking, am I right?" she said to her friend Kaitlyn.

"I can think of better ways," Kaitlyn said, and giggled. "Like watching the sunrise cuddled up with Marcus Cunningham."

"Come on." Sunny rolled her eyes. "Let's head this way and forget about your new hot squeeze."

"He's hard to forget!" And Kaitlyn proceeded to rhapsodize about the latest boy on her list of conquests.

Sunny was glad for her, mostly. Kait had gone through some terrible things in middle school, and had been treated badly by a few of the boys in town. With the help of Sunny and another friend, she'd gotten over it and the boys had been thoroughly punished. Now, Kaitlyn was happy and, as Mom said, "healthily boy crazy."

Even Mom thought it was normal to be obsessed with boys at her age. Well, too bad. Sunny had other things to do, and most of the boys she knew were dumb.

Speaking of boys…a few minutes later they passed the Blue House, and Sunny reflexively glanced over, just in time to see a flash at the window. Interesting. Did Caden have nothing else to do but spy on people from his hiding place? Come to think of it, probably not. It must be boring to be cooped up all day, hiding out from whatever he was hiding from at home.

Sunny and Kaitlyn kept going, and soon they were at the hiking trail that led off their little peninsula and into the woods. The ground was a mix of sand and dead leaves, and some of the trees sported tiny, pale green sprouts. The trail started out wide and then branched off into several narrower ones. Sunny was hoping she could get Kaitlyn to go a few miles.

"This is great," Kaitlyn said, waving her fancy watch. "I'll get in so many steps!"

Sunny blew out a sigh. "Can't you just do something for fun, instead of worrying about it being exercise or making you thin?"

"This *is* fun," Kaitlyn said, and hugged her. "*And* it's getting me fit to hike with Marcus, because he's, like, super outdoorsy."

"As long as I can help with *Marcus*," Sunny said, and immediately regretted her snotty tone. She didn't even know Marcus, beyond to say hi. Maybe he was an amazing human being. And Kaitlyn was a good friend, even if she was in an annoying phase. "Seriously, I'm glad you came."

They hiked for a while, and Kait asked Sunny about her mom, and her classes, and the school trip to DC, which had been cut short when some of the kids had been caught smoking pot. That had been a disappointment, but it would be rescheduled, and meanwhile, she was just glad Kait had agreed to do something else fun.

The sun rose higher, and with as fast as they were moving, Sunny was sweating and hot. The sound of frogs and crickets, and the rippling waters of a small creek beside them, cleared Sunny's head. She loved being outdoors.

A high-pitched yelp made them both spin toward a big

pine. There was a little movement and a flash of reddish-brown fur.

Fox or dog? Sunny rushed over, Kaitlyn behind her. It was the dog she'd seen before, the dog that had been bleeding, only now it was lying on the ground, struggling to move. Short hair, muscular, some white markings on its chest. A pit bull mix, most likely.

Its brown eyes were cloudy with pain and Sunny's heart nearly broke. "I've seen this dog before," she said as she knelt near it. "Someone dropped it off near…" She broke off, realizing she shouldn't tell Kaitlyn about the Blue House and its occupant. "Near Victory Cottage. It was bleeding then."

The dog, a medium-sized, short-haired beauty, snarled when she reached out her hand.

"Don't touch it," Kaitlyn said. "Dad says all animals will bite when they're hurt."

Sunny studied the creature's back, keeping a safe distance. "It's got a big cut."

"Its ear is torn, too." Kaitlyn pulled out her phone. "No service. We should go get help—my dad or the vet."

"Or the police," Sunny said. "I think someone did this to her." There were too many wounds in odd places. Maybe the dog had been hurt before and gotten attacked by a predator in its weakness.

"Come on!" Kaitlyn started backing away toward the path. "Let's get help."

Sunny bit her lip. "I don't want to leave her. You go."

Kaitlyn hesitated, then squatted down and studied the dog. "Okay. I will. Be careful." Kaitlyn jogged back the way they'd come.

Sunny sat down near the dog and slowly stretched out a hand to it. It strained toward her, then pulled back. She could see its ribs.

"Hey, be careful." The male voice startled her, and the dog yelped and struggled, trying to get to its feet.

Sunny turned and there was Caden, just a few feet away. "What are you doing here? Did you follow us?"

"I come out this way a lot," he said, which wasn't really an answer. He knelt down, a safe distance from the dog, and it stopped struggling and subsided back down with a sigh. "Maybe give her some water."

Sunny wished she'd thought of that. She pulled a water bottle out of her day pack, hesitated, and then poured the water into her cupped hand and extended it to the dog. From this angle, she could see that it was a female.

"I didn't mean in your hand! You're gonna get bit," Caden warned.

But the dog sniffed the water and then took a couple of laps, then a couple more. Sunny refilled her hand and the dog drank thirstily. "I wonder how long she's been here? And what might have happened?" She glanced at Caden.

He shook his head. "People are crazy."

"You think someone did this to her?"

He shrugged. "I've seen animals killed by other animals, and they don't look like her. If another animal hurt her to that extent, it would probably have done it for food, and…" He trailed off.

"And she'd be dead and half eaten," Sunny finished. Slowly and carefully, she refilled her hand once more and let the dog drink. "But it doesn't look like something a human would do, does it? And anyway, why? Why would anyone *do* that?"

Caden shook his head. "My mom used to volunteer at a shelter. She came home with all kinds of stories."

Sunny tilted her head to one side. "You said you can't live at home now. But your mom sounds nice, if she worked for a shelter."

He rolled his eyes. "Her *charitable activities* never last longer than a couple of weeks," he said. He nodded toward the dog. "See if you can pet her."

That was an obvious change of subject. Was Caden in trouble, so much that he'd gotten kicked out of his house?

The dog whined, and Sunny leaned forward and carefully rubbed her neck, taking the opportunity to study the torn ear.

Voices and the sound of bushwhacking warned of Kaitlyn's approach, and sure enough, she came into view. With her was her father and a police officer they knew, Trey Harrison.

"There they are!" Kaitlyn sounded out of breath. She led her father over to them, and he knelt and tilted back his head, squinting a little. He was mostly but not entirely blind, and he was good with dogs.

"Did you see anyone else around here when you found the dog?" Trey asked.

Sunny looked toward Caden, but he was gone, and she gulped. How could he be gone? He must have taken off the minute they'd heard the others.

"Nobody else was here," Kaitlyn said, relieving Sunny of the need to answer.

"Is its tail docked? Ears?" Kaitlyn's dad, Mr. Martin, asked.

Kaitlyn leaned one way, trying to see the dog's tail.

Sunny leaned forward again, studying its ears. The dog cringed away, quivering, probably scared of the newcomers. "It just has regular ears, I think," she said. "Small and flopping over a little."

"Tail's docked," Kaitlyn announced.

Trey knelt down beside Drew. "You're thinking dogfighting?"

"Just asking what we'd ask back in Baltimore," Mr. Martin said. That was where he and Kaitlyn and the rest of their family had lived before, back when he'd been a police officer. "We had some problems with it."

Trey shook his head, frowning. "I've heard of problems with dogfighting around here, but I've never seen direct evidence." He studied the dog, holding his hand out for it to sniff, and surprisingly, the little creature allowed it. "This doesn't look like much of a fighting dog, though."

"You think someone abused the animal?" Kaitlyn's dad asked, his voice going flat.

Sunny's heart was pounding now. Should she tell them that Caden had been here? Could he have abused the dog and then made up the story about his mom to cover it up?

But she didn't think so. She'd be able to tell if he were that much of a jerk. He'd seemed interested in the dog's welfare.

"Could be abuse," Trey said. He pulled out a leash. "Could be something else. I'm going to put this on her and we'll take her up to the pound."

"No," Sunny said.

Trey, Mr. Martin and Kaitlyn all turned toward her. "What do you mean, no?" Kaitlyn's dad asked.

"No pound for this girl," she said. "I'm taking her home to stay with my mom and me."

"NO WAY CAN we keep her." Bisky set down her grocery bags, parked her hands on her hips, and looked at two pairs of puppy-dog eyes, one pair belonging to a pitiful-looking medium-sized dog, and the other pair to Sunny. They were huddled together in the middle of her kitchen floor. "She needs veterinary care that's going to be really expensive, and even if she can get healthy, she's going to have a lot of issues."

Sunny cradled the dog closer. The white towel she was using to hold it—one of Bisky's new ones, of course—

was dotted with blood. "They were gonna take her to the pound, Mom."

"The pound would have the means to deal with a dog like that." Bisky knelt to look at the dog more closely. "What happened to her, anyway?"

"We don't know, but Kaitlyn and her dad think some-body abused her. That, or she was in a dogfight. Like, a professional one, you know? We found her in the woods."

Bisky drew in a breath to reiterate that no, they couldn't take this project on, when there was a pounding on the screen door. "Open up! Police!"

Since the door *was* open, Bisky heard another officer's comment. "Don't come on strong like that when you're just asking questions in the community! Hey, Bisky, you in there?"

She rose to her feet and went to open the door. "Sure am. Hey, Evan. Jimmy."

"Mind if we come in and ask a few questions?" Evan stepped in front of Jimmy as if making sure he didn't open his fool mouth again.

"Not if you grab a couple of those grocery bags outta my truck," she said, "since my kid is too busy to help her mom."

"That's not our job—" Jimmy started to say.

"No problem," Evan interrupted. "Jimmy will bring them right in."

Bisky smiled a little as she let Evan in the house, then held the door for the blustering and complaining Jimmy Colerain. "What's up, gentlemen?"

"We need to talk to your daughter." Jimmy thumped the grocery bags down on the kitchen table, probably break-ing Bisky's eggs.

Bisky stiffened. No way was she letting this pair take an aggressive tone toward her daughter. She stepped be-tween the officers and the spot where Sunny and the dog sat now; they'd shifted to the corner of the kitchen, and Sunny's back was against the wall.

"If you don't mind, that is," Evan said. He was relatively new in town, but he seemed like a sensible person, wanting to connect with the locals and help in any way he could.

Jimmy Colerain, on the other hand, had grown up here, and while he was only a part-time cop, probably one of the chief's projects, he had an inflated sense of his own importance.

"What do you want to talk to Sunny about?" She kept her arms crossed and stared Jimmy down. Sometimes, it was nice to be a bigger and taller woman.

"That abused dog there," Jimmy said.

Evan glared at Jimmy, then smiled apologetically at Bisky. "We'd like to talk to her a little more about what she saw and heard."

"And it takes two of you? Do you think she did something to the dog? Because I'm looking at a girl who had the courage to help a poor wounded creature, and I don't see why you need to come in here acting threatening."

Evan cleared his throat. "There are two of us because Jimmy's getting some mentoring about how to talk to members of the community," he said evenly. "He won't be participating from here on out, just watching. Isn't that right." He looked at Jimmy.

The younger man's face reddened.

Evan continued to stare him down.

"Yeah, that's right," Jimmy said finally.

"You can ask her a few questions," Bisky said to Evan, "if that's okay with her. What do you think, Sunny?"

"It's fine, Mom." *Don't embarrass me* was the implied subtext, which meant that Sunny was comfortable with the basic situation.

"We wanted to know if she saw anyone else hanging

around where the dog was found, or heard anything." Evan knelt down beside Sunny and looked at the dog, shaking his head. "We'd sure like to catch whoever did this to an innocent dog."

Sunny shook her head rapidly. "No, we didn't see anyone."

Bisky frowned. She knew her daughter, and Sunny had said that too fast. She was hiding something.

"No other teenagers?" Evan asked. Maybe he'd heard the lie in her voice, too.

"Some of the dock kids?" Jimmy said from his station by the door.

Bisky glared at him.

"C'mon," he said, "Y'all skin muskrats for fun."

Bisky tensed and glanced over at Sunny. She wanted to give Jimmy a piece of her mind, but she didn't want to embarrass Sunny or set a bad example.

"Shut up, Colerain," Evan said.

"Well, it's the truth! Y'all *do* skin muskrats."

Bisky opened her mouth to chew him out. This was exactly why the dock kids struggled.

Sunny cleared her throat. "Y'all," she said from the floor, drawing out the word for emphasis, "y'all eat hamburgers. Do you know about conditions in slaughterhouses? Because I can give you some details if you'd like. Show you a video, although it's pretty graphic. It might upset you, but it might also make you wonder who's really into abusing animals."

Evan winced, and Jimmy reddened, and Bisky smiled. *That's my girl.*

There was another knock at the door, and Bisky turned to see William there.

"Come on in," she said. "Join the fun. We're suspected of abusing animals now."

"What?" He looked from Jimmy to Evan.

"Because of how we supposedly skin muskrats for fun," Sunny explained. She was stroking the dog's head now.

"That's a cultural thing!" William frowned.

"You'll have to tell me about that some day." Evan looked from William to Bisky. He sounded genuinely interested.

William drew himself up to his full height, which meant that his head was practically scraping the ceiling. "I'm sure there's a demonstration you could attend, or a book you could read on the subject," he said to Evan. All of a sudden, he sounded like the professor he was, and he also sounded like he was scolding a student. Why, she couldn't fathom.

"Right. Well, I'll just ask Sunny a couple more questions." Evan settled into a sitting position and petted the dog some more. "Tell me again about the spot where you found her," he said to Sunny. "Do you know of anyone who hangs around that area? Any particular reason you went hiking there today?"

As Sunny denied knowledge of anything, Bisky was again conscious that her daughter was hiding something. She didn't suspect Sunny of hurting the dog herself. No way would Sunny have anything to do with abusing an animal, Bisky would stake her life on that. But as a mother, she could see that Sunny wasn't telling the whole story.

"We'll continue to investigate," Evan said, standing. "If you think of anything, let us know right away. We don't want anyone mistreating animals in this community."

Jimmy let out some kind of snort under his breath. Evan frowned, and the police officers left. Evan started scolding the younger officer as soon as they got outside.

"We're keeping this dog," Sunny said when the officers' car started up and they drove away.

Bisky frowned. William shrugged.

The last thing Bisky wanted in her house, as her responsibility, was an abused dog. She wasn't the type of parent who had trouble saying no, either.

But when she looked at Sunny's face, she blew out a breath. "This is probably a big mistake," she said, "but we'll give the dog a home for now."

CHAPTER SEVEN

WILLIAM PACED THE small kitchen of Victory Cottage. Looking out the window at the wind-tossed bay didn't provide the usual comfort.

He hadn't slept well and was still on edge. The scene at Bisky's yesterday had bothered him for reasons he didn't fully understand.

That cop who'd made comments about dock kids was irritating, but William knew the type, had grown up with them. A little better off than the families that worked the water, they'd trumpeted their superiority as a way to bolster themselves up. He'd had bigger problems back then, and the jokes had run off him like rainwater off a duck's back.

It hadn't been Jimmy Colerain who'd caused his insomnia. It was the other one. The good-looking officer who'd seemed all too interested in learning about Bisky and connecting with her.

He climbed up the stairs as Sunday morning church bells rang somewhere in town. He'd do his laundry and clean the place, pay his bills. Maybe he'd get to work fixing that broken segment of fence he'd seen yesterday.

The sound of the doorbell startled him and he realized he hadn't heard it since arriving in town a week ago. Who would be coming over this early on a Sunday? He barely knew anyone in town, these days.

He ran his fingers through his hair, went downstairs and opened the door.

There was Bisky.

He sucked in a breath. She wore a denim skirt, above knee length and fitted, with a red sweater that suited her coloring. Her face was pink and the breeze off the bay lifted her loose hair from her shoulders.

He'd wondered what she would look like with her hair down, and the answer was, good. She looked good.

He also couldn't help but notice her curves. When had Bisky turned into such a knockout?

She cleared her throat and smiled, looking a little nervous. "Did I wake you up?"

"No. Come on in." He held the door, gestured her into the kitchen and watched the sway of her walk, mesmerized.

She looked over her shoulder and frowned. "You okay? If you're not in the mood for company, just say so. Although I'm not here for a visit."

Stop looking at her like that, it's Bisky. "I'm glad to see you," he said truthfully, following her, "but if not for a visit, then what's up?"

"I'm taking you to church," she said.

He stopped. "I don't go to church."

"Maybe that's your problem. Come on." She softened her words with a smile. "There's a lunch after. Everyone brings stuff, and some of them are amazing cooks."

He looked out the window to stop himself from staring at this new version of his old friend.

Going to church. His family hadn't gone, ever. Like other kids in Pleasant Shores, he'd gotten dragged along with friends and neighbors sometimes, but he'd always felt like people looked at him funny, talking about the big dock kid in the ragged clothes, wondering what he was doing there.

When he'd married Ellie, it had been in a church, and they'd attended church on holidays. And later, in the dark months after Jenna had been killed, a couple of friends had practically forced him into counseling with a local pastor, who'd given him some books and bible passages to read and had prayed with him.

He couldn't say whether it had helped or not. Nothing had really helped, but the pastor had brought him back from the brink of despair, reminded him he had things to live for still, could do some good in the world.

In honor of that guy, and because it was Bisky who was asking, he nodded. "Okay," he said. "I'll go."

"Good." But when he grabbed his jacket, she just stood there, eyebrows raised. "Do you have anything nicer to wear?"

"I…" He looked down at his jeans and T-shirt, and it all flooded back to him. The dock folks had tended to dress up for church, while the richer town folks dressed down. "We still wear our Sunday clothes?" he asked.

She smiled and nodded. "You said 'we,'" she said. "You're one of us still."

So he had. So he was. He trotted upstairs and put on khakis and a polo shirt. "Is there time for me to shave?" he called down.

"If you hurry."

So he did a quick shave and added a sports jacket, and went downstairs, feeling better.

She smiled when she saw him. "You look like a professor," she said, and there was something that resembled appreciation in her eyes.

That put a spring in his step, and they walked out together into the early spring morning, keeping a brisk pace so they'd get there on time.

As they passed storefronts and yards with bushes starting to bud, he felt a wave of happiness, like he was waking up. The air smelled fresh, and somewhere above them, a bird sang a spring song: *too-WEE, too-WEE*.

William almost felt like he could sing, too.

Bisky had come to get him, bring him to church. She could have done the same to Officer Evan Stone, but she hadn't. She'd chosen him.

As they reached the church steps, he found himself smiling. Up ahead, a couple of teen girls giggled over something on a phone.

The sound of it crashed over him like a giant wave, bringing back memories and washing away his good mood.

Here he was feeling happy, when Jenna could never be happy again. What was wrong with him? He didn't deserve to have a nice, happy springtime Sunday.

Bisky had gotten a couple of steps ahead of him, and now she turned. She stopped, studied his face, and walked back. "What happened just then?"

She was too perceptive. "Those girls," he admitted, nodding sideways to the giggling pair. "Sounded just like my Jenna."

She put an arm around him, resting her head on his shoulder. "That must be so hard." She hesitated, then added, "I honestly can't imagine what you're going through. I don't know of anything to say to comfort you."

At least she wasn't telling him to get over it or remember the good times. "It's hard, but I don't want to bring you down."

"That's what friends are for," she said simply. "Come on. We'll sit in the back. Maybe the service will help."

So he followed her inside and they sat in the back corner, a little removed from the small crowd greeting each other, talking quietly. In the background, the organ played, something beautiful.

And he was broken. Broken inside. If only he hadn't left Jenna alone that day.

He looked through the church bulletin, trying to focus

on what it said, sucking in breaths to soften the tightness in his throat. Bisky was watching him, and he really didn't want to talk about Jenna and break down here, in public.

So he changed the subject. "Doesn't Sunny come with you to church?"

"Sometimes," she said. "This morning, she's taking care of the dog."

Right, the dog. "Are you keeping it?"

"I guess." She shook her head. "It's a pitiful creature. And it makes me mad that someone would hurt a dog like that."

"Yeah, and that people blame it on the dock kids."

She nodded. "There are still so many stereotypes. That's why I want to do the teen program. Why I want you to help, too. You made a decision yet?"

He blew out a breath.

"You get them," she continued. "A lot of people don't, but you do. You can give them hope."

Could he? What Bisky was saying was similar to what the pastor had said, back home. That he could be a good example to kids who hadn't had any advantages. That he had something special to offer because of the background he came from.

The pastor had even said God would use his rough childhood for a good end. He'd stopped short of saying God would use Jenna's death for a good end—probably sensing that William would deck him—but his words about William's background had made some amount of sense.

"I mean," she said, "I'm not going to push you into something you really don't want to do. If you can't, I'll find someone else to help out."

"Like Evan Stone, the cop?" he blurted out.

She gave him a strange look. "I hadn't thought of him," she said, "but he does seem like a good guy. He's new in town and not very connected yet. Maybe he *would* like to help." She looked at him sideways. "But I'd rather have you."

She'd rather have him. He straightened in the church pew. "All right," he said, "I'll do it."

AFTER SERVICES, BISKY led William to the church luncheon. He seemed to be doing better, at least a little bit, but she was worried about him.

How did you get over the death of your child? How did you manage to go on with life at all, let alone seize some kind of happiness? If anything ever happened to Sunny...

She couldn't even let that thought stay in her head for two seconds. It was weak of her, maybe, and as William's friend she ought to try, but she couldn't. She shook the idea off and looked around the church basement, where the luncheons were held in cold weather. "Do you remember coming to this with my family, years ago?" she asked William. If she could distract him, even in a small way, maybe it would help a little.

He looked around. "I do," he said. "The smell brings it all back. I'm pretty sure I ate way more than my share, but people were nice."

"As they should be. It's church."

He was right: the smell was mouthwatering. Someone was frying crab cakes, and the aroma of fresh-baked corn bread filled the air. Bisky's stomach growled. "I always skip breakfast when the church is having a lunch," she said. She opened a bag she'd been carrying and pulled out a plastic bin. "I made chocolate chip cookies," she said. "I love 'em, but I don't dare bake them when it's just me and Sunny to eat them. I run the risk of eating them all myself."

"You don't worry about your weight, do you?" His eyes skimmed over her. "You look good."

That gave her a funny little tingle in between her tummy and her heart. Which was ridiculous; this was William. What did it matter if he liked how she looked? "Every woman worries about weight a little, especially as she gets older," she said. "Come on, I see some people we can sit with. Pastor Steve will bless the food, and then they'll have us go up table by table, so everyone doesn't rush the kitchen."

Talking helped her get rid of that odd sensation of wanting William to like how she looked. It also felt like a good idea to have him sit with her amidst a whole gang of people, rather than going off by themselves. "Everyone," she said when they reached the table she'd targeted, "this is William Gross. He's back in town after a lot of years away." She nodded toward the closest family. "William, that's Paul, but you two already met, right? And that's his wife, Amber, and their son, Davey."

"I'm five," Davey informed William.

"Are you really?" William smiled at the little boy. "You're pretty big."

"And that's Ria and Drew and their daughters, Kaitlyn and Sophia. Sunny's not here today," she informed Kait, because the two of them were good friends.

"Did you let her keep the dog?" the teenager asked.

"Against my better judgment," Bisky said, shaking her head, and the others laughed.

"And this is Trey and Erica and their baby, Hunter," she said. "Who everyone always fights over holding, because he's so adorable."

William's face lit up. "I can see why," he said. "Do you think he'd come to me?" He knelt down beside Erica, making himself smaller.

"You're welcome to try," Erica said. "He's as heavy as if

he were made of bricks." She scooted Hunter toward William, who held out his hands.

Hunter studied him, his face impassive. William reached out gently and took him in his hands, then when Hunter remained calm, stood and swooped him into the crook of his arm. He bounced the baby and spoke quietly to him, and Hunter began to smile.

The sight of such a big man with a baby did something to Bisky's heart.

She'd used to wish for another child, a brother or sister for Sunny, but as the years had gone by, it had come to seem unlikely. She'd talked herself into being glad. As a woman alone, raising Sunny well, providing for her needs, saving up for college…there just weren't resources or space for another child.

She was thirty-seven now, late in the game for babies. She hadn't felt that maternal hunger for a long time. But watching William with Hunter was bringing it back, hard and strong.

She didn't want to let that happen, so she deliberately turned away and talked to Amber until William gave the baby back to Erica and the pastor prayed over the food. Bisky gestured William ahead of her, so he walked with Paul and Trey to fill his plate. She even hoped to put someone else in between her and William when they returned to the table, but everyone quickly grabbed their earlier seats, leaving her right next to him.

And he was hard to ignore, especially when he leaned close to tell her how good everything was. She caught the scent of his aftershave and felt the warmth that seemed to radiate from his body, and got almost dizzy.

What was wrong with her? She and William were friends, and that was all. What William needed most was a friend.

She was glad to see how well he got along with everyone. He'd matured since she'd known him as an awkward, angry boy. He was a man now, friendly and strong, someone others enjoyed talking with. It was a different side of William, and she liked it. Wouldn't mind seeing more of it, she thought, and then scolded herself for her foolishness.

"You look happy," Amber said, waggling her eyebrows at Bisky and giving a meaningful glance toward William. "Any particular reason?"

"I *am* happy," she said, ignoring Amber's implication. "William's going to work with me on the new program for teens." She looked over and saw that William was listening. "See, it's public now, you have to."

"I'm committed," he said, smiling. And she was blown away. When had he gotten so handsome? When had she started *noticing* he was so handsome?

And she was going to be working with him. Yikes.

The windows were open, with blue sky and sunshine visible outside. Around them, people were going back for seconds or dessert, walking around talking to people at other tables, laughing and enjoying the day. Kayla came over to their table.

"Miss Kayla!" Davey ran to wrap his arms around her legs, nearly tripping her.

"Davey's preschool teacher," Amber explained to William with a wry grin. "I count for nothing when she's around."

"Davey's pretty fond of you," Paul said, putting an arm around her. "You're his mom."

Bisky smiled at the obvious tenderness between them. There had been a time when Paul had asked Kayla out, before realizing that he and Amber were meant for each other. Amber had been jealous. But now, there was no awkwardness between them.

Davey's mother had died several years ago, but Paul was right: Amber was clearly Davey's mom now, and the little family were friends with Kayla and her mom. Which was good. Pleasant Shores was too small of a community for grudges to last long.

"Let's go get dessert," Paul said. Amber and Bisky declined, but Paul and William and Trey headed up to where pieces of pie and cake were being distributed.

"He's good-looking," Kayla said, smiling, as soon as the men were out of sight. "Adds to the great scenery in this town."

Bisky felt a primal sense of possessiveness. William was more than scenery, and Kayla couldn't have him.

And then she realized how ridiculous that was.

"He *is* good-looking." Bisky made herself smile at Kayla and Amber.

"And?" Amber asked. "How do you feel about him?"

"He's a friend, and that's all," Bisky said firmly.

Deliberately, she looked around, watching Davey run over to play with a group of kids who were climbing onto the stage and jumping down. People were starting to leave now, putting on coats and gathering dishes.

Bisky remembered when Sunny had been one of the children jumping around and playing. But that time was over for her. Sunny would soon be on her own, moving on.

"It goes fast," Amber said, reading her mind. Amber's daughter, Hannah, was away at college. Where Sunny would be soon, too.

From the next table, Primrose Miller beckoned to Bisky. Primrose was the church organist, and she was busy feeding one of Chelsea Carbon's twins while Chelsea fed the other. Primrose could strain Bisky's nerves because of how much she loved to gossip, but she was a sweet person underneath. Bisky went over to stand next to the woman.

"Who's your young man?" Primrose asked, still spoon-
ing food into the baby's mouth. She nodded in William's
direction. "The tall one. He looks familiar."

"He's not my young man." Bisky had to smile at the terminology, but then she noticed that other people were listening. No doubt thinking she and William were together,
and that, she had to dispel. "He's William Gross. He grew
up here, but he's been away for a while. Now he's here for
the Victory Cottage program." Not for Bisky. Definitely
not for Bisky.

She'd never been with anyone seriously and long-term.
And she didn't hold it against herself; she was strong, and
that was good, but men didn't like it. She was too much
for most men.

Suddenly, she wanted to leave. "I have to go check on
Sunny," she said to the ladies, and then repeated the same
excuse to William. Then she hurried up and left by herself. Maybe that would cut down on any gossipy idea that
she had feelings for William, or him for her. He wasn't her
"young man," as Primrose had said, and he never would be.

Now, she just had to make sure her own heart got the
memo.

CHAPTER EIGHT

As WILLIAM CAME to the edge of Pleasant Shores' downtown, or what passed for it, on Monday morning, the school bus emerged from the dock area, and memories flooded him. Getting on that bus and leaving the docks, going to school, had been the best part of his day when he was young. At school, he'd been able to think and read and learn in peace. He'd met teachers who cared about books and ideas.

That was where he'd learned there was another life besides the dirty and dangerous one in his troubled family.

There, and at Bisky's house. His steps quickened, taking him past the new diner that bridged the gap between the town and the docks. The smell of bacon wafted out the door as it opened and a couple of women in business clothes came out, talking and laughing.

He'd try the diner soon, he decided. He was getting tired of his own bad cooking. And he needed to support local businesses.

Today, he was going to work with Bisky to plan the program she wanted to develop for teens, following guidelines from the program up the shore but also tailoring it to the Pleasant Shores kids. Mary had okayed it as his volunteer gig while he lived in Victory Cottage, and the more he'd thought about it, the more he was looking forward to helping kids who might be in the situation he'd been in, feeling trapped in a life that didn't suit them. Maybe he could do some good, make something out of his time here, and help others as well as healing himself.

The only problem was the strange feelings he'd been having about Bisky. Yesterday, attending services and meeting up with her friends at the luncheon after, he'd gotten a little too intent on watching her. She was nice to watch, laughing and talking, obviously at home, wearing that red sweater that fitted in a way that had a lot of men giving her a second look.

It wasn't just how she looked, either. She'd automatically understood when he'd had that moment of remembering Jenna, there on the steps of the church. She'd known he needed to be away from people. She hadn't comforted him with false platitudes like so many well-meaning people tended to do.

Bisky was genuinely kind and empathetic. A good woman.

And he needed to remember that, which would also remind him that he couldn't get too lost in thoughts of how it would be to hold her close or come home to her at night. He was no good for anyone in a relationship, and he had to make sure he avoided any move in that direction.

Now, he saw her on the docks, doing something with her crab buckets. She wore jeans and a hoodie, her hair in a long braid down her back. She looked like a kid.

There were a few other watermen hanging around their own docks, scraping hulls or mending traps, probably because, like Bisky, they were taking a break between oyster and crab season. A couple of men stood smoking and talking; they looked in his direction and nodded as if they knew him. Maybe they did. He'd spent so much time with his head down when he was younger, reading a book or doing somebody's odd jobs or trying to avoid his father's wrath, he hadn't gotten close with most of the families who lived near the docks and worked the water.

Somehow, he'd gotten to know Bisky and her family, and it had been the making of him.

She looked over her shoulder and saw him watching her, and her forehead wrinkled. Great, he seemed like a stalker. "Let's get to work, figure this thing out," she said. "Once crab season starts, I won't have much time to sit down and talk."

"Right." He came over and sat down a respectable distance away from her. He picked up a crab pot, found a spot where the wire had come untwisted and started putting it back together. Rather than making small talk, he dove abruptly into the work they'd planned to do. "So, the teen program. We could take them crabbing once the season starts."

She tilted her head and frowned at him. "That's what they have to do whenever there's a day off from school anyway, most of them."

"Oh, right." His own family hadn't had a successful fishing business, but his dad had done a little crabbing, trying to make some money to supplement their welfare and disability payments. Not that Dad had been disabled, but back then, it had been easier to scam the government.

When William had grown up and left and thought back on it, he'd realized that his father was probably involved in some illegal activities, too. How else had he been able to afford to buy a boat and keep top-shelf liquor in the house?

"I'm thinking maybe we should teach them the history of this place," she said. "Give them a sense of pride in where they came from. You could do it. You're a teacher."

The idea interested him, but he had doubts. "Like more school? I doubt they'd want to listen to a lecture from some guy they don't know, telling them about the place they've lived all their lives. I mean, admittedly, there's some great history around here, but…"

"But teenagers don't care about it." Her hands moved quickly while she spoke, weaving a clean, white piece of twine into a W pattern on the side of a trap.

"What's that for?" he asked.

"Biodegradable," she explained. "If the trap gets lost, it disintegrates. Gives the crabs or whatever else gets caught inside an escape hatch. Government regulation these days."

"And you have to replace them every year?"

"Pretty much," she said, nodding. "I don't mind. It's a better way." Peaceful. She'd always seemed peaceful when she worked with her hands, worked near the water.

He watched how she did it and then grabbed another pot with a rotting twine section. He cut it away and then took a new length of twine and wove it through, tying a tight knot that his fingers remembered, even though he couldn't have said how he did it.

"Think back," she said. "What would we have liked to do as teenagers? What would have benefited us?"

"Knowing there's another place in the world besides here," he said immediately. With his words came a memory: the time they'd done a school trip to DC, and he'd caught the dream of escaping his family and doing something on his own, something different and maybe even better.

But Bisky was frowning. "I want them to see the good in this place, to stay here." She snapped her fingers. "Maybe the new museum," she said.

"We have a museum?" That was hard to believe. Pleasant Shores was a small town, and back in William's younger days, it had been rough around the edges, with most people just trying to get by.

She nodded, putting aside her work and facing him, cross-legged. "It's really cool. Mary donated the money to get it started. Drew, you met him yesterday, he's one of the curators."

"When did this happen?"

"It's new. It's focused on the history of the place, and the science, the ecosystems. They're still raising money to add more exhibits. It's only open a couple of days a week, now, but come summer, they're hoping to open up every day. Show the tourists that Pleasant Shores is about more than a beach and ice cream."

He smiled to see how enthusiastic Bisky was about their hometown. She loved it. She was a lifer here.

Just another reason they couldn't be together. William had no intention of staying in this area beyond the two months of the Victory Cottage program.

He refocused on her idea. "Having the kids help with the museum is a good plan. Especially if they could make an exhibit for it themselves, or otherwise get involved. Hands-on, that's the direction education is going in now, anyway. It's how people learn best, they're finding out."

"Y'all scholars are only now figuring that out?" She gestured at her stack of crab pots, then grinned. "I know what you mean. Sunny has a lot of projects these days." She frowned, her forehead wrinkling in thought. "Maybe they could do social media for the museum, make videos or something, appeal to the tourist kids and teens."

He high-fived her. "Great idea."

And then they were just smiling at each other like fools.

There was a bang from the dock next door. "If I can interrupt the gabfest," Rooker Smits called from the next dock, "I could use a hand."

William stood, but Bisky did too and put a hand on his arm. "I'll do this, it's personal," she said.

She made her way over to Rooker's dock and they disappeared into his shack.

That left William to finish twining the rest of the crab pots and stack them up. And reminisce, really experiencing all he'd left behind. The smell of the docks, oil and salt and fish. A seagull atop every piling. The clouds that scudded high across the sky, and the breeze that never really stopped, making it comfortably cool even in the height of summer.

He'd been away a long time, and he'd tried not to think about the Pleasant Shores of his childhood. But as he'd blocked out the rough parts, he'd also blocked out the good things. Like the beauty of the sun sparkling on the bay that stretched for miles. The way people helped each other, the easy invitations to church or supper, the slower pace of life that gave everyone time to stop and chat when the day's work was done.

Because of his friendship with Bisky and her family, he'd experienced some of that good side. He needed to be grateful for that.

He wished he could have introduced Jenna to this side of his background. She'd been so social. She would have loved it here.

Bisky and Rooker came out of his shed. Rooker said something gruff to Bisky and she nodded and patted his back. William couldn't make out the words, but he saw the old man look up at Bisky and smile, his face breaking into a thousand wrinkles. She was almost a foot taller than Rooker was.

She came back over to her own dock, and she was smiling too. "Thanks for finishing my work for me," she said.

He nodded toward Rooker. "What was that about?"

"He has trouble with his leg," she explained. "Kind of a lingering bacterial thing, and they're afraid it'll go to sepsis. He needs someone to help him change the dressing."

"You do that for him?"

"He's alone, except for his granddaughter, and she's

young and busy," she explained. "Doesn't want the nurse to come every day just for that, so I help him out."

"That's good of you."

She shrugged, then smiled. "While I do it, he pumps me for information about Mary. I think he wants to ask her out."

William looked over to Rooker's dock and watched him limp out toward his boat. "He's a little old for her, isn't he?"

Bisky shrugged. "Love's love," she said. "He's in his eighties, and she's only seventy. *And* she already has a sort-of boyfriend. But I don't discourage him. Mary deserves to have men flocking around her."

"She seems great."

"She is. And she's had a tough time." Her expression changed, softened. "In fact…she knows what it is to lose a child to violence. Maybe you and she will talk about it some day."

"I didn't know." William blew out a sigh. He was sorry, truly sorry, that Mary had gone through a trauma like he had. He also knew that connecting with other survivors was one of the only things that helped when you were drowning in the pain. "I'll talk to her. Maybe. Sometime."

"I'm sorry." She bit her lip. "Is it wrong of me to bring it up? I don't want to make you sad."

"I think about Jenna every day," he said. "I like it that you're not afraid to mention it."

At the same moment, they both reached out. Their hands touched, clasped. And then they were looking at one another, hard.

William felt that intense connection again, something he hadn't felt with anyone else.

Her lips parted a little, and he saw her suck in a breath. What would it be like to kiss her?

Too good, and that was bad. He pulled back his hand

like he'd touched a flame. They'd been talking about Jenna. Where did he get off having that kind of stirring when he'd been the cause of his daughter's death?

He stood, spun, and got very busy restacking the already-neat crab pots.

AFTER THEY'D WASHED UP, Bisky and William ambled through town toward the museum, hoping to get the chance to meet with someone there and assess their interest in getting the teenagers involved.

Bisky glanced up at William and smiled. It was pleasant to walk beside a man she could look up to physically. There were a fair number of men her same height, but not that many who were significantly taller. With William, she felt like a normal-sized woman.

It was around eleven o'clock. The shops that stayed open year-round were doing a brisk business. She pointed out Mary's bookstore and the struggling new toy store, and they talked a little about Goody's, which had been around forever.

She thought about offering to take him to the Gusty Gull, the bar-restaurant that stayed open all year and was where all the locals went to drink and dance, but she snapped her mouth shut. It might seem too much like she was asking him out, and that, she definitely didn't want to do.

Despite, or maybe because of, that weird little zing that kept happening between them.

William was a friend, part of her childhood. And he *needed* a friend more than anything else, as evidenced by the fact that he was still so grief-stricken about his daughter.

You never got over that, she was sure. But William's pain seemed acute, complicated. Maybe what she should do was set up William to take Mary to the Gull, where they could have a drink and Mary could share her wisdom about how to live on after you'd lost a child to violence.

She'd talk to Mary, see what she thought.

The point was, Bisky wanted to be a friend to the man beside her, and she didn't want to ruin that friendship with an attempt at a relationship that wouldn't work out anyway. Her relationships with men never worked out, and she'd resigned herself to that fact long ago.

Best to just enjoy the fact that they were going to be awesome working with the dock teenagers together.

At the museum, he held the door for her, and she wondered where he'd picked up a gentleman's manners. Definitely not from his father.

"Welcome," Drew Martin said from behind the museum's front desk. "Are you interested in a tour, or just want to look around on your own?"

"Hey, Drew, it's Bisky," she said as they approached the desk. She turned to see if William had caught on to the fact that Drew had a visual impairment. He hadn't seemed to notice yesterday.

He did now, apparently, because he quickly introduced himself. "William Gross. We met yesterday at the church lunch. How's it going?"

"Good, good," Drew said. "Feel free to look around, get a taste of our heritage here."

William smiled. "I'm somewhat in touch with that, since I grew up here. No, we're looking for a way to get some teenagers involved with the museum."

Drew raised his eyebrows. "Good luck with that. My daughters won't have a thing to do with it. Boring, they say."

Bisky explained the program they were planning with the dock teens. Then she frowned. "If your girls are bored with this place, our teens will be, too."

"Unless we can get them really involved, give them a stake in it," William said.

Bisky leaned on the desk. "What if they lead some tours? Or help with social media for the museum?"

"Now that, we could use," Drew said. "Neither I nor Mary is that good at social media, but we need to improve. Need a website, too."

"Do you think any of the dock kids are good at website construction?" William asked Bisky.

"Maybe a couple of them. But they often don't have wireless. Nor computers, in some cases."

"They could use our computers here. We've got pretty good service."

"Would that be a motivation?" William asked. "Giving them a chance to be more digitally connected, like their peers?"

"It's possible," Bisky said. She liked that William wasn't giving up easily. "I think we have to get them at least a little excited at the beginning, and then they might catch a real interest as they get more involved. But how do we do that, with a bunch of mostly boys?"

Drew looked in William's direction. "Pizza," he suggested.

"Yep. *Free* pizza," William said.

"Free food will motivate any teenage boy," Drew said. "How well I remember."

William laughed. "If we're on the same page, will you work with us on this? It's my volunteer gig for Victory Cottage and I'd like to do a good job for Mary's sake."

"Mary will get to you," Drew said. "She's great. Sure, I'll do whatever I can to help."

Watching them made Bisky's heart twist with a sudden ache of longing. She liked men, especially men like Drew and William. Somewhere inside her lurked the hope that she'd find love, find a man who would embrace her strength and size and still see her as a woman, and attractive.

She had more time than ever before now, with Sunny so busy. She was, she had to admit to herself, lonely.

But men like these wouldn't find her attractive, because she wasn't the petite, feminine type. Drew had Ria, who was curvy and womanly. William...who knew what he wanted, what his wife had been like?

Anyway, she needed to get off this track of thinking or she'd be depressed. She pretended to hear her phone, pulled it out and looked at the blank screen. "Hey," she said to William, "can you work out a few details with Drew and then find your own way home?"

"What about lunch at Goody's?"

"Rain check?" she asked.

"I'm off in a bit," Drew said. "I'll go with you. Could use a milkshake."

So that was that. William was fine, had made a new friend.

The fact that Bisky felt empty inside, well...too bad for her. She'd just have to get busy, find some new project to work on, maybe even check out a dating website and see if there were any interesting men over six feet tall in their tiny community or willing to travel there.

Yeah, right.

CHAPTER NINE

SUNNY WASN'T MUCH on delays, but even less did she like to hear the word *no*. So when she beckoned Mary to come out of the bookstore and talk to her, she had a good buffer against both: the new dog, Muffin, cowering on a leash beside her.

"Is this that poor dog that was abused?" Mary knelt and put a hand out to Muffin, who reared backward, quivering. "Oh, my goodness, she's so sweet and so scared."

Inside the shop, Mary's poodle mix, Coco, was clawing to get out. "Have you found out how she reacts to other dogs?"

Sunny shook her head. "Not yet. We're going to let her wounds heal before exposing her to other dogs. That's what the vet suggested." She cleared her throat. "Um, so I was wondering if you'd thought any more about the therapy dog program. Would you want me to try to start training Muffin for it, sort of as a test case?"

Mary frowned. "I can't see that, dear. She's scared of her shadow. Besides, she's what amounts to evidence in a police case. I don't think she should be involved in any kind of training program, really, until that's cleared up."

Sunny narrowed her eyes. "Plus, you haven't found anyone, right? And William's not a dog guy, so that's not working out."

Mary sighed and nodded. "I need to find an adult trainer, but it's not easy."

"Why not?" She sounded definite, but maybe if Sunny could get her talking about it... "Is the pay too low? The benefit of a teenager—me—is that we work for cheap."

Mary smiled. "The pay's actually good, but it's a part-time job in an isolated community. And to find someone who's entrepreneurial..."

Sunny nodded, pretending to know what that meant.

"It's tough because we want creative thinking, a dog person who works well with people, someone who's flex-ible and can accept feedback...it's a tall order."

Sunny wanted to scream, *I can do all that!*

Mary put a hand on Sunny's arm. "I know you want to do it, and you probably could, if it weren't for all the regu-lations and the trust factor. For those things, people need an adult in the role." She paused. "Tell you what, if there *is* a good adult leader found, and *if* he or she needs an assis-tant, you'll be first in line for the job." She glanced into the store. "I have customers. You take good care of that sweet pup, won't you? And Sunny," she added, "try to be a kid for once. Hang out with your friends. Do what teenagers do."

Sunny sighed as Mary went inside. The trouble was, she didn't really like doing what teenagers did. She didn't es-pecially enjoy hanging around her boy-crazy friends these days.

With nothing else to do, she texted Kait and her other close friend, Venus, and sure enough, they were together. The good news was, no boys were involved, for once. "Come over!" Kait ordered, and Sunny clicked her tongue at the dog and turned in the direction of Kaitlyn's house, right beside the Chesapeake Motor Lodge that Ria, her mother, owned and managed.

She held out hot dog pieces to Muffin, trying to encour-age her to stay at her side, and in fact, the dog seemed to be in favor of that. When a loud car went by, bass music rumbling, she practically slammed herself against Sunny's leg. And when another dog barked from behind a fence, she ran in the other direction, nearly pulling Sunny into the path of an oncoming car. For a medium-sized dog, she was strong.

And okay, maybe Mary was right: she did have her training work cut out for her. But she was fine with that. She wanted to help Muffin overcome her fears.

The afternoon was balmy, and she shed her sweater and tied it around her waist. Warm sun beat down on her. Summer, and tourist season, would be here before they knew it. With that would come the requirement to help Mom with crabbing, all day, every day.

Sunny didn't mind helping, working, but crabbing wasn't what she wanted to do with her life.

"Over here!"

Sunny looked over to where the voice had come from. It had sounded like Venus, but where was she? Then, as she headed across the lawn in front of Kait's house, she found her and Venus in the shadow of a big tree, a full-length mirror propped in front of them. They were decked out in shorts and bikini tops, with makeup and hair fully done.

"Come see us! We're doing a St. Patrick's Day photo shoot!" Kaitlyn posed, hands on her back, pushing out her rear end.

At that point, Sunny realized that their clothes—what little there was of them—were mostly green, and that Kaitlyn was wearing a shamrock headband.

Venus knelt beside the tree, snapping photos on her iPhone.

"Wait, do these shorts make me look fat?" Kaitlyn asked.

Sunny drew in a sigh. "No, you look cute," she said. "What brought this on?"

"We're just getting ready for summer," Kaitlyn explained.

Venus adjusted her long braids to spread more evenly across her bare shoulders. "Lots of hot tourist boys," she said. "I can't wait."

"First time you guys ever liked tourist season," Sunny grumped. Of course, neither of them had lived here their whole lives, like Sunny had.

"Hey, is that the dog we found?" For the first time, Kait noticed Muffin. She knelt down in front of the dog, then sat cross-legged, not reaching out a hand. "Is she doing okay?"

"Yeah. She's still healing, but the vet says she's doing really well. Skittish, though."

"Do you think she'd like to meet Dad's dog? She's right inside."

"Worth a try." While Sunny hadn't wanted to introduce Muffin to Mary's rowdy poodle mix, she thought Kait's father's former K-9, Navy, might be a good companion for Muffin. Sure enough, when Kaitlyn emerged with the golden retriever, it approached Muffin slowly, then sat a short distance away, just as Kaitlyn had.

Muffin cowered low, but when neither Kait nor Navy came any closer, she stretched her nose out toward Navy and sniffed. When the golden retriever moved, though, Muffin jumped back.

"Baby steps," Sunny said.

Venus, not as much of a dog person, had watched the exchange from a safe distance. "I can't believe someone would hurt a dog," she said.

"Me, either." Sunny got an idea the way she always did: fully formed and ready for liftoff. "That's why I want the three of us to investigate, find out who did it."

Kaitlyn and Venus looked at each other. Then Kaitlyn slowly shook her head. "I don't mean any disrespect, but what can we do that the police can't? Aren't they looking into it?"

"Yeah, in their free time, which is nonexistent." Sunny ran her hands over Muffin, letting it all play out in her mind. "We can poke around where they can't, see what we can find out."

"I don't want to." Venus lay back and stared up at the blue sky. "Maybe I'm lazy, but I just want to watch Netflix and try on clothes. School's been hard this year."

Sunny narrowed her eyes. "The three of us made a pretty good team when Kait was in trouble," she reminded them. It was a subtle dig: she didn't want Kait to forget that they'd helped her figure out who was circulating a bad video about her, and not only that, they'd gotten revenge on the boys involved.

"We did, and I'm grateful," Kait said. "It's just…I'm with Venus. Kinda tired."

Sunny didn't think she could do it alone, and she didn't want to. "There's actually a cute boy involved," she said, then immediately regretted bringing up Caden.

"Ooh, who?" Both of her friends snapped to attention.

What was done was done. So Sunny explained how Caden had come out of the woods just after Kaitlyn had run for the police, and had disappeared when the police came. "He's living—squatting, really—in the Blue House by Victory Cottage."

"Why?" Kaitlyn asked. "Isn't he rich?"

"All he said was that he needed not to live at home for a while."

"Now, that's a mystery I'd like to solve," Venus said. "He's yummy."

He *was* yummy. If Sunny had wanted to date, she'd have chosen a guy like Caden: built, countercultural, not full of himself, smart. "So will you come at least see what we can find out?" She'd get them interested that way and then they'd become the friends they'd been before, and help her solve the dog mystery. Sunny figured Caden wouldn't be at the Blue House, because she'd seen him at school, headed for the locker room. Probably, he'd hang with the soccer team or play some basketball with the group that spent all their time on the outdoor courts.

"What good will it do to go to the Blue House?" Kaitlyn asked.

"That's where Muffin was originally dropped off. Maybe we can find something out." The truth was, she didn't have a plan, but she hoped something would fall into place.

With a lot of groaning and whining, Kaitlyn and Venus stowed their photo shoot gear and followed Sunny to the street where Victory Cottage and the Blue House were. The sun was getting lower, and the air cooler, and Sunny listened to their complaints about being cold in their shorts without a whole lot of sympathy. She'd told them to put on jeans, but they both wanted to tan their legs. Which wasn't happening, not in March, but she didn't bring that up.

As a kid who spent a ton of time on the water, Sunny didn't try to get tan. She was already brunette, and she got dark soon enough with long days of crabbing. Mom usually made her wear a hat, like all the watermen did.

But Kaitlyn was a town kid—from Baltimore, actually, before her family had moved to Pleasant Shores a few years ago—and Venus came from up the coast. She was light-skinned but liked to get sun, because it brought out her freckles, which she thought were cute, and she was right.

They approached the Blue House, and Navy and Muffin lunged and barked at a gull pecking along the road.

Sunny felt like cheering. Muffin was acting like a real dog!

Then the door of Victory Cottage opened, and there was Mom's friend William on the steps.

"Go, go, go!" she said, urging her friends to hide behind the Blue House. She didn't want William to see her and report to Mom where she was and what she was doing. Almost immediately, she realized she should have just pretended they were out taking a stroll, but it was too late. Now, they were committed to hiding.

"Sunny?" came his voice. Great, he'd seen her. But maybe if they hid, he'd forget about it.

"Who's the giant?" Venus asked as they ran around the back of the Blue House.

"Mom's friend," Sunny panted. "Come on, we can go in."

"It'll be locked!"

"Let's just try it." She was pretty sure Caden didn't always lock the place, because no way did he have a key.

Sure enough, she pushed open the door easily and they all fell inside, laughing. "Close call," Kaitlyn said.

"This reminds me of old times," Venus added. "Remember when we hid in the window well of Chris Taylor's house and filmed him doing his dastardly deeds?" She was back to the fake British accent she sometimes used.

Sunny pushed herself to a sitting position. The dogs sniffed around, finding a few food crumbs on the floor.

"You said Caden wouldn't be here, right?" Kaitlyn asked. "Because he's not going to like us breaking in."

"You've got that right," came a voice from the hallway. Caden came in and stood, arms crossed. He glared at Sunny. "Why'd you squeal about my hiding place?"

"I…I…" Sunny felt bad. She'd done it, really, to get her friends' attention. "We're trying to find out about who dropped Muffin off here."

"Are you in trouble?" Kaitlyn asked Caden. "Why are you staying here?"

"It's just…not a great time to be at my house. I told my folks I was staying with a friend, and they're not the types to worry about me. But now that everyone in the world knows I'm here, I'll probably have to move on." He stomped over to the refrigerator and started pulling food out and loading it into grocery bags.

"No, stop!" Kaitlyn hurried over to him and put a hand on his arm. "We won't tell anyone. Right?" She looked at Venus and glared at Sunny.

"Right," Venus said. "We won't tell."

"Of course they won't," Sunny said. "You don't have to leave. You can help us! We're investigating what happened to the dog."

"I don't want to do that. Y'all get out."

"Come on," Venus said, tugging at Sunny's arm. "Let's go. You heard him. Leave him in peace. Don't ruin his hideout any more than you already have."

Sunny looked at the three faces around her, ranging from annoyed to angry, and realized she'd screwed up. How would she fix it?

ON TUESDAY NIGHT, William walked into the Gusty Gull and stopped in the doorway, surveying the scene. He'd expected a quiet dive, but the place seemed to be having a wild party. Loud music played, its volume belying the fact that the band in the corner was only three guys. The smell of fried food hung in the air, and almost every table was filled with talking, laughing, drinking people.

Once his eyes had adjusted to the dim light, he realized that there were shamrocks and green streamers everywhere, and that most people were wearing at least some item of green clothing.

Ooohhh. It was St. Patrick's Day, and here in Pleasant Shores, as elsewhere, the green beer was flowing.

He scanned the room and located Drew. They'd agreed at the museum yesterday that rather than getting lunch at

Goody's, they'd hit the Gusty Gull tonight. He approached Drew's table, greeted him and sat down.

"Place is packed," William said. "I think that's Mary in the middle of the dance floor. She's good!"

"Is she dancing with a bald man? Sharp dresser?"

"Uh-huh." William leaned to see past some of the other dancers. "They're doing something like salsa…he's twirling her and dipping her. They put everyone else to shame."

"That's Kirk James. He's crazy about her, but she doesn't want a boyfriend. Or so she says." Drew grinned. "Gotta get you up on the local gossip."

"It's good to see another side of Mary." As the song ended, the bald man held onto her arm, gesturing with his other hand. She laughed and shook her head, pulled away, and went to a table where a couple of other women were sitting. "Looks like she blew him off. She's back sitting with two women I met, but I can't remember their names. One's maybe Amber?"

Drew nodded. "Amber and Erica, most likely. Sisters, and they're good friends of Mary."

"Can I get you another, Drew?" The voice came from a frazzled-looking waitress. "What about you, sir?"

"I'll have the same," Drew said. "Thanks, Suz."

"Iced tea for me," William said, and when the waitress left, he explained even though Drew didn't question his decision. "Got too much of the wrong side of alcohol, growing up. Never developed a taste for it."

There were a couple of games on TV, hockey and spring training baseball. William was into baseball, always had been, and it turned out Drew followed the Orioles, too. After a while, they talked a little about the museum and how it could work with the teens. "Better not make too many plans," William said. "Bisky's taking the lead here. She knows everyone and everything about the community."

"You said you grew up around here, though?" Drew asked.

William nodded, then realized Drew couldn't see a nod. "Uh-huh. I was a dock kid of sorts, not that my family had a real fishing business. Dad made a little money oystering and crabbing." He didn't mention the welfare and disability payments, nor his father's other questionable activities.

"How'd you end up a professor?"

William smiled. "Would've surprised a lot of people if they knew," he said. "I dropped out and headed up the shore. Got my GED, met a mentor, and he helped me find a scholarship. It went on like that, all the way to a doctorate in education." The truth was, he'd gotten a lot of assistance on the way. That was part of the reason why he liked working at the community college. The teaching load was heavy, but the students made it all worthwhile. Many of them were like him, kids that couldn't afford a private school or even a state university. He tried to help along as many as he could, or at least, he had until they'd lost Jenna and everything had fallen apart.

"How's it going?" A voice from above their heads made William look up. There was Evan Stone, now in uniform. "Hey, Drew, it's Evan."

"Are you working the Gull tonight?"

"Yeah, keeping an eye on things. But I'll sit down for a few."

"Good luck keeping this crowd in line," Drew said.

"It's damage control at this point." Evan scanned the room. "See who's leaving drunk and make sure they don't try to drive home."

"Good man."

Evan turned his attention to William. "Heard anything about that dog?" he asked.

"No." William felt accused. "Why would I?"

"Just thought you might," Evan said mildly. "Since you were at Bisky's that night. People don't always want to talk to a cop, especially one who's new in town."

"I heard nothing."

"Trust me," Drew said, "you'll always be new in town if you didn't grow up here. But it's a welcoming town, anyway. There's just a difference between locals and newcomers, that's all."

"What about you?" Evan asked William. "Do you consider yourself a local or a newcomer?"

He's just doing his job, William reminded himself. "A little of both, I guess."

They talked a few minutes longer, and then Evan stood abruptly and headed after a couple who were leaving, falling-down drunk.

"You planning to leave as soon as your time at Victory Cottage is done?" Drew asked.

"Yeah, I am," William said. "Have a job back home. And this place holds a lot of bad memories for me."

"You might want to check it out, see how it's changed," Drew said. "It's a real friendly town. Nice place to raise a family."

"Uh-huh." William wasn't buying it, and anyway, what did it matter to him whether it was a nice place to raise a family? Did he want to be here in a pretty little town where everyone *else* had a nice family?

"Believe me," Drew said, "when I came back here, I didn't think I'd stay. I'm a former cop," he explained.

"Really?" That surprised William.

Drew nodded. "Uh-huh, until I got disabled in the line of duty. Couldn't go back to my old job, so I had to figure out how to make a life here. It helped that I remarried my wife," he added.

"And I bet your girls were glad about that." William

ignored the twinge he felt, thinking of Drew with his two teenage girls. Jenna had been deeply unhappy when William and her mother had separated. Now, he'd give anything to have stayed with Ellie, at least for the time being. He wished he could have made Jenna's life perfect.

"Uh-huh," Drew said. "If you don't mind my asking, are you and Bisky together?"

"Why do you ask?" William wasn't used to small-town nosiness anymore.

"To be honest," Drew said, "my wife and I were talking about it. She thought you'd be great together."

"Old friends," William said. "And that's all."

Drew nodded, seeming to catch on that William didn't want to spill his guts to a guy he'd just met. "Friends are good," he said, and they went back to focusing on the games and the dance floor action, which was getting wilder as people consumed more alcohol.

"Hey, gentlemen." Two women were suddenly sitting at their table. Both wore tight jeans, tight shirts and high heels. Both were pretty.

And drunk.

"We were hoping you'd like to dance," the blonde one said.

Drew laughed. "Not me," he said easily. "My wife's the only one who can handle my bad dancing."

Well played. William tried to think of a gracious turndown. He'd used to like to dance, when things were good with Ellie. They'd even danced at a few middle school dances they'd chaperoned, mortifying Jenna, but in a good way. Her friends had loved it.

"You're gonna have to find somebody else," the blonde said to her quieter friend, nodding sideways at William. "He's mine. I like 'em big."

"Uh, no thanks," William said, laughing a little. "I've had a long day."

"Way to objectify the man," her friend said. "Come on. Sorry, gentlemen."

After they'd left, William shook his head. "That was embarrassing."

"Were they pretty?" Drew asked.

"Oh, sure."

"Well, if you're not with Bisky, why not dance with some pretty women? You might meet someone that way."

"No thanks," William said. "I'm a bad bet for love."

"Are you now?" Drew frowned. "Nobody's perfect at it, you know. Just ask my wife."

William liked Drew, but he was a little tired of hearing about "my wife, my wife."

"Listen," he said. "I gotta go. You okay getting out of here?"

An expression of annoyance crossed Drew's face. "I'm fine."

"Sorry, man, of course you are." He should know better than to question a blind man's competence. He'd clearly gotten here okay on his own.

He walked out of the bar, through the happy, friendly people, feeling like a loser all around.

If he didn't have an appointment to meet with Bisky the next morning, he might have gotten in his car and driven right back to Baltimore where he belonged, or at least, where he could disappear into the crowd.

CHAPTER TEN

ON WEDNESDAY MORNING, Bisky met William downtown, halfway between their houses, and they walked toward the preschool.

They'd agreed to meet before connecting with Kayla. They were going to talk to her about whether her young students, some of whom stayed a full day in extended care, would benefit from being involved in the museum activities they were planning for their teenagers.

The breeze rustled through long-needled pines. The sun shone bright, and the occasional wild cry of a loon broke through the chirp and trill of spring's first robins. A perfect Chesapeake day.

Bisky breathed in the fragrance from hyacinths someone had planted around a mailbox. Beneath that, always, the salty smell of the bay. Down the street, they could hear children's voices. Recess time.

"You want to be out on the water, don't you?" William asked.

"How could you tell?" She smiled at the way he'd read her.

"You sniff the air like you used to when we were kids. I could always tell when you were going to try to talk me into borrowing somebody's boat."

"Busted." She loved the Chesapeake; it had been in her blood from a young age. "And yeah, I wouldn't mind being out right now. But crabbing season starts soon enough. Until then, it's nice not to have to get up early."

"I bet."

"Excuse me, have you seen a little boy?" A young, frazzled-looking woman rushed out from a picket-fenced yard in front of a run-down trailer. Roses tried to climb up a rusty attempt at a porch, and plastic ride-on toys were strewn around the yard.

"No." Bisky stopped. "What's the matter? Amy, right?"

"Yes, I'm Amy." The young mother was distracted. "It's my Bobby. He wandered off. Again."

"We'll help you look." Bisky scanned the area. "What's he wearing?"

"Bright blue jacket. He's a redhead with freckles. You've seen him, right? I'm going to the neighbors." Amy rushed toward the next trailer down.

As soon as she was out of hearing distance, William spoke. "Is it a safe family?"

Strange he'd go there first. Or maybe not. Bisky nodded. "They're nice people. Just poor and under stress."

"He's over there." William pointed at a line of bushes that separated the little trailer park from the preschool.

Bisky saw movement, a flash of blue, and they both hurried over. A grimy little boy, dressed in too-short jeans, came reluctantly out of the bushes at Bisky's order. William stayed back, which was good, because when the little boy saw him he blanched. A man of William's size could intimidate a child.

"You scared your mother. You can't just run off. Are you okay?" Bisky inspected the child.

"I'll go find his mom and tell her he's safe," William offered, and disappeared.

"What were you doing?" Bisky asked the little boy.

"I want to go to school!" He pointed through the bushes

at the colorful flashes of kids' bright clothing and the sound of happy voices from the preschool's playground.

Amy came rushing over, William trailing behind her. She swept the little boy into her arms. "I told you, you stay in our yard! This is dangerous!" She looked up at Bisky, then William, still holding her son close. "Thank you so much. He's always sneaking over here. Says he wants to go to school."

William looked from the little boy to the pristine preschool. Then he looked back at Amy. "There's a scholarship program," he said. "If you'd be interested. It's a nice school."

"I never heard about that." Amy looked skeptical, but there was just a little hope and interest in her eyes. "He's a handful, always wanting to talk and look at books and dig things up. I can't keep him busy enough."

Bisky had never heard of any such program, either. It would be strange if William knew about a local scholarship for little kids when Bisky didn't.

"Bisky will get you the information."

"Thank you. That would be wonderful."

Bisky gave Amy a weak smile as the woman walked away, still lecturing her son but with more of a spring in her step.

As soon as Amy was back in her yard, Bisky turned to William. "Why would you raise her hopes like that? Sure, there's a Headstart program up the coast, but I don't think she can take him there."

"Why not?" William propped his hands on his hips like he was ready to argue.

"Because she has three other kids. Maybe four, I don't know her that well." She frowned at him. "Now she's all excited her youngest might be able to go to preschool. And I'm going to have to be the one to disappoint her."

William put a hand on Bisky's arm. "Bisky."

"I mean, I get that you feel bad for her. You probably would have benefited from preschool yourself. But that doesn't excuse—"

"Bisky." He said her name softly, looking into her eyes.

She shut her mouth and looked into those eyes, and a feeling went through her she couldn't name. She just knew that she felt warm and breathless.

"I'm paying for the kid's preschool," he said. "All you have to do is figure out a way to get the money to her that she won't suspect."

She tilted her head to one side. "You're paying for it yourself? It's kind of expensive, I think."

He shrugged. "It's okay."

"Wait a minute. Are you rich?"

He laughed a little, shook his head. "Not at all. I just don't have a lot of needs." Something passed over his face then and was gone.

Bisky knew what it had been, too, because she was a single parent. When you had a child, and not a ton of money, any new expenditure had to be carefully considered, weighed against your child's needs, current and future.

But William didn't have to weigh that anymore, because he no longer had a child. "You were such a smart little kid," she said, wanting to distract him. "You always knew the answer before the teacher, from first grade on up."

"I was a smart aleck," he said.

"At times. Mrs. Grimstead thought so." She smiled to remember William being scolded and sent to the principal. On the way out of the room, he'd walked over to the chalk-board to correct her math error.

That had been before he'd quieted down. Either his dad hadn't been so bad, then, or his parents hadn't cared if he got in trouble at school. Probably a little of both.

"I'm glad you grew up to use your smarts," she said now. "And it's kind of you to help that child."

He shrugged. "It's better for him to put his mind to use at something productive, not running away and scaring his mom. Come on, it's time to meet with Kayla."

Obviously, he wanted to change the subject, didn't want to focus on his own generosity. But Bisky couldn't help thinking about it as they walked the rest of the way to the preschool. She kept stealing glances over at him and thinking about the man he'd become.

If she didn't know better than to let herself, she might even have fallen a little bit in love with him.

ON FRIDAY AFTERNOON, William picked up one end of a picnic table and, with Bisky at the other end, helped her move it from the backyard to the front yard. It was a big, solid old table, and William reflected that a lot of women would have trouble lifting one end of it.

Not Bisky, though. She was strong.

"Thanks for doing this," she said as she set down her end, not even breathless. "This should be good. This is where we usually leave it in the summer, in fact."

For a moment, William pictured summer here, sitting under the big shade tree, eating crabs and roasted corn. It sounded appealing; he could almost taste the traditional bay delicacies. Could imagine the feeling of being here with Bisky and Sunny and other friends he was making.

Except he wasn't going to be here for the summer, he reminded himself.

It wasn't summer yet, but it could have been: the temperature had climbed into the eighties, a rare hot day in March. The sun was still weak, but William could feel it on his shoulders. The yard sat a little higher than water level, sloping down to the road, and across the road was her dock and shed. That meant there was a great view of the bay, which shone like polished glass.

He'd avoided Bisky for a few days, citing counseling appointments and paperwork. It wasn't a lie, he *was* busy getting settled in, but he could have made time to meet and work on the program earlier. He'd just needed a break after they'd gone to the preschool to meet with Kayla, who was all in with having the preschoolers serve as the teens' first audience.

His avoidance couldn't last forever, though. Bisky had called him this morning and as much as insisted that he come over so they could start pinning down the details and get the program ready for after-school work with the teens starting next week. Now, she forked back her hair and apologized for being bossy. "Crab season's coming," she said, "and I'll have a lot less time. Unless you want to develop and run the whole program yourself, we'd better spend a few hours today getting the details pinned down."

"You're right. Of course." He tried not to look at her too closely. She was wearing shorts and a T-shirt, nothing fancy, but he hadn't seen her dressed for summer in years, and he was reeling from the impact of her long legs.

He was just a guy, right? Any guy would notice Bisky's legs.

And then that thought bothered him, too, because he didn't *want* other guys to notice her legs.

"Yoo-hoo," she called to him, pulling his attention back to their work. "The high school counselor gave me a list of kids who've tentatively agreed to come. Or their parents are making them," she added wryly. "Having another activity right after school isn't what every kid wants."

"We're not taking them out of sports or anything, are we?"

"Nope." She reached a hand out toward the dog they'd

taken in. William hadn't even noticed the animal, skulking around the edges of the yard, when he'd arrived. "None of the kids are on spring teams."

"Good." William hadn't been able to play sports, because his family couldn't afford the gear and his father hadn't wanted to sit down and talk to the coaches about ways to fund it. The truth was, William had been just as happy to read a book, but due to his size, everyone had always tried to get him on their teams. He liked using his body and had gotten into swimming and lifting weights back in the city. But that had all stopped after Jenna died. He hadn't been able to do anything more than the bare minimum to get by.

That was part of why he'd gotten so stressed out, he supposed. He should have kept working out. If he hadn't forgotten to eat half the time, he'd probably have gained a ton of weight.

"Hey, girl!" Bisky's singsong voice brought him back to the present, and he looked over to see the dog they'd taken in, Muffin, inching toward her, trailing a leash. "She's attached to me," Bisky explained, "but she's still terrified of most other people. She wants to come sit near me, but she's scared of you."

"She looks a lot better." William studied the dog. "You know, I'm not a fan of dogs, but this one's cute. And she's more afraid of me than I am of her." He reached out a hand, and she leaped back.

Bisky handed him a couple of dog treats. "Toss them toward her, one at a time. She'll start to see you as a good guy."

"So what are we going to do if some of these kids don't like history?" he asked as he tossed the dog a treat, pulling the conversation back to the teenagers and the program they were trying to plan. "Even though the museum focuses on this area, that academic of a topic isn't every-one's cup of tea."

"True." She tapped her pen on the table, considering. "We'll have to think of something else for them to do, some alternative activity. Like, the kids up the coast help older people with small-scale construction projects."

"Maybe they could build something for the museum, if they're more hands-on," he suggested. "It backs on the bay, but it doesn't look like there's a dock or anything."

"Good idea." She made a note.

They kept talking, figuring out what they'd do at their first meeting, how they'd present the program to get the most engagement from the kids. William had always loved planning lessons, and this was like that, only collaborative.

He kept reminding himself that he was here to get well and go back to his job. Not to stay and follow through with the teenagers when the school year ended.

Not to see what Bisky's legs looked like with their summer tan.

"I'm home and it's hot!" Sunny's shout came from the street, and then she came climbing up the green grass. "And it's Friday, woo-hoo!"

Bisky reached out a hand, and Sunny came over to sit by her, close. Bisky put an arm around her, and Sunny leaned in.

"How was school?"

"Kinda boring. We have the standardized tests next week so they're all trying to review." She looked at William, ac-knowledging him for the first time. "The better we do, the more money the school gets from the state of Maryland. Which, if you think about it, doesn't make sense. Schools where kids do poorly should get more money."

"Pleasant Shores Academy is private though, right?"

"Yes, but we get some state money. Because there are some scholarship kids there, like me."

William liked her opinionated ways, and he wondered whether Jenna would have turned out to have strong opinions, too. She'd been more in the awkward, "don't look at me" phase when she'd been killed.

Man, he wished he could have seen her grow up, gotten to know who she'd become as an adult. She'd had so much to offer the world. All lost with a drugged idiot's bullet.

He swallowed and looked down at the table while Sunny and Bisky chatted away.

The sound of a car stopping in front of the house made them all look toward the road. Muffin barked and then hid behind Bisky.

It was a police car, and Evan Stone got out and strode toward them.

This guy again. Seemed like he spent an awful lot of time seeking Bisky out.

"I have a surprise for you," he said, and William bristled even more. Was the guy bringing presents now? While on the town's payroll, yet?

Evan smiled and knelt, holding out his hand toward Muffin, who was trembling and letting out the occasional bark. "How does your dog get along with other dogs?"

"We don't know yet," Bisky said.

"She did okay with the Martins' dog," Sunny said. "Why?"

"I have someone I'd like for her to meet." He walked back to his car, opened the back door, and urged a black dog to come out.

The dog hesitated on the edge of the seat, but finally, lured by a treat, jumped down and looked around, cowering.

Why it was cowering was hard to say, because it looked fierce.

"Oh my gosh. Boy or girl?" Sunny hurried down the slope toward the car and approached the dog, slowly.

"She's a girl," they could hear Evan say.

Muffin growled, the hair on her back rising.

"What on earth?" Bisky spoke quietly to William, sounding exasperated.

"Looks a little like Diablo," William said. It was true: there had to be some German shepherd in the cringing creature.

"Part shepherd, part pit, if I had to guess." Bisky picked up Muffin's leash. "And Evan's getting Sunny excited about it. You just wait, she'll come up here and ask if we can keep it."

He was glad to hear her sounding annoyed with Evan, who was now making his way toward them. The dog hung back, and Sunny walked slowly on the dog's other side, giving it plenty of space.

"It's another injured dog," Evan said as he reached them, "with wounds similar to the ones your dog had. Picked it up over near Victory Cottage, actually. We're not sure what's going on, but I thought maybe you could take it in."

"No way," Bisky said. "I'm only now getting used to one dog, and she to us. There's no way we can have a second."

"Mom, we could," Sunny protested. "We have all the stuff. They could share a dish and we could use an old blanket for a bed. She could sleep in my room."

"No." Bisky crossed her arms and glared at Evan. "I don't know why you thought of me. It's not like I take in strays all the time."

Evan turned to William. "What about you?"

He lifted his hands, palms out. "No way. Me and dogs don't get along."

"Maybe it's time to get over Diablo," Bisky teased.

Sunny's eyes widened. "You knew Diablo? Mom used to use him as a reason we couldn't get a dog."

"Not only did I know him, he was my dad's dog," William said.

"But Mom said…" Sunny trailed off and looked at her mother.

"I said he wasn't treated well. That wasn't William's fault."

Bisky was right about that, mostly. He'd hated the way his dad had been toward the dog. William's few efforts to befriend Diablo had resulted in terrifying snarls and growls, and he'd given up too easily. He just hadn't had the knowledge of how to help a dog like that. "My dad's mistreatment made Diablo into a mean dog, but it wasn't the dog's fault," he said. "That responsibility rests on my dad."

Evan watched the exchange closely. Did he want to learn about shore culture, or find the dog a home…or get to know Bisky better?

"I didn't like dogs much, for a long time," Bisky said. "The way we grew up, people treated dogs differently."

"And then came Jonathan the puppy raiser," Sunny said slyly.

Bisky reddened. "No need to go into that."

"I know, but it made you not afraid of dogs," she said.

William wondered if he'd ever find out who Jonathan the puppy raiser was and what his connection to the family might be.

Probably not, but he couldn't help being curious.

The black dog approached Muffin, who snarled louder. Then they both started barking, pulling at their leashes to get at each other, and not in a friendly way.

"Look," Bisky said over the din as Evan led the black

dog a few paces away, "they don't even like each other. No way could we take that dog in."

"You're right." Evan walked the dog down to his cruiser, put it inside, and then came back. "Sorry to bother you folks. It was a good try."

"What will happen to the dog?" Sunny asked.

Evan frowned. "I guess I'll have to take her to the pound," he said. "My apartment doesn't allow dogs, and it's hard to place a pit."

Sunny nudged William. When he looked at her, she nodded at the black dog and gave him a meaningful look.

He could read it, easily, because he'd had a daughter. A daughter who'd had him wrapped around her little finger. A daughter who'd talked him into doing all kinds of things he didn't want to do, from playing with dolls to going to a father-daughter dance to buying her shoes that cost more than a week's salary.

Once a sucker, always a sucker. He cleared his throat. "If Sunny will help me manage it," he said, "I'll take the dog."

CHAPTER ELEVEN

FRIDAY NIGHT WAS always hopping at Goody's, but tonight, with the unusually warm weather, it seemed like everyone in town was there.

Sunny had scored a table by the window, ignoring the dirty looks people were giving her because it was a big table and she was alone. She was waiting for Kaitlyn and Venus, but they were running late.

No doubt they were lingering over their hair and makeup. Oh, well. That couldn't ruin Sunny's good mood.

She was thrilled she'd talked William into taking in that poor injured dog. Not only that, she'd gotten the gig of helping to train him. William had even said he'd pay her for her time.

It was a step in the right direction. She sucked on her milkshake, savoring the rich, creamy chocolate.

"Hey." Above her, Venus's voice sounded and then Kaitlyn chimed in with her own unenthusiastic "Hey. We're getting our shakes."

She could tell from their voices that they were still mad. Oh, well. She daydreamed about using her skills to train William's new dog, maybe even make him into a therapy dog, just like she hoped to do with Muffin. Like Mom always said, there was more than one way to skin a muskrat.

William was okay. More than okay, because he'd saved that dog from the pound. She just wished there weren't such weird vibes between him and Mom.

"Earth to Sunny, we're sitting here," Venus said, and Sunny realized her friends had slipped into the chairs across from her while she was spacing out thinking about dogs.

"Hey, I'm glad you could come out. Great night, huh?"

Kaitlyn frowned. "Don't you care that you upset him?"

Sunny didn't pretend not to know what Kaitlyn was talking about. Caden. "Of course, I'm sorry, but he won't talk to me. I think he wants to be left alone."

"We should go get him and apologize," Venus said. "Nobody really wants to be left alone. Plus…he's hot."

Kaitlyn sucked on her straw, hard, and nodded. "What's he doing, staying at the Blue House by himself, anyway?"

"He told his parents he was staying with a friend," Venus reminded them. "But why wouldn't he just do that?"

"Does he even have friends?" Kait asked. "I mean, the kind you could stay with?"

"Who knows?" Sunny shrugged. She didn't think going to get Caden would go well. And she hated all that boy-crazy stuff.

Although if she *were* going to be boy crazy, it might be about Caden.

"If we all go together, maybe he'll get over being mad at you," Venus pointed out.

Sunny did kind of want to see what was going on with him. "Okay, we can go," she said.

"Yes!" Kaitlyn stood up. "Come on," she said to Venus. "Let's go before she changes her mind."

They walked through town, which was almost crowded right near Goody's. Even as they got to the quieter residential streets, there were people out on their porches or walking their dogs. Everyone seemed to be in a good mood, happy for spring.

When they reached the Blue House, Sunny paused, unsure of what to do. "I don't think he'll come to the door," she said. For the first time, she realized how hard it must be for him to be in there all alone, keeping the lights out at night so he wouldn't be detected, without a TV, maybe even without wireless.

"I'll message him," Venus said, and did.

"What did you say?"

"I told him to come out and we'd buy him a milkshake, so I hope y'all have money."

"He's not going to…" Sunny trailed off, because the door was opening. Caden came out and approached their group. "Hey," he said to Venus and Kaitlyn. He ignored Sunny.

"You came out!" Kaitlyn sounded happy.

"I was going nuts," he said. "Plus, ice cream. Were you serious?"

"Of course! Let's go." Venus didn't mention the fact that they'd just come from Goody's.

What made Sunny happy was that Venus and Kaitlyn were smiling. They, at least, seemed to have forgiven Sunny.

They walked the long way back through town, swinging down toward the docks, where lights and voices made things lively. The warm night, plus the fact that their local waterman's festival was tomorrow, meant that things were hopping here.

"Are you and your mom doing the boat-docking contest?" Kaitlyn asked.

Venus leaned around from Caden's other side. "If you are, we'll come cheer for you."

Caden looked blank. "Boat docking? What's that even mean?"

"Jeez, Caden," Kaitlyn said. "Don't you ever leave your fancy neighborhood? This is the local version of the summer outdoor festival. Sunny and her mom have won the boat-docking event before."

"Beating all the men," Venus said, dancing around.

"Yeah, I've seen your mom," Caden said. "She's pretty tough."

"Sunny's tough, too," Venus said. "She can beat all the boys at push-ups, when they test us in gym."

Sunny sighed. "I stopped doing that last year, because of getting teased."

"You should be proud," Kaitlyn said.

Her friends weren't mad at her anymore, but Caden probably was. Sunny still felt embarrassed, as if Caden was looking at her and how big she was. He was no taller than she, and probably weighed less. It wasn't like *he* worked for a living.

"Let's play on the playground!" Kaitlyn said, gesturing toward the swing set and the slides in the tiny park that marked the border between the town and the docks.

As one, they all ran over there. Sunny and Kaitlyn jumped into the swings and started pumping. Caden climbed the slide and stood on top, while Venus snapped pictures.

As the swings swung higher, the wind blew through Sunny's hair and she felt like a kid, screaming and laughing. This was better than having weird worries about Caden, thinking about whether he thought she was too big and tall. She jumped off, flying out into the grass and landing on bent knees. Kaitlyn jumped, too, landed off balance and rolled sideways, laughing.

"You guys are nuts." Caden sounded happy. "I've been so mind-numbingly bored inside that place."

After a little more swinging and sliding, they settled down and continued walking toward Goody's. There were little clusters of people, mostly family groups, but there was a group of men who sent up Sunny's inner warning signals.

She'd never seen any of them in town before, and in Pleasant Shores during the off-season, that was rare.

While her friends joked and talked, she eased to the side of her group and tried to listen to what they were saying. She heard the words *side bets* and *dogs*.

The men saw her and moved away, one of them glaring first, so she turned and pretended full involvement in her friends' conversation.

Inside, though, she was pondering. What did dogs have to do with betting? She'd heard of greyhound racing, and one of her friends had rescued a former racing greyhound, but there were no tracks around here. So what had the strangers been talking about?

SATURDAY MORNING, BISKY pulled her waterproof jacket tighter around herself as she approached the public docks. It was going to be a warmer-than-usual day, which was a blessing for their annual boat-docking competition, but right now, the morning breeze cut to the bone.

Bisky participated in the timed contest most years. It was fun, navigating from a standstill to a docking slip as fast as possible without wrecking. The last couple of years, Sunny had been the mate, meaning she lassoed all four corners to the pilings, as fast as possible. The sport had been popular on the Chesapeake for years, and some communities got fancy about it. Here in Pleasant Shores, during the off-season, it was informal. No prizes, just bragging rights.

The group of men standing near their boats called out greetings.

"You're the only lady in the competition this year," old Henry Higbottom said.

"Better leave it to the men," another guy said.

"Save it for the water," she advised, pulling her hair back into a messy ponytail. She joined the group, sizing up the water conditions, talking about the boats. They'd use two docks for this one to keep things moving along. Even though most of the watermen were between seasons, everyone had work to do, with only a little over a week left until crab season started.

"Take to your boats," Henry called out. He'd finally decided he was too old to compete, so they'd made him the whistle-blower and timekeeper.

Bisky sent another text to Sunny, who'd groaned and begged for ten more minutes of sleep when Bisky had knocked on her bedroom door this morning. The girl needed to get down here, now.

She looked up from her phone and saw William approaching the docks.

He wore jeans and a flannel shirt, all neat and clean and handsome, and here she was in her work clothes, hanging with the men. Typical, and she shouldn't let it bother her. She waved at him and turned away, and then her phone pinged.

I'm not doing it.

Her eyebrows drew together and she punched her phone. You said you would! It's about to start!

I'm sorry, I'm sick.

Skeptical, Bisky typed in What's wrong? Need me to come home?

No! Just cramps.

She sighed and shoved her phone in her pocket. Sunny wasn't the type of girl to be sidelined by a case of cramps, unless she just didn't want to do something.

"Where's your crew?" Henry asked.

"My first mate bailed," she said. "I'm out."

Immediately, everyone started talking.

"You gotta compete!"

"We like to beat you!"

She snorted at that. "Get beat, more like." But she was glad the men wanted her to compete. She'd worked with most of them, or their families, all her life. She'd do anything for them, and they for her.

"I'll crew for you," young Johnny Anderson said, his eyebrows waggling suggestively. "Course, there'd be a cost."

She rolled her eyes. "Thanks, but no thanks." Most of the men didn't bother to flirt with her. Having known her for so long, they looked at her more like a sister. But a few of the younger or newer guys hadn't yet forgotten she was a woman.

"I can lend you my crew." Ralph Everson shoved his son forward.

Bisky looked at the boy's miserable face. "Divided loyalties. Can't make him do that."

"Hey, Bisky." There was a little stirring at the edge of the small crowd as William made his way through, moving slowly. She'd noticed that about him: he was extra careful to be polite and gentle, maybe because he was so big.

Finally, he reached her. "I'll crew," he said.

She felt her jaw drop. Around them, there were murmurs of curiosity, a few whispered conversations.

"You've got to be kidding me," she said. "Do you even know how to lasso a piling?"

He lifted a shoulder. "No guarantees about ability," he said, "but I've seen it done. I'll try, if you don't have anyone else."

"Let's get started," Henry brayed through his megaphone. "Draw lots for the order, and we'll start with Dock A and alternate."

The wind chose that moment to kick up as everyone drew lots, reported their numbers, and then went to their boats. She looked at William. "You're sure about this? You might get dunked."

"I can swim," he said, grinning. "Let's do it."

"Okay!" She jumped onboard and showed him the dock lines and hitches. Then she headed to the helm and started the motor. They'd switched over to crabbing gear, which made the boat lighter, but she hadn't run it this way in months. She wasn't expecting to win anything; it was all just fun.

Especially fun now that William was involved.

Her phone pinged. Sunny. Are you mad at me?

Instead of answering the question, she snapped a picture of William in the back of the boat and sent it to Sunny.

Two boats went in front of them, making good time, and she stood with William and strategized. "Watch the order. Sunny does front, then back, but some of these guys lasso clockwise. Your choice." Henry blew the air horn to signal a successful completion and then called out the time.

And then it was their turn. Her heart pounded as the crowd cheered and clapped and catcalled. There seemed to be a lot of people watching, especially women, probably because she was the only female.

And because of William. Word had gotten out that he was a former dock kid who'd made good. No doubt there was a lot of curiosity about whether he'd turned into a snob or could still get his hands dirty.

She glanced back toward William. Standing in the back of the boat, sleeves rolled up to reveal massive forearms, hair blowing back in the stiff breeze, he looked strong and sexy.

And he was crewing her boat, as a favor to an old family friend. And that was all, she reminded herself as she took another look at him.

"Ready?" she asked.

He gave her a nod and a grin.

The air horn sounded and she started, black smoke rising as she gunned the boat, pulled forward, swung around, and backed into the slip.

"Go!" she yelled, and William was running, aiming the circle of rope at the piling.

He got the first one, and there was a roar from the crowd. He dove across and lassoed the second.

On the way to the rear tie-ups, he looked back at her. "Pull closer," he called.

She eased the boat back, but the wind caught and pitched it.

Pitched William into the water.

There was another roar from the crowd, laced with sympathetic laughter this time. Someone came onto the dock and reached out a hand to him, and he climbed out, laughing and shivering and shaking off like a dog.

He thanked the man who'd helped him and then looked at her and lifted both hands, palms up. "Sorry," he called.

"You tried." She was laughing as she pulled her boat back down to her own slip, leaving William to make his way through the noisy group of spectators.

He was a good sport to have participated. It showed he was willing to make a fool of himself, something a lot of men had trouble doing. He was comfortable in his own skin.

She tied up, grabbed a couple of towels and headed back down toward the competition. William met her halfway. "Sorry I ruined the chance of the only woman competing today," he said. "I got some flak from the ladies in the crowd." He was blushing a little, and she could just imagine what kind of flak he'd gotten.

She handed him a towel, and he rubbed it over his hair

and bare arms. He'd untucked his flannel shirt and now, he squeezed water out of it. She handed him the other towel and he rubbed his chest underneath, giving her a tantalizing glimpse of taut abs. Not like the skinny male models Sunny liked, but thick, sturdy muscles, a man's muscles.

She sucked in a breath and looked up at his face, and realized he'd caught her admiring him.

It's William, she reminded herself. They'd played together as kids, gone swimming and fishing. She'd seen him bare-chested dozens of times.

Never like this, though. "You should take off that wet shirt," she said before she could stop herself. Her voice sounded a little high and silly.

His eyes narrowed as he looked at her. "Should I?"

It was like there was no one but the two of them in the world, all of a sudden. The roars of people down by the racing slips, the cawing of gulls, the sun emerging from behind a cloud…all of it was just a blur compared to the man in front of her who was looking into her eyes with a question in his.

She felt a girlish urge to laugh, deny what was going through her mind, but this was William. He'd see right through any effort to brush him off. She bit her lip, her breath coming faster than it should.

He took a step closer to her, reached out a hand and touched her chin. He was looking into her eyes still, but now there was intent behind his gaze.

The darkness of his eyes, the way he studied her, as if he were assessing her…the salty, docky smell of him, his wet shirt clinging to muscles that were way too spectacular for a professor…more than anything else, the confidence and certainty in the way his hand moved to brush back a lock of her hair…yeah. This was a William she didn't know.

Though she wanted to. She *really* wanted to.

She drew in a breath and his gaze shifted to her mouth. He was going to kiss her.

Her phone warbled out the opening of Beethoven's Fifth. Sunny's ring.

She took a step back. "I…it's Sunny. She said she was sick." She kept looking at him, though, and he at her, right up until she pulled the phone out of her pocket and took the call.

"Did you guys really compete? Did he fall into the water?"

She ran a hand through her hair, feeling flustered. "Yeah. You feeling okay?"

"I'm fine. I'm sorry I bailed on you. Come home and I'll make you pancakes."

Bisky drew in a breath and let it out and gave William a regretful little smile. "Sure, honey," she said. "I'll be right home."

William was already backing away as she ended the call. "I'm heading for a hot shower," he said. "Tell Sunny we'll set up some dog training soon." He gave Bisky a quick glance and then strode down the road.

Bisky turned back to her ordinary life and her responsibilities, wondering what had just happened.

CHAPTER TWELVE

On Monday afternoon, home from a planning meeting with Drew at the museum, William knelt beside the dog's crate and tried to lure him out with a piece of jerky. "You know by now I'm not going to hurt you," he said, keeping his voice low and quiet, keeping himself small.

The dog inched forward, sniffing. She wanted the food.

William stayed perfectly still, and the dog advanced closer. Today, William's hand was just six inches outside the crate.

A loud car drove by outside and the dog shrank back inside. She'd come out of the crate occasionally, if lured by food, enough that William could snap a leash on her and take her outside to do her business. But progress was slow. And that was why Sunny was coming over soon, right after she got out of school.

He wasn't thinking about Sunny, though; he was thinking about Bisky. He couldn't get her out of his head, and unfortunately, he had to have a lot of interaction with her in coming days as they started the teen program.

He'd come so close to kissing her. His mind had left the building and his body had taken over, after the excitement of the boat-docking contest. The way she'd looked in her shorts and man's shirt with the rolled-up sleeves, the way she'd looked at him…because she *had* looked at him with something like desire, he was sure of it…all of it had lit a fire that hadn't gone out since.

The dog crept forward again, and this time, got close enough to grab the jerky out of William's hand and immediately withdraw into the crate to eat it. The sight of those big teeth in close proximity to his own flesh made William's heart pound, made him sweat. It was a visceral reaction. The dog had ears that half pointed up like a shepherd, and half bent over, which gave her a rumpled look. Her dark eyes were alert. She was a beautiful dog, if only he could get past his fears.

He backed away from the crate, grabbed his jacket and the dog's leash, and opened the door. She loved to go outside, and sometimes came to look out, which she did now, and he snapped the leash on her and took her outside.

He couldn't allow his newly awakened and totally misplaced desire for Bisky to hide the realities: she was a friend. Relationshipwise, he was a failure; he'd failed at marriage, failed to take care of his wife, failed terribly at taking care of his daughter. He wouldn't inflict himself on his worst enemy, let alone a friend.

The dog lay down to chew on a stick, and William grabbed a lawn chair and set it close by her. He'd chill here until Sunny came, let the dog enjoy some time out of her crate.

"How's it going?" Sunny asked a few minutes later, from the side yard. She held their dog, Muffin, on a leash.

His dog let out a bay that sounded like fear and then strained toward Muffin, barking and snarling. Sunny's dog abandoned her calm demeanor and began snarling, too, dragging Sunny closer.

The loud barking and growling and sharp white teeth reminded him of Diablo, brought back an image: his father, wading into a fight between Diablo and a neighborhood dog that was even bigger. Dad had kicked both dogs repeatedly until the other one had slunk off. He'd given Diablo a few more kicks before stomping inside.

It had worked, sort of, but William couldn't bring himself to take the same approach.

"Okay! Leave it!" Sunny's voice rose above the doggy rumble. She tugged at her dog, pulling it over to the other side of the yard. "Sit!" she ordered, and repeated it, and amazingly, the dog did sit for a few seconds before lunging at William's dog again.

"Take her away and give her treats for being quiet." Sunny tossed William a baggie of small treats.

William did as she told him, walking his dog to the other side of the yard, and indeed, the dog calmed down some. He looked over and watched how Sunny lured her dog into a sit, holding a treat at her nose and then moving it up and back until the dog had no choice but to sink down on its haunches.

He tried the same to his dog, and sure enough, she slowly lowered herself into a sitting position. He felt a surge of satisfaction. And relief, because both dogs had quieted down.

"Keep doing that," Sunny said, and brought her dog closer, holding a treat to its nose. William kept rewarding his dog for sitting, and aside from one little growl, she continued to do it.

"I can't believe this is working," he said once Sunny was within earshot.

"She's food motivated, and that's good. What did you name her?"

"I didn't. Not yet."

Sunny's jaw dropped and her eyebrows shot up. "Loser!" she singsonged. "Four days and you haven't named that poor girl yet."

The way she said it was exactly like Jenna had used to tease him, and the mix of joy and sorrow almost knocked him flat. He put out a hand toward the lawn chair and sank down into it.

The two dogs pulled toward each other, but Sunny's dog's tail wagged and then William's did, too. They sniffed each other cautiously, end to end, and then William's dog jumped back.

"You did good with her," Sunny said. "You should be proud of yourself. What's wrong? Did I hurt your feelings, calling you a loser?"

He shook his head and forced a smile. "No. You're right, I need to find her a name."

She didn't seem to buy his cheerful tone. Instead, she frowned and sat down in the lawn chair across the firepit, studying him. "Mom says sometimes when you see me, you think of your daughter."

"Yeah." He leaned back, letting his hand dangle over the dog, petting its side a little. The dog glanced up at him and then lay down beside his chair.

"Would she want you to be all sad?"

The question hung in the air while he thought about it. Pictured Jenna and imagined what she'd say to him. "No," he said finally. "She'd probably call me a loser for it."

Sunny grinned. "If the shoe fits…"

He laughed a little, and then they just sat there in the sun. They were both wearing winter jackets but the sun was warm and there wasn't much of a breeze. The crisp air carried along the scent of some spring flowers that were blooming, lined up against the back of the cottage.

"Hello?" A voice came from the same side of the house where Sunny had appeared, and the dogs went into a frenzy of barking again. At least they were doing it at someone else and not at each other. The woman who'd called out was about William's age and wore jeans and a green jacket, her hair tucked under a hat. "William Gross?"

"Can you hold them both?" he asked Sunny, and she held out her hand for his leash.

He walked over to the woman. "I'm William Gross," he said, holding out a hand.

She shook it, quick and businesslike. "Suzanne Brady. I've been hired as the new trainer for the therapy dog program, and Mary Rhoades said you have a dog over here that might be a candidate, if it's not too fearful."

He looked back doubtfully at his unnamed dog. Sunny was walking toward them now, holding both dogs' leashes.

"Which one?" Suzanne asked.

William shrugged. "Both of them, I guess."

She frowned, and Sunny's whole body tensed beside William.

"Let's see what they can do," Suzanne said, and walked toward the dogs.

William's dog yelped and jumped back. Sunny's didn't jump, but reared away a little.

"We're just getting started with them," Sunny said. "They were abused."

"Not sure they're going to be good candidates then," Suzanne said.

William's dog still cowered, as far away from Suzanne as she could get. William didn't like the woman's attitude. He stepped between the dog and the trainer, feeling protective.

Sunny looked crushed.

"Show her what Muffin can do," he urged. "I'm no expert with dogs," he added to Suzanne, "but Sunny is. She's made a ton of progress with Muffin in just over a week."

Sunny led her dog a few steps away and gave commands: sit, down, give paw. The dog obeyed each one.

Sunny's smile got increasingly broad, and William's

heart lifted. He was proud of Sunny, and he knew her mom would be even prouder. Bisky was a good mother, allowing Sunny to have her own space and activities and be independent. The result was a strong, competent teenager.

Suzanne was studying Sunny and Muffin. "Uh-huh," she said, not sounding impressed. She walked over to Muffin, knelt and snapped her fingers.

Muffin cringed away from her.

Suzanne frowned. "See, she's going to have a hard time. She needs to be able to meet new people with enthusiasm. I just don't want you to have false expectations."

She turned toward William's dog and repeated the finger-snapping.

The dog bared her teeth.

"Oh, no, no, no," Suzanne said, standing, backing up and shaking her head. "We can't have that. She's not going to work out."

William felt like baring his teeth, too. "How can you make that judgment?"

"Yeah, after less than five minutes?" Sunny chimed in.

The woman raised her eyebrows, her mouth twisting to one side as she looked from Sunny to William and back again. "I do have years of experience," she said. "I assume you don't."

Sunny bent down and started petting her dog, not talking back.

"Thanks for stopping by," William said, and took a step forward. It wasn't much by way of intimidation, except that given he was double Suzanne's size, it probably felt threatening.

Which he normally avoided, but this time, it was intentional. It was no more than Suzanne had done to both dogs, and the size differential was bigger there.

At least he hadn't snapped his fingers in her face.

It worked; she backed away. "Right," she said. "Nice to meet you." She turned and walked rapidly toward the street.

Sunny muttered a word under her breath, one William was pretty sure she wasn't allowed to use, but he didn't correct her. "I didn't like her, either."

"I could tell," Sunny snickered. "I think you scared her."

He shrugged. "What do you think we should do?"

"Mom says you'll always have naysayers," Sunny said. "And that you can't let them run your life."

"Your mom's wise," he said. "Always had been. So do you think we can prove Suzanne the trainer wrong?"

Sunny grinned. "I'm ready to try. You?"

He nodded. "If you'll help, because I have no idea what I'm doing."

"I do," she said confidently, reminding him so much of Bisky as a girl that it hurt his heart. "But you definitely have to choose a name for your pup."

"Something tough," he said. "She kind of needs a boost."

"Raven?" Sunny suggested. "Xena? Athena?"

"Xena," he decided. "Short and sweet."

"Not so sweet," Sunny said. "She's a warrior princess. Mom and I streamed the series last Christmas."

That made him happy, the idea of Bisky and Sunny watching a TV series about a strong, powerful woman, together. "Xena it is," he said.

ON TUESDAY AFTER SCHOOL, Bisky looked at the six teens lounging around her heated sunroom in various stages of sullenness or boredom. Had she made a mistake?

It didn't help that Sunny had begged off participating. "It's fine if you do it, Mom," she had said, "but it's not my thing. I'm not an at-risk student. I have direction. I'm already planning to go to college."

Which was true, but without Sunny's fun presence, Bisky wasn't sure how to attract this group's interest. She'd explained that the school was offering credits for it, which meant they could get out of a class next year. It was too late to get anything going with college credits for the two seniors in the group, but the school counselors had told the seniors it would look good on their resume.

The parents had all been enthused, or at least accepting, of having the kids participate. The kids themselves, though, would need to be convinced to give the program more than halfhearted energy.

When in doubt, go with food...but William was bringing it and he was AWOL, too. Fortunately, Bisky had been on a baking spree. She grabbed a plate of cut-up brownies and another of sugar cookies and started passing them around.

Within minutes, the mood in the room lifted. The kids started talking and joking.

Thank heavens for the fact that food was the way to a teenager's heart. There were four boys and two girls, which was another reason Bisky had hoped Sunny would participate, but oh, well. She watched as the kids joked with each other. They were good kids, and she'd known them all their lives, knew their families. None of them were close friends with her and Sunny, but around the docks, you knew everyone. Olivia was one of seven kids, and Bisky knew her parents struggled to put food on the table. Elijah had gotten in some minor trouble with the law; he was the type of kid that always got caught, most recently for smoking pot.

Aiden and Avery, the twins, spent a lot of time helping their mom with her cleaning business, mainly working in the big houses on the other side of Pleasant Shores. They were quiet, and Avery in particular was known for being really smart.

Rounding out the group were Connor, a football player almost as big as William who was sometimes stereotyped as being the not-so-bright athlete, and Syd, pierced and angry. Syd was going to be the biggest challenge, Bisky suspected.

William banged through the door from outside, holding a stack of pizza boxes. "Sorry to be late. Xena got out."

The teens got quiet, as was their way when an outsider breached their fortress.

Bisky, on the other hand, felt strangely warmed by the sight of him, thrust back to that day last weekend on the water, when he'd seemed like he was going to kiss her.

Which would have been a huge mistake, she reminded herself. She brushed her hands together and stood. "Pizza time," she said. "So we had dessert first, that's not a sin. Everyone get some and then we'll talk."

Quickly, the teens flocked around the boxes William was opening, and they were soon settled on chairs or the floor with paper plates of pizza and soft drinks.

Bisky needed to avoid thinking too much about William, so she jumped into talking about their plans for the coming weeks. "We were thinking you could choose what you want to do in this program," she started. "Have some input, at least. It's prevocational, so think about what you might want to try for work. Or part-time work, if you're going into a family business."

"Mom says we can't make a living on the water much longer," Olivia said.

"My dad is making me stay," Connor said. "Says I can haul twice as much as anyone he could hire."

Bisky didn't doubt that. "You could also learn more about some angle of the business," she said. "Accounting, or PR, online marketing. That way, you can stay, but also grow professionally."

The twins were quiet, so she nodded toward them. "What about you? Any future plans?"

The twins looked at each other. "We can't wait to get out of here," Aiden said. "Some way or other, we're going to college."

"That's a great option, and I know you can make it happen," Bisky said.

"Nah," Syd said. "You're never going to get out."

Bisky gestured at William. "He did."

"He's not from a water family."

"Yes, he is," Elijah said, "but…" He trailed off, his face darkening with a blush.

"Shut up." Olivia elbowed him. "It's rude to…" She realized everyone was listening and cut off whatever she'd been going to say, looking embarrassed.

William smiled ruefully and spoke up. "I come from a water family, but not the best. Whatever you heard, or whatever you were going to say about them, was probably right, or too mild. Things were pretty bad."

Elijah put down his pizza and leaned forward like he wanted to hear what William said next. Elijah's family was one of the rougher ones on the waterfront, though nowhere near what William had come from.

"Your family still around?" Connor asked.

Aiden and Avery glanced at each other, causing Bisky to wonder what they'd heard.

William shook his head. "My mom's passed on, and my father is long gone. We're out of touch." He frowned, looked out the window for a beat. "Anyway. I left before I graduated high school, which isn't the best way. I ended up getting my GED, and then I got a scholarship for college."

"Full ride?" Avery asked. "Because that's what we'd need."

"Full ride on tuition," William said. "I worked, and lived pretty cheaply, so I could pay room and board and books." He looked around at the teens, most of whom were listening closely. "That's one thing you learn, growing up as a dock kid: how to work hard."

There were grunts and groans of agreement.

Bisky leaned in. "That's a good thing. Not all young people know how to work hard, but you do. It's a strength you'll be able to capitalize on whatever you do."

"Right." William smiled at her.

Bisky sucked in a breath. He had no idea how handsome he was. *Stay focused*, she scolded herself. "You got support to get your PhD, too, right?"

"What's that?" Elijah interrupted.

"It's an advanced degree that allows you to teach in a college," William said, "and yes. I got my tuition paid and living expenses, too, in exchange for teaching some introductory classes."

Aiden and Avery were visibly impressed, but Syd snorted. "College. I don't know why anyone would pay for school. I can't wait to get out of there. When I'm done, I'm done."

"Which is good," Avery said, "because you don't have the grades to go to college."

Not wanting an argument to start, Bisky jumped in. "You don't have to go to college to make it around here," she said. "I didn't. I took over my family business."

"Which means you're still getting up in the middle of the night to work," Aiden pointed out.

"Yeah," Bisky said, "that's true, but look around you. I'm living in the lap of luxury."

That made them all laugh, which was what Bisky had

wanted. She wasn't struggling, and her house was fine, but it was the same one she'd grown up in and the age showed. It was clean and functional, but no one would ever call it fancy.

They went on eating, and chatting generally, joking around. When she noticed a couple of kids checking the clock, she decided to get down to practical business. She passed out more brownies and cookies to keep the mood upbeat. "Okay, everyone, listen up," she said. "So far, you have three choices. Work at the museum, work with training dogs or do something with the preschool kids who stay late for extended care. And the dog training isn't up to speed yet, so basically two choices."

"I love kids," Connor said.

"I can't stand them, because I have to take care of my three little brothers all the time." That was Olivia.

"We could take maybe one or two to work with dogs, my dog that is," William said. "Sunny's going to help, so you'd need to follow her guidance. But I'm bad with dogs, so I need all the help I can get."

His vulnerability warmed Bisky's heart. The kids here, especially the boys, didn't see enough adults admitting weakness, didn't know that that in itself was a kind of strength.

"I think the museum's cool," Olivia said. "That's what I'd like to do. I like history."

"Perfect, then," Bisky said. "It's history, and it'll be real to you because it's the history of what your grandparents did. And it's not just history. The museum also focuses on the bay and the, you know, nature. The environment, the science of the area." She hadn't explained that well, and her own lack of education bothered her for the first time in a long time. She knew why, too: William. While they'd grown up the same way, he'd gone on to better himself and broaden his education. She hadn't.

"You should do the museum." Aiden nudged Avery. "You're good at science."

More of the kids were talking about it, and only a couple looked scornful or bored. This was probably the time to end things, while enthusiasm was relatively high. "Nobody has to decide right now," Bisky said. "Just think about it, and we'll meet again Thursday after school. And let's meet down at the museum so you can get an idea of what it's like. Sound good?"

"No pizza?" one of the boys asked.

Bisky glanced at William, eyebrows raised.

"We could probably spring for some kind of food," he said. "Maybe not dinner, but…"

"Milkshakes!" someone said.

"Yeah!"

"Museum, then Goody's," Bisky said. "Sounds like a plan." She looked at William. "And it looks like we'll have to talk to Mary about a food budget for this crowd."

"They're ravenous," William agreed, snagging another large piece of pizza from the box, causing the kids to snort.

After the kids were all gone, Bisky beckoned William back out onto the sunporch and threw herself down into a chair. "How'd you think that went?"

"You were great." William sat down in the chair next to hers. "I think they're going to like it, most of them, but it'll take effort to keep them positive and on track."

"We have our work cut out for us," she agreed.

"Let's reassess after Thursday," he said.

An idea sprang into Bisky's head. "Why don't you come over for dinner on Friday," she said. "Family dinner with me and Sunny. We can talk over next steps, and get Sunny's ideas as a teenager."

The moment she'd said it, she held her breath. Why had she put herself out on a limb like that? He wasn't going to want to spend his Friday night with her.

He tilted his head to one side, studying her, and his eyes darkened. She could see him struggle.

"Don't feel obligated," she said quickly. "It's fine, we can just talk about it over the phone or whatever."

He put a hand over hers. Just lightly, but it burned like fire. "Bisky," he said. "Shhh. I'd like to come."

Their eyes met, held, in the moonlight. Outside, crickets and a late-night waterbird made the only sounds.

He'd like to come. He'd like to come. The singsong joy of it echoed in her heart for hours after he'd left, which was *not* a good thing. Not good at all.

CHAPTER THIRTEEN

SUNNY KNELT IN the corner of the kitchen Friday afternoon with a handful of dog treats while her mother stirred something good-smelling on the stove.

"So," Mom said, "William's coming to dinner."

Something about Mom's elaborately casual tone made Sunny's eyebrows shoot up. "I wondered why you were cooking something fancy."

"It's not fancy," her mother protested. "It's oyster stew."

"Smells great. Is he bringing his dog?" If he did, then Sunny wouldn't mind him coming over. The more chance she had to work with both dogs, the better.

"I don't know. Text him and tell him to, if you want."

"Can I use your phone?" Sunny kind of wanted to scroll through their messages and find out if the vibe she sensed between them was real.

"Sure," Mom said, and nodded toward it.

Which meant there was nothing even PG rated in their messages. She punched in her mother's password, found William G in her contacts. *William, it's Sunny. Bring your dog so we can prove Ms. B**** wrong.* She hit Send and grinned. It was up to William how he would fill in the blanks, since the woman's last name started with a *B*. She scrolled through the few messages between William and her mother. Aside from the occasional smiley emoji, it looked like strictly business. No hearts or lovey-dovey words. She put the phone back onto the table.

She made Muffin sit, and then moved the treat backward over her head to get her to sit up on her haunches, something that she hadn't been able to make happen yet. Muffin lunged toward the treat, and Sunny pulled it away.

"Don't frustrate her," Mom scolded from the stove.

"I know what I'm doing, Mom."

Two more tries, and she proved herself right as Muffin raised up onto her haunches, propping her paws on Sunny's arm for support.

"Look, Mom," she said, low, and Mom did and clapped.

A few minutes later her own phone buzzed in her pocket, and she checked it. Going boy hunting tonight, want to come?

"Ugh, my friends drive me crazy," she complained. "All they want to do, think about or talk about is boys. Listen to this, from Kait." She read her mother the text.

Mom laughed. "I'm sure Ria would be appalled to know her daughter claims to be boy hunting," she said as she stirred the soup. Then she turned and leaned back against the counter, taking a long swig of iced tea. "But, honey, boys can be great. I know what you mean about the boy-crazy stuff and centering your life around men, that's ridiculous and too many women do it. But they have their place, men do." She smiled a little. "I maybe didn't communicate that to you clearly enough."

"Men like William?"

"No!" Mom blushed. "He's a friend and that's all."

"Uh-huh." Sunny stood, grabbed a spoon, and tasted the oyster stew. "Delicious." Mom wasn't a gourmet cook, but she did a good job with all the local specialties. Sunny didn't do much cooking, so far, but she knew how to make oyster stew. Mom had insisted on that.

"Yoo-hoo." William rapped on the open front door, and

Muffin let out a loud, baying bark and rushed to the door, jumping at it.

Sunny went and pulled Muffin back. "Come on in," she said. "Oh, good, you brought Xena."

William opened the door and came in, but Xena held back.

"Come on, girl, you remember Muffin. She's your good buddy." Sunny led Muffin back into the kitchen and grabbed some treats. William half enticed, half lifted Xena through the doorway.

Sunny scattered treats on the floor for Xena, and then another bunch in another area for Muffin. "I was reading that sometimes being with a more confident dog is good," she said. "I guess Muffin is confident compared to Xena."

Mom smiled at William, then went back to her cooking.

William held up a bag. "I brought ice cream from Goody's," he said. "For tonight, or you two can share it later."

Sunny took the ice cream, checked the flavor—chocolate—and stuck it in the freezer.

"I also worked out a group discount for anytime we want to bring the teenagers in," he said. "Yesterday almost broke the bank."

Sunny read another text from Kait and rolled her eyes. More boy-crazy stuff. I'm training dogs, she texted back, hoping that would be boring enough to end the conversation.

She watched Mom and William as she focused on her phone and the dogs. They didn't seem like they were dating, but still, Sunny got a funny feeling that they liked each other. Not just as friends, either. It was something about the way Mom laughed, something about the way William touched her back as he reached into the top shelf of a cupboard to get something down, which Mom absolutely did *not* need him to do; she was plenty tall enough to reach everything in their kitchen herself.

It started to annoy her. "Come out here and work with your dog for a few," she ordered William. He smiled and came outside readily, and then she wondered whether she'd imagined his connection with her mom.

No matter. He'd been working with Xena to sit, and once Sunny and Muffin were far enough away not to be a distraction, Xena followed William's command and sat. She refused to lie down, but William said she'd done it occasionally for him at home.

"Even so," he said, "I can't see her becoming a therapy dog, to be honest. She's so scared of everyone and everything. She's starting not to be scared of me, but that's all."

"She's made progress, right? And you've only had her for a week." Sunny frowned, thinking. "Maybe we should have her around people at a distance, and let her see they're not going to hurt her. Like, at the edge of the park, or something."

"Makes sense." He handed Xena a treat.

"She's food motivated, so every time she's around another person, give her lots of treats. Like you're doing now. She'll start to associate treats with people."

"Do you really think she'll get there?"

"I don't know," Sunny admitted. "But I want to try. Do you?"

"Sure," he said. "Truth is, I'm getting over some fears myself. Not a dog person, like I told you all before."

"Dinner's on the table," Mom called, and they both went in, said grace, and dug in. Mom had made biscuits to go with the oyster stew, and a salad, and it was all good.

"My daughter loved biscuits," William said. "It was her favorite breakfast."

"What exactly happened to her?" Sunny asked. Mom

looked at her sharply and she felt bad. "That was rude of me. You don't have to answer. Sorry."

"It's okay," William said, his voice quiet, but steady. He drew in a breath and let it out, then went on. "She was shot by a guy who broke into our house," he said. "I'd left her home alone, which I'll regret to my dying day, and she was taking a nap. She came out while he was hauling off our TV, as near as anyone can tell, and he shot her down."

Mom put a hand over his, briefly. "It's a parent's worst nightmare," she said, "but you shouldn't blame yourself."

He shrugged. "I was the one who left her alone."

There was an awkward silence then. Both Mom and William were quiet, and they'd both stopped eating.

"Tell him he's wrong," Sunny finally said to Mom.

"I have."

William shrugged and looked away.

Xena crept over to his side and lay there.

"Look," Sunny said, amazed the two of them couldn't see it. "Kids are left alone all the time. She was, what, fifteen?"

He nodded.

"Mom was leaving me alone when I was eleven or twelve, isn't that right?"

"That's right," Bisky said. "Mostly in the daytime, but sometimes in the evening. Every morning, during oyster or crab season."

"So it could just as easily have happened to me," Sunny said, and then swallowed, because that gave her a strange feeling. Especially when she looked at her mother's stricken face.

Neither adult answered, so Sunny jumped up and started clearing dishes, and she was relieved when they started talking about the teen program they were both working on and what activities would work best. She felt bad for William, of course, but she also felt an urge to get away. She checked her phone, which she wasn't allowed to do at the table, and found three messages, two from Kait and one from Venus. "Come over," was the upshot.

Sunny got the dishes into the dishwasher while Mom and William talked in low voices. "I'm going over to Kait's for a while, okay?" she said as soon as she was done.

"Walking over?" Mom frowned out the window at the twilight.

"I'll leave now, and they'll meet me." It was their usual arrangement, visiting each other's houses during the dark season.

"Call when you want a ride home," Mom said. "Before ten thirty, okay?"

"Eleven?" she asked. "Or I could take the car myself."

"I'll come get you." Mom was old-fashioned that way and liked to be involved in Sunny's life, preferring to drive her around rather than send her off in their one car.

Her phone buzzed again and she checked it.

Hurry up. We're trying to figure out who's abusing dogs.

Galvanized, Sunny rushed to grab a coat. "Later," she called, and headed out the door. She'd give anything to figure out who'd hurt Muffin and Xena, and to make sure it didn't happen to any other dogs.

WILLIAM WATCHED SUNNY hurry out the door and then smiled at Bisky. "They don't slow down and ponder things like adults, do they? Jenna used to rush off the minute a friend called or texted."

"They have their priorities." She touched his hand. "I'm sorry Sunny reminds you so much of Jenna. That must be hard to deal with."

Her hand on his was warm, and so were her eyes. He

turned his hand over and squeezed her smaller one. "It's not a bad thing. I have a lot of good memories I'd nearly forgotten. Sunny brings those out."

"I'm glad." Bisky's eyes were thoughtful as she looked from his face to their clasped hands and back again.

He opened his mouth to say something and then closed it again, because he didn't really know what to say. He felt close with her after sharing a family meal, but what was the good of telling her that when there was nowhere it could go?

She pulled her hand away, rose, and looked into the kitchen. "She cleaned everything up, or most everything."

He rose and stood behind her, looking at the neat kitchen. "Good kid. And that *doesn't* bring up a memory of Jenna. She hated housework, just like her mother did."

She looked over her shoulder at him. "Has to be done," she said. "How'd you manage if neither of them liked it?"

Well, he and Ellie had fought a lot at the beginning. "Eventually, I started doing most of it myself. It was a good break from my desk job."

She met his eyes, and it was as if she knew there was a story there, but she didn't want to ask him about it. She stepped away almost like she was nervous and walked across the kitchen. She rearranged a few things on the counter. "Do you think we have the next steps figured out okay?"

He nodded. "What we talked about at dinner should work."

Muffin ambled around the kitchen, sniffing. Xena came in and stood for a moment by William's side, and then tentatively took a few steps to snag a crumb of bread.

Bisky knelt down to feed Muffin a treat. Then she tossed one to Xena, too. She stayed down on the floor, rubbing Muffin's back. "I guess you're mine, huh, girl? Sunny's the one who wanted you, but is she here for your evening walk? No, she's not."

The singsong voice Bisky was using made Muffin's tail start to wag.

"I swear she knows the word *walk* already," Bisky said. "You're a smart girl, aren't you? Yes, you are."

Following her lead, William knelt down and hesitantly stroked his dog in the same way Bisky was stroking hers. He couldn't quite bring himself to talk the singsong baby talk, not with a witness, anyway. But Xena nonetheless rolled onto her back to give him access to her belly, which felt like a win.

He looked up to find Bisky watching him. "I like it better than I thought," he said, "having her."

"They grow on you."

And then there was an awkward but somehow wonderful silence where they were smiling at each other.

Finally, he broke it. "I should go, but...would you want to walk them first?"

"Sure," she said easily, without hesitation.

Moments later they were walking down the shore as the sun set, heading deeper into the dock area rather than back toward town. It was cool out, and they were both wearing jackets and hats.

William felt way too strong of an urge to pull Bisky close. To quell it, he turned down the inland dirt road.

Bisky hesitated, then followed him. "Are you heading where I think you're heading?"

Was he? He'd walked this road a thousand times, as a child. But he hadn't been back home since the day he'd left Pleasant Shores for good. "I guess I am," he said. "Have you been back here lately?"

"No. I used to walk by every now and then, digging

sang—wild ginseng roots—but I got too busy lately." She touched his arm. "It's not what it was. Just so you know."

"It never *was* much." The idea that the trailer he'd grown up in had deteriorated beyond the dilapidated state it had been when he'd grown up…that was hard to fathom.

The sun had set, but the moon cast a silvery light over everything.

The dogs sniffed and barked a little as they went deeper into the marshland. Frogs chirped and plopped into the water, and something rustled through the undergrowth that made Xena lunge, with Muffin immediately following suit. All of it was thrilling stuff, apparently, to the canine crowd.

"Sunny's right, you know," Bisky said out of nowhere. "You don't have to feel so guilty about what happened to your daughter. It's not your fault. It's awful, but it's not your fault."

William had heard that sentiment before, but he'd always disregarded it. Now, maybe it was what Sunny had said about kids often being left alone, or maybe it was the way the past was rising up to greet him on this moonlit road, but he started to let it in.

If Jenna's death hadn't been his fault, then what?

If it were just some random, horrible thing that had happened…a wave of grief washed over him, tightening his throat. "It *is* my fault," he said once he could speak again.

Because feeling guilty was better than just feeling devastated.

"There it is," Bisky said, gesturing toward a structure ahead where moonlight glinted off metal.

It was his family's trailer, all right, practically buried beneath vines and branches. A section of vines by the door was torn away, as if squatters sometimes made use of the place, but there was no light, no sign of life. It seemed to be deserted now.

They both stopped to look at the trailer while the dogs sniffed madly, pulling at their leashes.

"William?" Bisky was right beside him, close enough to touch, but she didn't do it. "What really happened when you left Pleasant Shores?"

He turned his head to look at her. "You don't know?"

"No one does. Just, one day you weren't here and neither was your dad."

For the first time, he wondered how that had felt for her. They'd matured beyond being childhood playmates by the time he'd left, but they'd remained friends, had seen each other a couple of times a week, had shared their cares and woes.

He tugged Xena, making her stay close, and slowly, he and Bisky and the dogs started walking around the trailer. "Mom always told me to leave Dad alone. To tend to my studies and keep the peace."

"I remember," she said. "Your mom was so sweet."

"Too sweet," he said. "Too sweet for her own good. That day I left, Dad beat her to within an inch of her life."

Bisky sucked in a breath. "No one knew where she'd gone, either, but she came back a month or so later, without either of you. I don't know if she talked to anyone about what happened, but if she did, my family never heard about it."

"Your uncle never told you what went down?" He'd expected word to get out, via her cop uncle.

"Uncle Nate?" She shook her head. "He took me aside and told me you were okay, and that I wasn't to ask questions or talk about you being gone."

That sounded like Nate. "Do you really want to hear the story?"

She nodded.

He stared off into the darkness, and it started to play out in his mind, like a movie. "I was the one who pulled him off her." He hated revisiting that day in his mind and rarely did it, but being back here brought it all back: the screams, the blood, his father's rage as he stood over William's bleeding mother. "Your uncle said I saved her life, and that was why he didn't take me in for what I did to my dad."

"What did you do? You didn't…" She trailed off, staring at him, her eyes huge.

"I didn't kill him, but I came close. As close as I ever have or ever hope to again." He swallowed down bile. "Once I'd knocked him unconscious, I stood there over my two bloody parents and thought, I have to get out of here or this place will make me into my father." He blew out a sigh and looked at Bisky.

She was watching him, quiet, waiting.

"I called your uncle. He'd been kind before, and I thought… I just didn't want my father to wake up and finish the job on Mom, and I was worried she'd bleed out." He remembered his own mix of rage and self-loathing and fear, and it tightened his throat. He swallowed, and coughed, and was able to go on. "Once Nate said they were both alive and would survive, and got her an ambulance, told me he'd hook her up with domestic violence people…I changed my bloody clothes and filled a suitcase with my things and left."

They were standing right in front of the trailer now, and Bisky put an arm around him and squeezed a little. "It sounds awful."

"It was." But talking about it, at least to Bisky, wasn't as bad as he'd imagined it would be. Maybe it was the way she accepted what he said and didn't jump to judgment or condemnation.

"Where'd you go?" Bisky sank down onto the metal steps that led up to the trailer door, looking up at him. "How'd you survive? You were only sixteen."

He nodded. "I was big and strong enough to find work.

I took Dad's car, and made it about a hundred miles. When it died near Stahlstown, I walked the rest of the way into town. Slept on a park bench until the cops found me and told me about a shelter for runaway teens."

"That was lucky."

He nodded. "Very. I stayed there while I worked day labor and earned enough to get a room in a rooming house. That was quieter. The woman who ran the place saw how hard I worked on my GED studies, and she got me to apply for college. I'm still in touch with her. I owe her a lot."

"Wow." Bisky moved over to make room for him on the steps beside her. "You had a time of it, didn't you? Did your dad ever try to find you?"

He shook his head. "Mom got some counseling at a domestic violence center, and she ended up coming back here to live. But I guess you know that."

"She's the one who told people you taught in a college. She was real proud."

That made him smile a little. "Dad…well, your uncle gave him the choice of staying away, forever, or facing charges for manslaughter."

"Manslaughter?"

He swallowed. "Mom was pregnant."

"Oh, wow." She rubbed his back, gentle circles that felt good. Soothing, and something more. He liked her touch.

He turned to look at her. In the moonlight, her eyes shone.

He felt tender, exposed. "Would you do something for me?" he asked on impulse.

"What?"

"Would you take down your hair?"

Her eyes widened and she just looked at him for a long moment. Then, slowly, she reached behind herself and pulled the elastic from her ponytail. She never took her eyes off him as she spread her hair over her shoulders.

The two dogs had lain down at their feet. The call of a loon sounded in the distance, the night alive with small, natural sounds you'd never hear in the city, but they were sounds he'd grown up with.

He reached out and took a strand of her hair in his hand, lifted it, let it fall.

"It's soft," he said. "Pretty."

"Thanks." Her eyes had gained a knowing, now. They darkened, and her breathing quickened. He was alert to her because he was feeling the same changes in his own body.

He reached higher and tangled his fingers in her hair, and leaned closer. He could smell a slight, flowery cologne.

This was Bisky, his dear old friend. Who also happened to be an incredibly beautiful and warm and desirable woman.

He shouldn't kiss her, right? But he was raw after telling his story to her. Too raw to choose the sensible, careful route.

Slowly, he leaned forward and brushed his lips over hers.

CHAPTER FOURTEEN

BISKY FELT LIKE she was melting.

William's lips moved over hers and her heart rate ratcheted up. Dizzy, she clung to his broad shoulders, a steady anchor in the storm of her own feelings.

Wanting to get closer, she lifted up to meet him, increasing the pressure of the kiss. His responding groan sent vibrations through her entire body.

His face was rough, stubbly, but his lips were gentle. His hands on her back stayed high, kneading her shoulders a little, tangling in her hair.

This is William. And she knew it was her old, dear friend. She felt a depth of caring for him she'd never experienced for any other man. The things she'd known about him before melded with the things she'd seen in him since he'd returned to town, the horrible things he'd shared tonight. All of it made her want to draw him near, help him, soothe him.

Except he didn't need soothing, because he was a strong, powerful man, and he was kissing her like a strong, powerful man. He was making her entire body throb just from kissing. Her breathing went ragged and her heart pounded to where she felt like she might pass out. She tugged away. "Wait a second, William," she said.

"Too much?" He studied her, his eyes dark with what she could tell was desire, his own breathing rough. "I never want to be too much for you."

She swallowed. *This is William. He needs a friend, not...*

The old arguments started to rear their heads, but she didn't want them back, not just yet.

"Come here." William was sitting on the steps, and he urged her, half lifted her, until she was sitting on his lap. Then he cuddled her against him as if she were a child.

She'd never have dared to sit on a man's lap before. She was too big, too much.

But for William, she wasn't too much. He was substantial enough to handle all she was. She leaned against his broad chest and listened to the strong beat of his heart.

I've never been happier, she thought.

He stroked her back slowly. "What I feel right now..."

She waited for him to elaborate, but he didn't, and that was all right. He was telling her with his gentle hands and warm embrace. He was showing her that he cared.

And not just in a friend way, either. She'd stirred him as a man, and that gave her a delicious feeling of power and joy.

They sat like that for a few minutes. Tangled together, kissing a little, warming each other with half comfort, half desire. Bisky wanted more, and she knew enough about men to be certain William did, too. But he was strong enough, man enough, *good* enough to hold back, and slowly, the real world gathered in around them: the night sounds, crickets and frogs; the moonlight, the dogs at their feet.

Muffin stood and gave a short bark, and Xena leaped to her feet on high alert. Bisky squeezed William's shoulder and then, reluctantly, stood. "Probably some critter in the woods," she said, "but that's my cue to get back. I need to pick Sunny up soon."

William stood, too. He draped his arm around her shoulders, and it felt amazing and good to nestle under his arm. She'd never been able to do that before, not really. William was the perfect fit.

Then he stiffened. "Did you hear something?"

She tilted her head. "No...wait." She held up a finger. There was a low laugh, the clink of a bottle. The dogs went nuts again.

"Come on. Stay behind me." He led the way toward the noises, walking lightly and quietly for a man of his size. With the dogs barking, there was no question of their sneaking up on anyone, but as they got closer to the main road and came to an old camp circle, it was apparent that sneaking wasn't important. These were teenagers, and they were drinking. A lot, guessing from the empties and the slack attitudes. A couple of them even noticed Bisky and William, but beyond nudging each other and nodding in their direction, they didn't seem to care that adults had shown up.

Several of the teenagers were kneeling around something. As William and Bisky approached, they backed and shuffled away.

All except for one kid, who continued holding a dish for the dog to lap up.

"Quit it," one of the others yelled, nodding sideways at Bisky and William. And the kid looked guilty and tossed the dish away.

Xena and Muffin continued growling and letting out the occasional bark, but they stuck close to their humans.

"Look out, it's Big Bisky," someone said, and Bisky's stomach tightened for just a minute before she reminded herself that it didn't matter if intoxicated teenagers called her names.

The dog that had been surrounded by kids turned toward Xena and Muffin, but staggered a little and then sat as if it didn't remember how it was supposed to act around other dogs. It stood and walked a few uncoordinated steps, and then lay down clumsily.

Muffin and Xena surged forward.

"Hold them," William said to Bisky, and strode forward. "What did you do to that dog?" he asked the teenagers.

Bisky had her hands full with their own two dogs, now pulling and barking, but she skimmed the faces of the teens in front of her. There was Elijah, and another kid she recognized as his cousin who visited often. There was Syd, and another girl and two boys she didn't know.

The teenagers didn't answer William's question. They whispered among themselves. A couple of them staggered almost as badly as the dog, which William was now examining. Bisky alone knew how much courage that took. William was overcoming his fear of dogs, but he wasn't there yet.

This dog wasn't growling or snarling, though. She was relaxed and sleepy looking. As Bisky studied it more closely she realized she had seen it in the neighborhood. It belonged to a family who lived in a mobile home at the far end, and it was an escape artist, often digging under the fence and running away. Peppy was the dog's name, she was pretty sure.

"Is it hurt?" she called over the sounds of their dogs. Elijah started to slip away, but she stepped in front of him. "No. Uh-uh. You stay here until we know what's going on and what we're going to do."

"No wounds, but..." William leaned closer and sniffed, then leaned back and glared at the teenagers. "Were you feeding that dog alcohol?"

One of the girls giggled, and a couple of the others looked sheepish and nodded.

"Idiots." Bisky didn't know whether alcohol was fatal to dogs, but it couldn't be good for them. And she knew enough about teenagers to understand they probably hadn't meant it any harm, but seriously?

"All right," William said. "We either call the police now, or you give me your names." He made them each say their names into his phone, and Bisky confirmed the ones she could. "You can go," he said after they'd all shared their names, "but expect to hear from us."

"We should take the dog to the emergency vet," Bisky said. "And for sure, you kids are paying for it. It's not cheap."

Several of the teenagers glared and others muttered to each other as they took off.

That left William and Bisky to care for the intoxicated little hound. "Let's get out to the main road where there's better cell service, and we'll call the vet," she said.

So they did, and were quickly able to get a vet on the line. "Watch the dog," she said. "It may be fine, depends on the size of the animal and how much it ingested, which you probably have no way of knowing." She rattled off signs and symptoms that should prompt a visit, and then Bisky ended the call.

They walked back to Bisky's place. William held their two dogs, now calm, while Bisky cradled the little hound in her arms.

"I'll take it home," William said.

"No, I can keep it, it's from around here." Then she snapped her mouth shut. There she went, being bossy again. Big, bossy Bisky. Insecurity rose up in her as they reached her house. "Sorry, it's just that I think I know where it lives. I'll give them a call in the morning, take it home."

"That's good, then," he said. "Listen, Bisky, I apologize."

"For what?"

His forehead wrinkled like he was worried. "For kissing you," he said. "I shouldn't have done it."

He regrets it. He doesn't really want you. And that's fine, you don't need him.

"It's no big deal," she said quickly, not wanting him to

explain further. "The moonlight, talking about the past. I get it. It was a fluke."

He looked at her for a moment, his head tilted to one side. "Right, a fluke," he said. "See you. Thanks for dinner."

"Sure." She opened the front door and went inside, taking the little hound and Muffin with her. She glanced back in time to see William's quick wave, and then he and Xena walked down the street.

Bisky stood in the doorway and watched him go. He was walking slowly. She still admired his size, his form, his strength.

She put her hand to her mouth and let herself relive the kiss. It had been wonderful. Even now, she felt a remembered glow from just thinking about it.

But he'd retracted it. He'd said he shouldn't have done it.

That was right. He shouldn't have done it, and she shouldn't have allowed it. Had they ruined their friendship?

She cuddled the sleepy little dog against her and slowly shut the door.

THE NEXT MORNING, William browsed the shelves at Lighthouse Lit, waiting for Mary to finish ringing up a customer's purchase. They were meeting to assess William's progress in the program and make sure things were going well.

And things *were* going well. Almost too well. He couldn't stop thinking about last night.

Kissing Bisky had been one of the high points of his life. It had been like magic, there in the place where all his childhood misery had happened. She'd basically transformed that misery into joy. Now, he'd never have only bad memories of his home place; he'd always be able to think of Bisky and moonlight kisses.

Except that it had been a mistake, and it couldn't happen again.

A relationship with Bisky was unthinkable. She was a dear, longtime friend, and he couldn't do that to her. He didn't deserve her. He couldn't keep her and her daughter safe.

That last thought made him pause. He hadn't kept Jenna safe, and he'd always, always regret that. At the same time, he'd heard what Sunny had said and it was true: parents left their teenage kids home alone all the time. He couldn't have stayed chained to Jenna's side forever, every moment, protecting her. It had just been rotten bad luck that the intruder had come that day, and she'd woken up.

But that was excusing himself for his inadequacies, wasn't it? Trying to talk himself into the fact that he was a decent man who could earn the love of a good woman.

He couldn't.

Bisky had agreed that the kiss shouldn't have happened, that it had been a fluke. She hadn't taken it seriously.

A text from her pinged into his phone, and his heart leaped.

Dog is fine, no ill effects. Evan is getting in touch with the teenagers' parents.

Evan. Great. His stomach soured.

He tried to focus on the bookshelves in front of him rather than on the thoughts of last night. He ran a hand over the thrillers, his preferred type of books, but he'd gotten turned off by them since Jenna's death. He hadn't been reading much, and he should. He should buy some books and take them home and spend more of his evenings reading, and less time thinking about Bisky.

"Need help finding something?" Mary asked.

"Yeah," he said. "I'm off the violent books, but I like a page-turner."

She nodded. "Science fiction, maybe? Space opera?"

Maybe it would be good to visit another world entirely. He'd liked that type of books when he was younger. "Sure. Help me pick one out?"

She led him over to the science fiction shelves and talked him into buying the first book in a couple of trilogies. "I have something else you might like, too," she said, and led him over to the memoirs. She pulled a thick volume off the shelves. "This man had a terrible crisis in his life, and he went into the woods for a year to think. Worked everything out. Want to try it?"

"You're going to break the bank," he complained jokingly.

"Just doing my job," she said. She led him to the counter, where he found a fourth book, this one a political analysis. He handed her his credit card and was soon the owner of four new books, considerably poorer, but he was looking forward to digging into them.

"Let's sit down and meet while we can. Julie, my assistant, should be here any minute, and then we know we won't be disturbed."

"Sure." He followed her to the little circle of chairs and sat down.

"Now," she said, leaning forward. "Tell me how things are going. Are you all right?"

"Yes, doing fine. I'm grateful for the program."

She waved a hand like that wasn't what she'd meant. "Are you going to your counseling? What did you think of the dog trainer?"

"Counseling's going well. The trainer, not so much," he said, and told her about it.

She nodded. "I wanted to hear your side of it. She reported back to me that I'd misunderstood her in the interview and she could really only work with puppies, not, quote, damaged dogs."

"I'm sure she had a thing or two to say about me and Sunny as well."

One side of Mary's mouth quirked up in a half smile. "She did. I'm doubting that she's the right choice, but frankly, she was the only applicant. I'll talk to her. Meanwhile, are you getting along with Bisky, working okay with her?"

"Yes, it's fine," he said quickly. He didn't dare say too much about Bisky, not when things were so oddly intense between them.

"Don't let her do all the work," Mary warned. "That's her tendency."

"Of course." He frowned. Was he doing that? "Do you think I'm not shouldering enough of the responsibility, say for the teen program?" He was all too familiar with colleagues who didn't take on their fair share of the burden. He'd always tried to do a little more than his share, which was, he'd been told, the key to succeeding at a job as well as succeeding at relationships, like marriage.

Of course, his efforts to do more than his share in marriage hadn't worked out too well.

Mary leaned back in her chair. "I think you're doing just fine, but why don't you tell me about what you're planning for the teens?"

So he talked about the museum work and the childcare option for kids that didn't want to do the museum stuff. How they'd planned to offer the choice of working with dogs, but weren't clear on whether that was an idea that would work.

Mary listened and nodded. "As a temporary third option, I could take on a couple of the kids to do some work in my shop. I'm opening out walls for a new office and building some shelves and flowerboxes in front, too. Do you think your kids could help with that?"

"Probably." He was grateful she was getting involved, giving more ways for the teenagers to be of use. "I'm not a super handyman or carpenter, but I'm good at watching YouTube videos and figuring things out."

"Perfect." She studied him. "So is working with our teenagers going to be helpful to you, in terms of your healing?"

He hesitated, and then, slowly, nodded. "I think so," he said. "It's difficult, though."

"Because of your daughter." It wasn't a question.

"Exactly."

Mary nodded. "It took time before I could be around young children after losing my daughter."

He tilted his head to one side. "Bisky mentioned something about that."

"It's not something I talk about very often. Although more often than in the past." She gave him the shadow of a smile. "My daughter was killed in an on-purpose car crash when she was five years old. The perpetrator was hired by my ex-husband."

He blew out a breath. "Wow. I'm sorry." That might be the only thing worse than random violence: violence initiated by a family member. All of it turned his stomach.

"Thank you." She slipped off her shoes and pulled her legs up under herself. "I struggled quite a bit with guilt. Thinking what he'd done was my fault. Going over and over all the things I could have done differently that day."

"Me, too." He leaned forward, propping his elbows on his knees. "That's exactly what I do. If only I hadn't gone to the store that day. If only I'd taken her with me. If only I'd called to check that my ex was picking her up."

Unlike most people, Mary didn't jump into saying he was wrong and telling him he shouldn't blame himself. She just nodded ruefully. "I know. If only I'd insisted on going along. Because, yes, I wished I'd been in that car with her. To share her last moments, and a lot of times, I wanted to die myself."

"I'd have taken a bullet for Jenna anytime," he agreed. "And there were many times I wanted to die."

Mary looked concerned. "You're not having suicidal thoughts now, are you?"

He thought. "No, not anymore. I think being here is healing. The counseling is helping, but so are all the people in Pleasant Shores."

"I felt the same." She waved to a woman who'd come in and stationed herself behind the counter. "Don't be surprised," she said, "if things get worse before they get better. Because you *will* get past the guilt. But not past..." She trailed off.

"I *am* getting past the guilt, at least a little. But what were you going to say?"

"Just that...when the guilt goes, the grief can flow in even more, for a while. Part of your mind's been using the guilt to keep the grief at bay."

That was food for thought. "Do you have a picture of your daughter?" he asked.

She smiled, stood, and beckoned to him. "Take a look at our children's nook," she said.

Indeed, she'd set up a lively children's book area, with colorful rugs and cushions, and picture books face-out on the walls. Above the whole thing was a banner that said *Daisy's Corner.* And on a high shelf were framed pictures of an adorable girl who looked to be about five years old.

"Take one down," she urged him. "I can't reach them."

He reached for the nearest one. It was your standard

LEE TOBIN McCLAIN 169

baby-with-teddy-bear portrait that it seemed like every parent had made, when their kid was at a cute toddler stage.

He'd had one of Jenna. He wondered what had happened to it.

"She was beautiful," he said.

Mary's eyes shone with unshed tears, but she smiled. "She was. I never want to forget the good times. She loved reading her little books, even as young as she was." She cleared her throat and brushed fingertips under her eyes. "Anyway. We keep a collection going and donate books to low-income children. Including some of those right here in Pleasant Shores."

He looked around. Could he ever get to the stage where he'd do something in Jenna's memory?

"Do you have a picture of *your* daughter?" she asked.

He nodded and scrolled through his phone. He found one he'd always loved: Jenna and one of her friends, laughing as they mugged for the camera on a sunny day when he'd taken them hiking. The hike had devolved into wading in the creek and sunbathing, but she'd been happy, and that was what mattered.

"Lovely," Mary said. "She was how old when she was killed?"

He appreciated that she didn't gloss over what had happened, because it meant he didn't have to tiptoe around to avoid upsetting her. "Fifteen," he said.

"Heartbreaking." She put an arm around him as they both turned toward the door. She was a tiny woman, and almost twice his age, but they were connected in a way most people never would be. He admired her spirit. Maybe he could learn something from her.

"Keep me updated on the teenagers," she said. "And if you ever need to talk, you know where to find me."

"Thanks." And William walked out into the sunlight of a warm day, feeling emotional, but better.

He walked through town slowly, taking in the shore birds overhead and the neighbors walking and the flowers pushing their way out of the earth. Not thinking; just enjoying.

He passed the Blue House and there was Victory Cottage. Maybe for the first time, he appreciated what it was, what Mary was doing for the community. She was something else.

He started up the sidewalk to the front porch and then stopped.

Sitting on the front stoop, in the shadow of one of the evergreen bushes, was his ex-wife. She didn't look happy.

CHAPTER FIFTEEN

THAT SUNDAY, BISKY focused on cleaning up after the church luncheon. She wasn't going to think about the fact that she hadn't seen William all of yesterday, nor that he hadn't come to services today.

Sure, he'd come to church on his own last Sunday, had stayed for the lunch. That didn't obligate him to come every week, did it?

She wiped down the last of the long tables. It was actually good he hadn't come. For one thing, she'd been on cooking *and* cleanup duty and wouldn't have had time to spend with him. If he'd even wanted to spend time.

For another thing, she'd agreed to stay and help get the church gardens ready for flower planting. That might take up all afternoon.

He could have helped.

But why should William help? He wasn't really connected in this town. He was here temporarily.

And he'd thought it was a mistake to kiss her. He'd apologized for it.

That was over.

At least, probably. The trouble was, she couldn't help remembering. Couldn't help touching her mouth when she remembered the feel of his lips on hers. Couldn't help the squiggly feeling in her stomach when she thought about how his broad back had felt beneath her hands. Couldn't help the way her heart warmed when she remembered how he'd held her on his lap, as if she were a precious treasure and a desirable woman, all at once.

She'd brought an old T-shirt and sneakers for gardening, so she put them on and went outside and got to work hauling wheelbarrows of mulch while the men argued over how to work the old rototiller and the other women went ahead and turned over the soil by hand. They had flower beds in front of the church, but in back, they cultivated a big garden for church members and community folks in need. It was one of Bisky's favorite service activities to do for the church. She wasn't much for committees and arguing over budgets, but she was strong and liked to be outside.

The dirt smelled good. Kayla was here, and Mary, and when Bisky took a break, she sat down beside them. They were pulling early weeds in one of the flower gardens.

"I'm surprised you're here," she said to Mary, because Mary attended the Catholic church in town.

Mary smiled up at her. "I like your church's activities, and there's no reason I can't do both. Besides, sometimes I have to escape Kirk. He's terrific, but overwhelming."

"I wish I had someone overwhelming," Kayla said, and then slapped her hand to her mouth. "Did I really say that? I don't even mean it."

Bisky and Mary looked at each other. "It's okay to have mixed feelings about men," Mary said. "Lord knows, they warrant it."

"Agreed." Bisky didn't want to say more. Mixed feelings definitely described how she felt about William right now. She loved her old friend, but the new version of him roused feelings in herself she didn't understand, didn't necessarily like. Warm, tender feelings that could make you weak, soften your shell like a just-molted blue crab, the most vulnerable of creatures.

Behind them there was a squeaking sound and heavy

breathing as Primrose Miller came along the path on her new, bright red motorized scooter. "Doesn't that look pretty," she said, leaning back in her seat to survey their work. "I sure do miss gardening. I used to love it."

That made Bisky feel ashamed for her occasional desire to avoid Primrose and her gossip. "I remember your flowers from when I was a kid," she said. "Mom always said you had the prettiest roses on the Eastern Shore."

Primrose flushed and smiled. "Thank you, dear. Your mama used to walk you by to look at them, when you were just a little girl."

The memory tightened Bisky's throat. "I miss her every day," she said, which was true. Her mother had succumbed to cancer at sixty, without much of a fight. Bisky was pretty sure her mother's speedy death had to do with the fact that she didn't want to go on without Bisky's father.

"That William Gross used to walk by, too," Primrose said. "In fact, if I'm not mistaken, you and he ran through my flower beds a time or two, trampled things down."

"I remember throwing a ball that landed in them," Bisky confessed. "William took the blame. Said he should have caught it, and we both tried to straighten out the flowers."

"I remember. It was hard to be mad at the two of you, you were such a cute pair." Primrose frowned. "I always thought you'd end up together. Wondered if he'd come back to town for that purpose, actually, but…" She trailed off.

Bisky glanced at Mary. She kept quiet about her programs and the backgrounds of the people who made use of them, and in Primrose's case, that was a good thing. She shot Mary a smile to show she wouldn't spill any secrets about William and the reason he'd come to Victory Cottage.

"I was surprised to see him with a woman yesterday," Primrose said now. "Tiny little blonde thing. Never saw her around town before."

Bisky studied Primrose's face. Was she making up stories?

"Oh, yeah, I saw them too," Kayla said. "I wondered who she was."

Bisky's heart lurched, which was absolutely ridiculous. There was no reason to feel strange that William had been seen in town with another woman. It wasn't as if he and Bisky were dating or had any obligation to each other.

Mary bit her lip, and Bisky could tell she knew something about the woman. Her stomach started to churn. She'd eaten too much at the church luncheon, maybe.

"So I asked around," Primrose said, her voice excited with the news she had. "Turns out she's his ex-wife."

Bisky had to move, had to get away from Primrose and the others. She stood and started shoveling mulch into a heap in the flowerbed.

It was good that Mary and Kayla were able to get Primrose onto a different subject, because Bisky was busy thinking. Thinking as she worked, which was always the best way. Giving herself a good talking-to, as Mom had always encouraged.

Men were more of a sideline, at least in her life. They weren't the main thing. Her needs for warmth and companionship got fulfilled by her woman friends and the men she worked with, and most of all, Sunny.

Sunny won't be around forever.

She stopped that thought right in its tracks. Sunny was an independent girl—woman, really—and would move on to live her own life, though God willing, they'd always be close.

So William had kissed her. No big deal.

He was hanging around with his ex-wife. Again, no big deal.

It was all fine. Bisky emptied the wheelbarrow in record

time and went back for another load and tried to put enough energy in her step to cure the ache in her heart.

ON SUNDAY AFTERNOON, Sunny flopped down on Kaitlyn's bed and regarded her two friends, Kaitlyn and Venus. Music blared from Kaitlyn's speaker and the air reeked with perfume spray.

As usual these days, Venus and Kait were trying on clothes. "After this, will you do my makeup?" Kaitlyn begged Venus. "You're so good at it."

"At your service," she said. "I'll do yours too," she offered Sunny.

"Sure," Sunny said, surprising herself.

Kaitlyn's jaw dropped, but Venus smiled. "You have to get ready for when *Caden* comes over," she said.

Sunny sat upright. "He's coming over? Why?" She narrowed her eyes at Kait, then wiped the angry expression off her face. Did Kaitlyn like him? Did Venus?

"She invited him for *you*, idiot! We know you're crazy about him."

"I'm not crazy about him! I don't get like that!"

"But wouldn't you like to know him better?" Venus asked. "We saw how you looked at him."

If she was looking at Caden weirdly, she needed to stop. No way would she moon around about boys, the way her friends did.

"I don't know if he'll even come," Kaitlyn said. "I just figured...because I invited Marcus, too, and it would be good to have another boy."

"And I'll be the fifth wheel, as usual." Venus let out a windy sigh.

As Kaitlyn punched at her phone to change the music, Venus beckoned Sunny over to the mirror, which they'd set up by the window for natural light. "Hair back," she said, handing Sunny a scrunchie. "Good heavens, girl, you need to stop being out in the sun all the time, you're brown!"

Sunny shrugged. "A lot of people pay for this kind of tan," she said, echoing what her mother always said. Although Mom *had* gotten more careful with sunscreen lately.

Sunny was glad Venus and Kait had invited her to hang out. They were all getting along better for whatever reason.

Venus was just getting ready to apply the facial masque she said Sunny desperately needed when the doorbell rang. The dog barked, and there was the sound of Kaitlyn's dad talking to someone, and then heavy footsteps tromping on the stairs. A rap on the door, and Caden and Marcus came in.

"Keep that door open," Kaitlyn's dad called up the stairs.

"Dad!" Kaitlyn rolled her eyes. "You'd think I was twelve."

"I heard that," he called.

"I just love your dad," Venus said. "He's adorable."

Sunny winced. She'd once made the mistake of describing old Rooker Smits as adorable, and her mom had yelled at her for fifteen minutes about respect and dignity and treating older people like people, not puppies.

Anyway, she wouldn't have thought of Mr. Martin—a big former cop who took no flack from anyone—as adorable. But it *was* sweet how close he was with Kait and her sister. Sometimes, it made Sunny wish she had a dad.

Caden and Marcus hunched together over a video game, and Kaitlyn abandoned the other girls to join in. Venus decided to forgo the facial masque. Instead, she went ahead and put a little makeup on Sunny, then put her hair into French braids.

"How's it going, staying here?" Sunny asked. Venus was living in the Martins' spare room most weeks.

"It's great. Better than that awful island."

"Teaberry Island is cool," Sunny protested. They went by it pretty often when they were fishing, and its quaint, two-street downtown was interesting. Only a few recluses lived there all year round, according to Mom. "Why'd your mom move there, anyway?"

"She needed to take a break. For her art." Venus rolled her eyes and then squirted a little hairspray over Sunny's head. "There. Perfect."

Sunny studied herself in the mirror. Having her hair in a fancier style, wearing a little mascara and blush, did make her look better. Less like a kid or one of the guys.

"Thanks," she said. "So you don't like the island?"

"No way," Venus said. "It's totally boring. There's nothing to do."

Sunny felt like there wasn't much to do in Pleasant Shores, either, but at least it wasn't deserted and there were other teenagers. "Do you have any of your mom's art? I didn't even know she was an artist."

"She left a perfectly good job to do pictures of dogs," Venus said. She gestured at Kaitlyn's wall. "Kaitlyn loves them, so I kinda permanently loaned them to her. I don't want 'em in my room, but I don't want to hurt Mom's feelings."

Sunny walked across the room to the pictures Venus had indicated, sucking in her stomach. Mom always said she shouldn't slump, that slumping just made her look like a miserable tall girl, so she kept her shoulders back and tossed her head.

From the side of her eyes, she glanced at Caden. Was he looking at her?

He *was*. She blushed and hurried the rest of the way to the pictures.

She studied the first one and frowned. It wasn't what she'd thought of as art before; it was more like a comic book version of a dog. Not a kids' one, but not exactly manga, either. The dog portrayed looked a little bit like the one Mom and William had found, and Mom had brought home overnight.

She moved over to the next one. She didn't recognize the two dogs there, but they were fighting in a kind of pit while men leaned over watching, leering.

"What's with the dog pictures?" she asked Venus.

"Oh, Mom's like an animal rights activist. In her spare time." Again, Venus rolled her eyes.

"I'm out." Caden put down his gaming console and walked over to where she and Venus stood looking at the pictures. "Hey," he said, "isn't that Peppy?"

"Maybe," Sunny said. "You mean the dog kids were trying to get drunk, right?"

"Oh, yeah, that." He looked down.

Wait a minute. Mom hadn't named names of any of the kids she'd seen. "Were you there?"

"Uh-huh, but don't tell anyone," he said. "I sorta sneaked off."

Just like he'd sneaked off when they'd found Muffin in the woods. She narrowed her eyes at him. "That's wrong, feeding a dog alcohol!"

"I wasn't *doing* it," he said. "I'm just…" He trailed off.

"You're just what?" she asked.

"I'm just looking into things," he said. Then he turned away and marched back over to where Kaitlyn and Marcus were still playing video games. They'd leaned closer to each other, so that now, their shoulders touched. "Marcus was there, too," he added defensively.

Sunny threw up her hands. "You guys are awful."

"Yeah," Kaitlyn said, "but they're cute." She pinched Marcus's cheek, and Venus giggled, and Kaitlyn was back to thinking her friends were complete idiots.

She, on the other hand, wasn't so distracted by a cute boy that she forgot about the mystery they were trying to solve. Was the dog in the woods, the one these yokels had gotten drunk, somehow related to Xena and Muffin and whoever had hurt them? And was Venus's mom somehow involved?

CHAPTER SIXTEEN

"WILLIAM!"

The lilting voice outside Victory Cottage made William want to hide his head in his hands. His ex-wife was *still* in town?

He'd seen Ellie Saturday and Sunday. Monday, she'd promised she was leaving. But here it was Tuesday afternoon and she was knocking on his front door.

"William? I know you're in there."

And Ellie was nothing if not persistent. He pushed aside his laptop where he'd been reviewing plans for today's museum work with the teenagers and trudged to the front of the cottage. He opened the wooden door but not the screen. "You said you were leaving."

Her face fell, and a reflexive guilt gripped him. Ellie was fragile, easily hurt.

"I just wanted to say goodbye." She smiled winningly. "I just have a little time before I hit the road, and I thought…"

He sighed. "I'll take you out for a milkshake before you leave town," he said. "If you promise me you're all packed and ready to go." He glanced at the time on his phone. "If we go now, you can be on the road by three, and home well before dark."

"You're so sweet to take care of me. I can just come in and say goodbye."

"No." He knew what that would be like, because she'd

already tried to get him into bed twice. "Out in public, or forget it."

"Oooh, you're so *firm*." She smiled. "I really like that."

He sighed. "Let me grab my things so I can go straight to work from there."

Minutes later, they were walking through town. It was a warm day, the last day of March but more like May, and people kept glancing at them.

It stoked his memories. Partly, they were conspicuous because he was so big and she was tiny; they made an odd couple. But partly, people noticed them because Ellie was gorgeous. Model-thin, with blond hair to her waist and a ready smile and laugh.

It had taken him a while to realize that the thinness was due to a problem with anorexia that dated back to her high school days. The laugh, as often as not, was related to her drinking in the middle of the afternoon.

He hadn't smelled any alcohol on her so far, so hopefully, she'd restrained herself today. If she hadn't, he wouldn't be able to encourage her getting in a car and driving.

"I'm glad you'll be done with this program soon," she said, grabbing his arm and squeezing it, leaning close. "I can't wait for you to get back to Baltimore."

"Ellie." He pulled his arm out of her grip. "Even when I come back, it's not going to be you and me together."

"But I'm sorry! I told you I was sorry." She clutched his arm again. "I was devastated, and I needed a distraction. You can understand that."

He shook his head, pulled his arm away again and urged her past the shops toward Goody's. "Even when we were together, I wasn't what you wanted."

"How can you say that? You know I adore you!"

He shook his head. "After your earlier two affairs, I took

you back. For Jenna's sake, so we could have a family. Now, with her gone…" He trailed off.

"But our marriage wasn't all about Jenna."

For him, in the end, it had been. But telling her that—again—wouldn't do any good. She was in one of her non-listening phases.

He ushered her into Goody's and held up two fingers toward the woman behind the counter. "Chocolate," he said, and led Ellie to a table. Thank goodness, the place was nearly empty.

In their discussions the previous couple of days, William had surmised what was going on and why Ellie had appeared in Pleasant Shores now. Her latest boyfriend had left her. And she was one of those waiflike creatures who couldn't manage without a partner supporting and adoring her.

He got the milkshakes, paid for them and carried them back to the table. He set one down in front of her.

She frowned at it. "I can't drink that. I'll be as big as a house."

"Doubtful." He could tell she wanted more attention and praise for her slenderness, but he wasn't going to encourage that. "What are your plans for when you get back? You said you have an apartment lined up?"

"Kind of," she said, her voice veering toward a whine. "I was hoping we could live together."

"We're divorced, and we're not getting back together. You need to take charge of your life, honey." He slipped back into the endearment and could have smacked himself.

Her face lit up in a smile. "I love it when you call me honey," she said.

"It was a mistake. And I'm saying you need to find a place to live and a job. Until then, you'd better stay with your parents."

"They kicked me out," she said.

Something about the way she said it made him think she was lying. "I still have their number," he said, pulling out his phone. "I can call them and talk them into taking you in."

"All right, all right, they didn't kick me out and I can stay with them." Her lower lip stuck out. "But you should take me in. You owe me."

How had he ever found her attractive?

"It was your fault Jenna died," she said, her voice going shrill as she repeated a refrain he'd heard constantly in the weeks and months after Jenna's death. "You should have been there."

The truth was, *she* should have been there. She was supposed to have picked up Jenna within an hour of William's departure, but she hadn't come. She'd hedged enough about why she'd been late that he'd figured out she'd been preoccupied with her latest man of the month.

"You should have waited till I got home," she accused now.

Maybe he should've. He'd known what Ellie was like, how unreliable she was.

But he'd had to go to his faculty meeting, and Jenna had said she'd be fine, she was going to take a nap, and he'd headed off to work without a worry in his head.

He'd arrived home after a few hours at work to police tape and a misery so enormous he could barely take it in. Only later had Ellie arrived and collapsed into hysteria.

Deep inside, she probably blamed herself. But she never really *did* blame herself, so she'd blamed him.

Ellie was dependent, and childish, and wanted a man to lean on and pet and baby her. She easily found them, too, because she was so beautiful.

He'd been shocked that she'd wanted him, when he was

working on his graduate degree all those years ago and she was a student. She'd loved how big and strong he was, how protected he'd made her feel.

His head had been turned, he admitted it.

Now, looking at her as she cried a little and flung her hair back and leaned forward with her low-cut shirt, he didn't feel flattered or attracted at all; he felt trapped.

An image flashed into his mind: the last time he'd been here with Bisky. Bisky, strong, happy, enjoying life. Now that he knew himself, knew more what life was about, he realized *that* was what he wanted. That was what he would choose if he could have anyone.

He couldn't, of course. Ellie was right about one thing: he should have protected Jenna, and he hadn't. Hadn't succeeded in protecting and keeping and reforming Ellie, either, for that matter.

"Can't we try again?" Ellie begged.

He studied her and made himself consider her plea one last time. He'd been swayed by her tears and promises twice before. They'd gone to marriage therapy and things had been okay for a while, until someone else caught her eye.

Now, without Jenna, he had no motivation to take her back, and no desire to, either.

He took her hands. "Look at me."

She did, through long, teary lashes. "You're saying yes?"

"I'm saying no. This is no and this is forever. We're through."

She stared back at him and her throat worked and he remembered loving her.

Not anymore.

"Go home," he said. "Go home to your parents and get yourself on your feet again. You'll figure it out." Even as he said it, he could predict exactly *how* she'd get on her feet:

with the next man who took her out and bought her things and told her she was pretty.

"William!" The words were hissed from the doorway, and he looked up to see Sunny. She tapped at her wrist where a watch would have been, if she'd worn one. "Time to start!"

He scanned for Bisky and there she was, outside Goody's. Her back was to him, but something about the stiff set of it told him she'd seen him with Ellie.

He was still holding Ellie's hands, and now, he pulled his own hands away and stood. "I have to go."

Sunny walked out of Goody's and over to her mother. She put her arm around Bisky and they walked toward the museum.

Ellie cleared her throat, a choking, crying sound. "I...I don't know what I might do to myself," she said, her voice trembling.

Those words clutched at his stomach, just as they did every time he heard them. He couldn't be responsible for another woman's death.

His therapist had told him the suicide card wasn't valid, that those who used it to keep a relationship were emotionally abusive. He'd practiced a response—"that's your choice, and I can't stop you from making it"—but now, the words stuck in his throat.

He sighed. "Look, I'm going to call your parents and tell them you're here," he said. "Unless you'd rather I call... Roscoe, was that his name? Raymond?" She'd flung it at him as she'd left, but he'd pushed it out of his mind.

She tilted her head to one side, considering. "I guess I'll call Roscoe," she said. "If he knows I came down here to see you, he'll be pretty jealous." She pulled out her phone.

Translation: she could manipulate him. "I'll call your

parents, too, just to make sure you're safe," he said. "Good-bye, Ellie."

She gave him a sulky pout, and then started speaking into her phone. As he called her parents and relayed the situation and Ellie's location, he watched Ellie's pout turn into a smile. Roscoe had evidently caved.

He gave Ellie a little wave and strode out of Goody's. He needed to find Bisky and make sure she hadn't misinterpreted what she'd seen. He couldn't be with her, no, but he *had* kissed her; the least he could do was clarify that he wasn't with someone else less than a week later.

Bɪsky walked toward the museum beside Sunny, barely listening to her daughter's indignant rant. "What was he doing with that woman? I thought he and you liked each other! Man, if he's treated you badly…"

"It's his ex-wife," she interrupted.

Her own voice sounded dull, as dull as the day. Low clouds hung over the Chesapeake, blocking the sun and seeming to muffle the town's bright colors.

"Oh." Sunny sounded surprised and went quiet for a minute, then started up again. "If she's his ex, then he shouldn't have been holding her hands like some lover-boy. What a jerk! I thought he was one of the good ones."

"He has every right to do whatever he wants," Bisky forced herself to say. "He and I aren't seeing each other."

"You've been *talking*," Sunny said, and Bisky knew that was teenage parlance for some kind of romantic connection, or the start of it.

"Besides," Sunny continued indignantly, "he's late! What a jerk."

Despite herself, Bisky smiled at her daughter's loyalty. "He'll probably be here in a few," she said. "If not, we can get started without him."

"He's not who I thought he was," Sunny said.

Me, either. And Bisky had known him since childhood.

That was the huge mistake of getting involved with an old friend. When the inevitable breakup happened, you didn't just lose the romance; you lost the friendship. That thought made her throat tighten up.

Ahead, six or seven teens milled around outside the museum. Even on a day that had gone cool and gloomy, most of them would rather be outside after a day at school.

Food for thought. She'd see if Drew had any outdoor projects to complete around the museum. She found that she didn't want to be inside, either, especially if William was going to be working there.

She cleared her throat and forced a smile. "Hi, everybody, glad you could come." She was, too. This was what was important. Not some *man.* "If you want to work with Mr. Martin inside the museum, come with me and I'll get you set up."

"I'll work with Mr. Martin anytime." Serena, new to the group, waggled her pierced eyebrow up and down.

"Ewww, he's Kaitlyn's *dad*," said blonde Olivia, lightly slapping Serena's arm.

Serena and a couple of the boys headed inside with Bisky, and she spoke with Drew about finding them some work while they waited for William to come take over.

"No problem," he said immediately. "You okay?"

"Yeah, thanks, I'm fine." She went back outside, just in time to see Kayla approach with a line of six preschoolers, walking two by two, each pair holding hands. Bisky smiled at the little ones, noticing their cuteness with some outer part of her brain that wasn't hurting. "I think we're going to have a craft in the museum basement. Elijah, you said you wanted to help with the children, right?"

Truthfully, she didn't know what was supposed to happen between the teenagers and children; that was William's part of the plan. "William isn't here yet," she said to Kayla. "Any chance you can keep them occupied until he gets here with the supplies, if he gets here?"

"No problem," Kayla said. "You okay?"

"Yeah, thanks, I'm fine." But she obviously wasn't, and obviously, people could tell.

Have some pride, girl. It was what her father had said when she'd experienced teasing about her dock kid heritage.

She could do it, too. She could pull herself together.

No way would she let William see what he'd done to her.

But that kiss... Some weak, girlish part of her cried, deep inside. That kiss had been beautiful, and so full of promise. To have that level of romance and attraction, *plus* the beauty of an old friend who'd known her parents and understood her love of the water and had felt the same joys and sorrows of all the families around here... *That* would have really been something. Something beyond what she expected or deserved.

But what men wanted was a fragile little blonde, not her.

The bay tossed and churned, slate-gray, beautiful even at its worst. Above, the gulls flew and cawed. On a good day or a bad, they still had to work for their food.

A throat cleared beside her. It was Connor, big and burly and shy. "Is there something else you want us to work on?"

She nodded hard, cleared her head. "Yes, we're going to have the third group work on the flower beds. If you want to join that group, I'd welcome you. Lots to haul."

"Sure. I like to work."

So she, Connor and one of the twins, Aiden, started on the flower beds. She set Aiden to work digging holes while she and Connor each took an end of a two-by-four from the stack beside the building to the front of the flower bed. "We're going to build a low little wall with these," she said, panting as they carried it across the grassy area and put it down in front of the would-be flower bed.

"I can do that, Miz Castleman," Aiden said. He was small and slight, but he'd been raised to help a woman, especially an older one. Most of the dock kids were the same.

"It's okay. You get the holes dug, and we'll be in good shape."

She and Connor were hauling the fourth big two-by-four when William approached. "Let me do that," he said, his voice gruff.

"I'm plenty strong." She continued with Connor, and they set the big piece of wood down, in front of the second flower bed.

Sunny had been with the inside group, but now she rushed outside. "You're supposed to be inside," she said to William, her voice a little snotty. "Mr. Martin can't do it all alone." She stepped between Bisky and William as if she were physically blocking him from her mother.

Bisky shook her head and whispered "Manners." She appreciated Sunny's support, but she also just felt weary and sad.

William gave her a long look, but she turned away. "Ready, Connor? We've got the side pieces to bring over yet."

"Sure." The two of them walked over to the stack of lumber, leaving William to stand with Sunny for a minute and then walk inside, shoulders slumped.

She didn't care. The physical work felt good. It almost distracted her from the ache in her heart.

Half an hour later, though, William came out again. She was drinking water, a little apart from the teens who were all now planting flowers, and she couldn't avoid him.

"Listen, Bisky," he said. "About what you saw…"

She raised a hand. "Forget it. It doesn't matter or interest me."

"Bisky." He stepped closer.

She couldn't keep up the fiction that what she'd seen meant nothing to her. So she stood her ground and put her hands on her hips. "I have too much pride to be your side chick. You should know that."

"It's not like—"

"I know what I saw," she interrupted. "Leave me alone." And before he could answer, argue more, break her heart, she spun and walked over to the gardens, determinedly turning her face away from him.

CHAPTER SEVENTEEN

ON SATURDAY AROUND NOON, Sunny guided her boat into one of the open slips at Teaberry Island and ignored the slight unease in her chest. "Tie up," she ordered Caden.

Aside from a bank of clouds to the south, the sky was blue. It was a warm day, and Caden wore a snug-fitting tee that made it look like he'd been working out.

You're not here to gawk at him, you're here to find out what Venus's mom knows about the dogs.

"You sure you know what you're doing?" He stood above her on the dock, looking down, hair shining in the sun.

Sunny swallowed. "Of course." She climbed out of the boat, wondering if he was checking her out. She was wearing her cutest jeans, and she probably should have worn something warmer on top, but right now, at noon, her short T-shirt was fine.

"Come on, let's check out this place," she said. "Have you been here before?"

"Are you kidding? My folks only hit the high-price resorts." The corner of his mouth quirked to one side, indicating he didn't share their tastes. "How about you?"

"Mom and I came a couple of times. I guess she used to hang out here when she was a kid. There was more to the place then." Just like most of the Chesapeake islands, Teaberry was shrinking as its shoreline eroded.

Strangely, though, as it had shrunk, it had become more of a vacation spot and artist's colony, which was why, she assumed, Venus's mom was here. There was a little down-town consisting of a short block with a couple of galleries, a diner, a café and a souvenir shop. Branching off from it were a few residential streets. In the distance, you could see a couple of bigger houses on a bluff above the shoreline.

"So you think we'll just happen to find Venus's mom?" Caden was such a boy, always skeptical and thinking he knew what was what.

"She said her mom lives in a pink house. How many of those can there be? And I know her mom's not rich, not like your folks, so it's probably going to be one of the little places close to downtown."

"Okay, Sherlock," he said, and there might have been grudging respect in his voice. "Look, there's a pink house." He looked around. "The only one I can see."

"That must be it!" She gripped his arm, and then dropped it immediately, not wanting to seem like a flirty girl.

"So what do we do now?"

"I have to think." She led him into a park that backed on the pink house and sat on a park bench, patting the seat beside her.

He sat. "What exactly are we trying to find out?"

"What Venus's mom knows about Peppy and the other dogs she painted," she said. As she articulated the plan, she realized it sounded full of holes, but she pushed on. "I don't know for sure if that one painting was Peppy or not, but she also did pictures of dogfights. I want to find out why."

Caden frowned. "I wish you'd told me the plan before-hand. I wouldn't have come."

"But you said you were looking into what happened to the dogs in the woods. I figured you'd want to help them."

"Sure, I mean, who doesn't want to help dogs? But this is stupid. You're going to, what, walk up to this stranger and ask her, hey, are you involved in dog abuse?"

"No! I'll be more subtle." She frowned. "I'm not saying she's a criminal or anything. Maybe I just want to see what else she's painted and if this is in line, or something new. I mean, if she's an animal rights activist, then maybe the pictures *are* just generic. But if not..."

"So you think we should snoop in her house?"

"No! I don't believe in breaking and entering."

"Could have fooled me." He grinned, and then she remembered she'd basically broken into the Blue House.

"I would only do it for a good cause." Sunny realized that was true. If she had to break into Venus's mom's place to help the dogs, she would.

She was having fun being with Caden like this, casual and fun, not romantic but not *not* romantic. It was...interesting.

A woman came out of the little pink cottage and walked toward them, then past them. She was curvy, with long dreadlocks, and she wore a loose, brightly colored dress. "Do you think that's Venus's mom?"

"Could be. Looks like her."

"And looks like an artist."

"Look, if she's a famous artist, we could find her online." Caden pulled out his phone, then frowned. "No service."

"I already looked," Sunny informed him loftily. "But all her art's behind a firewall. Which, to me, is suspicious. Why wouldn't she be public about it if she's trying to sell it?"

"True. If we're breaking in, we should go do it before she finishes her errands." Caden stood and led the way to the pink house, moving stealthily. For the first time, she realized that he must have broken into the Blue House, too, and that he was good at hiding; he'd succeeded in staying away from his family this whole time. "Hey," she said, "how come your family isn't looking for you?"

"Long story. Come on." He climbed the concrete back

steps and tried the door. "Open." He looked at her. "Are you sure we want to go in?"

Sunny's throat felt dry. "Um…no?"

The door flew open. "That's a good thing," came a voice, a man's, "because you'd get yourself shot that way."

Sunny gulped to see a heavyset, muscular man, dressed in gym shorts and a ripped T-shirt. His gun was pointed at them.

Caden took a big step back, bumping into Sunny, and then they both nearly fell off the steps. "Uh, hi," he said, "we're, uh, friends of Venus Jackson."

Sunny nudged him. They shouldn't be giving any identifying details.

"Yes, and? That somehow gives you the right to walk into our home uninvited?"

"We weren't…" Sunny trailed off, because they most certainly *had* been planning, or at least hoping, to go in.

The man glared at them. "Stay right there," he said, then went inside to a landline and placed a call.

Moments later, the woman they'd identified as Venus's mother was hurrying toward them. "What's going on?"

"They were trying to break in." The big man had his arms crossed over his chest.

"We weren't…we just…"

"We were looking for more of your pictures of dogs," Sunny blurted out, figuring that, at this point, it was better to get everything out into the open.

"How do you even know about those?" The woman crossed her arms.

"Because…we love dogs?" Caden tried.

She tilted her head to one side, her lips flat. "Not credible."

"Do you know someone who's abusing dogs?" Sunny asked, and then, when the woman's face drew up into a frown, she regretted it.

"Of course not," Venus's mother said. "Don't you think I'd report it? I get my images off the internet."

The man came out onto the porch. "You kids get on out of here before I call the police. You're upsetting her, and she's sensitive. She's an artist."

"You know my daughter?" the woman asked, her voice softening a little.

"Yes. She's a good friend."

"Is she all right?"

Why hadn't Sunny been up front and just asked Venus to come? "She's fine. Great."

"She'll get a piece of my mind for telling anyone where I am," the woman said. "Look, keep my location to yourselves, okay? I've gotten harassed for publicizing those dogfighting images. That's why we're taking a break, living here for a year."

"That's not their business." The man put his arm around her. "You kids get on out of here. Scram." He shooed them away as if they were a couple of annoying flies. That made Sunny mad, and she tried to stand her ground. But the man puffed up threateningly, and almost as a unit she and Caden turned and ran.

They didn't stop until they reached the boat. "Get in," Sunny called, and started the motor.

Only after they were five minutes out from shore did Sunny's heart stop pounding double time. At that point, she realized the sea was too choppy for comfort. But they'd make it home; they had to. Because no way could they go back to Teaberry Island.

By MIDAFTERNOON ON SATURDAY, William had argued with himself long enough, and he couldn't talk himself out of going to see Bisky.

She'd avoided him again on Thursday, even though they

were working with the teens together. So it was harming the program, because the kids definitely noticed.

Mostly, though, he wanted to make things up with her.

He knew he had to leave and go back to his real life. One month of his time here was already almost gone.

He knew he couldn't be with Bisky, couldn't inflict himself on her. But he deeply, deeply regretted hurting her, and he wanted to explain. Maybe they could at least part as friends when his time in Pleasant Shores came to an end.

He approached her open back door, tapped on the screen, and then looked inside. Bisky was there, and she was walking around fuming. "What do you want?" she snapped.

"Is something wrong?"

"Yes, something's wrong. Sunny's got a doctor's appointment up the shore, but I can't find her." A text came in and she looked at the face of her phone, frowned, and texted back, then looked at him. "That was Kaitlyn. Neither she nor Venus knows where she went. When I find her, I'm going to strangle her."

"You've looked all around inside?" Alarm bells were going off inside William.

"Of course." She frowned. "So I guess outside is next." She plowed past him. "You can help, but don't think that means we're friends again."

That almost made him smile. They walked around the outside of the house and then down to the dock. Bisky hurried faster the closer they got, and then muttered something, sounding angry.

"What's wrong?" he asked.

"She took out the boat." She lifted her hands, palms up. "She knows she's not supposed to do that without letting me know where she's going. No way is she going to get back in time for her appointment."

"They left about eleven," Rooker Smits contributed

from the next dock. "Told her a storm was coming, but you know kids. She didn't care. Too busy flirting with her young man."

William's gut tightened as he looked up at dark, low-hanging clouds.

"Who'd she go with?" Bisky asked.

Rooker shrugged. "Didn't recognize him."

"Any idea where they were headed?"

"They went toward Teaberry Island," Rooker said.

William's eyebrows lifted. He'd been there, but it wasn't exactly close by.

A gust of wind caught them, and William looked out at the choppy bay. Dread tightened his stomach. If something happened to Sunny… He couldn't even bear the thought. "She's good at navigating a boat, right?"

"Sure, but not…" Bisky broke off and bit her lip, her forehead wrinkling. "Can I take your boat?" she asked Rooker. "She's probably fine. I'm sure she is."

"Take it." He tossed her the keys.

"If you know anyone who's free," William said to Rooker, "maybe they could come help search."

Bisky opened her mouth like she was going to protest, then snapped it shut again and nodded.

Rooker pulled out a big phone and started pushing buttons, squinting.

The boat pitched and tossed as Bisky steered it, and a cold wind whipped the hat off William's head before he could grab it. The temperature was dropping.

Icy water hit the side of his leg, and his heart sank lower. No one could survive for long in these temperatures; hypothermia would soon set in.

"Let's call in the Coast Guard," he said as big drops of rain started pummeling them.

Bisky grimaced, looking up at the sky. "Hate to do that, but…"

William knew why: they weren't sure that Sunny's boat was in distress, and they also didn't have a location. The watermen were careful not to tie up the emergency channel with general calls.

A voice came over the radio set. "I'm west of Teaberry up through Kentstown. No sightings."

"That sounds like one of Rooker's buddies." Bisky steered them toward Teaberry Island.

"I'll try to contact her," William said, because there wasn't much he could do to help. He felt useless, ineffectual. Like before.

Bisky shook her head, water flying off her as if from a wet dog. "Just monitor Channel 16." She gripped the wheel and guided them through a swell, and then spoke again. "Why didn't I get a fixed-mount radio with GPS?"

He beat back his emotions and pushed buttons, trying to figure out Rooker's radio, while Bisky fought the rough water. Waves slapped them hard, rocking them from side to side, and the sky let loose with torrents of rain. Finally, he heard a call on Channel 16. "Coast Guard, Coast Guard, Coast Guard," came the thready female voice. He was pretty sure it was Sunny. "She's okay, she's calling the Coast Guard, but not Mayday," he yelled to Bisky, but she was focused on managing the boat and, amidst the wind and rain, didn't hear him.

He knew enough not to muddy the channel with talk, but he listened to her describe their location. She insisted she wasn't in distress, but was taking on a little water, which sure sounded like distress to William. The Coast Guard watchstander sounded calm, though, and told Sunny to switch to a nonemergency channel where they could communicate without jamming up the emergency one.

He made his way to Bisky and told her Sunny's location. "She's okay, she says, but they're taking on water. Should I contact Rooker?"

"Anyone searching will be monitoring Channel 16," she said, and turned the boat so sharply that he nearly fell.

The sky seemed a dark blanket over them, spitting rain in sheets now, and William's hands ached with the cold, but he shook it off. How would Sunny be able to manage?

"I see her boat!" Bisky gunned the motor, and the boat churned ahead toward a dark spot William could barely see, and then he could. The boat seemed to be foundering. "Sunny!" he yelled. "We're coming for you, don't give up!"

"She's overboard!" Bisky said, and William ran to get the rope and life preserver.

He tossed it carefully, but the waters swept it past.

Sunny was floating—thank God she was wearing a life jacket—but her eyes were wide and scared. "I don't know what happened to Caden!" she screamed.

William threw the life preserver again, and this time, Sunny grabbed it and held on. He hauled her in and lifted her into the boat where she collapsed on the deck, shivering.

"See if Rooker has any blankets below," Bisky cried, but William was already there, digging in the storage bin, finding a couple of old wool blankets and a poncho. He went back up and helped Bisky wrap Sunny in the warm materials.

Sunny fought off the blankets and tried to stand, then collapsed again. "Caden... I don't know where Caden is." She was so out of breath she could barely talk.

"Was he on the boat or overboard?" Bisky spoke sharply.

"On the boat...but he might not...be anymore."

William looked over to where Bisky's boat was now listing and bobbing in the rough waters. "Pull over there close and I'll try to climb across."

"Stay here," Bisky ordered Sunny, and then rushed back to steer Rooker's boat into position.

The moment the two boats touched, William crossed the gap between the boats and climbed over, barely making it, the slippery railings nearly sending him into the churn. On the boat, he squinted and searched around, reeling and falling on the slippery deck, his vision hampered by the rain. Finally he found Caden sprawled in the boat's tiny cabin, barely conscious. "Hit my head," he grunted out, rubbing the side of it, and then closed his eyes.

William picked up the boy, no easy feat, and carried him to the deck. "Found him, he's hurt," he yelled.

Bisky pulled the boat close again and William threw an arm over the rail and held them together. Bisky reached over and gripped Caden under his arms, Sunny holding her from the back by the waist of her pants. Between them, William pushing and Bisky pulling, they got the boy over to Rooker's boat. Sunny pulled him to the deck, checking him, while Bisky took over holding the two boats together and William climbed across.

"We made it!" Bisky was laughing and crying.

William looked back at Bisky's spinning boat, decided he'd better focus on getting the people to shore, and went for the helm as Bisky knelt by the two teenagers. He managed to steer the unfamiliar boat in the direction they'd come, Bisky calling out supporting instructions.

But as they headed toward Pleasant Shores, the storm already waning, William's heart was heavy in his chest. He'd helped, but not enough. He hadn't saved Sunny; Bisky had. Without Bisky, he would have been totally ineffectual, as he had been with his daughter.

CHAPTER EIGHTEEN

BISKY WASN'T SURE HOW, but somehow, they made it back to land. William steered the boat while Bisky hugged and fussed over Sunny and her friend, a kid Bisky didn't even know, who'd apparently hit his head in the tossing boat. He now appeared to be coherent and hopefully okay.

It seemed like all of Pleasant Shores had learned about the search and gotten involved. Several other boats flanked them on their ride, one of them towing Bisky's waterlogged boat. As soon as they reached Rooker's dock, there were people ready to help them tie up and climb off the boat.

William carried Sunny inside and upstairs, and thank heavens for that, because Bisky was jelly-boned after all the terror and excitement. The other teen—Caden, his name was—was shivering and panicky, and maybe he wasn't as okay as he'd initially appeared, because he was spouting nonsense while his parents helped him into their fancy car and drove him away.

It all blurred in Bisky's mind. She was dimly aware of Mary and Kayla hustling her off into a hot bath, bringing in tea and cookies to get her strength up. They ignored her protests that she needed to tend to Sunny. "Put on your own air mask first," Mary scolded. "Anyway, Ria's giving her the same treatment. She showered her off and put her to bed. The tea they made Sunny will help her go to sleep."

Bisky stopped midsip and held her cup toward Mary. "I don't want to sleep."

"No, your tea is regular green tea," Kayla assured her. "A little caffeine, not much."

As soon as she'd stopped shaking, gotten cleaned up and warmed up, she put on warm flannel pants and a hoodie and made her way upstairs to see Sunny. Ria was sitting in a chair by the bed while Sunny dozed. She jumped up and hugged Bisky, told her Sunny was going to be fine, and then left them alone.

Bisky leaned over the bed and put her arms around her daughter, and the shaking of Sunny's shoulders told her Sunny was crying a little, just as she was. Finally, she let Sunny sink back down onto her stack of pillows and settled herself on the edge of the bed, holding her beloved daughter's hand.

"Am I in trouble?" Sunny sounded weepy.

"Absolutely." Bisky tried to make her voice steady and firm. "We'll figure it out later, and yes, there will be consequences. But…" She felt her throat tightening. "I love you so much, kid. I was so scared."

They hugged again, and the feel of her warm, healthy, alive daughter in her arms was bliss.

"I was scared too, Mom," Sunny said, sinking back down again. "It was all my fault. I'm sorry I sank our boat."

"You didn't sink it. The twins' family hauled it in. It took on a little water, that's all."

"Oh, good." Sunny's wide smile was momentary, and then she frowned again. "Is Caden okay? He needs us to take care…of him." Sunny's voice was fading. That sleep-inducing tea must be taking effect.

"He's fine," Bisky said, stroking Sunny's hair back from her face and adjusting the blankets around her. "He's going to be just fine, and so are you. Now, get some rest."

Downstairs, more of her friends had arrived: Ria's husband, Drew; Amber and her husband, Paul; Bisky's cousin

Gemma and local hardware-store-owner Isaac, newly an item. Everyone fussed over her, making her sit down while they brought her hot oyster stew and saltines and a glass of wine, asking her to recount what had happened. She thanked everyone and looked around for the one person she *really* wanted to thank. "Where's William?" she asked.

"He *was* here," Kayla said, looking around.

"Pretty sure he went home to shower," Paul said.

Of course he must have. He'd been soaked. Bisky chatted a few more minutes and then excused herself, stepped into the dining room where she could hear better, and called him.

The call went to voice mail, which was disappointing. When his greeting ended, she left him a message: "Thank you for everything you did today. Come back over if you want some food and company. Most everyone's over here."

She went back out and talked with her woman friends, told the story over and over, accepted their congratulations and hugs. It was warm and wonderful and she had another glass of wine. This was why she loved her hometown and always would. They pulled together and helped each other.

And her daughter was safe. She kept looking upward, partly toward Sunny's bedroom, but partly to offer repeated prayers of thanks.

Drew sat close to Ria, and Amber was actually in Paul's lap. Seeing the happy couples made her wish William would come back. And she didn't want to examine exactly why she wanted that, or what it meant. She'd figure that out another day. All she knew was that she longed to be close to him.

She checked her phone, but he hadn't called back, so she texted him another message and waited to see if he'd respond.

No answer.

In the living room, people were still talking and laughing, most starting to drift out now, waving, hugging her, telling her to get some rest.

She waved back and smiled and hugged, but she kept checking her phone and there was still no response.

He'd probably gone straight to bed, exhausted. But a feeling of unease settled in her stomach and wouldn't go away.

SUNNY WOKE UP sore in every muscle. At first she thought her head was just pounding, but then she realized the pounding was at her bedroom door.

Bright sunshine poured through her window and slowly, the previous day's events came back to her. Ugh. Her stomach knotted. She'd really screwed up and for a minute there, she'd thought she might die. And cause Caden's death too.

Where *was* Caden, anyway? Had he gotten any of the help and support she'd gotten from Mom and her friends last night, or had he trudged home to the Blue House alone?

"Let me in!" It was Kaitlyn, and Sunny sat up, blinking, relieved to see a friend.

"I'm so glad you came over."

"Here." Kaitlyn thrust a bag of donuts at Sunny. "My mom made me bring it." She spun and walked toward the door.

Sunny sat up and swung her flannel-clad legs to the side of the bed. "Wait! What's wrong?"

Kaitlyn turned back. "Besides the fact that you ruined Venus's and Caden's lives?"

Sunny's stomach lurched. "What do you mean? Caden's fine, right?"

"His parents found him, because of all the calls that went out about your boat being gone. Someone knew he was on it and let them know."

Sunny's heart sank. "Oh, no. Where is he now?"

"They took him home. And he's not answering his phone."

Sunny closed her eyes and leaned back against her pillows. "What about Venus?"

"Her mom's boyfriend came over this morning and dragged her back to the island. She might have to homeschool there. Or else the whole family might have to move."

"What? She wants to stay here!"

"Exactly. But apparently, her mom and her boyfriend got mad that Venus let you see those pictures. They were supposed to be private because she's gotten harassed by dogfighting people. Now, she's afraid word will get out where she is."

"I wouldn't tell." Shame welled up in Sunny. She'd caused that with her thoughtless actions.

Muffin nudged her way into the room and jumped up on Sunny's bed, and she cuddled the dog close. She wished she could go back to yesterday morning and start things over.

Kaitlyn turned as if to leave and then spun back. "Why did you go over there without us? Without even telling us?"

"I…" Sunny trailed off, because her own reasoning wasn't clear in her own mind. If you could even call it reasoning. In truth, she'd just gotten the idea and run with it.

"Don't answer," Kaitlyn said, pacing from one side of Sunny's bedroom to the other. "I know you wanted Caden for yourself."

"That's not true…" She trailed off. It *wasn't* true. Was it?

"You've been acting like me and Venus are idiots for being boy crazy, but you're just as bad. Worse."

Sunny stared down at her quilt, ragged now. It was a Dutch Doll pattern her grandmother had made, out of her baby clothes.

She longed for those days, when she was a little kid and

Mom made all her decisions and no one got mad at her, except maybe for spilling her juice.

Now, she was old enough to seriously screw things up. And she had. Her throat tightened and tears welled in her eyes.

She looked up at Kaitlyn. "How can we fix it?"

Kaitlyn lifted her hands, palms up. "We can't."

Sunny thought. "What if we go over to the island and talk to Venus's mom? Tell her how sorry we are. I mean, how sorry I am. Explain that we're not going to tell anyone where she's at."

"Pretty sure she doesn't want to talk to you. And what about Caden?"

The thought of him, back at home with his parents in that vague bad situation he'd run away from, turned Sunny's stomach into a tight knot. "I'll think of something," she said, but weakly.

"Count me out," Kaitlyn said. "I'm sick of your big ideas." She stomped over to the door and left.

Muffin leaped off Sunny's bed and followed her.

Sunny sank back down onto her bed and cried a little into her pillow. Even the dog had abandoned her.

She could smell the salty dirtiness of her own hair. Last night, she'd only rinsed it. Downstairs, Mom was banging pots and pans. She heard her talking to Kaitlyn, both sounding cordial. So Kait was making nice, not wanting to involve Mom in the drama. Though Mom would probably find out some of it, at least.

Anyway, Sunny would probably be grounded for the rest of her life, or else kept so busy with chores that she had no time to see her friends or fix anything.

If she even had any friends left. She pretty much didn't. And now that that was the case, she could admit it: she'd really liked Caden. Had thought that maybe, if their friendship came along and worked, she'd like dating him.

But she was just like Mom, who sometimes claimed she was too big and bossy to have a relationship. Men didn't stick around women like them.

At least Mom kept friends, though. She could hear, now, that someone else was in the kitchen. It sounded like Mary.

They were laughing. Because Mom was a good friend who didn't screw up other people's lives.

Sunny wasn't.

After a few more minutes crying under her covers, she sat up. Enough. She was going to figure out some way to help Caden and Venus. *And* find out who was abusing the dogs.

She didn't know how, but somehow, she was going to do it. Or die trying.

CHAPTER NINETEEN

WILLIAM SPENT THE next while trying not to think. In a rote manner, he went through his responsibilities with the teenagers, fixed a couple things around Victory Cottage. When he ran out of things to occupy himself, he contacted Mary and asked if she needed him to do anything else.

He'd expected her to put him to work fixing up things around her store. Instead, she suggested he start to do a few repairs on the Blue House. She also suggested that he ought to get Paul, Trey and Drew to help him.

He didn't have it in him to call the other men, but he whistled to Xena. They trudged over to the Blue House together so William could look things over.

To his surprise, he found evidence of a squatter there. Not a messy, partying or drugged-up squatter, but someone who washed his dishes and folded his sleeping bag and, evidently, used the shower.

He was pondering all of it when Xena barked, and then Sunny walked through the door, Muffin following behind her. He was surprised, but genuinely glad to see her. He hadn't talked to her since the boating disaster.

The two dogs greeted each other, tails wagging.

"I'm glad to see you're okay," he said, then looked at her closely. She had the swollen eyes of someone who'd spent a lot of time crying. "*Are* you okay?"

"I'm fine." She was clearly lying. Listlessly, she wandered over to the sleeping bag and duffel, knelt and started looking through it.

Xena walked over to her hesitantly and sniffed her shoe, then nudged her hand. Sunny rubbed the dog's head, absently, and then Muffin pushed her way in, obviously looking for her share of attention.

"So...what are you doing here?" He walked around looking at the window frames. He was guessing the loose screen on one of them was how someone had broken in.

She didn't look at him. "I know who this stuff belongs to," she said. "I'm going to take it to him."

He frowned, considering what she'd said. Why would Sunny know a squatter? "Is it a kid?"

"My age."

"Is it the kid you were boating with?"

She nodded.

"Where is he now?"

She cleared her throat. "He's at his parents' place. I heard. I haven't talked to him."

It sounded like there was a story there. "Look, Sunny, I don't want to get all into your business, but it sounds like someone's in some trouble. You, or someone else."

She lifted one shoulder. "I don't know." Then suddenly, she turned around and faced him and scooped Xena into her lap. "He says his parents are bad news, but they're really rich. He lives all the way over on the other side of Pleasant Shores, and I'm sure he's mad at me, if he even has time to think about me, because I outed him about where he was. Or at least, dragging him along on that trip outed him."

"But his parents must have been searching for him. If he was missing, you'd think everyone in town would be looking for him. Look how they all came out to help when you were in trouble."

"He told his parents he was staying with a friend, and

they didn't check into it." She sank down onto the floor and urged Muffin to sit beside her. "They don't care about him."

William couldn't believe that. "Any parent of a sixteen-year-old would confirm it with the other kid's parents before letting him stay for, what, several weeks? Unless something is really wrong."

"Then I think something's really wrong. He comes to school and everything, or he did, but his parents don't seem to be in the picture."

"I wonder why they showed up when you guys had the boating issue?"

She shook her head. "Didn't want everyone to know what bad parents they are? By the way," she added, "thank you for what you did. You pretty much saved our lives."

Funny she'd look at it that way. That was a kid's perspective. "I just helped. Your mom did most of it."

"That's not what she said." She studied him shrewdly. "How come you and her aren't getting together as much anymore? And how come you're hanging with your ex-wife?"

All that seemed like a lifetime ago. "To answer your last question first, my ex is troubled," he said. "She was between men, so she came looking for me. She doesn't feel right unless a man is taking care of her and fawning over her."

"Yuck," Sunny said.

"I agree. And I'm done doing it. So now she's gone, but I think your mom misinterpreted what she saw."

Sunny rolled her eyes. "Ya think? You were holding hands with her."

"Trying to get rid of her."

"Maybe tell Mom that."

"I tried. She won't listen. And anyway…" He shook his head. "I'm not what she, or what you guys, need. Better if I stay away."

"I will never understand men." Sunny started gathering up the boy's things.

"So, you're going to haul all that stuff across town on foot?"

She shrugged. "What choice do I have? I'm not supposed to even be here. I can only leave the house if I'm working."

He frowned. "Did you tell your mom you were working?"

She wrinkled her nose and nodded. "Yeah. Said we were training the dogs."

"Then that's what we have to do." He didn't want to undermine Bisky's discipline. "And then I'll drive you home, and we can swing by your friend's house on the way, see what's what."

"You'd do that for me?"

He shrugged. "Yeah. Besides, Xena needs the training. Look how she noticed when you were upset and came to comfort you. She'll be a great therapy dog, but only with training."

He had the feeling that Sunny needed to get involved in something positive, anyway. Maybe this would be that thing.

And God help him, if he could see Bisky, even from a distance, it would be worth it.

"No, Muffin!" Sunny clenched her fists, frustrated, then took a couple of deep breaths to calm down before kneeling in front of her dog to rub its head and comfort her.

Halfway into their training session, things weren't going well. It didn't help that Sunny felt totally distracted. She kept checking her phone to see if Caden had answered. She checked again now, for the tenth time. He hadn't.

William had taken Xena off to the side of the yard and was commanding her to sit, then rewarding her each time she did. He looked up at Sunny and grinned. "I'm practically a dog whisperer now, huh?"

"Right." She couldn't help smiling, too. William was a pretty good guy. Didn't think he knew everything like most men, and was willing to listen to a teenager. Of course, he'd been a dad.

Sunny tried to imagine how her mom would react if she herself died, and the whole thing was so awful that she pushed it out of her mind. Last night, although Mom had been mad at her, she'd mostly hugged on Sunny. She'd even cried a little, which Mom *never* did.

Sunny had always taken it for granted that she was the center of her mother's universe. Now, she thought about the flip side to that kind of love: what if a parent lost a child?

What if a child lost a parent? What if *Mom* had gone overboard yesterday?

William strolled over, Xena at his side, and Sunny's eyes widened. "She's heeling!"

"Yeah. I watched that video you sent me, and I've been working with her. She can sit and heel pretty good." He knelt and rubbed the dog's sides.

"That's really good. Let's see if she can sit while Muffin walks by. And then we'll trade places."

The first time, Muffin got excited and lunged, and Xena cowered.

"Again, but farther apart," Sunny said, and they put about eight feet between the dogs. The lunge and the cowering were both much reduced, and the third time they tried, it went perfectly.

"Now it's just a matter of moving a little closer, slowly," Sunny said. "We'll see if we can make it work five times, a step or two closer, and then end on a success."

"You're pretty good at this, you know?" William said.

Sunny looked at him quickly to see if he meant it or was faking, but his expression looked sincere. They got the dogs to make successful passes in front of each other at six feet, the sitting dog holding position and the walking dog staying calm.

"We did it!" She high-fived him. "Let's stop there." She sank down onto the ground cross-legged and checked her phone. Nothing from Caden, and nothing from Venus or Kaitlyn, either. She bit her lip. She was happy about training dogs, for sure, but she *really* wanted her friends to like her again.

"What's wrong, no answer?" William asked.

"Caden hasn't answered, and that scares me. And my girlfriends are mad at me."

"I'm a good listener," he said, "or I used to be. What's up with your girlfriends?"

She hesitated. He'd lost his daughter. Would talking to Sunny about her problems kick up old wounds?

On the other hand, he'd offered, and she had no one else to talk to. "Can you keep a secret?"

"Unless it puts you at risk, sure."

"It doesn't. That trip we took, me and Caden? I was trying to play detective, find out from my friend Venus's mom what she knew about the abused dogs, since she's like this graphic design artist, and she did pictures of dogs like ours."

"Abused ones?" William's head jerked around and he stared at her.

She shrugged. "I thought so, but now I'm not sure. Anyway, she and her boyfriend got upset that Venus let us see her art, because she's gotten threatened for doing it. She doesn't want anyone to know where she is, but Venus told us. And then I insulted her by asking about abused dogs. Anyway, she made Venus come and live with her on Teaberry Island, which is absolutely not where she wants to be. And if she gets harassed again, they'll probably have to move somewhere else."

William was sitting on the step now, drawing in the dirt

with a stick. When she stopped talking, he looked up at her. "That's not good," he said, "but has Venus ever done anything that made her mom mad?"

"Like sneaked out at night without permission? Yeah." Sunny smiled, remembering the time when they'd gone after some guys who were teasing Kaitlyn.

Kaitlyn. "Anyway, my friend Kaitlyn, she blames me for all of it. Says I'm too bossy—which I am—and that I took Caden on the boat and didn't tell them about it because I have the hots for him."

He raised an eyebrow. "Do you?"

She blew out an exasperated snort. "I don't know. I like him, but I'm not the type to rush into the whole boyfriend thing. Anyway, he's got too much on his plate to think about a girlfriend. Like his parents." She frowned and checked her phone. "He hasn't answered me yet. I'm worried he's in trouble."

"Then let's go over there." He stood and held out a hand to pull her up, and a moment later, they and both dogs were in his car, Xena in the back seat and Muffin in the front. They headed for Caden's side of the peninsula.

Sunny's heart pounded. She had Caden's stuff in the trunk of William's car, but should she get it out and take it to his door? Was there anything incriminating in it that his parents would find? Would he want his stuff, or would he want her to leave it alone?

When William, following her directions, pulled into the Shoreline Estates development of expensive new homes, he glanced over at her. "Pretty fancy," he said.

"I know. I've never even been over here before." She checked the address she'd found in an online school directory. "That one up there. With the pillars."

He pulled up and stopped his car. "I can go up with you or not."

"It's okay." How would she explain William? Caden would probably just be mad she'd gotten someone else involved. Now her stomach churned with all the things that could go wrong.

She grabbed his duffel from the trunk and walked up to the massive front porch, feeling like she was going to throw up. Really, she just wanted to run home and hide in her bed, hide behind her mom. She half turned, then straightened her spine and drew in a deep breath. *You have to help him. You can do this.* Fingers shaking, she rang the bell.

A woman who looked about Mom's age, but with perfect, unlined skin, neat chin-length hair and tourist clothes came to the door. "Yes?"

"I… I'm here for Caden," she said. "Are you his mom?"

"I am. But Caden can't come out." She glanced at the wide, polished-wood staircase behind her.

"Is he okay?"

She was opening her mouth, eyes concerned, when a voice came from behind her. "Who is it, Pauline?"

A moment later, Caden's dad was there. He was a handsome man; even Sunny could see that, comparing him to the dads she knew. Hair in a stylish short cut, with only a little gray; athletic build, nothing like the paunchy fathers of some of her friends; a square jaw like a movie star.

And blue eyes that were as cold as ice.

He tilted his head to one side. "You're the girl who was in the boat with Caden yesterday, correct?"

She nodded and swallowed. She wasn't sure why this guy terrified her so much, but she could clearly see why Caden hadn't wanted to live here with him.

Not only that, but she feared she might have made things worse for him by coming here. "I, um, I'll come back later," she said.

She kept glancing behind him at the staircase, hoping

Caden would appear, but there was no sound from above. For all she knew, this cold dude had hacked up his son into a million pieces and thrown him into the bay. Or sent him to reform school.

What was for sure: he hadn't questioned Caden's lie that he was staying with a friend during all the weeks he'd been at the Blue House.

And she was suddenly sure she didn't want to give Caden his stuff back. She wanted him to be able to escape and go back to his hideout ASAP.

She turned to leave, trying to conceal the duffel with her body.

"What's that? Is that something of Caden's?" Caden's dad opened the screen door and stepped outside.

"Um, no, it's nothing." What if there was something incriminating in the duffel, pot or a diary or porn?

"I'll take it," he said, and took another step toward her. She stepped back.

And felt a hand on her shoulder, the slightest squeeze.

"I'm William Gross, how are you?" He held out his hand to Caden's dad and took the duffel from her. There was no threat in his voice, but Caden's dad stepped back anyway. Compared to William, he looked small.

"We were hoping we could get Caden to join in a program for teenagers I'm running," William said.

They *were*?

"We don't need anything like that." Caden's dad's mouth twisted into a slight sneer. "Truth to tell, he's in trouble for the stunt he pulled yesterday."

"It's not for fun," William said. "It's making the kids work on local projects."

Caden's dad was opening his mouth, obviously about to say no.

"My mom put me in it as a punishment," Sunny blurted

out. Which wasn't a complete lie; Mom had threatened her with that several times. "It's gardening and helping babysit little kids and building retaining walls, stuff like that. It's really hard." She held her breath.

There was a sound behind Caden's parents. Caden, creeping down the stairs. He was moving slowly, strangely. She glanced at William.

He'd noticed, too. "I have to report to the high school up the coast, as well as their school—" he gestured to Sunny and Caden "—every student I invite and the parents' response. Part of the grant's requirements. They're going to interview some of the people whose parents say no, just to find out more about how to make the program effective."

"It's after school Tuesdays and Thursdays," Sunny offered. "Caden's coming to school tomorrow, right?"

Then they both stood looking at Caden's parents.

"It might be a good punishment for him," Caden's mom said timidly.

Caden's father's eyes narrowed and he turned and looked at Caden. "You're doing a work program with the dock kids," he said.

Caden nodded. He looked past his parents to her, but his expression was unreadable.

A phone dinged, Caden's father's. He pulled it out and looked at it. "Figure out the details," he ordered his wife, and stalked toward the back of the house.

Caden crept up the stairs again. And as William gave the time and place to Caden's mom, Sunny slipped down to the car and put his things back in, hoping she hadn't just made things even worse for her friend.

CHAPTER TWENTY

WILLIAM SPENT MOST of Monday brooding. He felt marginally better after working with Sunny and the dogs, but he was also worried about that kid they'd tried to help. He'd recognized the careful way the kid moved, and was pretty sure the boy had been beaten. William had been beaten hard himself, plenty of times, before he'd grown big enough to fight back. The very thought of a child receiving the treatment he'd gotten made his blood pressure shoot up.

But he didn't have any evidence against the family. He hadn't liked that father, but that could be because the guy was obviously rich and had the arrogance to go along with it.

All he'd been able to think of was to tell the dude that someone would be coming to his house to talk to the family. If the man were truly an abuser, he'd hate that. And sure enough, that had been the key to getting him to say yes. William hoped that they could get to know the kid during the teen program and maybe do something to help him.

Of course, that would involve him interacting with Bisky, which he didn't intend to do, even though he wanted to. He was trying not to think about that.

At Sunny's suggestion, he'd also gotten in touch with Trey's wife, Erica, who taught at the school. Informally, she'd agreed to ask around and see if Caden displayed any signs of being abused.

Maybe Caden was just a runaway, in trouble for other

reasons. Maybe his parents were just struggling parents of a teenager.

When the doorbell rang Monday evening, he didn't want to answer. But he knew what kind of a town this was. Whoever was outside would persist.

He opened the door to find Paul standing there in gym clothes. "Come on," he said. "Time to work out."

"We didn't have a plan to do that. Did we?" Maybe William had spaced it out.

"We do now. Come on, we need a fourth so we can partner up and spot each other."

The reasoning wasn't that convincing, and he had the feeling Paul had made an excuse to check up on him. On the other hand, William didn't have anything else to do.

That was how he ended up at a local gym with three former cops who seemed intent on making a big deal of the fact that he was a professor and therefore likely out of shape.

"What are you benching?" Paul asked him.

"It's been a while. Let me warm up."

He watched the others. Paul benched 200, and then Trey benched 180 and got teased for it. Then Drew lay down and beat them all out with a 220-pound rep.

"Your turn, you can't put it off anymore," Paul said.

"Go ahead, try to break my record," Drew urged.

William lay down on the bench and put his hands on the bar. It had been a while since he'd had the energy to work out, beyond the occasional run, but there was a time when he'd done it religiously. He'd always wanted to be strong enough to take on anyone who was bothering him or his.

Like his father.

But it had turned out that he hadn't been there when Jenna had needed him the most.

Picturing the guy who'd come in and shot Jenna, William nodded at Paul. "Stack on some more."

Paul put another couple of plates on the barbell. "That's 240," he said. "Sure about that?"

"Yeah." He'd been able to bench 300 at one time, but he'd been younger and working out hard, several times a week.

William grimaced and lifted and did six reps.

He'd be sore tomorrow, but it was worth it to see the expressions on their faces. Respect. Every man wanted it.

They worked around the gym, doing a circuit, and William stopped trying to impress anyone. His muscles would be crying tomorrow.

On the way out, they stood in front of the gym's TV where a baseball game was on, watched a couple at bats. "So what are you doing once you're finished with Victory Cottage?" Paul asked.

"Kids are sure going to miss you in the teen program," Drew said. "Seems like it's going good."

William shrugged. "Back to the community college," he said. Funny, it didn't sound quite so imperative as it had before. He'd talked to his old boss, who'd told him his temporary replacement was working out.

"You ready to go back?" Drew asked.

"Good question." William paused, looked around to see if he could get out of talking about it. But the other three men were looking at him, obviously expecting an answer. "Don't know if I'm healed," he said finally. "In fact, I don't think I'll ever get healed from losing my daughter and blaming myself for it. But I'm better."

"Makes sense. Man, you never *would* heal from losing your child." Drew's voice was thoughtful. "I can't even think about it. Makes my problem I came here for—losing my vision—makes that seem like a walk in the park."

"I was here for a back injury," Trey said, shaking his head. "That's nothing."

"Yeah," Drew said, "though you're still using it as an excuse for not lifting worth anything."

Paul frowned like he was thinking. "You know," he said, "there's a lot you could do right here, if you would decide you wanted to stay," he said. "You do developmental ed, right? Kids who aren't quite ready for college?"

"That's right." And he loved it; it was his passion. He felt for the kids who hadn't had advantages and were still trying to better themselves.

"We have a lot of kids like that around here. Some you're already working with, in the teen program, but there are others, as well, here and in nearby towns."

Trey drank from a water bottle, then nodded his agreement. "Erica was saying there's an opening in a college prep program upshore," he said. "She asked me if I knew anyone who'd be interested, because they're having trouble finding someone with the right background. I could put your name in."

The idea of it tugged at William. To help teens from the same background he'd had, to give them the kind of support he'd received, that had made him successful. "I don't know," he said. "It does sound good, but I don't think I can stay."

Paul waved at a couple of guys, then turned back to their group. "I've heard all good things about your work here," he said to William.

"If it was just work involved, I'd stay in a heartbeat," he heard himself say, and was shocked. This place had been drawing him closer than he'd realized.

"Problem with Bisky?" Drew asked. "I'm just guessing, but I hear my daughters talking, and they seem to think you've got something going on with her. She's a great lady."

"She is." And William was proud of her, that she was

so highly regarded in the town. "I'm not good enough for her. I screw up right and left. Like with the boat thing."

Paul looked confused. "I heard you helped save the kids," he said.

"Helped," William said, disgusted with himself. "Bisky did most of it."

Drew laughed. "I get that. You grew up thinking men ought to do everything themselves, while the women cooked dinner and admired you."

The blunt description made William smile. "You pretty much nailed it." Although in the home where he'd grown up, the woman had mostly cowered in fear and tried to avoid the man of the house.

"Turns out," Drew said, "things go better when you work at it as partners, not the man trying to do everything. I had to learn that fast when I lost my sight."

"Doesn't seem to hurt your marriage."

"Nope. Better than ever."

Paul had grabbed a couple of hand weights and was curling with them. "I came here with PTSD, and I needed a lot of help."

"No kidding, you were a wreck." Trey grinned, showing that he was joking, but Paul still tossed him a hand weight, making him dodge to catch it.

There was a bases-loaded triple in the game then, and they all watched, and a few other people came to see what was going on, so the personal conversation stopped.

"Beer at the Gull?" Drew suggested. He turned his face in William's direction. "You, too."

To William's own surprise, he wanted to go. "Sure."

It would be nice to stay on in Pleasant Shores. He'd like to hang out with these guys. Maybe even learn something from them. Because maybe they were right, and it was okay that he'd just helped Bisky rescue her daughter, not taken over and done it all himself.

Anyway, knowing Bisky, she wouldn't have allowed herself to be excluded or for him to take over. And that was kinda great. Took some of the pressure off of him.

But he still didn't feel like he could do it to her, give her himself, all damaged, up and down. And anyway, he'd probably screwed it up too bad already.

AT GOODY'S MONDAY NIGHT, Bisky paid for two milkshakes and sucked on her straw, and the chocolaty goodness calmed her distressed emotions. She looked over at Sunny and could tell the same was happening to her. By mutual agreement, they headed to Goody's new outdoor seating area. Goody had one of those heating lamps up, trying it out, but so far, nobody else was brave enough to sit outside this late in the evening.

"See, I was right," Sunny said. "Chocolate is the only thing that'll help us stop picking at each other."

"When we both have PMS," Bisky said.

"Hey."

"Am I wrong?"

Sunny tried to frown but ended up laughing. "Nope. Not wrong."

The sun was setting over the bay, making the sky a watercolor painting of purple and orange and pink. A few late customers straggled into Goody's, and a few more people strolled the bike path across the road on the bay side. But it was quiet enough to talk, which was what they needed to do.

"So what's up that made you so upset?" she asked after she'd judged Sunny to be chocolate-happy again. She knew Sunny felt the boat escapade had been a disaster, and she was right, it had been. Additionally, she'd heard Sunny and

Kaitlyn yelling at each other. And from Sunny's veiled remarks, Bisky knew she was worried about Caden, who apparently had been staying somewhere else before the boat escapade had alerted his parents to his whereabouts, causing him to have to be back home. That was the most worrisome, a kid possibly at risk.

"Have you heard anything more from Caden?" she asked now.

Sunny swallowed another mouthful, then spoke. "William invited him to do the teen program," she said. "So maybe we'll find out more when he does it, if he's even allowed to do it."

Just the mention of William made Bisky wince. He'd seemed set on apologizing to her for being caught with his ex-wife, but then Sunny's rescue had taken their attention all away from that, and now, he didn't seem to want anything to do with her.

"Are you and William friends again?" Sunny asked.

Bisky shrugged. She didn't want to inflict her adult problems on her daughter, who had plenty to deal with in her own life.

But Sunny had put her finger on the issue: *were* they friends?

A breeze swept their napkins off the table, and Sunny jumped up to chase them down. Bisky steadied Sunny's nearly empty cup while she thought about the question.

If they weren't talking to each other, how could they be considered friends?

Besides, she'd never figured out what was going on between William and his ex-wife. If he was still involved with the woman, then no way could his relationship with Bisky be anything more than friends. And truth to tell, since they'd kissed, she was miserable at the thought of him going back to his ex.

She never should have let that kiss happen.

"Earth to Mom." Sunny was back in her chair and tapping Bisky on the arm.

"Sorry," she said. "A little distracted."

"You and William seemed to be getting along okay on the boat, when you were hauling me and Caden in," Sunny said. "He's pretty strong. I was glad he was there."

"I was, too," Bisky said. Had something happened on the boat that had turned them off? Before they'd discovered Sunny was in danger, he'd been trying to apologize and she'd been cranky, putting him off. And then the emergency with Sunny had blotted out everything else. After that, he'd turned away and was refusing to speak to her.

"I don't know," she said slowly. "I guess something did happen on the boat ride. Maybe he didn't like me being in charge, which would be just like a man." Then she felt bad for saying that. She hated to teach her daughter to believe something negative about a whole gender.

"That's my problem too!" Sunny burst out. "I'm too much in charge with *all* my friends."

"Really?"

"Yeah. Kait and Venus didn't like me making the decision about going to the island without them. They thought I was trying to keep Caden for myself."

Bisky fought back a smile. "Well, realistically, for him to date all three of you would be a little much for him."

"No kidding. But also, Venus got sent to Teaberry as a punishment, and she might have to stay with her family instead of living in Pleasant Shores. That would be a disaster."

Here, at least, Bisky could provide some good news. "Ria said Venus is staying with them again, so it seems like that punishment didn't last long."

"She *is*? That's great! She always did say she could talk

her mom out of grounding her." Then Sunny's face fell. "But why didn't they tell me? They must still be mad."

Bisky nodded. "It's soon for them to give up being mad. Girls can hold a grudge." And there she went again, generalizing about a whole gender. "*Anyone* can hold a grudge," she corrected herself.

They sat for a few minutes, the heat radiating down from the standup heater, a couple of customers coming out of the shop, licking ice cream cones. "Look," Bisky said, "being a strong woman can be hard. It's against stereotype."

Sunny sucked the last bit of milkshake from her cup. "What's *that* mean?"

"Sometimes your friends want to act all girly. And there's no problem with that, but you might not want to do it, and you don't have to. You'll still have friends if you stay strong."

"Not Kait and Venus, apparently."

"I bet they'll come back," Bisky said. "Especially if…" She trailed off, knowing that any advice she offered would likely fall on deaf ears.

"If what?"

"If you let them in on your decision process. If you listen, as well as telling other people what to do." She held up a hand against Sunny's protest. "And I know, it's hard. We both have pretty good leadership qualities, and usually, we do have a better plan than a lot of people. But if people don't feel heard, they don't want to come along."

"Voice of experience?" Sunny asked.

"Yeah." Bisky looked up at the sky, where a couple of stars were just appearing, then smiled at her daughter. "There are always some ladies who don't care for the way I am, but real friends will let you be yourself." She thought of Ria, Amber, Erica, Mary. They were all so different, and different from her, but they liked her as she was. They'd made her life warmer, made her feel more supported, in recent years.

"I need to get some real friends, then," Sunny said.

"I bet Kait and Venus will come around. You three have been through a lot together."

"I hope."

"For now, focus on what's working. You said the therapy dog training is going well?"

"Yeah," Sunny said, visibly cheering up, "it's been great. You can't believe how much William is doing with Xena. It's like *he's* come around, too."

I wouldn't know, Bisky thought, and then felt like a teenager herself, and not in a good way.

"And you know Muffin's better all the time." Sunny went on, talking about the desensitizing she was doing with both dogs, and how they planned to take them out into the community more and more, to teach them how to manage around distractions.

Bisky loved seeing Sunny's enthusiasm, and she was pretty sure everything would turn out well for her daughter. And the fact that every mention of William hurt, well... Bisky would just have to learn to deal with that.

Until he left.

The thought of him leaving made her heart ache like it was going to fall out of her chest, and she realized, uncomfortably, what a mistake she'd made to let herself care for him that much.

"Will you, Mom?"

She'd spaced out again. "Will I what?"

"Will you come and see my dog training with William tomorrow?"

"No." That was the last thing she wanted to do. "You can't do it tomorrow, anyway, because it's the teen program day. And I want you to start coming."

To her surprise, Sunny didn't complain. "Maybe I'll make some new friends there. Plus, Caden will be there, I hope, so maybe he and I can make up."

"Good." She stood and patted her daughter's back. "Thanks for being good about it. I think we should head home, though, because Goody's trying to close up."

"Okay." But as they tossed their cups in the trash and started home, Sunny looked over at her. "Will you come see the training on Wednesday, then? I really want you to."

Bisky blew out a sigh. Sunny wasn't going to let up on this. "Okay, sure," she said. Even though the thought of seeing William, her old friend William, made her stomach twist with nerves.

CHAPTER TWENTY-ONE

SUNNY BREATHED OUT a sigh of relief the next afternoon as she and the twins headed toward Mary's store.

Working with the other teenagers in her mom's program didn't seem like it was going to be that bad. She liked the twins, and she liked Mary and the bookstore. Apparently, there was some work Mary needed done outside the place, and Mom had volunteered them.

That meant she didn't have to watch the awkward interactions between her mother and William. Couldn't they just admit they liked each other and get on with it?

It also meant she didn't have to work with Caden and feel guilty about getting him discovered by his weird parents. That was a relief, especially since he wouldn't even look her in the eye.

And then she heard a voice behind them. "Hey, hold up," William called. "Caden's going to be on your crew."

They all looked back, and there came Caden, trudging toward them with all the enthusiasm of a prisoner on his way to the electric chair.

"What's *he* doing this program for?" Aiden asked. "He's not a dock kid."

"He's nice," Avery said, and that made Sunny look at her with narrowed eyes. Did Avery *like* Caden?

"How do you even know him?" Aiden asked.

"Math Camp, a few years back. Hey, Caden."

Caden brightened for a second, seeing Avery, and then frowned again when his gaze met Sunny's. He looked away.

"Know anything about working with tools, building stuff?" Aiden asked. "Working *at all*?"

Sunny figured Caden would take offense at Aiden's tone, but he just snorted. "Unfortunately. My parents are crap about fixing things, so I had to learn."

"You fix stuff at *your* house?" Avery asked. "I'd have thought you'd get workmen in."

"Sometimes it's easier to just do it myself." Caden clearly didn't want to talk more about it.

And sometimes, Sunny thought, when your parents have issues, neither you nor they want outsiders to come in. That was why, according to William, the threat of having someone from the school interview Caden's parents had pushed them into letting him do the program.

They reached the bookstore and got their instructions from Mary. She wanted big window boxes for flowers built, to cheer up the front of Lighthouse Lit. They hauled out her supplies and tools, and then they all stood looking at the stack of wood.

"Um, well…" Sunny actually wasn't good with tools herself. She'd volunteered for this gig just because she liked Mary and the bookstore, not because she knew how to build things.

"Video?" Avery pulled one up on her phone and they all gathered around.

Except when Caden ended up next to Sunny, he made an excuse and moved to the other side of Avery.

Fine. She ignored him as they sketched out a plan and started sawing boards to the right length.

It was actually kind of fun. It was sunny, warmish, and lots of people stopped to ask questions and even admire their work. Pretty soon, they'd nailed together a couple of decent window boxes and were taking a break before figuring out how to paint and then attach them.

"So," Avery said, "that was a pretty spectacular fail on your boat the other day."

Sunny glanced at Caden. "Yeah, it was my fault. I was being stupid."

"Why'd you do it?" Aiden asked.

Caden focused hard on his phone. Probably a blank screen, or he was telling someone how annoying Sunny was.

Obviously, he was leaving the explanation to her. "We were trying to find some information about the dog abuse."

Caden frowned like he didn't know what she was talking about.

Avery nudged her twin. "We heard about that. There's some weird stuff happening to the dogs around here."

Aiden nodded.

"Like what?" Sunny asked.

The twins looked at each other. "Sometimes we sneak out," Avery said finally.

"Yeah?" Caden looked interested in that part. "Where do you go?"

"Ever go back to Victor's Hummock?"

"Not for a while," Sunny said. She knew the place as an old hunting and camping spot.

Caden looked up from his phone. "My dad used to take me there when I was little."

"Weird place for a rich kid," Aiden said.

Caden shrugged.

"Anyway—" Avery glanced at the two boys and then focused on Sunny. "There's some dogs out there, in cages. They're not treated very well."

"A lot?"

"About five or six." She paused, then added, "We think

there might be dogfighting. There's this pit, like, and some benches around it."

Sunny's jaw dropped. "Here? That's awful!" She'd seen a TV special on Michael Vick and it had given her nightmares afterward.

Not to mention that Venus's mom had done a painting of dogs fighting in a pit.

"There has to be an audience for that," Aiden said, "and money. It's all about betting."

"So there's gotta be some people around here who know about it," Avery said, "but we've been asking around the docks, and so far, nothing."

Avery looked at Caden. "Maybe it's not dock families. You need to ask around the rich neighborhood, see what you can find out."

"Considering I'm totally grounded except for this, that won't be easy."

"Hello, social media? Message some people." Avery rolled her eyes.

"If we find out there's dogfighting, what do we do?" Sunny asked slowly. "People who would organize that can't be very good people." She thought of the wounds on Xena and Muffin. "Anyway, our dogs are nice. How could they be trained to fight?"

Aiden shrugged. "Used as bait."

Fury rose in Sunny, and Caden looked mad, too. "You don't mean that."

"Pretty sure it happens," Aiden said.

"We have to find out about this and stop it," Sunny said. "We should go to the police."

"They're not going to believe us, without evidence," Aiden said.

"Then we find out when the next fight is," Avery said, "and get the evidence."

On Wednesday, William felt a little happy about the fact that Sunny and Muffin were coming over for another training session. Working with the dogs helped him shut out his confusion for a short stretch of time each day.

Yesterday, he'd hoped working with the teens would provide similar solace, and he and Bisky had managed to avoid each other, but he'd still been incredibly conscious of her. Conscious of how she was keeping her distance, so he had, too.

He wasn't even sure why anymore. He just knew that being around her made him risk staring at her in longing, or sweeping her into his arms, and neither seemed appropriate when he felt like such a bad bet for a relationship.

He liked Pleasant Shores. He didn't know if he wanted to go back to his old job. He even felt like he was getting better, mentally and emotionally. Like maybe life could be worth living even amidst his pain about Jenna.

It was being around Sunny and Bisky that did it, but the good feelings weren't unmixed. The connection with them was in equal parts wonderful and painful. He wanted a family, but he didn't trust himself with one.

He was out in the yard, putting Xena through her paces to get her warmed up, when he saw Sunny and Bisky approaching with Muffin trotting beside them.

Immediately, he went hot and cold inside. Xena whined.

He watched them come, trying to settle himself. "Didn't know we'd have an audience," he commented when they were within earshot. Then he could have smacked himself in the head for how unwelcoming that sounded. "Want something to drink?"

"You didn't tell him I was coming?" Bisky scolded. "Sunny, you know better than that. You can't just bring an unexpected guest to someone else's house."

"You're not an unexpected guest, you're an old friend,"

Sunny said, shrugging. "Anyway, I figured if I asked, he'd say no."

"I wouldn't have said no," William protested. He looked at Bisky, who looked back at him and lifted her hands, palms up. *Kids, you know how they are*, was what her gesture implied.

He *did* know how kids were, because of Jenna. He remembered her blundering ahead doing something that turned out to be socially awkward for him and Ellie. The memory made him smile a little, because Jenna's "so what" shrug had been so similar to Sunny's.

"Let's train!" She brought Muffin closer to Xena. "We were about, what, six feet apart last time? Is she warmed up?"

"Yes and yes," he said.

"Watch how she'll let Muffin get closer this time," Sunny said confidently, so William commanded Xena to sit, showing her the beef jerky she'd get for good behavior.

Sunny walked Muffin past, first at about five feet away, then about four.

"Good girl!" William fed her the jerky and rubbed her chest. "She got a little tense on that last pass. Maybe we should stop there for right now."

"You're doing good!" She high-fived him. "You're reading dog body language. Pretty soon, you'll be a pro."

He smiled at her enthusiasm. She was a good kid. A great kid, really, and so much like her mother that he felt like he was looking at Bisky sometimes, instead of Sunny.

"Here, Mom, hold Muffin. We'll do the 'Come when called' command. Xena can practice not getting hyper about it." Sunny walked to the other side of the yard. "Let her go when I call her."

"Really?" Bisky hesitated and looked at William. "Won't she run away?"

"Nope. Your daughter is good."

"Okay." When Sunny gave a high-pitched call, Bisky let Muffin go, and sure enough, the dog ran directly to her.

"Now do it with Xena," Sunny ordered.

"Hope you don't mind being bossed," Bisky said to William as he handed her the leash.

"Not by someone who knows what she's doing. Sunny's terrific." In fact, he thought Sunny was ten times better with dogs than the woman Mary had hired. Though, apparently, that woman had gotten angry when Mary had given her feedback, and she hadn't gotten along with a couple of other dog owners she'd spoken with. It didn't look like she'd be in the job for long.

His hand touched Bisky's as she took the leash, and William felt the contact all the way from his fingers to his heart. He had to fight the desire to grab her and hold on.

He tore himself away and jogged over to Sunny's side of the yard.

"Call her," Sunny encouraged.

He did, and Bisky let go, and Xena came racing to him, tongue flopping out of her mouth, what looked like a smile on her face. She barreled into his arms and he rubbed her scarred sides, his heart contracting with something like love.

"Give her a treat," Sunny said, "but her real reward is getting that attention from you. You've built a bond with her."

It was true, and William realized that whatever his future plans included, Xena would have to be a part of them.

They banged some trash can lids together to practice having the dogs stay calm despite loud noises. Then Sunny had Bisky approach to pet Xena, to make sure she could sit politely rather than hiding behind William.

It worked, and Bisky looked up at him, still petting Xena. "She's doing great."

"She is," he agreed, and knelt to pet her as well. She'd sat politely for Bisky, but when William petted her, her whole back end wiggled, a clear display of happiness.

"Look at that! She's crazy about you!" Bisky's genuine happiness made William smile, and she was smiling back.

William got a little lost in Bisky's eyes, and then it was like they both remembered their issues. Simultaneously, they looked away and backed apart. William's face felt hot.

"I'm taking the dogs inside for a drink of water," Sunny announced. "You two make up."

"But…"

She was gone.

Bisky looked up at him. "Whatever I did to offend you, I'm sorry," she said.

"You didn't offend me," he said. "I just…" He trailed off, not sure how to explain his complicated feelings about the boat ride and Sunny's rescue. How he'd wanted to do more, do it all himself, but how he was starting to realize that he might be looking at things the wrong way.

She raised a hand. "It's okay. I understand."

Did she, though? Did she get how much he cared for her, how he wanted her, but wanted the best for her?

"Hey," he said, and reached out. They hugged, and he patted her back.

"I just miss the friendship," she said against his chest.

"Me, too." She felt so good in his arms.

Maybe it wasn't *just* the friendship he missed.

CHAPTER TWENTY-TWO

BISKY CAME OUTSIDE to meet the teens on Thursday afternoon, her hair wet from the shower, wearing jeans and a T-shirt. Normally, she'd have needed a nap on the couch after a full day on the water. She was grateful that she'd gotten her boat fixed in time for crabbing season. And since she and William had straightened things out, she was feeling like everything was right with the world.

Avery and Sunny came toward her the moment she sat on the edge of the porch. "We have something really intense to show you," Avery said.

"What's that?" She looked up and saw William coming toward them with a couple of the boys. "Are they in on it? We should wait."

William looked so handsome. He still dressed a little preppy, with a polo shirt that he had to have gotten at some big and tall store. He wore khakis, but they couldn't disguise the fact that his legs were basically tree trunks. Bisky felt warm all over, just watching his approach.

"Come on, come on, we're telling them," Sunny said, and gestured William to sit beside Bisky.

Bisky eyed her narrowly. Was she imagining it, or was Sunny trying to play matchmaker?

The kids fell all over themselves explaining that they were pretty sure they'd discovered a dogfighting ring, and that was why the dogs had been hurt, and there was supposed to be a fight *tonight*. And they needed to go, all of them, to film it and get evidence for the police.

"Now wait a minute," William said. "Don't you think the police should be the ones to do any spying and filming?"

Caden gave him a look. "You think the cops will listen to us?"

"Good question," William admitted. He looked at Bisky. "Consultation?"

The two of them walked over to the side of the porch and stood close enough together that the kids couldn't hear them. Close enough Bisky could feel heat radiating from his body.

She had it bad.

She could admit, now, that she wished for more than friendship from William. But if that was all they could have together, then she'd take it. Anything would be better than distance and coldness between them.

"It sounds risky to me," he was saying. "I know next to nothing about dogfighting, but I can't imagine they're decent folks involved. If we let the kids go, they'll be in danger."

"You're right," she said. "I'd like to support them, but I just don't think it's a good idea."

They went back over to the kids and announced their verdict. "We're really impressed you figured this out," Bisky said, "and we want to support you, but it's too risky. We should tell the police. Maybe if William and I talk to them, they'll take it more seriously."

The kids glanced at each other. "Okay," Avery said, "but don't call the police yet. I'd like to find out a couple more things from the kids I talked to, and then, um, we'd like to tell them ourselves."

Bisky and William looked at each other and it was like they could read each other's expressions. She remembered being a dock kid, not looked at with respect, and William had to remember that double.

"They'll learn more by taking charge of this project for themselves," William said. "That's what all the education theorists say."

"It's what I say, too," Bisky said, without benefit of theory. "I guess we can let them talk to the cops themselves."

"All right!" the kids said. "We're out of here!"

"No, uh-uh." Bisky raised a hand. "You have obligations at the bookstore. Right?"

"Right, but it's quick," Sunny said. "You guys don't have to come if you don't want to."

William narrowed his eyes. "I trust you," he said, "but I need to follow up with Drew at the museum. Bisky, I can walk down there with those who are working at the museum while the rest of them finish up at the bookstore. You've worked all day. You deserve to take it easy."

It didn't feel like a rejection; it felt kind. "Thanks," she said, giving him a smile before he headed off with the kids.

She went to lay down on the couch, but she couldn't sleep. She had a slight feeling of foreboding she didn't understand.

LATER THAT NIGHT, Bisky was talking to Mary on the phone, checking up on the kids. "Did they do a good job finishing the planter today?"

"They did a terrific job on Tuesday," Mary said, "but they didn't come by today."

Bisky frowned. "That's funny. I'm sure Sunny said they were going to finish today. I guess something must have come up."

They talked a few minutes more and Bisky tapped her phone against her hand and looked up at the ceiling. Sunny was upstairs in her attic bedroom, working on homework, and Bisky hated to accuse her of lying, but she needed to know what was going on. "Hey, Sunny," she called up the stairs.

No answer.

"Come on, girl," she said to Muffin. "Let's go see Sunny!"

Muffin got to her feet gamely and followed Bisky up two flights of stairs. Bisky knocked on Sunny's door. "Honey? Need to talk to you."

No answer. Bisky rolled her eyes. No one could sleep as much as teenagers, especially during the day and early evening. She turned the knob and walked in to wake up her daughter.

But Sunny wasn't there. "Honey?" She walked around the house calling, growing more uneasy. She looked outside.

Then she texted, then called Sunny's phone. But there was no answer. She could tell from the tone that the phone was turned off.

William was the first person she wanted to call, probably because he'd been there when Sunny had taken the boat out. Rather than second-guessing herself, she did it.

Heart pounding, she told him Sunny was missing and hadn't shown up at the bookstore. It was news to him, as she and the twins had said they were going there to finish the job and had walked off in that direction. "Can you come help me find her?"

He hesitated. "I want to come," he said, "but I have… another obligation. I'll see what I can do."

"Okay, let's stay in touch." He sounded weird, but she didn't have time to focus on that.

She called Avery and Aiden's parents, who checked the twins' bedrooms and found that their kids were out, too. The other teenager who'd been supposed to go work at Mary's bookstore was Caden, but she didn't want to call his parents. Caden had already gotten in plenty of trouble through Sunny.

The twins just lived down the street. Their parents walked down, and Bisky went out front to meet them. To her relief, William pulled up in his car and hurried toward the little group. He checked his phone and then shoved it back into his pocket.

His presence released a little bit of the tension in Bisky's shoulders. She took deep breaths, trying to stay calm. "Sometimes Sunny just turns off her phone."

The twins' mother nodded. "Aiden and Avery share a phone, and it's old. Loses power fast, so that could be why they're not answering."

William frowned. "I hope they didn't take it on themselves to investigate that dogfighting ring."

"What?" The twins' father barked out the word.

William quickly explained what the teenagers had told them earlier this afternoon.

"But they weren't going to go." Bisky shook her head hard, even as her palms began to sweat. "We told them not to do that. They were going to go to the police."

"But didn't they say the fight was tonight?"

The twins' parents glanced at each other. "Where was it? Somewhere local?" the mother asked.

William pounded his fist in his hand. "I wish we'd gotten the exact location from them."

"Me, too." Bisky nodded. "It can't be anything big-time, but still...not the kind of place you want your kids to go." The thought of Sunny being anywhere near illegal, organized dogfighting, no matter how small-scale, tied her stomach in painful knots.

"Right," the twins' father said, his voice going grim. "One of my friends has talked about betting on dogs. Let me see what I can find out." He walked away, scrolling through his phone.

The rest of them kept trying to call the kids, but there was no answer.

The twins' father came back with a worried frown. "If it's the same thing," he said, "it's out at Victor's Hummock."

"Call the police," William told them. "Wait here and direct them, tell them everything." He turned toward his vehicle.

"Where are you going?" Bisky asked.

"I'm heading out there." He started walking.

She marched after him. "I'm coming too."

"No, it's not safe. I'll be able to scout the area more easily if I'm alone."

Bisky looked back to where the twins' parents were both on their phones. "Not true," she said. "I can look one way, you can look the other. If one of us is in trouble, the other calls for backup. Besides," she said, her voice catching, "it's my daughter."

He'd opened his mouth, obviously intending to argue with her, but at her last words, he went silent. He looked at her, and she knew he understood her sheer terror: Sunny was at risk.

"All right," he said abruptly. "Get in."

They drove at high speed over the rough roads toward the old gathering area known as Victor's Hummock. Bisky did an online search for dogfighting and read out some of the details: gambling, illegal in all fifty states, still very popular on both a small and a large scale.

She got a text from the twins' mom. The two cops on duty in their small department were both out at a bad wreck on the highway, but one of them, at least, would come as soon as possible. She texted back, suggesting that they try to contact Trey, then had to add a "never mind" when she remembered he was out of town.

When they got close to Victor's Hummock, William slowed down, and when he came to a couple of cars pulled off the road, he stopped, backed up, and pulled his car behind a clump of bushes. "We'll walk from here," he said. His phone buzzed, but he ignored it.

She was glad he didn't try to tell her to stay in the car. They made their way, slowly and quietly, up the road, aided by moonlight and guided by the sound of people talking and laughing, the smell of barbecue. "That's what the stuff I read said," she whispered. "They make an event of it. Admission charge, food, beer."

"Sick." William held out a hand. "We're close. Let's stay to the side."

His phone buzzed again, and this time he pulled it out and looked at it. His forehead wrinkled.

"What's wrong?" she asked quietly.

He glanced at her, glanced down at the phone, and shook his head.

They crept forward and soon got to a point where they could see a small crowd, probably twenty adults, gathered. Most were men, but Bisky spotted several women. Clothing was mixed; some wore plain, functional cargo pants and sweaters, while others had on more expensive-looking outdoor gear. Bisky didn't see anyone she knew, and of that, she was glad.

The sounds of dogs barking came from a row of dog crates, and Bisky's jaw clenched. To watch a couple of dogs fight, possibly to the death…to think about how they'd been trained to do so…

And if she was sickened, Sunny would be, too, and Sunny might be out here somewhere. Not discovered by the adults, thankfully; everyone looked relaxed, in a partying mood, oblivious to any teen or adult spies. "Maybe they're not here."

"We can hope." He checked his phone and frowned. "No service."

"Who's been texting you?" Bisky asked him. "That's not Sunny or another one of the teenagers, is it?"

He shook his head, sucked in a breath, and let it out. "It was my ex," he said without looking at her. "She says she needs me."

Hurt and resentment washed over Bisky. The woman was his *ex*. They were divorced. And she, Bisky, needed William more, now, to help her daughter.

Still, she tried to be fair. "What's going on with her?"

"She said her live-in is going to hurt her." He looked at Bisky and his face was tight. "I don't… I can't…" He looked from his phone to the crowd of dogfight spectators in the distance and then back to her.

He wanted her to absolve him of any responsibility here, she could see that in his eyes. But she needed him. She needed help.

You can handle it alone. You always have. He isn't responsible for your kid.

She looked into his eyes—haunted eyes—and drew in a breath, straightened her shoulders. "If you need to go, go," she said. "I'll take care of things here."

"I want to help you."

But he wanted to help his ex more; she could see that. "Go ahead. They're probably not even here. It's fine."

He pushed the keys of his car into her hand. "You need a vehicle. I'll run back."

"And do what? You need to drive to get to her." It was hard to choke out the words. Bisky *did* need a vehicle, in case Sunny were here and they needed to make a quick escape. She fumbled in her pocket. "Here. Run the back way to my place and take my car."

"Okay. Okay." He squeezed her shoulder, looking hard into her eyes. "You're strong. You can handle anything. Right?"

"Of course I can." She felt sick inside.

"If you need me, though, call me. I'll get back as fast as I can. And I'll call the police, push them to come out here, as soon as I'm back in range."

"Go," she said through a tight throat.

He nodded and started back down the road at a dead run.

Bisky watched him, blowing out a sigh. He admired her strength, but when it came to a choice, he'd picked the petite, beautiful, needy woman.

WILLIAM DROVE UP the peninsula toward the Bay Bridge, doubting himself. Why had he agreed, again, to help Ellie? Especially when Bisky needed him?

Yes, he'd called the police, emphasized that they needed to get to Victor's Hummock as soon as possible. The dispatcher had put him through to a frazzled Evan Stone, who'd promised to try. But there had been sirens and voices in the background, and Evan had hung up quickly. He was clearly in the thick of investigating a serious accident.

With all his heart, William wanted to be the one who was there for Bisky and Sunny. Wanted to help them and yes, take care of them.

The reason wasn't hard to find: he loved Bisky. Sometime in the weeks of living here and working with her, talking with her, remembering the past, he'd fallen in love.

It was an outgrowth of his childhood friendship for her, but it was so much more. Now, he admired her as a woman, felt passion for her unlike anything he'd ever felt before.

Even now, in this turbulent situation, his body quickened at the thought of her, loving and concerned and strong.

So why had he abandoned her in favor of Ellie?

That answer wasn't hard to find, either. Rushing to Ellie's aid had everything to do with the way he hadn't been able to rush to Jenna's. If only Jenna had realized someone was in the house, had stayed in her room and called him, he might have been able to save her.

Every time Ellie needed his help, he replayed the same drama, always hoping he could make Jenna's outcome different.

But Ellie wasn't Jenna. Yes, they looked a little bit alike; yes, they'd been mother and daughter. But Ellie was weak and, he had to admit it, manipulative. She didn't call him because of real emergencies. She called because she wanted to see if he was still willing to drop everything and come to her aid.

So far, he always had been. But now, driving through the darkness, looking ahead to the distant lights of the Bay Bridge, he had a realization: nothing he did to help Ellie would bring Jenna back. He could never replay that scene. He could never make it so that it was Jenna calling him. He could never reach Jenna in time.

He pulled to the side of the road and called Ellie.

"Are you here?" she asked, sounding breathless.

"No," he said, "and I'm not coming. If there's a problem with your boyfriend, you need to call the police."

She didn't answer for a moment, and then he heard her say "It's William," to someone else in the room.

There was a little shouting then, and William had a flashback: one time, during a fight with Ellie, she'd flaunted her phone and told him she'd called one of her many exes, that he was coming to get her.

Was Ellie doing the same thing now? "You're still on Parkside Lane?" he asked.

"Yes. Come quickly." Her voice sounded breathless, but he couldn't hear blows, and even the shouting had stopped.

"The police will be there."

"No, don't—"

He ended the call, placed another to her local police, and turned his car around.

BISKY STOOD WATCHING the rowdy crowd of dogfighting spectators. One man knelt by a big, ice-filled galvanized tub, throwing beers to others nearby. Two men sat on the tailgate of a truck, a money box between them, a couple of others talking to them, handing them cash. Obviously placing bets. A couple stood by a line of dog crates, the woman leaning in close to the dogs, then jumping back and clinging to the man's arms when they snarled and flung themselves against the wire.

Bisky had stayed long enough to be reasonably sure the teenagers weren't here, and she was absolutely certain she couldn't stop this event on her own. She'd go where there was cell phone service and call the police. Yes, the twins' parents were supposed to be calling them, and so was William. But she felt like she could add urgency to the plea to get at least one officer out here, even if they had to call in an off-duty officer.

Suddenly someone grabbed her arm and her heart almost burst. She let out a yelp and quickly stifled it.

"Mom! What are you doing here?" Sunny's whisper was sharp. She tugged at Bisky's arm. "Come on!"

Sunny was safe. That fact wiped away Bisky's hurt feelings about William, because Sunny was the important thing. "*You* come on," Bisky said. "You have to get out of here!"

"Can't. Everyone's here. The twins, and Caden."

Bisky held Sunny's arm. "You're putting yourself and your friends at risk. We have to leave, now."

"We're not leaving," Sunny said. Her eyes were cool and focused. "We're not going to let this continue. We're stopping it now."

Anger at her daughter's defiance warred with doubt that she could do anything about it. Could she drag her daughter away without revealing her whereabouts, revealing all the kids' presence, to the group of criminal, undisciplined, probably armed dogfight spectators? "Where are the others?" she asked, keeping her voice low.

"Come on," Sunny said again and led Bisky toward a weathered shack, raised on wooden stilts, some kind of hunters' blind. They climbed up, and there were the twins and Caden, too.

"You're in big trouble," she whispered to Sunny, and then squeezed her close for just a second. "What possessed you to come out here? We told you not to get involved!"

"Caden's been out here before, and he remembered this place. Figured it would be a good hiding spot. We've been here for hours, before they started getting set up."

"It's a small operation from what we can see." Caden kept his voice low, quieter than the racket being made by the spectators and dogs.

"I want you well away from the action." Bisky glared at each teenager in turn. "In fact, I want you all out of here."

"We'll leave soon," Caden promised, and the others nodded, too vigorously to be believable. "We want to be witnesses, get evidence."

Bisky pressed her lips together, then turned to Sunny. "You didn't answer your phone."

"Turned off," Sunny explained. "I didn't want to give us away." Their voices were low, and the crowd on the ground was getting louder, the penned dogs barking and yelping. There wasn't much risk of being overheard.

"They're about to get started," Avery said from her observation point, and they all crowded together to look out the narrow top window, made so that hunters could observe their prey without being seen. The crowd below was mostly in darkness, but a pit ringed by rope was spotlighted.

There were long moments of waiting for something to happen. The crowd talked and partied, laughing, drinking and betting. A pickup and a car pulled up, the occupants spilling out and joining the group.

Bisky kept trying to talk Sunny into leaving, tried to talk them all into it, but they flat-out refused.

So, rather than leave them alone, she stayed with them in the blind. She kept expecting the police any minute, but when they didn't come, she wondered whether William had even remembered to call them, given his preoccupation with his ex.

Every few minutes, the crowd noise surged and the dogs yipped more frantically, and it seemed like the fight was about to start. She was afraid of what the teenagers might do when that happened.

Then someone started shouting through a megaphone, and although the dogs' barking escalated, the people's voices quieted down.

"We're startin' with a warm-up," the voice called.

A few of the people cheered.

"We've got this scrappy little pup wants to try her strength against Moloch," he said. "Even though Moloch outweighs her by just a little…"

There were catcalls and laughter from the crowd. Bisky looked at Sunny, eyebrows raised. Now what?

Sunny pointed at Avery, who had her phone out and was videoing the proceedings. So that was their plan for gathering evidence. Okay, but had they thought it through? Had they considered what it would be like to watch, helpless, while two dogs tried to kill each other?

"She's small, but she's game." There was roaring from the crowd, and growling and barking from the dogs, and Bisky leaned forward, squinting, trying to see what was going on. There were two handlers, each holding a dog back on either side of the illuminated sand pit. One of the dogs was much bigger than the other.

The megaphone man was speaking again. "Now Moloch, here, never lost a fight. But there's a first time for everything."

"Takin' bets," one of the pickup truck guys called out.

Bisky looked at the other dog, half Moloch's size, and she had heard enough. "Come on, let's get out of here. You've got your evidence." She didn't want Sunny to have to listen to the fight, see it. Didn't want that for any of the kids.

"Face your dogs!" came the cry from ringside.

Then everything happened at once. The handlers let the two dogs loose on each other, and the crowd yelled and cheered for their favorites. Sunny stood watching the vicious fight, her face growing more and more horrified. And then she twisted out of Bisky's grasp and scrambled down the ladder.

"Wait!" Bisky called sharply. Sunny paused, and Bisky turned to the twins.

Avery was still at the window, holding up her phone. Bisky took the girl's shoulders from behind. "You and Aiden go get help," she ordered. "I'm going after Sunny."

"I have to stay and film," Avery protested.

Bisky glanced behind her and when she saw that Sunny had started to climb down the ladder, her stomach turned over.

"I have a better phone camera," Caden said, moving to stand beside Avery. "I'll video the rest."

"Promise. Now." Bisky had to get to Sunny, but she wasn't fooling herself she could fight this battle alone. "Call Evan Stone, any cop, your parents. We *need* you to do this."

Avery glanced over at her twin, and they seemed to communicate without words. "Okay. We will."

Bisky scrambled down the ladder after Sunny then, just in time to see her reach the edge of the ring. A big man grabbed her. "Whoa, little lady," he said, pulling Sunny back from the fray as if she were a small child.

Bisky jogged toward them, her heart nearly exploding, trying to make a plan.

Sunny struggled against the man. "Let go of me!"

The man's expression went from jovial to suspicious, and he pulled Sunny back from the pit. "You can't go in there. Who are you? What are you doing here?"

"I'm trying to save those poor animals," Sunny yelled.

That caught the attention of another man who seemed to be in a similar, guarding role, and he walked over and stood on Sunny's other side. "What's going on, sweetheart?"

Bisky slowed down, then stopped. She was still hidden by the trees. How could she best help Sunny?

A few people glanced toward Sunny and the two men, but most seemed content to let the bouncers handle it. The crowd was focused on the snarling, yelping dogs.

Wait. Think.

When the newly arrived bouncer ran a hand through Sunny's hair, though, Bisky couldn't stop herself; she charged in. "Don't you touch her," she ordered. "I'm her mother. Let her go."

A meaty hand grabbed her arm and spun her around. She struggled and kicked, but the man held her at arm's length, impervious to her efforts. "Cut it out or we'll hurt your kid," he grunted, and Bisky immediately went still.

Struggling against these men was futile anyway, Bisky

realized as she caught her breath. She was strong and fit, and so was Sunny, but both of the guards had guns, and they were both burly, muscular men. They shoved Bisky and Sunny farther to the edge of the crowd and then stopped, one standing behind each of them, guns poking at their backs. "Deal with 'em after," one guard muttered to the other. "I got a grand riding on this fight."

Twenty yards away, the dogs screamed and snarled in the ring, and the dogs in crates on the other side of the ring barked and threw themselves against the doors as if they wanted nothing more than to get in on the fight.

Bisky berated herself for letting things go this far. She didn't *think* the men who were now holding them captive would actually shoot them, but having her daughter beside her facing this kind of risk lodged her heart in her throat.

Sunny was crying now, watching the dogs tear into each other, teeth bared and flashing, muscular bodies hurling into each other with audible thuds. "That big dog's going to kill the little one," she choked out. She didn't even seem that scared of the man who'd grabbed her, so strong was her protective instinct toward the dogs.

The man orchestrating the fight looked somehow familiar, but Bisky was too scared and distracted to think about how she might know him.

And then the man guarding Sunny went tense. He said something to Bisky's guard and nodded toward the edge of the crowd.

There, in the shadows, was William. He scanned the crowd, and clearly, he hadn't seen her and Sunny yet. Relief, anger and fear for his safety warred within her. She wouldn't call out to him, not yet.

"Keep an eye on these two," the man who'd been guarding Sunny grunted to the other, and headed toward William.

No one in the crowd seemed to notice him, too caught up in the wildly yelping dogs in the ring.

She looked from William to the megaphone man who'd seemed familiar, and suddenly, she realized *why* he looked familiar.

The man orchestrating the fight and riling up the crowd was William's father.

CHAPTER TWENTY-THREE

WILLIAM SCANNED THE CROWD, his mind racing between concern for Bisky and shock that he was seeing his father for the first time in twenty years. He'd intended to come back only long enough to ascertain that the teenagers weren't really here after all and that Bisky was safely away. And then he'd realized that the man managing the fight was his own father.

He'd aged hard. His scruffy beard was entirely gray, his thick hair salt-and-pepper and long enough to look disheveled. Bushy eyebrows topped narrowed eyes and a red, weathered face. He was skinnier than William remembered; that much was visible despite the ragged, fleece-lined jacket he wore. His tattered jeans hung off skinny hips.

William remembered his father young and strong, and he hadn't considered what age would do for him; truthfully, he'd never expected his father to have a long life. Seeing him this way, worn out and prematurely old, wrung William's heart.

At the same time, his father's energy was high as he whipped the audience into a frenzy, and his crows of delight as the dogs ripped into each other turned William's stomach.

He had to stand up to his father one more time, but how?

The crowd was mostly occupied with the snarling, yowling dogs in the ring, and William was trying to figure out his next move when another man grabbed him roughly by the back of the shirt. "Who're you?"

William turned. The man who'd approached him was dressed in camo, an automatic weapon visible in a sling on his back.

"Just here to watch," he temporized, his adrenaline surging. This wasn't just some guy who liked to carry a concealed handgun; this was a man ready to take some people down.

Where were Bisky and Sunny and the teens? He could only hope and pray that they'd gotten away.

"No unregistered spectators," the armed man said.

Then William would pretend to be a spectator. "I just want to see the show," he said, and reached for his wallet. "I'll pay."

The man frowned, and William pulled out his wallet and handed over a fifty.

"Who's your money on?"

It took William a minute. Then he nodded at the ring. "The underdog," he said.

The man snorted and pocketed the money.

William stepped to the side and scanned the spectators, relieved that he didn't see Bisky and Sunny and the other teenagers. They'd gotten away. That settled, he focused again on the man with the megaphone who was revving up the audience.

Listening to his patter, watching him read the crowd, William suddenly remembered that his father could be charming. He caught the edge of a memory: his dad at the center of a circle of men, telling some story, making them roar with laughter.

William had felt proud to be his father's son that day.

As if he knew he was being watched, William's father looked up. He caught William's eye and visibly started.

Slowly, he lowered his megaphone to his side and stared, shook his head, stared some more. Finally, he started walking around the ring toward William.

From the crowd, there were shouts that sounded like dismay, and from the corner of his eye William saw the man in camo stand straighter, hand going to his weapon.

There had been a time, right after Jenna had died, that William had wished to be shot, as she had been. He didn't want it now, though.

He'd never get over his grief, but he had gotten over his death wish. He wanted to live.

"Who's that guy?" someone called, and there were more shouts as his father made his way through the small crowd. People were noticing this break from the usual protocol, apparently, and they weren't happy about it. A few even seemed to be gathering up their things, making ready to leave.

The dogs continued fighting, jaws snapping, snarling. The larger dog knocked the smaller one to the ground, again, again.

So this was where his father had ended up: orchestrating a cruel blood sport, hurting innocent animals. It shouldn't surprise William. His father's lack of morality and compassion had been a given as long as William could remember.

But it turned William's stomach anew. He couldn't let this go on. He'd stopped his father before, and he'd do it again.

A few car doors slammed and engines started up. Yes, people were leaving, afraid of being caught at their illegal activity. But at least half the spectators were still watching and yelling about the fight, ignoring the drama between father and son happening on the sideline.

Thank heavens Bisky and the kids had made it out.

His father finally reached him. "Son?" he said. "How'd

you find us out here?" He was staring at William, looking him up and down. "You don't belong here."

"Stop that fight," William ordered.

"Can't." His father glanced at the truck tailgate where two men still sat, one watching over the scene, and the other counting out cash. No doubt, that was where people had placed their bets. Now those in charge of the gambling seemed to be preparing to end things quickly if needed.

The yelping, snarling dogs turned William's attention back to the ring. The two dog handlers stood on either side of it. While others yelled drunkenly, these two were sharply focused, eyes going back and forth between the two fighting dogs. One of the men had his arms crossed. The other held a stick with a flattened ring. He was the ticket to stopping the fight, because if William wasn't mistaken, that stick was how they could separate the dogs.

William heard more talk, yelling, another car engine. A man and woman shouted at each other on the edge of the crowd.

More of the audience headed away, while others, women and men both, cheered for their dog, ignoring any interpersonal drama.

William's father turned back toward the ring and lifted his megaphone. "This one could go to the death, folks," he yelled. "We're still takin' bets."

William hadn't seen his father in twenty years. He was much bigger and stronger than the man now, and even back then, he'd managed to knock his father out.

He wanted to do it again. But now there were others involved, and guns. "You need to put a stop to this," he said to his father. "Please. The police are coming."

In the ring the smaller dog fell and the bigger one gripped its hind leg in his jaws. William watched, horrified, as the big dog bit down and the smaller dog screamed.

His old fears of the flashing teeth and angry eyes of Diablo warred with his new love of Xena. He started toward the dog owner with the stick. If his father wouldn't stop this travesty, William would.

The camo-clad man who'd initially questioned William stepped in front of him. "Don't even think about it. Or we'll take you out just like we're gonna take out those two."

He gestured with his gun toward the side of the crowd.

William reeled back, staring, his heart turning over. Bisky and Sunny were there, side by side, and a big armed man stood behind them. Sunny was crying. Bisky kept glancing from William to Sunny.

Not only hadn't they escaped, but they were here under guard and targeted for killing. He took a step in their direction, and the gunman grabbed him and pressed the weapon into William's side.

His father's eyes narrowed. "That's the way to get him outta here," he said out of the corner of his mouth, his eyes never leaving William. "That's his woman."

Interest flared in the gunman's eyes. "Well, well. Try anything funny and we'll shoot your woman." He grabbed William's arm and poked his weapon in William's back, shoving him toward Bisky and Sunny.

William braced for the biggest acting job of his life. "I barely know her," he said loudly. "She's not my woman."

The gunman nudged him, laughing. "Can't blame you. She's a big 'un."

Bisky had heard that; he could tell by the flash in her eyes. But she was strong, she'd know he was trying to save her, she could take it.

"Let them go," he said, waving a careless hand in their direction. "They're nothing to me. Nothing to worry about, either, from the looks of things."

"He's lying," the camo-clad man warned.

At the same moment, William dove toward the guard behind the two women, taking him down.

"Go!" he yelled to Sunny and Bisky.

"Come on!" Bisky put an arm around Sunny and started running into the darkness, crouching down. Something cracked William in the head—the butt of a rifle—but he grabbed it and shoved it aside, looking in the direction Sunny and Bisky had disappeared. He let out a sigh of relief. Whatever happened to him, at least they were safe. He hoped.

I BARELY KNOW HER. She's nothing to me.

She's a big 'un.

William's words, and his acknowledgment of that other guy's words, beat at Bisky's heart as she ran into the woods with Sunny.

Ahead of her, Sunny stopped and held up a hand. "Nobody's chasing us," she said.

"Let's get a little farther." Bisky was panting, and she led the way up a narrow path that came out onto the dirt road.

There, they both paused to listen. In the distance was the cheering and shouting of the crowd, but there was no one behind them, not that Bisky could hear. And she didn't think those men who'd been guarding them could have moved silently.

"They don't think a couple of women could do anything." Sunny sounded disgusted.

"You're probably right." The only time the men had shown any real concern or interest in her and Sunny was when they'd thought Bisky was William's woman.

Which she most definitely wasn't. He'd made that clear, both by leaving to go to his ex, and by his careless words.

She felt in her pocket for the key to William's car. "Come on," she said, "let's get out of here, get help."

"I don't want to leave," Sunny said. "I want to sneak back there and take pictures of license plates. Get more evidence for the cops."

"Too dangerous," Bisky said.

"We'll be careful." Sunny grabbed her arm and looked into her eyes. "We've come this far to help those poor dogs. We can't give up now. We have to do what's right."

Bisky looked at her daughter, her heart seeming to swell in her chest. Who *was* this activist she'd raised? "It'll be dangerous."

"I know." Sunny held her gaze steadily. "I accept the risk."

Bisky sucked in a breath. She wanted to protect her daughter. But she had to acknowledge that Sunny was grown, grown enough to make risky decisions of all sorts. At least she was making them for a good cause.

"If we stay together," she said, "and if you promise to listen to me and run if I say to."

Sunny hesitated.

"I'm your mom. I want to fix things, too, but I won't go along with it if you're going to be impulsive and stupid."

Sunny nodded quickly. "Fine. I'll listen."

"Then let's go." Bisky's heart was in her throat. Sunny said she'd listen, but would she? As an emotional teenager, if she saw something that upset her, would she really be able to exert self-control?

Bisky hoped this wasn't the biggest mistake she'd ever made.

WILLIAM WATCHED THE PIT as the dogs snarled and snapped. The smaller one struggled toward the bigger one, dragging her hind leg. She'd been trained to fight to the death, trained out of caring for her own safety. Horrifying.

"Yeah, Princess!" the man who'd been guarding William yelled. "Lookit her! She's gonna be a great fighter."

"Whee, she got game!"

"She'll give 'im a run for his money!"

The crowd grew frenzied. William's father started waving his hands up and down, riling people up even more. The avid expressions on some of the faces suggested that there was probably a lot of money on the fight.

He stepped back to where his father stood. "Make them stop, now. I don't want to see that dog killed."

His father frowned. "I can't call the fight," William's dad said. "Who would get the purse?"

"The police are on their way, stop it!" The voice was Sunny's, and William looked back, his heart sinking because he'd thought they'd escaped to safety.

"Sunny, get out of here!" he yelled across the shrinking crowd.

"Not until they stop the dogs from fighting," Sunny said, and in her fierceness, he saw how much she was like her mother. She came toward him then. "Make it stop, William," she said, her voice low now, tears in her eyes. "Make them stop hurting each other."

He studied her face for a moment, then nodded and turned toward the ring.

There was the sound of a gun being cocked.

He wished he'd confessed his love to Bisky.

More car doors slammed and more engines started. When William looked toward the jumbled cars, he realized that the twins were there, too, snapping pictures of license plates.

Then the truck that had held the betting operation pulled away.

Cursing, the big dog's handler waded in with a stick and got his dog to clamp on it. He tried to guide it away, but it turned back to the injured smaller dog, now panting and bleeding on the ground.

William saw tubs of ice, mostly devoid of beer cans now and partially melted, and something he'd read came back to him. People used buckets of water, or a hose, to stop dogfights.

He grabbed the largest tub and flung its contents onto the fighting dogs.

That allowed the handler to pull the confused big dog away. The other handler hurried toward a vehicle; apparently, he'd decided to abandon the injured dog in the ring.

William stepped closer and saw the small dog bare its teeth. He didn't want to go near it, but he thought of Xena—now that he'd seen a dogfight, he was guessing she'd been a bait dog or unwilling to fight—and he took off his coat and used it as a blanket to wrap the dog a little, protect himself from those teeth as he lifted the dog into his arms.

"You're still softhearted," his father said.

"And you're still cruel to creatures who can't defend themselves."

To William's shock, his father looked ashamed as he waved a hand around the area, now deserted. "I don't like doing this stuff," he said. "I just need the money."

William shook his head. "I can't forgive you for what you did to Mom."

"I wanted to take care of my family," his father said, staring at the ground. "I just…couldn't. It did something to me, made me crazy."

Shaken, William realized that he felt exactly the same. He had wanted to take care of Jenna and even of Ellie, but he hadn't been able to do it. And it had done something to him, too. Maybe he had more in common with his father than he'd realized.

It wasn't a good thought.

The sirens got louder, and a police car swung across the

road. Two officers emerged, one headed toward the few remaining cars and the other, Evan Stone, toward William and his father. Evan glanced down at the megaphone William's father was still holding. "Is this the man behind it?"

William looked at his father, who wasn't making any effort to get away. "He's involved," he said slowly, "but if you're looking for the mastermind, I don't think he's it."

Evan nodded and began firing questions at William's father.

Moments later, the other cop came and said something to Evan, and Evan turned to William. "Go on, see to Bisky."

William turned, and sure enough, there was Bisky. She stood in the emptying parking area, arms around Sunny, who was crying.

He wanted to help them in the worst way. But he was a failure. He'd nearly let them get killed. When the time for decisive action had come, he'd abandoned them to go off on a wild-goose chase after his ex.

As usual, he'd made the wrong choice.

Evan was patting down William's father now, but he met William's eyes and jerked his head sidewise. "Go on, see to them," he said.

They were better off without him. "No, no interest," he said, loudly and clearly. He looked at her as he said it. Better to be direct, make sure no softheartedness on her part made her think there was anything remaining between them.

The expression on her face told him she'd gotten the message.

William turned away, the little dog in his arms, and walked slowly back toward Bisky's car.

He laid the dog gently in the back and thought what to do. He'd drive it to an emergency vet. Yes. Once he got into an area with better cell phone service, he'd find a vet and go.

What he really wanted was Bisky. Too weak to stop himself, he turned toward her.

But the place she'd stood was empty. Bisky was gone.

CHAPTER TWENTY-FOUR

SUNNY WAS RELIEVED when it all settled down. Finally, she and her friends finished talking to the police and their parents. All of the teenagers had gotten lectured at, but everyone had also done a lot of hugging. When Sunny had asked if everyone could stay around and have a bonfire, the parents had conferred and then agreed. The girls were allowed to sleep over, too.

Now, Sunny stared at the flickering flames of the bonfire and then looked around at her friends. She, Kaitlyn, Venus, the twins and Caden all lounged around the firepit at her house, in lawn chairs and on blankets. The smell of wood smoke mingled with the deep chocolate taste of the s'mores they just finished making and eating, and Sunny felt sleepy and content. It was 1:00 a.m., and it felt like they'd all been together for days.

Earlier tonight, she'd wondered if she would even make it home alive. She'd never been so terrified in her life as she'd been with a gun poking her in the back, watching the dogs tear each other apart.

"I'm still totally freaked out." Avery took a big drink of soda and looked around. "Anyone else?"

"My heart hasn't slowed down yet," Sunny admitted.

Kaitlyn nodded. "Mine, either, and all I was doing was waiting for you guys to get back."

"I feel good," Venus said. "You saved some dogs at any rate."

"Yeah, we *are* kind of heroes," Caden said.

"Except that our parents hate us," Avery reminded him.

"As do the cops, don't forget," Sunny said.

Caden poked the ground with a stick. "They should be grateful," he said. "We sped up their investigation by about six months." Apparently, the police had been monitoring the online activities of the group behind the fight and were gathering information to try to shut them down permanently and also find out whether they were connected with a bigger, more professional dogfighting organization. They'd lectured the teenagers about taking on things that weren't their business, interfering with an official investigation and putting themselves at risk.

That was fine, the police had a point…but meanwhile, they'd been willing to let some dogs be sacrificed, and even if it was for the greater good of the investigation, Sunny thought that was wrong.

She leaned back in her lawn chair and looked up at the stars, then around the circle of her friends. No one was saying they weren't mad at her anymore, but it was clear that they weren't. That was a huge relief. It was over, and she still had friends.

William had taken that poor little brown dog to an emergency vet. Sunny had texted him, and he'd told her what he was doing and said he didn't need any help.

She didn't know what was going on between him and her mom, because they seemed to be at odds, again.

But Sunny was through trying to mastermind everything, trying to be in control. It had worked tonight, sort of, but it sort of hadn't, and she had decided she needed to take a rest from being in charge.

She started scrolling through her photos. Mostly, they were of cars and license plates, and they'd turned out dark and blurry. Still, the police wanted them to send all the pictures and videos in.

Caden was sitting beside her, and when he saw what she was doing, he leaned closer. He looked over her shoulder, and as she scrolled to the big car at the scene, the one that looked almost like a limousine, he put a hand on her arm and gripped, hard.

She looked back up at him. "Something wrong?"

"Let me see that one." He leaned closer. "Yeah," he said, his voice growing grim. "That's my dad's car."

"Was he there?" Kaitlyn had been listening and now she came over to kneel on the other side of Sunny, also looking at the phone.

"Your dad was there betting on the dogfight?" Sunny kind of winced. She hated the thought that anyone she knew was there, but for it to be Caden's father... How awful.

"I don't think he was betting on it," Caden said slowly. "I think he's behind it."

Just as he said it, there was one of those natural silences that punctuates every group conversation. The fire crackled. A small animal rustled in the nearby bushes.

"Behind it? Your dad's behind the dogfighting ring?" Kaitlyn's voice was loud with surprise. The others had been looking at each other, but now everyone laser focused on Caden.

"But your dad is rich," Sunny said.

"Maybe that's how," Caden said slowly. "He hasn't gone to a regular job in the past couple of years, but the money seems to keep rolling in." He shook his head. "I knew he was up to something. Always sneaking around, turning off his computer screen when me or Mom came in, going into the other room to take calls." He frowned. "I actually thought he was having an affair, because that's what Mom thought."

"She told you that?"

"No, but I heard them fighting."

How awful it must have been at his house. No wonder he'd moved out and gone to the Blue House to stay for a while.

Kaitlyn sat back and wrapped her arms around her knees. "I heard that new cop, Evan Stone, say that there must be a bigger group behind this, that it's a pretty small potatoes organization here on the Eastern Shore. Could your dad be involved with something bigger?"

Venus stared from Caden to Kaitlyn and back again. "You mean like the mob?"

"Maybe. I don't know." He looked miserable, hunched over, like he was trying to make himself smaller.

Sunny thought about how Caden's parents had acted when she'd gone over there. His dad had seemed awful, and his mom wasn't much help. Neither of them had seemed to care about Caden's well-being at all.

She itched to try to fix the situation. But, she reminded herself, she was through taking control, taking over, being bossy. She held out her phone. "It's your dad. It's your call. Delete it if you want to."

Everybody was quiet then. The only sound was the frogs croaking, quietly at first, then getting louder, then sinking back down.

Caden stared out across the bay, his forehead wrinkled. "I won't delete it," he said finally, not looking at any of them. "But don't send it to the cops quite yet. I need to text my mom and tell her to get out of there."

"Does she have somewhere to go?" Kaitlyn asked.

"I have an aunt who lives up the shore. Maybe she can go there."

They all waited while Caden texted his mom. "Where are *you* going to stay?" Sunny asked. "Because I doubt you want to go home just now. And you can't go back to the Blue House. That's the first place people will look for you."

"You can stay at our house," Aiden said, and Avery nodded.

"Thanks." Caden's phone buzzed and he looked at it. "My mom says she can be out of there in half an hour," he said. "She must have already known. She's not surprised."

Sunny bit her lip, looking at him. His mom hadn't even called to see if he was okay. She thought of her own mom, coming to check on her, getting involved, helping all the kids. Sunny was lucky, and she was grateful.

"Should I send it in?" she asked. "Or wait till tomorrow?"

"Send it in," he said grimly.

Sunny did it, then squeezed Caden's hand, and then they were all standing and hugging each other. They had been through a lot together, but they *were* together and they'd come out ahead. That was something to be thankful for.

THE MORNING AFTER the dogfighting mess, Bisky sat in the diner across from her cousin Gemma, pushing around a pile of scrambled eggs. "He said it loud and clear," she explained. "Said he didn't want me and that he wasn't interested. Three times!"

Gemma took another bite of pancakes and then put down her fork. "It just doesn't make sense. When I saw you together, at the boat-docking thing, it seemed like he really, really liked you. Plus, he doesn't seem like the kind to be mean, from what I remember about him as a kid."

Bisky moved her plate to the side and pulled her coffee cup closer, wrapping her hands around it, feeling like she needed the comfort. Feeling cold.

"There was really no mistaking it," she said. "First off,

he left me and Sunny there to handle those thugs by ourselves."

"Yeah," Gemma said, frowning, "that wasn't cool."

"His ex needed him." Bisky pushed out the words past the tight feeling in her throat and face. "I mean, I get it. I'm stronger than his ex, and I'm good with that. But if it means he's always going to be running back to her when she calls..." She propped her cheek on her fist. "Face it, I'm never going to have the kind of great relationship you have. I'm just not made for it. Men don't feel that way about me."

"Come here." Gemma stood and started tugging Bisky's arm.

"What? Where are we going? We have to pay the check."

"Just to the ladies' room." Gemma waved to their waitress. "We'll be right back," she said, and the woman nodded.

Gemma was small, but she was determined, and she wasn't going to stop pulling on Bisky from the looks of it. So Bisky unfolded herself from the booth and let Gemma usher her into the ladies' room.

Gemma guided Bisky toward the sinks and stood beside her. "Look," she said, pointing at the mirror. "What do you see?"

Bisky looked at herself, the circles under her eyes, the plain ponytailed hair, still wet from the shower. "I see a tired woman who's not as young as she used to be," she said, "and her annoying cousin." To soften her words, she put an arm around Gemma. "You're sweet to try to make me feel better."

"I'll tell you what I see," Gemma said, undeterred. "I see a strong woman who's taken care of her family and earned a living ever since she hit eighteen. A woman who's made it in a man's world and stayed good and kind. A woman who's been a great role model to her daughter, and..." She leaned her head on Bisky's arm. "And who was a huge help to me when I needed it."

"Thanks, hon." Bisky meant it. Gemma's words did buoy her up a little.

"And men *do* like you. Maybe William's just a warm-up, and your prince is just around the corner. You never know."

That made Bisky smile even while her heart twisted. She didn't want a prince; she wanted William. "You always were a little unrealistic. Come on, we'd better pay and then I need to get home and make sure Sunny's okay. That was quite a night the kids had."

"You think about what I said."

"I will, promise. I'm glad you're here, Gemma."

"Me, too."

And it was true, Bisky reflected as she left the diner, waving to people she knew, giving Gemma one last hug. She was thankful for her town, her daughter, her cousin and her friends. She had a good life here, and she'd continue to have that, she knew.

It was just that, right now, there was a hole in her heart. A William-shaped hole.

She had too much self-respect to chase after him or put up with what he'd done. But oh, she was going to miss him.

WILLIAM HAD NEVER visited a jail before, but it seemed a fitting end to the last twenty-four hours. Prior to that, he'd never been to a dogfight, nor an emergency vet, so why not finish things out by visiting his newly incarcerated father?

His emotions were raw. Part of it was about Bisky and trying to understand what had happened between them. Trying to understand how he felt, and trying to figure out how she felt, too. He knew that he cared about her, and up until now, he thought that meant he needed to stay away from her for her own sake, that he was a bad bet. Now, he wasn't sure if that was the case or not. But he was pretty sure he had ruined his chances with her by some of the things he'd said last night.

He'd thought hurting her was the right thing to do, to push her away. But his gut told him he'd been wrong, wrong, wrong.

Great move, Romeo.

The other thing that had his stomach in knots was his father. He'd honestly never expected to see the man again, had figured that he had probably passed away. To encounter him on the Eastern Shore, so near where their family had lived long ago, had been a complete shock.

And then he'd realized he should have expected it. His father had always scrambled to earn a living, finding all kinds of ways to make a buck, never worrying too much about the legality of it. And now that William thought about it, he wondered if it had been his father living in the old home place.

Even to find the man participating in a deplorable blood sport shouldn't have shocked William, because his father had attended local prizefights whenever he could and had never really known how to take care of animals, had always thought of them as creatures to be used—and abused—not cared for.

Some of the puzzle pieces were falling into place, but not all of them. Strangest of all was the way his father had acted when William had talked to him. He hadn't seemed to hate William. It was a marked difference from the angry attitude his father had held toward William his whole life. Ever since William had beaten him up, all those years ago, and called the police on him, he'd expected his father to hold a huge grudge.

William was sitting on one side of a piece of Plexiglas, and there was a phone, just like on TV. Beside him, an older woman cried as she talked to a younger man, maybe her son.

There were all kinds of ways a parent could get their heart broken.

And then his father was in the chair opposite him, on the other side of the Plexiglas, and all his musings flew away as he stared at that face, familiar because he'd grown up with it, and familiar because it was almost the same face he saw in the mirror himself, every morning. He and his dad had always looked a lot alike, and even as weathered and haggard as his father looked, the resemblance was obvious.

His father picked up the phone, and belatedly, William did the same. His father's first words surprised him. "I appreciate you coming in," he said.

Since when did his father appreciate anything?

"Did you get that pup to the vet?" his father asked.

It took William a minute to realize that his father was asking about the health of the dog he had heartlessly put into the ring.

"Yes. Looks like she'll be okay. Eventually."

"Too bad she got hurt like that." His father did sound a little sorry, but also matter-of-fact. Hurt dogs must be fairly normal in the dogfighter's world.

"Why did you do it?" he asked his father.

His father actually looked confused for a minute. "What, the dogfighting?"

"Yeah," William said.

His father shrugged. "Got in over my head and couldn't get out." He rubbed a finger across what looked like a spot of dirt on the table in front of him. "I couldn't get out, but I never did like it. Hey. Did you get the brown-and-white pit and the black pup I brought you?"

William frowned at him. "What are you talking about?"

"I brought you a couple of dogs, first the brown-and-white one, then a black one. Hope you took care of them."

All of a sudden the truth dawned on him. His father was talking about Xena and Muffin. "How do you know about those dogs?"

"I saw you were in town," his father said. "Knew you had a soft heart. I remember how you tried to make friends with Diablo. So rather than killing 'em, like I was supposed to, I dropped them off near your place." He looked vaguely ashamed. "I just hated for them to die when they didn't need to. Guess I'm getting soft like you, in my old age."

William stared at his father, trying to understand.

His father was getting soft…meaning he would watch dogs get mauled, but he didn't want to kill them. It wasn't much of an improvement, but still, William would never have believed it based on the man he'd known.

It must be true, though. His father had brought William injured dogs because he knew William would take care of them. He'd changed from the man who'd kicked and mistreated Diablo.

It was going to take him a while to process that. "If you really have a soft heart toward animals, you need to cooperate until the police find out who's behind this fighting conference." William had done a quick bit of internet research on dogfighting and had picked up some of the terminology.

"Well now, I just might," his father said. "Looks like I'll be in here awhile, either way, but maybe I can put an end to some of that sick stuff."

"I hope you do."

There was a little silence then, awkward. There was both too much and too little to say. "What will you do now, son?" his father asked finally.

Hearing his father say that one word—*son*—made William's throat tighten. "Back to my job in Baltimore, I guess." His time in Pleasant Shores was nearing an end. His therapist had commented last week about how well he was doing. Impulsively, he said, "I lost my daughter. She got in the path of a thief with a gun. She was fifteen."

His father's eyes widened. "I'm real sorry to hear that." After a minute of silence, he added, "Your mother lost a child. Miscarriage. Baby girl."

Anger reared up inside of William. "I know, and that was your fault." What was he thinking, starting to see the good side of his father, when his father was essentially a murderer?

"You mean from that fight you stopped? No." His father shook his head. "I know that's what you and that cop thought, but she'd already lost that baby. I found her seeking comfort in a bottle and another man, that last night. He ran off, and she and I fought."

William thought back to the scene, the last time he'd seen his mother alive. Could that be true, or was his father lying, making excuses?

"Still doesn't make it forgivable," his father said. "I treated her bad, right up until I got kicked out of town."

William stared at his father while his view of the man as a horrible monster made a shift.

Yes, his father had been abusive, mean and hurtful. He'd done indefensible things. But maybe he hadn't caused the death of a child after all.

Something nudged at William then. Was his view of himself as a guilty monster just as wrong?

"What about Bisky Castleman?" his dad asked.

That startled William. "She's safe," he said. "She left with her daughter. Nobody hurt her."

"No," his father said, "that's not what I meant. I meant, what about her and *you*?"

William tilted his head to one side. "What do you mean?"

"Always thought you'd end up marrying that girl, close as you two were," he said.

"I very much doubt that," William said, although the idea of marrying Bisky filled him with a longing that almost made him breathless.

The pair next to them stood. The mother cried openly, and the prisoner-son wiped tears from beneath his eyes. He walked away slowly, turning once to wave. The woman watched him go and then turned and trudged toward the exit.

"How come you doubt you'll marry Bisky?" William's father asked.

"Because I screwed up pretty bad with her."

"And? We all screw up. I couldn't fix my screwup, but you could fix yours."

"I'm no good for her," he said. "I pushed her away for her own sake."

His father shook his head. "That makes no sense," he said. "You're a good man. Not perfect, but good. You sure you're not just punishing yourself for not being perfect?"

"I wouldn't—"

"Trust me, you would," his father interrupted. "From the time you were small, you took the weight of the world on your shoulders. Took responsibility for way too much, and blamed yourself when things went wrong. Even when those things were my fault, not yours." He shook his head. "Don't mess up your life and your chance at happiness, son. Give yourself some grace. And give Bisky some grace, too, if you want to. She's a good woman just like you're a good man."

"Time's up," called the guard from the side of the room.

William's father put his hand to the glass. William didn't follow suit, he couldn't. After a minute his father nodded, and then the attendant was escorting him out.

William watched him go, saw the slump of his shoulders, and knew his father was an old man.

It was enough to make anyone think. What did he want his own life to look like going forward? Would he get to the age of his father and be as alone as he was?

How badly had he screwed up with Bisky, and could he fix it at all?

ON SATURDAY, THE GUSTY GULL opened its outdoor seating because it was such an unusually warm day. Seventy-one degrees in the early afternoon, and Bisky, Amber, Erica and Ria met for an afternoon cocktail and gabfest.

They were all a little shaken, or at least Bisky was, by the events of the previous week. She was glad to get together with her friends, because she was feeling a little melancholy and felt the need to get out of her house.

After they'd all hugged and ordered summery drinks, Bisky sat back and looked at the clear blue sky over the Chesapeake Bay. "Breeze feels good," she said.

Erica gestured out at the bike path across Beach Street. "It's great to see Sunny so happy again, with her friends," she said.

Bisky looked over and saw her daughter with Kaitlyn, Venus and Avery. They were walking the path, talking a mile a minute, and giggling, all wearing too-short shorts and too-skimpy tops for the weather, but that was kids.

Bisky was so proud of Sunny for what she'd accomplished with the dogfighting, even while she was mad at her for taking such risks. Mostly, she just felt grateful that Sunny was safe.

Ria was watching them too. "The girls are growing up so quickly. I'm going to miss being so actively involved in their lives. I love being a mother. Although…"

Something in Ria's voice made Amber and Erica tune in. "Although what?" Amber asked.

Ria hesitated and blushed. "Drew and I aren't using protection, if you know what I mean."

"Whoa now!" Amber clapped her hands, then pumped her fist. "Baby, baby, baby!"

Erica was laughing. "As fertile as the two of you are? We're going to be having a baby shower right here at the Gusty Gull in nine months, if not sooner."

Ria held up a hand, smiling. "Hey, I'm not twenty-five anymore. I bet that it won't even happen, but we both love kids so much."

Bisky felt an unusual surge of jealousy. She had always envied Ria, a little, for her loving husband. But she suddenly envied her this opportunity to start anew on motherhood. Not that Bisky would want to do that herself, but it would just be nice to have something big, the possibility of a baby, to look forward to.

Their drinks came then, and the conversation got more general, but Bisky kept coming back to the thought.

Sunny was getting more and more independent. She'd asked if she could spend Easter with Kaitlyn and Venus, who had a plan to help serve Easter dinner and do an egg hunt for some of the disadvantaged families in their community.

Of course, Bisky had said yes. She was proud that Sunny wanted to do something like that. She'd opened her mouth to offer to help, but had stopped herself in time. Sunny and her friends were plenty old enough to do the activity on their own. They didn't need mothers interfering.

It meant Bisky would spend Easter by herself, and that was fine. Maybe she'd cook up an Easter dinner anyway, or take a book outside into the hammock and spend the afternoon reading.

"Hey, lady." Amber nudged her. "How are things going with William?"

"Yeah," Ria said. "I got the impression you and he were pretty close." She waggled her eyebrows up and down.

The good mood Bisky had been grasping at slipped away. "Not happening," she said.

"Why not?" Erica tilted her head to one side, looking concerned.

"Oh, he doesn't want a woman like me," she said.

Amber raised an eyebrow. "Oh? What kind of a woman is that?"

Bisky didn't intend to tell these women all her business, but somehow, the words spilled out of her. "Someone big and tough and take-charge," she said.

"What would make you think he doesn't want those qualities in a woman?" Ria frowned. "I think most men these days appreciate having an equal partner. Even macho types, like Drew."

"Not William," Bisky said. "The other night, at the dog-fight, he made it very clear he wasn't interested."

Amber's eyebrows lifted. "Are you sure?"

Bisky recounted the multiple comments he'd made. "Plus," she went on, "did you see his ex-wife?"

"No, and what does that matter?" Erica asked. "She's an ex for a reason."

Bisky shook her head. "The minute she called him for help, he took off. Even though Sunny and I actually needed him."

"Did he know that, though?" Amber frowned. "You have a way of acting like you're totally independent and fine, all the time. Which is great," she added, raising a hand, "but it can maybe make a man feel superfluous."

Bisky shrugged. "He might not have known I needed him, but…"

"But what?" Erica leaned forward, elbows on the table, studying her.

Bisky sucked in a breath and then the words just came. "I would scold Sunny if she said anything like this, but the woman was tiny. Tiny and delicate and blonde… The exact opposite of me. That's apparently what William likes."

"Stop." Ria jumped in. "That body image stuff can be deadly. Comparing yourself to other women. Believe me, I know."

"True, of course," Bisky said, and took a long draw on her drink. "I know that."

But she didn't believe it in her heart. Didn't believe William could want a woman like her, and she had the evidence to prove it.

"Self-image," Amber proclaimed, and waved a hand for the waiter. "It trips us all up. Makes us limit what we can have in the future."

"Well, sure, but if it's accurate…"

"It's not! That's the problem. We get stuck in particular views of ourselves and it's hard to change. Like, I thought I was nothing but a party girl. You can imagine that a guy like Paul seemed out of reach."

"But he wasn't, because you're so much more than a party girl," Erica said, patting her sister's arm.

They ordered appetizers and another round of drinks, and the conversation went on to other things, but Bisky thought about it. Of course, Amber was more than a party girl even if she'd thought she was not. And of course, Ria had a lovely body and spirit, and her husband's love for her was apparent every time Bisky saw them together.

Those women, smart and worthy of respect, had had mistaken views of themselves. Their men—and their friends—had helped them realize that they were more than their shrunken and negative self-images.

Bisky would have considered that could be true of her as well, but she had direct evidence from William. His words at the dogfight rang in her ears, blocking out any chance of a future together.

SUNNY WAVED AT her mother, sitting with her friends on the outdoor deck of the Gusty Gull.

"Our moms are having a little too much fun." Kaitlyn waved up at her mom, too, who was doubled over laughing at something Amber or Erica had said.

Sunny noticed her mom wasn't laughing. She didn't even seem to be paying attention; instead, she was looking out over the bay, her expression thoughtful.

Mom had seemed a little sad lately, and Sunny wondered what it was about. Was it William, or something Sunny had done? She definitely had broken some rules lately, made some mistakes. She probably shouldn't have asked to spend Easter away from Mom. When you were a family of two, you had to look out for each other.

But maybe it wasn't about her at all. Who knew, with a mother? She rubbed Muffin's sides, and her dog looked up at her with adoration.

"Make her do her tricks," Kaitlyn said, and Sunny obliged, putting Muffin through her paces: give paw, roll over, sit pretty.

"You love bossing that dog around," Venus said. "I think you figured out the right line of work."

Sunny laughed. She was just glad Venus wasn't mad at her anymore, that they were all friends again.

"Hey," Kaitlyn said, pointing across the street, "isn't that the new trainer lady?"

Sunny looked in the direction Kaitlyn had indicated. Sure enough, the trainer that had been so hard on her and William and the dogs was walking along the other side of Beach Street, her border collie in lockstep beside her. Ugh. Mary approached the woman and started talking to her. Double ugh.

Sunny had wanted to be the person Mary chose to train the therapy dogs, had wanted it desperately, but it wasn't going to happen.

She waited for depression to hit her as she watched the two women talk, but it didn't come. She realized with surprise that she was okay with that. She'd still be able to work with dogs, and there were different ways that could happen, and it was okay.

Mary and the trainer continued talking, and from the looks of things, it wasn't going well. They were shaking their heads and frowning. Sunny felt a little glad in a mean way, but then pushed aside her thoughts.

She talked with her friends for a while—about boys, of course—and then Mary crossed the street and approached them. "May I speak with you?" she asked Sunny.

"Sure."

Mary pulled her off to the side. "Are you still interested in working with the therapy dog program?" she asked.

Sunny's heart jumped. "Absolutely! But I thought you hired that woman." She gestured in the direction the trainer had gone.

"It didn't work out." Mary frowned, then knelt to rub Muffin's sides. "We've decided to part ways. So, I could start from the ground up looking for another candidate, or..." She bent down and gave Muffin's ears a rub. "I admire what you've done with Muffin. You've turned her around. William's dog too."

"Thanks!" Sunny didn't think she could smile any bigger. "But you said before that we need an adult to do the program?"

"That's still the case, so we'll need to have an adult supervisor," she said. "I was thinking about William, actually."

Sunny thought about that. She'd started out with mixed feelings about William. But he'd worked really hard to overcome his fears about dogs, and he'd been amazing in helping them break apart the dogfighting ring. He was kind of funny, in an old guy way.

The other thing was that she was pretty sure her mom liked William, but for whatever reason, the two of them couldn't seem to get it together. Maybe she could help. "I'd be glad to work with William," she said. "I'm sure I can talk him into it. At least, if he's staying in town."

Mary smiled a little. "If anyone can, you can," she said. "His time at Victory Cottage is almost up, but I'm hoping he'll decide to stay in Pleasant Shores permanently."

Did Sunny want that? Even if it meant he might be around her mom permanently?

She looked over at Kaitlyn and Venus, talking and laughing. She was settled in with them, settled in for these next couple of years until they all went their ways to different colleges, the military or work. She hoped that even after graduation, she could stay friends with both of them, for the next few years and beyond.

She wanted Mom to be happy, too. And if being happy meant her mom had a boyfriend, even a husband, Sunny just might be okay with that. "I wouldn't mind him sticking around," she said.

"Good. Come to the shop Monday and we'll pin down some details." Mary shook her hand, all professional, and then crossed the street and headed up to the deck of the Gusty Gull where Mom and her friends still sat.

Of course, Kait and Venus wanted to know what the conversation with Mary had been about, and she ended up telling them about the therapy dog gig and also about how

William might be involved. When she said she was going to talk him into doing it, Venus laughed. "Still bossy for a cause," she said.

"I guess I am," Sunny admitted. "So shoot me. I get things done."

They continued to tease her. That was what friends did.

And friends also helped you when you couldn't help yourself. That was why she was going to help William figure out a way to get back into Mom's good graces.

WILLIAM WAS DOING something he should have done a while ago, and he didn't know if he was going to be able to handle it.

But now that he'd worked things out, in some kind of way, with his father, it was time to make peace with Jenna.

That was why he was just outside of Baltimore, climbing through the hilly cemetery toward her grave.

He hadn't visited often. Hadn't been able to. He wasn't one of those people who thought you should visit a loved one's grave every week or even every month; he didn't think Jenna would care. Still, when he saw that some weeds grew along the base of her gravestone, his stomach tightened and he knelt and pulled them out.

Then, carefully, he set a container with her favorite flowers, spring daffodils, alongside the grave. He noticed that some of the other plots had spring flowers coming up naturally, and he decided that he'd plant daffodils in the fall, so they'd come up next year.

He sat and traced the gravestone's etching with his forefinger: *Jenna Gross. Gone too soon.*

He closed his eyes for a moment, because she most surely was gone too soon. Cut down when she was full to the brim with life.

He lowered his head, letting it sink into his hands. He

didn't feel like he needed to make peace with his wife in order to try and move forward into a relationship with Bisky. But he did feel like he needed to make peace with Jenna before he could be any kind of a father figure to Sunny if, God willing, Bisky and Sunny accepted him in that capacity. He wanted Jenna to know he wasn't replacing her, that Sunny wouldn't be his daughter in quite the same way that Jenna had been. That he'd never forget Jenna, that her picture would always hold a place of honor in his home, that he'd remember her birthday, would watch her videos, would play her favorite songs even as time moved on and those songs weren't on the radio anymore.

"I'm thinking about starting a scholarship in your name," he said. The words sounded rusty. He wasn't the type to talk to a dead person.

But this was Jenna. Jenna, who had been so bright, and so social. Jenna, who had already decided she wanted to attend a Big Ten university so she could join a sorority and go to the football games.

She'd never get to do that.

But William still had his half of Jenna's college fund, still in the college fund account. He hadn't been able to make himself withdraw it. Now, he would build on it, maybe even do a little fundraising, and start a scholarship to be given yearly to one of the dock kids, to help them get started as he had been helped.

He told her about it. He called up her favorite song on his phone and played it, and the memory of her singing along in her slightly off-key voice brought tears to his eyes.

He regretted every moment of impatience he'd shown her, every time he'd been too busy to play basketball or dolls with her, even though those moments had been few and far between. He hadn't treasured her enough. But he had treasured her a lot, had shown her a lot of love.

And he'd always regret, terribly, that he had left her alone on that last day. But he had come to realize that it was more bad luck than his fault. Still, he told her he was sorry.

And then it was as if he could hear her voice, only it was a little mixed with Sunny's. "Dad, you can't be with me every minute. I'm fine staying home alone. Everyone does it."

With a start, he realized that she had said some version of that, sometime in the weeks before she died. And he had lightened up the restrictions on that a little bit, not wanting to hover over her and be a helicopter parent.

"I know I couldn't be with you every minute, but I wish I had been with you then." His throat went thick and the tears came then, a lot of them. He hated so much that she'd died alone.

After a long time, William said a prayer of his own, wiped his eyes and blew his nose, and stood. "I'll be back," he said. "I'll tell you how the scholarship goes, who gets it."

She didn't answer, of course. But he felt a little more at peace as he turned away and walked back to his car.

Could he move on now? He didn't know. But the lighter feeling in his heart told him he wanted to try.

CHAPTER TWENTY-FIVE

WILLIAM STRAIGHTENED HIS collar and loosened his tie. It had been a long time since he'd worn a dress suit, but Easter seemed to be the right occasion.

Oh and then there was the small matter of proposing to Bisky, which he'd decided to do right after church. As in, now.

He had tried to listen to the sermon, and he'd sung along with the hymns, but his mind was preoccupied. He just wanted to do it already. He tried to make his way through the after-church crowd, but everyone seemed to want to talk.

Mrs. Decker, wearing a wide, flower-covered hat, plucked his sleeve and stopped him. "You clean up well," she said approvingly.

That was one vote of confidence, but he definitely didn't feel secure. Bisky wasn't answering his calls, so Sunny had suggested that church would be the right spot to get together with her.

He couldn't believe it, but Sunny and several of the other teenagers were involved in making this proposal work, or at least they knew about it.

"Hurry up, William!" Sunny gestured to him, and he tried harder to get through the crowd. It wasn't easy at his size, but the advantage was, he could see over the other people.

He saw Bisky and immediately, all his courage left him.

She wore a beautiful blue dress that hugged her curves, and she, too, had a hat on. Despite her height, today she was wearing heels. She wasn't taller than William, but she was taller than most of the people in the church.

Including Evan Stone, with whom she was having an intent conversation. Jealousy shot through William's body and his courage came back. He made his way to where the two of them were standing.

According to Sunny's plan, he was supposed to get Bisky to come to the front of the church, but it wasn't going to happen. Right now, he just had to get her away from Evan.

"Can I talk to you?" he blurted as soon as there was a break in their conversation. He was being awkward, maybe rude, but he didn't even care.

Bisky tilted her head to one side and narrowed her eyes. "Why now, William?"

"It's important." He didn't answer the question, because how could he?

"Give us a minute," she said, her voice cool.

Sunny was texting him, making his phone buzz repeatedly. While Bisky and Evan continued their conversation, he read the messages, which boiled down to "hurry up!" and "Tell her to come to the front of the church!"

Sunny had assured him that the little church's altar would be the best backdrop for him to pop the question. He was pretty sure that she had organized some of the teenagers to watch, and he knew that she planned to photograph the event.

But that wasn't what William wanted, he realized now that he was in the moment. He wanted privacy and he wanted to be outdoors. He'd ask to walk her home, he decided just as Sunny approached, and he told her so.

"That's not social media worthy!" Sunny whispered the

words so only William could hear, tugging at his sleeve. "Just get her inside!"

He turned around and put his hands on Sunny's shoulders, gently. "I appreciate your help, and I'm glad you're on board with my asking her. But I need to do it my way, not yours."

Her mouth was open to protest, but she snapped it shut and nodded. "Okay," she said. "Sometimes I get a little overenthusiastic."

He grinned. "I like that about you." He did, too. He liked everything about Sunny, and he hoped he'd get the chance to know her better, to join her family. He patted her shoulder once more and then turned back to Bisky.

She was saying goodbye to Evan, and it seemed like they were making plans to get together. William hated that, but it wasn't his place to tell her who she could get together with. His place was just to try to encourage her to get together with him.

"Can I walk you home?" he asked. "I need to talk to you."

She hesitated.

The clouds were thinning out and the day was warm. He looked down at her shoes. "Can you walk okay in those?"

"Not fast, but sure." She was studying his face and the frown on hers said she wasn't buying any excuses for his bad behavior.

Well, she was worth fighting for. He held out his hand, and after a short hesitation, she took it. And he drew her away from the crowd and toward the street that led to the docks and home.

WHAT DID WILLIAM want with her?

He looked so serious. And so incredibly handsome. She'd never seen him in a suit, wouldn't have thought he could wear one well, as big as he was, but it fitted him perfectly and he looked self-assured and comfortable and really, really good.

Her mouth went so dry that she dug around for an excuse to slow him down, to go inside and pull herself together. "I left my coat in there," she said, gesturing toward the church. "I'll get it."

"I'll come with you," he said.

So much for pulling herself together. She hurried inside, leaving him to follow behind her. She took her time walking to the coatrack.

He stopped in the entryway, and spoke to a small group of the teenagers. Sunny was among them, and they seemed to be having a somewhat heated debate, but everyone was smiling.

She had to admire how he had embraced the work with the teenagers. They really liked him. Despite having every reason to back off from them, considering the trauma in his past, the loss of his daughter, he'd powered through and stepped up.

Sometimes courage wasn't rushing into a battlefield or carrying somebody's pet cat out of a burning building. Sometimes, courage was staying where you were and doing what you had to do, no matter how much it hurt.

William had that kind of courage.

As she walked back to the group, William was shaking his head and waving the teenagers away. "Get out of here, I'll do it my way."

Do what?

As the kids left, looking at her and laughing a little bit, William beckoned her over to a picture on the wall of the church. It was among many others that depicted the history and life of the church and its congregation.

"Can you find us?" he asked.

She looked at the pictures. She had walked past them for

years without studying them closely, but now, she saw that one of them was from a long-ago church picnic they'd both attended. They were young, maybe eleven and twelve, and they were playing beach volleyball with other kids. Bisky had worn her serviceable tank suit, and William, who probably didn't even own a swimsuit at that time, was wearing shorts and no shirt.

They were high-fiving each other, laughing.

"We had it made as volleyball players," Bisky said. "That must be one of the rare times we were on the same team. Usually, they didn't allow that."

"Everybody wanted one of the tall kids," he said. He bit his lip. "Actually, that's probably one of the few times I spent an afternoon just goofing around."

She nodded. His family hadn't had the space for that type of fun, physically or emotionally. "Did you end up talking to your dad?"

"I did." He took her hand again and turned toward the exit. "I visited him in prison, had a surprisingly good talk. Want to walk?"

An icy hand clutched Bisky's heart.

He must be getting ready to break it to her that he was leaving.

She tried to count back in her head. How long had it been since he'd come? How long did the Victory Cottage program last?

If he wasn't leaving now, he would be soon. And even though she was mad at him, the thought of him not being here sucked all the air out of her chest.

She had to admit it: she'd fallen for him. He was so good with Sunny, with the teenagers, with everyone in town. He was her old friend.

And he was much more than that, in her heart, but she

didn't want to dwell on that, even inside her own head. He had said he wasn't interested, and she had her pride.

Numbly, she followed him down the street, winding through the little residential neighborhoods, picturesque with spring flowers and warm sunshine and white picket fences. In one of the yards, a group of kids shouted, running around with baskets in their hands, clearly on an egg hunt.

Now that they were walking, now that her hand was warm in his, he didn't seem to be in any hurry to say anything. But she wanted to get this over with. "Just tell me," she said.

He looked sideways at her. "Do you mean that?"

"Yes!" She turned to him then, pulling her hand out of his, putting both hands on her hips. "I'm not going to stroll through town all day waiting for you to drop some kind of bombshell."

He was looking at her in such an intent, intense way. She didn't know what it meant, but it took her breath away. His eyes took her breath away.

Something about the way he looked at her... Yes. She'd fallen for him. She'd fallen in love with him, and he was leaving.

All of a sudden it came to her with breathtaking clarity, the thing she'd been wanting, but had never articulated to herself before: to grow old with him. They'd been kids together, and in some part of herself, she had wanted that to go on, to be with him across the lifespan, to watch his hair grow gray and see what other changes age might bring to both of them.

She wanted to weather those changes together. But it wasn't going to happen, and her throat tightened at the thought of losing him.

"All right." He led her to a bench that looked out over

the bay. He waited until she'd sat down, and then sat down himself, next to her.

She looked at his dear face, tears prickling at her eyes.

He touched her face, wiped a tear with his thumb, and then she realized she was already crying.

"Why are you sad?" he asked. "It's a happy time."

"Not when you don't want me."

He looked puzzled. "Why would you think that?"

Tears were running down her face now. "What you said at the dogfight," she managed.

"I didn't mean any of that." He shook his head, gripping her hand. "I wanted to protect you. To protect you and Sunny, and they were getting more violent when they thought we were connected. That's all. I never meant to hurt you." He took her hand and brought it to his mouth for a light kiss. "I *am* sorry I left you alone to deal with that situation. Really sorry. Going to try and help my ex was bad judgment, and it won't happen again."

She studied him. "Why'd you do it, then?"

He shook his head. "I know how competent you are, and how incompetent she is. I thought you could handle everything yourself, but even if you could, you shouldn't have to."

Did he mean it? "I thought she was your priority. It sure seemed that way."

"Nope. You are. I'm going to try to ensure that you never doubt that again. Because the thing is, Bisky, I love you."

"You what?" She sucked in a breath, and heat seemed to spread within her. Her heart raced and she couldn't say anything more. She could only watch his face.

She must have imagined hearing that. Pure wishful thinking.

"I love you." He repeated the words, so yes, she'd heard them correctly, but they didn't compute. Didn't match what he'd said at the dogfight. Dismantled in a flash all of her carefully constructed arguments for why she'd be fine, just fine, without him.

He clasped her hand in both of his. "Sunny is on board with this, by the way, although I doubt she'll approve of my doing it without a bunch of cameras on us."

Doing *what*?

He looked directly into her eyes. "I love you for your strength and your goodness. I love you because we have a past together and because you're a friend, my best friend." He reached out and brushed a finger across her cheek and through her hair. "And you're beautiful, that's part of it. An important part, but not the main thing."

Was she dreaming? She had to be dreaming. Somehow, it was a lifelong dream she hadn't known she had, and she didn't want to wake up.

He took both her hands then, and sank down onto his knees. "I know there's not much chance that this will work or that you'll say yes, but I have to ask. Will you marry me?"

"I thought you were leaving." Bisky stared at him, her heart pounding so hard that it was difficult to breathe. "Did you just ask me to marry you?"

He nodded. "I did." He reached into his pocket and pulled out a little box and opened it. And that was what convinced her that she wasn't, in fact, dreaming, because the ring he was offering was a pearl. A natural pearl in an antique gold setting, the rarest, most joyous find for an oysterman. How perfect.

She looked from the ring to his dear face, tears prickling at her eyes as everything she'd ever wanted came together, like a puzzle. She *did* have William. She wasn't losing him. William and Sunny got along. She'd have companionship and company and love in her coming years, and it was wonderful.

"You're probably thinking about whether I can help support the family," he said.

She shook her head, but he went on. "There's a new job opening up, helping to prepare some of the shoreline kids for college. I heard about it from Trey's wife, Erica. I'm going to apply for it. But if I don't get it, I'll find work. I would work at anything to be with you."

"Oh, William." She slid down then, right into his lap, and he wrapped his arms around her and planted his lips on hers, and it was a kiss for the record books, so powerful and intense and full of love.

Finally he lifted his head and wiped her tears with his thumbs. "Did you say yes?"

"No, but yes. Yes, yes, yes."

It wasn't until they'd stood and started walking back to her place, she leaning her head against his shoulder, he with his arm around her, that Sunny came running up the street behind them, calling "Mom, Mom, wait!" She had Kaitlyn and Venus with her, and they all were holding up their phones. "Thanks for making it incredibly hard on us," Sunny accused William. "All we got was distance shots. How are we going to post that?"

He turned, Bisky at his side, to face her daughter. "Don't you even want to know what she said?"

Sunny laughed. "I don't even have to ask. It's written all over your faces."

And in our hearts, Bisky thought as she reached out to include her daughter in their embrace. In our hearts.

EPILOGUE

THE DAY THEY dedicated the Blue House dawned hot and clear.

Bisky walked ahead of William and Sunny, who were dawdling, discussing Xena and Muffin and their training as their dogs heeled perfectly beside them. It was nine o'clock in the morning, early for a teenager to be up, and she and William had just gotten back from their Rocky Mountain honeymoon two days ago. They'd been married three wonderful months, but they'd delayed their honeymoon until crabbing season was over. They'd hiked, and kayaked, and made love under the stars. It had been wonderful.

Mary stood on the porch of the Blue House amidst the small crowd that had already gathered, and when she saw William, Bisky and Sunny, she beckoned them to join her there. "Come on, you're the stars of the show," she said as she led them toward what was the effective center stage, the top of the steps.

The real stars, though, were the dogs: Xena, Muffin and the two additional pit bulls they'd rescued from the dog-fights. Those two were staying at the Blue House, along with the caretaker they'd gotten just recently, Mandy Smith. She claimed not to be a dog trainer, but she liked dogs and was willing to watch over the small kennel they were developing.

Sunny was doing the training with William's help, and loving it.

As Mary made a little speech, thanking everyone who had helped either financially or physically with getting the

Blue House into shape, Bisky looked around. There were Ria and Drew with their daughters. Paul and Amber stood, young Davey at their side. And Erica and Trey were beside Ria and Drew, holding little Hunter.

As Mary wound up her speech, Sunny hugged her, said a few poised words of her own, and then hurried down the steps to be with her friends. Venus and Kaitlyn gathered to one side, with Caden and Avery beside them. Caden was also helping with the Blue House, staying with Aiden and Avery.

"What's the name of the dog program going to be?" someone called out.

Mary looked over at the teenagers. "Do you want to announce it, Sunny?"

Sunny smiled and nodded. "Fighters to Friends," she said. "Because if all goes well, we'll be training these fighters to be therapy dogs."

There was general applause, and then people broke up to look around the facility and partake of the food that Goody had catered: pastries, and fruit, made-to-order omelets and coffee.

Bisky didn't love the heat, so she sat down in the shade to cool off. Immediately, William was there to hover over her. "Are you okay? Is this too much for you?"

Bisky laughed. "I'm not a delicate flower."

"I know that, but you *are* in a delicate condition, as they say," William said. He couldn't keep the grin off his face.

Bisky put a hand to her stomach, knowing her own smile matched his. "Shh."

Sunny came over and knelt in front of her. "Are you getting overheated?"

Bisky threw up her hands. "Between the two of you, this pregnancy is going to drive me crazy," she said. Sunny and William were the only ones who knew, but they were as fussy as a whole army of relatives and nurses.

"Oh, my, are you expecting already?" Primrose Miller must have motored up silently on her scooter and now, her eyebrows were raised high.

Bisky put a finger to her lips, groaning inside. "We're trying to keep it quiet until I pass the three-month mark."

"Of course, dear," Primrose said, although her forehead wrinkled. That would be a real strain for Primrose, since she loved to be the first to share spicy news.

The dogs went crazy over a cat who had streaked across the front lawn, and William and Sunny got busy trying to calm them down. Then, they took Xena and Muffin through their tricks to the delight of the crowd.

Avery came and sat beside her. "They're really doing well," she said, nodding at the dogs.

"How are *you* doing?" Bisky asked her. The teenager was getting ready to leave for an early prep program at her college. She was the first recipient of the Jenna Gross Memorial Scholarship, and Bisky was sure she would make good use of it.

What Avery didn't know was that they'd done enough fundraising to double the scholarship. Bisky beckoned to William.

He was instantly at her side. That was one thing she was still getting used to: how attentive he was, how attuned to her. She thought it had to do with their long friendship, but she also was awestruck about his capacity for love and caring. Not only that, but she was discovering in herself a capacity for being loved, for letting someone in, for opening herself to someone else's caring and even, sometimes, taking charge.

"Do you want to announce…" She nodded sideways at Avery.

He frowned for a moment, and she read his emotions

easily: it would be hard for him to talk about the scholarship in front of a crowd.

"You don't need to do it publicly," she said. "Maybe we could just tell the twins."

"No, I can do it. I'll announce it if Mary will do it with me, since she's such a big donor. Let me talk to her." He squeezed Bisky's shoulder and walked over to where Mary was standing. They had a short conversation.

And then William put his fingers to his lips and gave a piercing whistle. As soon as the crowd quieted down, he began to speak, Mary standing beside him.

"Some of you know that, a few years ago, I lost my beautiful daughter, Jenna," he said, and the few conversations that were still going on came to a halt or were shushed. "Today, we want to announce the first recipients of the Jenna Gross Memorial Scholarship." He cleared his throat, and Bisky worried that he might break down, but he didn't. "It's a four-year college scholarship," he went on, "given to someone raised in Pleasant Shores who exhibits need."

"And aptitude," Mary said. "We had several applicants this year, all of whom show a lot of promise, but two stood out as just exactly the kind of young people we want to encourage and support."

Avery looked confused. She'd been told about the scholarship privately, but there had been no mention of a second recipient until now. At the last minute, Mary had decided to double her contribution so that both twins could attend college.

"Everybody," Mary went on, "please congratulate Avery and Aiden Sanford!"

There were cheers and hugs all around. Aiden and Avery gave short, teary speeches of thanks.

As the celebration continued, Kayla drifted over to talk to Bisky. "I just wanted to be the first, or one of the first, to congratulate you," she said.

"Oh, that's sweet," Bisky said. She studied Kayla. "But you sent such a nice wedding gift already."

"Not about the wedding, about the baby!"

Bisky's jaw dropped, and then she narrowed her eyes. "Primrose?"

Kayla nodded. "I'm sorry, was that supposed to be a secret? Because I think everyone knows."

Bisky let out a sigh. "Of course they do."

Kayla smiled at her. "You're already a terrific mom, and I know you'll be a terrific mom a second time. How does Sunny feel about it?"

"She's kind of taken over. This week, she's painting the nursery. I'm trying to talk her into still wanting to go away to college, but she says she doesn't want to be far away from her little sister or brother."

"That's sweet. You're very lucky." Kayla blinked a couple of times and then made an excuse and left.

Bisky watched Kayla walk away. She hated that Kayla seemed so lonely, and promised herself she'd round up the ladies for a night at the Gusty Gull this week. She'd be drinking juice or tea, but that was fine, drinking wasn't what it was all about. It was the friendship.

She watched William as he stopped to talk with Caden, who had been skirting the edge of the crowd. Caden still felt a little awkward in town gatherings, since his father had been taken away to prison so publicly. But Pleasant Shores was the kind of town that helped people recover and made allowance for problems in the background, and Caden was basically being embraced by the community.

Especially by William, who knew all too well what it was to have a difficult family life and a problematic father.

William's own father was serving time, but William visited him every month. Bisky and Sunny had gone once, too. He was a troubled man and he'd done horrible things to his family, but through therapy and an understanding pastor, and time to think, he seemed to be reaching a better place. Bisky felt like his father's rehabilitation was helping William heal.

William looked in her direction, clapped Caden on the shoulder, and came back over to sit beside her. "How are you, beautiful? Are you happy?"

"So happy." She leaned into him, enjoying his warmth and strength.

He put an arm around her and pulled her close. "Me too. I never thought I'd be happy again, and I definitely never thought it would be in Pleasant Shores."

"With the childhood friend you used to have adventures with," she said. "Who would have figured?"

He leaned closer and kissed her cheek and then growled into her ear. "Here's to new adventures with old friends."

Muffin ran over and nudged her leg, and Xena did the same to William. The breeze cooled her skin.

Bisky nodded, unable to speak. Overcome with emotion, and maybe it was because of the child she was carrying inside her.

She'd always been a happy person, and she'd had so much that was good in her life. But now, her heart was full to bursting.

She looked at him and admired the strong line of his jaw, the thoughtfulness of his eyes. He was a strong man, and a deep man, with a big heart.

"I feel blessed," she said.

"I love you," he said at the same time.

And then, completely disregarding their friends and family and neighbors around them, they shared a slow and tender kiss.

* * * * *

SECOND CHANCE
ON THE CHESAPEAKE

CHAPTER ONE

"TIME TO CELEBRATE our freedom," Gemma McWharter informed her elderly Chihuahua mix, Fang, tucking him more securely against her side. She put down her suitcase so she could ring her cousin's doorbell. Then she stepped back and inhaled deeply.

February on the Chesapeake. Cold, but not the same kind of cold as she'd left behind in north-central Pennsylvania. The air smelled salty and felt a little balmy, and it took her back to childhood summers spent with the poorer—but happier—branch of her family.

She knocked on the door again. "Bisky? Are you there?" Did she have the wrong day? Her ex would've said it was just like her—always screwing up, spacing out, getting things wrong.

Fang gave two short yaps, and she kissed the top of his head and set him down. Only then did she see the note, a torn spot on top suggesting it had fallen down from the nail it had been hanging on.

Come on in, make yourself at home, you know where everything is. I'll be home by six, with wine. We'll have a blast.

Relieved, Gemma smiled and let herself in. Bisky was still Bisky, her favorite cousin. She'd been right to come.

Fang trotted ahead of her into the living room and then

looked back, panting. His open mouth revealed his single tooth, the reason for his name. "Go ahead, explore," she encouraged him, and he began sniffing the perimeter of the room.

Gemma kicked off her shoes and looked around Bisky's big, comfortable home, its lived-in style a far cry from the McMansion Gemma had lived in with her husband, or her parents' grand estate. A couple of boat paintings adorned the walls, but the house wasn't overdecorated with nets and shells and fake crab pots, like the tourist places.

A month ago, during a phone conversation, Bisky had mentioned she wanted to redo her attic as a surprise for her teenage daughter, Sunny, while she was away on a school trip. Gemma had jumped at the opportunity to help. Bisky did okay with crabbing and oystering, but there wasn't money for luxuries. Gemma could be useful for her strong, confident cousin, for once.

Besides, she needed practice at redoing spaces for an actual client, and the before-and-after photos would add to the meager collection on her new website.

Visiting the Eastern Shore would give her a break from her family while she decided on her next move. The week away would give Mom time to recover from the fact that Gemma—quiet, backward Gemma—had done what Mom couldn't: leave a marriage to an unfaithful, unloving husband. It would also give her bullying brother, Ron, time to cool down about her divorcing his best friend.

Fang didn't do stairs as well as he used to, so Gemma carried him up the two flights to the attic to get a preliminary look at the week's project.

The scent of newly cut pine came through the open door, and dust particles danced in the slanting beam of late-afternoon light. A dormer looked out over the bay. This was going to be a gorgeous room for a teenager.

She set Fang down and he ran across the space, yapping. She followed him and then recognized all the hazards: sawdust, an open can of paint and even a couple of scattered nails. "Fang, come!" she ordered, but the indulged little dog trotted into the attached bathroom, ignoring her, still yapping.

She hurried after him and felt something sharp pierce the arch of her sock-clad foot. "Ow! Ow! Ow!" She hopped to the wall, watching her step this time, and reached down to disentangle the carpet tack strip that had attached itself to her wool sock and punctured her foot in what felt like several places. "Fang! Get back here!"

Of course, he didn't listen.

She limped toward the bathroom to save him... And ran directly into an enormous, flannel-clad chest.

"Whoa!" She double-stepped back, her heart pounding.

The giant stepped back, too, and picked Fang up. Fang growled, and the man deposited him in her arms. "Sorry to startle you, ma'am."

That voice was so familiar. She looked more closely at the man in front of her and felt her face heat. "Isaac?"

"Gemma?" he said at the same time. "Are you all right? What happened?"

Fang yapped madly at him from the safety of Gemma's arms while Gemma tried to collect herself. What was Isaac doing here? How had he gotten even better looking than when they'd been friends in their teenage years?

Were he and Bisky an item?

Tucking Fang into the crook of one arm, she gestured toward her foot. "Stepped on some carpet tack," she said. "I wasn't watching where I was going. Are you...do you live here?"

"No!" He laughed like that was funny. "I'm just remodeling the bathroom and putting in a window seat, a few things like that," he explained. "Bisky pulled out the carpet yesterday. I'm sorry I didn't clean up—"

She waved a hand. "Not your fault. I'll be fine."

"That has to sting, though." He frowned down at her foot, then looked at her face. "I didn't know you were visiting Bisky."

"I'm decorating," she said. "Here from Pennsylvania for a week." She stepped backward—she still felt too close to him with his considerable physical presence—and winced as her injured foot hit the ground.

"Come, let me take a look." He gestured her toward the bathroom. "Sit on the edge of the tub and take your sock off. The least I can do is offer first aid."

She did as he'd said and then wished she hadn't. The bathroom was small, and Isaac… Wasn't. She cuddled Fang, and the little dog alternately cowered close and then craned his neck to try to sniff Isaac.

Isaac knelt in front of her and lifted her foot to look underneath. "Those tacks got you a couple of places," he said. "Nothing deep, and they're bleeding pretty good, so you shouldn't need a tetanus shot. Let me clean them up and put something on them."

"It's okay," she said, but he was already wetting a clean white rag. He added hand soap and then gently lifted her foot.

Her heart thumped. "You don't have to—"

"Gemma. I feel responsible." He looked up at her and she sucked in a breath. Oh, those eyes. Soulful brown eyes that had romanced her into her first kiss—what was it—twenty years ago?

He washed her foot gently and then rinsed the washcloth and wiped the soap away. "Sit still while I grab my first aid kit," he said, and walked out of the bathroom.

Gemma might not have been able to move, anyway. She felt a little limp from the shock of discovering Isaac here.

"Antibiotic and bandages." He came back into the bathroom, knelt down and smeared ointment on her injuries.

"So," he said as he fitted a square of gauze to her foot, then taped it into place, "what have you been doing for the past twenty years?" He looked up at her with a grin, and then she remembered his dimple. Warmth spread through her.

Oh man. She did *not* need to be thinking about how cute he was. This vacation was about her being *free* from men, not getting attracted to an inappropriate one just weeks after her divorce had finally gone through.

"This and that," she said airily. Because, really, what *had* she accomplished? She'd gone to college, married a man pre-approved by her parents and older brother, and lived miserably with him. They hadn't been able to have children. He hadn't wanted her to work. "I'm starting a redecorating service, and Bisky is one of my first clients. Well, I'm doing it for her for free, since she's family. Plus, she's putting me up for a week at the shore."

"Fair enough." He patted the bandage and then pulled her sock on again, carefully, as if she were a child. "There you go. All better."

"Thank you." She started to stand, and then he was too close and she sat down again.

Immediately, he backed out of the little bathroom. "I'm going to sweep this place up right now," he said. "Hold on to your dog. I wasn't expecting anyone else here, which is why it's such a mess. Careless of me."

"I'm surprised Bisky didn't tell you I was coming." She looked around, frowning. The room was finished, but bare bones. It needed a lot of work.

Footsteps sounded on the stairs. "Did I hear my name?" Bisky asked, walking in from the hall. "Hey, girl, you're here!" She opened her arms, smiling hugely.

Gemma's shoulders relaxed, and she walked into her

cousin's arms for a big hug, Fang growling indignantly as he was squashed between them.

"Girl, you're a sight for sore eyes." Bisky stepped back and studied her. "You let your hair grow! And you've got so much style."

"Thanks." Gemma glanced down at her floral dress, then back at her cousin, clad in a plain, long-sleeved T-shirt and jeans. Bisky was the definition of a natural beauty. "And you're looking great, too. I thought you'd be coming from work."

"Believe me, I wouldn't smell this good just back from a day of oystering. Today I was off. Had to visit a friend and pick up wine." She looked around the attic. "Are we really going to get this done by the time Sunny gets home?"

Gemma studied the room doubtfully. "Depends what you're doing to the floor. If we have to restain it, then I don't see how."

Bisky shook her head. "She likes carpet," she said. "So Isaac's going to put that down, and finish the bathroom and the window seat. Right?" She looked at him. "Can you get away from the hardware store for that long?"

"I can work here every evening. We asked a couple of the part-timers to put in more hours, so I can squeeze in a couple full days as well." Isaac gave her a reassuring smile. "Don't worry, we'll get 'er done."

"Terrific. But what am I thinking? We don't have to stand here." Bisky backed out of the room, beckoning to them. "Come downstairs, and I'll open the wine, and we can figure out how you two are going to get this project done in a week."

Gemma tilted her head and glanced at Isaac, whose brow was furrowed. Obviously, he hadn't known he'd be working with her, just as she hadn't known she'd be working with him.

And how uncomfortable was that, working with the guy

who'd given you your first kiss? They'd left things on a weird note all those years ago, and then Gemma had only been back to Pleasant Shores a couple of times—once when a distant relative had married, and once when Sunny was born—to help for a couple of weeks. She hadn't seen Isaac either time. She had no idea of whether he was married or single, what he'd done, how he'd changed.

It was going to be an interesting week.

CHAPTER TWO

ISAAC SAT AT Bisky's kitchen table, turned down the offer of wine and studied Gemma, the woman who'd reappeared in his life after twenty years.

He'd have known her anywhere: porcelain skin, mahogany curls and that shy way she turned her eyes away. He'd thought her gorgeous as a teenager, and she still was, maybe more so. She'd been sweet and kind inside, too, or so he'd thought.

But his family had been right: it was a mistake to get involved with the summer people. Technically, she was more than a summer person; being Bisky's cousin, she wasn't exactly a tourist. But still, she was from a different world. She had expensive clothes. She hadn't had to work. She'd had the accents and speaking style of someone who attended a fancy private school.

And she'd gone on to marry a rich man, just as his mother had predicted. The same man who'd shown up the last week of the last summer with Gemma's brother, Ron, driving a Porsche and throwing his money around.

So what was she doing back here now, without a wedding ring?

"I'm sorry to spring this on both of you," Bisky said. "I'd thought Isaac would be done with his part by the time you got here, Gem, but it didn't work out that way."

"My fault," Isaac said. "We had a flood at the store, and cleanup had to take priority."

Bisky winced. "Yeah, that was rough. I know you must have taken a financial hit, too. You're good to still make the time to do my project."

Of course he had; he liked Bisky, but additionally, he had to take on all the work he could manage just to keep his mom and his aunt and his store afloat. There was no time for leisure.

No time for dating. No time for a woman like Gemma, who no doubt was used to being wined and dined. She probably lived in a gated community, and he knew from Bisky's updates over the years that she'd traveled the world.

Isaac, by contrast, lived in the house he'd grown up in and had done nothing except stay home and work.

He needed to get his old feelings for Gemma right out of his mind.

"So," Bisky said, reaching for a folder stuffed with papers and magazine clippings, "here are some pictures Sunny showed me a few months ago, when she was begging me to redo her room. I made like I couldn't afford it. So this is going to be a surprise."

Gemma studied the pictures. Isaac leaned over to look, too, and ended up getting a whiff of something flowery from her hair. Resolutely, he moved away.

"Looks like we'll need to do some shopping," Gemma said to Bisky. "Or maybe you'll just send me out for stuff, if you have to work. Then, honestly, it'll be a full-time job to get it all done this week."

"True for me, too," he said.

"Can you work together," Bisky asked, "or will you just be in each other's way?"

Gemma looked at him the same moment he looked at her, and their gazes tangled for the briefest of moments. Doe eyes, that was what she had. As wild and shy as the sika deer that roamed the Eastern Shore.

"We can work together, I think." Gemma bit her lip. "I mean, I can."

"Me, too." He looked away from her pretty mouth and thought about spending the next few days in close quarters with her. Heat coursed in his veins.

It was going to be quite a week.

AFTER ISAAC LEFT, Gemma glared, only half-jokingly, at Bisky. "Did you plan this?"

"Plan what?" Bisky raised her eyebrows, a smile tugging at the corners of her mouth.

"This! Me and Isaac, working together all week!"

"Nope." Bisky held up her hands, palms out. "It truly was an accident. I thought he'd be done by the time you got here. But—" she grinned "—now that it's happening, I think I like it."

"I don't!" Gemma picked up Fang and put him on her lap, where he rolled onto his back for a belly rub. "I'm supposed to be celebrating freedom from men. And now I'm thrown together with Isaac Roberts. The handsomest man alive!"

"He *is* handsome," Bisky agreed. "A really, really good guy, too."

Gemma looked quickly at her cousin. "Do you... Is there anything between you?"

"With Isaac? No. No way. He's like a brother." She paused. "But everyone in town knows how much he's sacrificed for his family. That's all I meant. He's one of the good ones."

Gemma felt unaccountably relieved. "How about you? Are you seeing anyone?"

Bisky shook her head. "You know me. I'm busy raising Sunny and working."

"I thought you sometimes dated when Sunny was away." Gemma took a sip of wine.

Bisky leaned back in her chair, shrugging a little. "It gets old, these short-term things."

She sounded a little sad, and that wasn't like Bisky. "Did something happen?" Gemma asked.

"I just grew up, I guess. Don't worry about me. I'm fine. My life is full." She refilled Gemma's glass and then her own. "But my life's also boring, whereas you... Man, girl, sounds like you've had some excitement. How'd you get the guts to dump *el jerko*?"

"My friend, the high-powered lawyer." Gemma rubbed a finger around the rim of her wineglass. "She told me exactly how to get my money and paperwork together and then file when he was off on a so-called fishing trip. He didn't want to end the marriage because of how it would look, but he also didn't want to be any kind of a husband to me. Not when I'm so boring compared to his special friends at the club."

Bisky snorted. "I assume the special friends were in their twenties and blonde?"

"And busty," Gemma said. "Turns out he likes busty." Which Gemma wasn't.

"Told ya so," Bisky said, but lightly. It was true; on the night before Gemma's wedding, Bisky had taken her out for drinks and had a talk with her.

"Why are you marrying him?" she'd asked bluntly. She'd come up for Gemma's wedding, had only just met Jeff, but she'd disliked him on sight.

"No one else is going to ask me," Gemma had said. She was echoing what her mother and brother had told her, but she knew it was true. She was shy and backward and not that pretty. "I want kids."

"You can have kids other ways." Bisky had sounded completely exasperated. "You have a college degree. Use it! Move somewhere away from your family and get a job.

Come to Pleasant Shores and stay with me! Just don't marry a man you don't love."

In some part of herself, Gemma had known she should take Bisky's advice. But the relationship and the wedding had built up a momentum of its own. She hadn't had the courage, back then, to put a stop to it.

"You were right," Gemma said now, rubbing Fang's ears.

"Men." Bisky reached out for Fang, and Gemma passed him over. "You're the best little man, aren't you, buddy?" She held him like a baby, which he tolerated for only a moment before struggling to right himself. Bisky handed him back to Gemma. "You know, I'm generally not that big of a dog person, but I like your little guy. He has attitude."

"He's been great. My best friend through all this."

"I'm glad you have him, then." Bisky gave a great yawn. "Sorry. I can't wait to spend more time hanging out, but for now, I have to go to bed. Four in the morning comes early. Let me show you where you're sleeping."

They cleaned up their glasses and then headed to the second floor, Bisky leading the way, Gemma carrying her suitcase. On the threshold of the guest room, Gemma's throat tightened.

All along one side of the room was baby stuff: a crib, a changing table, a rocker.

"Sorry it's got so much junk," Bisky said. "I cleared out the attic and didn't have anywhere to put this stuff... Oh, hon, what's wrong?"

Gemma shook her head and cleared her throat. "It's nothing. It's just...we were going to adopt, and I had the nursery all ready, and then it fell through." She swallowed hard. "Twice."

"Oh no!" Bisky folded her into a hug. "I'll sleep here, and you take my room."

"No, it's fine. I'll be fine."

"I can't believe you went through that without telling me."

"I actually couldn't talk about it. Still can't. You need to go to bed." She turned her back on the baby furniture, put her suitcase on the bed and opened it.

"Are you okay?" Bisky still had a hand on her shoulder. "To stay in here and to do the attic?"

"Of course! I'm fine. I'll make the attic great for Sunny," Gemma promised.

She'd just have to figure out a way to do that without going crazy working in tight quarters with the man she'd never forgotten.

A WEEK WORKING closely with Gemma McWharter was going to be even tougher than Isaac had thought.

He'd kept busy finishing the bathroom update as soon as she'd started work on the bedroom, but he couldn't caulk all night. He was supposed to get the bedroom's window seat fitted and planed out today, but she was out there painting walls, cute and sexy in a skimpy tank top and jeans. He wasn't going to be able to pretend she wasn't there.

"Do you need help painting?" he asked finally.

She looked down from the sheet-covered chair she was standing on. "I wouldn't turn it down," she said. "But don't you have things to do yourself?"

"Can't put in the window seat until the walls are done," he said. "May as well help you get there."

"Then sure," she said promptly. "Trim or roller?"

"Roller," he said, and so she continued painting along the edges while he poured paint into a pan and started rolling it onto the wall she'd already edged.

"I'm glad Bisky didn't choose bright purple or pink," Gemma said. "I thought girls usually liked those kinds of colors, but apparently, Sunny prefers neutrals. The gray is going to be gorgeous."

"Sunny's a great kid," Isaac said. "Works hard and helps her mom. And funny."

They painted in silence for a little while, and then she spoke. "If you don't mind my asking... How come you didn't get married and have kids?"

He glanced back over his shoulder at her. He rarely got this question anymore, since everyone in Pleasant Shores knew him and his situation. "I don't even have time to date, what with taking care of Mom and running the store."

"What's going on with your mother?" she asked as she carefully ran her brush along the woodwork that framed the window. "You don't live with her, do you?"

"I do." He stood back to examine the wall he'd just finished painting, looking for bare spots. "Not many women want to date a thirty-seven-year-old man who still lives with his mother. She has Parkinson's," he clarified, "and she can't stay alone anymore. Works for both of us."

He glanced over to see that she'd stopped painting to look at him, her lips turning down. "I'm so sorry. How is she doing?"

"Her spirits are good. She does as much of the housework as she can. Still cooks a mean lasagna."

She clapped her hands lightly. "I remember! Hers was the best."

"Still is," he said, although the truth was, Mom struggled to remember the ingredients these days. It wasn't to the level of cognitive impairment, but she had trouble focusing. "Tell me about you. What's been going on?"

She smiled a little. "Uh-uh, you don't get to change the subject yet," she said. "You don't have kids, and you don't date much, okay. What *do* you do?"

He moved to the next wall and started rolling on paint. "I work," he said.

"At the store?"

He nodded. "Plus I do side jobs like this one."

"So you're putting in, what, twelve hours a day?" Her tone was joking.

He nodded. "At least."

"Is that necessary?" She sounded shocked. "Wow." After a moment's silence, she added, "I'm sorry. I've never been in need, and I don't know what it would be like to work two jobs."

He looked back over his shoulder at her. "We're not in need, exactly. It's important to me to build up enough savings that Mom would be taken care of, if anything happened to me," he said. "Plus, the store has been in the family for decades. It's an important part of the town, but it barely scrapes by."

"Why? Are people hitting the big box stores instead of staying in town?"

He nodded. "Some support us, but it's always a gamble as to whether we'll be in the black any given month. So we don't want to hire outside managers. Me and my aunt, between us, we cover the shifts."

"Isn't she getting kind of old?"

He grinned. "Don't let her hear you say that. She feels and acts young. She's been climbing ladders and lifting boxes her whole life, plus spending most of every day talking to customers. Seems to be a recipe for good health."

"Good for her."

They painted a little while longer, and when he'd done all he could, he put down his roller. Standing beside the sheet-covered dresser in the middle of the room, he took a long draw from his water bottle. "This place is looking good."

She came to the center of the room and turned slowly around, scanning it. Then she smiled up at him. "Thanks for helping me get the painting done. I'll help you with your part however I can."

Their gazes met and held. He could see the gold circles

around her pupils, the pink flush across her cheeks. His heart thumped, then settled into a rapid pounding.

He remembered the first time he'd kissed her, how hard it had been for him to work up the courage, how surprised he'd been that they both seemed to know what to do and that it felt so good.

He should be smoother now, but he wasn't. "You have paint on your chin" was what came out of his mouth. He pulled a bandanna from his back pocket and wiped at it.

He was so close now that he could smell her lemony perfume.

His eyes flickered down to her lips and then back to those gorgeous eyes. He remembered more than the first kiss now; he remembered how quickly things had intensified between them as the summer had gone on, and how hard it had been to pull back.

Her eyes darkened, and he could tell she was remembering it, too.

Mom and Aunt Jean had warned him against getting so close to her, and in the end, they'd been right. Which was why he shouldn't kiss her now.

She made the decision for him. "Well, hey, thanks again!" She stepped away, her cheeks going pinker.

Thanks for what? For almost kissing her? For *not* kissing her? And then he realized she was talking about the painting. "You're welcome. Think I'll go home and check on Mom." His voice sounded a little funny.

As he walked home, he wondered about it. He knew what had made him hesitate, but what had made her back away?

CHAPTER THREE

THE NEXT DAY, Isaac walked into the hardware store two minutes late, knowing he'd hear about it, rubbing his eyes. Trying to rub away the image of Gemma and her full, pretty lips, but that was futile.

"A little help here?" His aunt—great-aunt, really, his mom's aunt—was struggling with a large box.

He hurried over to take it from her. "You should have waited for me."

"I might've," she said, "but Goody is out back waiting for us to load this into her car, and you know how impatient she can get."

He did. He carried the box through the store to the back entrance and loaded it into Goody's ancient, wood-paneled station wagon, trying unsuccessfully to stifle a yawn.

"Glad you saw fit to finally wait on me," Goody snapped as she drove off. Goody ran the local ice cream shop and was known for being cranky.

Aunt Jean glared after Goody's car, then sighed. "We can't afford to alienate her."

"Sorry I was late." Isaac knew that all too well. If they couldn't offer better service than the big box stores, that was where people would go, and they'd be out of business.

As they walked back inside, she put an arm around him. "You've been working extra, haven't you?"

He nodded. "Things are tight."

He didn't need to say more; Aunt Jean understood. As

small business owners, they bought their own insurance, and even the minimal plan was hard to afford. When his mom needed extra treatments, each one was an expense.

"What are you working on?" she asked.

"Bisky's converting her attic into a new bedroom for Sunny. I'm doing some of the woodwork and plumbing."

"I hear her cousin Gemma is there." Aunt Jean frowned.

Isaac nodded. "She's starting a redecorating business. Kind of practicing on Bisky's project."

They'd reached the middle of the store now. A few customers had come in and were strolling the aisles, shopping, but no one was ready to check out yet.

They both walked around then, checking on people, making sure they could find what they needed. Then Aunt Jean came to straighten paint cans beside Isaac. "So you're working with Gemma, spending time with her?"

"A little, looks like. We have to get the remodel and the decorating done this week."

"Bad idea." Aunt Jean shook her head. "I don't like it."

"She's changed. She's nice."

"You stay away from her," Aunt Jean said darkly. "She's not our kind."

"Are we really still doing that?" He pulled out a rag to dust the bottom shelf paint cans. "Separating people out into categories, our kind and the rest?" Gemma had seemed nothing but sweet last night. Sweet, and beautiful.

"Our type and the rich snobs," Aunt Jean snapped. "Like Gemma McWharter and her family. She treated you like dirt before, and she'll do it again. You don't deserve it." She patted his shoulder. It was her version of a hug and he smiled at her.

A movement down the aisle caught his eye as he looked over at his aunt. Gemma stood there, her little dog in her arms, her face stricken. Clearly, she'd overheard.

GEMMA STARED AT ISAAC and his aunt. *Our type and the rich snobs. Like Gemma McWharter and her family.*

Was her family viewed that way still? Was she?

It wasn't that far from the mark with her family, she had to admit. Money and status were everything to them. But she was different. Wasn't she?

Reflexively, she hugged Fang closer. She'd thought Isaac liked her, thought he was going to kiss her, but if this was the way he felt…

"Gemma." Isaac stood and approached her, his face compassionate. "Are you okay?"

"I'm fine." She nodded. Best to pretend she hadn't overheard. She didn't want him to pity her.

"Aunt Jean, she's…" He gestured behind him, where his aunt had disappeared. "She's got some outdated views."

He was trying to make her feel better. But that was because he was nice, not because he cared.

He reached out and rubbed the top of Fang's head, the movement of his hand mesmerizing. "Can I help you find something?"

"Uh, yeah." Why was she here again? She fumbled in her pocket. "I need three more screws like this, and a couple of boards sawed to size, if you do that."

"We do that. Screws first." He led her to the area filled with drawers of nails and screws. He held out his hand for her sample, and within seconds, had supplied the size she needed. "Three, you said?"

She nodded, feeling shy as a memory came back to her: shopping for a little project she'd done back home, she'd encountered a hardware store employee who couldn't stop making jokes about screws, loudly, nudging her and making another male employee laugh.

Isaac wouldn't do that, though.

He slid three screws into a tiny plastic bag, then beckoned her to the back of the store, where boards and two-by-fours sat near an old sawhorse. "What length do you need?"

She pulled out her phone, where she'd noted the measurements. "I'm making a hook row and teenagers always have a ton of clothes, so... I think six feet."

He lined up the board she chose and sawed it, and she had the pleasure of watching his very nice muscles play underneath his olive green T-shirt. Fang struggled, and she put him down. "Now be good," she ordered him. "Stay close to Mama."

"That dog is a hazard." Isaac's aunt bustled over, not meeting Gemma's eyes. "No dogs in the store."

Fang looked directly at her as he lifted his leg.

"No, Fang, no!" Gemma swooped him up just in time. "I took you potty right before we came in. You know better."

Fang looked at Aunt Jean and growled.

"I'll ring you up while Isaac finishes cutting those. I suppose you'll want them delivered, since your little sports car isn't meant for hauling?"

Gemma lifted her chin. "Yes, please." If Mrs. Decker thought she was a snob, she might as well play the part.

As she followed Isaac's aunt to the front of the store, though, her shoulders slumped. Yes, she had to make this redo work. And she would.

But no, Pleasant Shores wasn't going to be an uncomplicated safe haven for her. There was too much backstory, too much history. She didn't fit.

No one but Bisky would love her here.

Her shoulders slumped as her thoughts spiraled. Would anywhere else be any different?

Mrs. Decker rang up her purchase, and Gemma paid with her card. Then, Mrs. Decker looked past her and out the front window of the shop. "Here it comes," she said, her voice disgusted. "Roll out the red carpet. Summer people are starting to show up at all times of the year, more's the pity."

"Nice car," Isaac commented from behind her. "And we need the summer people's business, Aunt Jean. Paste on that smile." He patted the older woman's shoulder.

Gemma sighed. She herself was one of the summer people that Mrs. Decker was complaining about.

As she walked out the front door, Fang trotting beside her, the door of the expensive dark sedan opened.

When her brother emerged, Gemma's stomach lurched. "Ron! What are you doing here?"

"I saw your note on Bisky's door," he said. "I've come to take you home."

"Come to take me… No. Forget it."

He nodded implacably and gestured toward the car. "Come on, now. Jeff is very upset. So's Mom."

She raised an eyebrow. "Are they, now? And why's that?"

"You've never known where you fit in. We care about you. No one here does." He put an arm around her—something Ron never did—and she had a flash of thinking that maybe he was sincere and wanted what was best for her. That maybe she did fit in better with her family than with the people in this town. People like Mrs. Decker, now glaring through the front window of the hardware store.

No one in this town cared about her the way her family did, difficult as they were.

"Maybe you're right." She sighed and glanced up at Ron's face, seeking comfort.

She didn't find it. Instead, he was smiling, a big, self-congratulatory smile.

It made her pause. Was she really that easy to persuade? "I'll think about what you've said." She stepped away from him. "I'm not sure what I want to do."

"Of course you're not," he said impatiently. "You're never sure."

His tone brought back all the things she didn't like about living with her family. She walked a few feet away.

It was as if the distance removed the spell he'd cast on her. She could leave Pleasant Shores, yes. She probably would. But she'd made a commitment to Bisky, and despite any issues with the people here, with Isaac, despite any reputation her family had, she needed to fulfill her obligation to her cousin.

She opened her mouth to say as much to her brother when he stepped forward and picked up Fang.

"Hey," she said, "he doesn't like it when—"

"I'll just put him in the car," Ron said smoothly, and walked it that direction.

She held on tight to the leash. "Wait a second! You can't—"

"Come on." He pulled on the dog.

Fang's collar tightened and he yelped. The pull on his neck was hurting him. Gemma dropped the leash.

Ron strode faster toward the car.

Gemma's heart turned over. Could Ron really be so awful as to… "Fang!" she cried. "Ron, give him to me this minute!"

But Ron tucked the dog under one arm and opened the car's back door.

ISAAC STRODE TOWARD the exit of the store. He couldn't let her jerk of a brother take her dog.

"Don't involve yourself." His aunt followed him, putting a restraining hand on his arm. "Nothing but heartache that way."

He appreciated his aunt's loyalty: she'd stood by his side, in so many ways, especially running the store and caring for his mom. But she wasn't right about everything. He stopped and gave her shoulders a little squeeze. "Have to help," he said, and marched out, reaching the big dark sedan's back door just as Gemma's brother—Ron, if he recalled correctly—was starting to close it. Inside, Fang whined pitifully.

Isaac shoved the man out of the way and looked across the car at Gemma. "Do you want Fang in here?"

"No!" She rushed around the car, reached in past Isaac and picked up the dog. She cuddled the quivering little creature close to her chest as she walked away from the car, then looked back at Isaac. "Thank you! My poor baby!"

Ron glared at Isaac. "Hands off my car."

Isaac lifted his hands immediately and held them up. "Not interested in your car."

Ron snorted. "Nicest car you'll ever see, working at your mom's hardware store. You locals."

Mom can't work here anymore. But he didn't put words to the thought. That wasn't of interest to Ron, nor to Gemma either, most likely.

And what Ron had said was true: he *was* a local, a small-town man tied to a family business. Gemma and her family were out of his league.

"Loser." Ron's lip curled.

It was what had happened before, years ago: Ron and his friend had made Isaac feel small, and he'd given up. But now, as he looked at Gemma, something reconfigured in his mind, like the pieces clicked together differently.

He looked at Ron's sneering face. "I earn an honest wage and I help people." Maybe it wasn't what would impress this family, including Gemma, but it was who he was.

"That's right." Goody had come out of her shop and now stood beside him. "He keeps the store running, and we need a hardware store here in Pleasant Shores."

"Wow, he keeps a small-town store running?" Ron's snotty implication was clear.

"He gave up everything for his family," Aunt Jean said from the other side of him. "He's worth ten of you."

Isaac stepped back and put an arm around each of the two older women. "Thanks," he said, meaning it, although his feelings were mixed. Someday, it would be nice to impress a woman his own age.

Someone like Gemma. But he wasn't going to wait around for her reaction. He gave Goody and Aunt Jean another quick shoulder squeeze, then turned and went back inside. He had a store to run.

"HE SAVED THE DAY, is what I heard!" Bisky lifted her glass of wine, and Gemma clinked her own against her cousin's. "He's your hero!"

Gemma shook her head. "He would have done the same for anyone. You should have seen how fast he got out of there."

"What did Ron do then?" Bisky asked, frowning. She and Ron had never gotten along.

"He cussed me out and left." Gemma shrugged. "Typical Ron. He doesn't like it when he doesn't get his way." She ran a finger around the edge of her glass. "They look down on me, you know."

"Who?"

"Isaac and his aunt," she said, and told of the remark she'd overheard.

"Oh, Mrs. Decker…" Bisky waved a hand. "She's a fixture in this town, and she's great most of the time, but she does get a little negative about tourists. Outsiders, really. You're not a tourist."

"But I *am* an outsider."

"You don't have to be." Bisky waved at the waiter and held up two fingers. "You know what, you should stay here."

"I *am* staying. I promised you I'd get Sunny's room remodel done, and I will." Although how she was going to work with Isaac, she didn't know.

Oh, he'd saved Fang, but that had been a general act of kindness. He'd left right away, without even responding to her thanks.

"That's great, but I meant you should stay on permanently."

Gemma looked out the window, where the bay shone like a silvery mirror. "Live here, you mean? Mom and Ron would never put up with it."

"Your mom and Ron aren't on your side. They never have been."

"But they're all I've got." Even as she said the words, bleakness settled in on her.

"Gemma. Think back. They shipped you off here every summer because they didn't want to deal with you, but you took what they did and made it a positive," she said. "And we love you. I love you. Sunny and I are family, too."

Gemma's eyes filled. "Thank you. I love you guys, and I love Pleasant Shores."

"It's a wonderful town," Bisky went on. "And I know, I think that because I live here, but everyone who gets to know the place falls in love with it. You could stay with me and Sunny until you got on your feet." She grinned. "You'd have to redecorate her old bedroom, but that's right up your alley."

"How would I get on my feet, though? It's not like I'm struggling, but I do need to earn a living, eventually. And I don't have the skills for most of the tourist-related jobs…"

Bisky waved a hand. "You don't want a tourist job. They last only six months of the year, so it's an incredible scramble for most. No, you should start your decorating business here."

"In Pleasant Shores? Who would pay me to decorate?"

"There are more and more wealthy people here, on the

other side of the peninsula. You could drum up a good business, helping them decorate. They're second homes for most, and they don't have a lot of time to devote to them."

The idea was actually intriguing. But Isaac… Could she live in the same town with him, see him often and know he scorned her? Could her heart take that?

She took a sip of wine and shook her head. "I just don't think I can do it."

CHAPTER FOUR

THE REST OF THE WEEK, Isaac and Gemma managed to avoid each other. Which was good, Isaac thought as he approached Bisky's house on the day Bisky's daughter, Sunny, was supposed to come home.

Bisky had insisted that both he and Gemma be present for the big reveal. Which meant he'd see Gemma today, probably for the last time.

He ran his fingers through his hair, always unruly, and knocked on Bisky's door.

Gemma answered, wearing red jeans and a white gauzy shirt, her hair loose around her shoulders. His mouth went dry.

Fang scampered out from the kitchen, barking madly, and she scooped him into her arms.

"Come on in," she said, and she sounded awkward, as awkward as he felt.

He wished things could have been different, wished she could stick around, that she wasn't from a family that had given her such high expectations.

He walked in. "Where's Bisky?"

"She went to Sunny's friend's house to pick Sunny up. She should be right back."

He cast about for something neutral to talk about. "Is everything ready?"

"For the big reveal? Yes, I think so."

Fang strained in her arms, staring at Isaac, struggling toward him.

"Do you want to take him?" she asked. "He's been touchy since the Ron thing."

"Sure." He felt fond of the dog by now, glad he'd been able to protect him from Gemma's brother.

She held out the dog, and Isaac tucked him snugly against his chest. Surprisingly enough, the dog settled immediately.

"We're home!" Bisky's voice came, loud.

"Who are you yelling to?" Sunny sounded cranky. Uh-oh. From what he'd seen of family groups at the hardware store, there was no cranky like teen girl cranky.

"We have company," Bisky said, ushering the girl in the door.

Sunny quickly concealed the irritated expression on her face, but not quickly enough that Isaac didn't see it. Oh well. Sunny was a nice girl, but she'd just gotten back from a school trip. She probably wanted her mom to herself.

"We'll be on our way soon, I promise, hon," Gemma said, giving Sunny the briefest of hugs. "I'm all packed."

She was packed? She was leaving?

She couldn't leave. Something close to panic rose up in Isaac's chest.

"So," Bisky said, "we need to head up to the attic for just a minute. These two are taking a box with them, and I want to make sure it's okay with you."

It seemed like a fairly ridiculous excuse. Sure enough, Sunny balked. "Whatever it is, it's fine," she said, yawning. "I just want to take a nap."

"Soon," Bisky said firmly, and to her credit, Sunny didn't protest anymore. She just sighed and stood up.

They all trooped up the stairs. Sunny glanced into her bedroom and did a double take. "What did you do to my room?"

"I'll explain in a minute. Up here, hon." Bisky ushered Sunny to the stairs that led to the attic. Isaac and Gemma trailed behind.

Bisky stepped aside so Sunny could go first.

Sunny wasn't paying a lot of attention, but when they got to the top, she stopped still, almost causing a pileup of people behind her.

"Mom? What did you do?" Sunny rushed to the window, then spun and looked at the bed, now covered with a pristine white spread and blue pillows. Gauzy curtains hung in the windows, and the carpet he'd put in looked nice, all newly vacuumed. No TV—Bisky had been adamant about that—but there was a low bookshelf holding schoolbooks and paperbacks.

"Just a little surprise," Bisky said, smiling with what looked like satisfaction.

"But how could you…money's so tight…" Sunny burst into tears and flung her arms around her mother. "I love it so much, Mom. Thank you."

Bisky looked shiny-eyed, too, as she held her daughter. Isaac felt more rewarded by this job than he had in ages. It was great to make a family happy.

Deep inside, he longed for a child of his own, because moments like this were what it was all about. Doing things for each other, making each other happy.

He felt an arm snake around his waist and looked down to see Gemma smiling up at him. "Good stuff," he said, and draped an arm over her shoulders.

She felt absolutely, perfectly right at his side.

Sunny was moving around the room now, looking into the bathroom, raving over the wall hangings.

And Bisky was laughing. "Don't give me too much credit," she said, gesturing toward Gemma and Isaac. "It's these two who did all the work."

Sunny came over then and hugged them both. "I can't believe you did this for me," she said. "I can't even tell you how happy I am right now. I'm going to love having this privacy and space."

Isaac saw Bisky's happy expression slip, just for a moment. Maybe she hadn't thought about it, but Sunny was going to spend a lot of time up here, away from her mother. It was right, and the nature of things, but it couldn't be easy for a single mom of one.

Bisky got a phone call and walked over to the far corner of the room to take it. Sunny grabbed Gemma's arm. "I'm worried about Mom."

"Why?" Gemma studied her.

"She had a week to herself. She used to, you know, go out and have fun, but now…"

"Now she just focuses on you?" Gemma smiled at Sunny. "You're a sweet child to care so much about her, but she'll be fine."

"But," Sunny said, her eyes filling, "I'm growing up, and I'll go away to college, and who will take care of her then?"

Funny that Sunny thought she took care of her mother rather than the reverse. "Your mom's pretty resourceful," he reminded her.

"And she's strong and smart and beautiful. If she wants companionship, she'll have it. Male or female." Gemma hugged Sunny. "Listen, I'm going to take off," Gemma said. "So glad you're happy with your new space, Sunny. Bisky," she called to her cousin, who'd just ended her phone call, "thanks for all your hospitality and for giving me the opportunity to do this."

"Thank you! It's perfect!" There was more hugging, and then Gemma started down the stairs.

She was leaving. He might never see her again. "I'll walk her out," he told Bisky.

She narrowed her eyes, studied his face for a minute and then nodded. "Sunny and I will be up here," she said. "Go."

GEMMA STEPPED CAREFULLY down the stairs, since her eyes were blurry with tears.

She was so happy for Bisky and Sunny. The satisfaction she felt at what she'd created—what they'd created—made her certain that starting her own interior design firm was the right thing to do. Homes helped families, and she wanted to help people have the perfect home.

She had to admit, she wanted a perfect home and perfect family for herself, but it wasn't going to happen. She'd tried and failed. Failed as a wife, and lost her chance as an adoptive mom.

Fang slept in a sunny spot by the window. She picked him up and made her way out to the car, but when she opened the door of it, there was Isaac behind her.

And that was what would make it really hard to leave. She loved it here, and she cared for Isaac a lot, but it wasn't going to work. He didn't feel the same.

The bay breeze was cool, the sun sparkling brightly on the water. She looked out across it and then turned to face Isaac. "Thank you for everything," she said. "That was a great project to do."

"It was," he said. "But Gemma…" He reached out and pushed back a lock of her hair.

He was going to kiss her goodbye. Just like he had before. It had rocked her teenage world and she'd never gotten over it.

"I wish you wouldn't go," he said.

She turned away and set Fang down into his little dog seat on the passenger side of the car. She had to avoid Isaac's kiss. Maybe then, she wouldn't be so sad.

"Gemma." He said her name forcefully, so forcefully that she turned back to face him. He was so handsome, and his eyes were so warm.

She felt like she couldn't breathe. "Yeah?" she managed to say.

"Gemma, I mean it. Don't go. Stay and let's see if we can make something of this."

His words soothed a sore, aching part of her heart, but she still felt insecure. "Your aunt said it. I'm not your kind. I won't fit in."

"You fit in perfectly. You *fit* perfectly." And then he was pulling her close and tucking her against him, and they *did* fit perfectly together.

He lowered his mouth to hers.

The kiss was epic. Of course, because it was the last.

After a moment, she pulled away. "I can't stand it," she said. Tears pressed at her eyes, but she wouldn't cry. Wouldn't let herself cry.

"You can't stand...what?" He looked puzzled, hurt.

"I can't stand for you to kiss me and leave me feeling so much when it's never going to work."

Fang barked behind her. She needed to get on with her drive, with her life. The trouble was, the life she was going back to seemed cold and desolate.

Isaac took her hands and held them firmly. "I just want you to explain," he said. "Okay, you're going to leave, but why? What is it? You don't like it here? You don't want to get involved with a man who's middle of the road in looks and success and income?"

He thought *he* was middle of the road? "Don't you see, Isaac, that I'm an outcast?"

He tilted his head and studied her, so closely that she felt self-conscious and looked away.

He touched her face, let his hand tangle in her hair. "No. I don't see that."

"Then you're not looking."

"I *am* looking. I see a woman who's stronger in the broken places. A woman who's gone through things and has scars, sure, but who's more beautiful for all she's been through.

A woman who's creative and funny and yeah, different, but different is good."

She gulped in a breath. "I *want* to believe you, but…" But she'd heard the reverse for most of her life, first from her family, and then from the husband they'd picked for her.

"I can make you believe if you'll stay and try," he said. "Stay and try." He held out his arms, but he didn't come closer. It was up to Gemma to decide.

She hesitated. There would be adjustments to make, efforts to fit in that might or might not work. A business to start.

A relationship to try, to take a chance on.

Back home there was… Familiarity? The comfort of knowing where she fit in, even if it wasn't a good place?

She looked at Isaac's strong, open face, his warm eyes. *Yes*, everything inside her said all at once, and she stepped forward.

Fang barked as they kissed again, and then Bisky and Sunny came out of the house. "You're still here!" Bisky sounded happy.

"I think…" Gemma said. "I think I'm going to stay in Pleasant Shores for a while."

"You are?" Bisky opened her arms wide. "I'm so glad. Let go of her, Isaac. I want to hug her, too."

"Yes!" Sunny pumped her fist. "You can keep Mom company."

Fang whined from his dog seat, and Isaac reached into the car and picked him up. "What do you think, dude? Stay awhile and get to know me better?"

Fang barked, and they all laughed, and hugged, and Gemma cried a little, happy tears.

She'd never felt a part of things, not really. But now…

She leaned against Isaac's chest, and he put a strong arm around her.

This, her heart said, and it came to her: this was what

home felt like. This place and these people, and most of all, this man.

Finally, after a lifetime of longing for it, she was home.

* * * * *

*Read on for a sneak peek at the next book
in Lee Tobin McClain's The Off Season series,
coming this Christmas!*

CHAPTER ONE

KAYLA HARRIS CARRIED a bag full of snowflake decorations to the window of her preschool classroom. She started putting them up in a random pattern, humming along to the premature Christmas music playing quietly.

Yes, it was Sunday afternoon, and yes, she was a loser for spending it at work, but she loved her job and wanted the classroom to be ready when the kids returned from Thanksgiving break tomorrow.

Outside the window she was decorating, November wind tossed the pine branches and jangled the swings on the Coastal Kids Academy's playground.

Then, another kind of movement from the playground caught her eye.

A man in a long army coat, bareheaded, ran after a little boy. When she pushed open the window to see better, she heard the child screaming.

Heart pounding, she rushed downstairs and out the door of the school.

The little boy now huddled at the top of the sliding board, crying. The man stood between the slide and a climbing structure, forking his fingers through disheveled hair, not speaking to the child or making any effort to comfort him. This couldn't be the child's father. Something was wrong.

She ran toward the slide. "Hi, honey," she said to the child, keeping her voice low and calm. "What's the matter?"

"Leave him alone," the man barked out. His ragged jeans

and wildly flapping coat made him look disreputable, maybe homeless.

She ignored him, climbed halfway up the ladder, and touched the child's shaking shoulder. "Hi, sweetheart."

The little boy jerked away and slid down the slide. The man caught him at the bottom, and the boy struggled, crying, his little fists pounding, legs kicking.

Kayla pulled out her phone to report the possible child abduction, eyes on the pair, poised to interfere if the man tried to run with the child.

One of the kicks landed in a particularly vulnerable spot, and the man winced and adjusted the child to cradle him as if he were a baby. "Okay, okay," he murmured in a deep-but-gentle voice, nothing like the sharp tone in which he'd addressed Kayla. He sat down on the end of the slide and pulled the child close, rocking a little.

The little boy stopped struggling and lay his head against the man's broad chest. Apparently, he'd gained the child's trust at least to some degree.

For the first time, Kayla wondered if she'd misread the situation. Was this just a scruffy dad? Was she maybe just being her usual awkward self with men?

He looked up at her then, speculation in his eyes.

Her face heated, but she straightened her shoulders and lifted her chin. She was an education professional trying to help a child. "This is a private school, sir," she said. "What are you doing here?"

He didn't answer, maybe because the little boy had startled at her voice and was crying again.

"Is he your son?"

Again, no answer as he stroked the child's hair and whispered something into his ear.

"All right, I guess it's time for the police to straighten this out." She searched for the number, her fingers numb with the cold. It didn't seem, now, like this merited a 911 call, but she'd leave that for the police to decide.

"WAIT. DON'T CALL THE POLICE." Tony DeNunzio struggled to his feet, the weight of his tense nephew making him awkward. "Everything's okay. I'm his guardian." He didn't owe this woman an explanation and it irritated him to have to give one, but he didn't want Jax to get even more upset. The child hated cops, and with good reason.

"You're his guardian?" The blonde, petite as she was, made him feel small as her eyes skimmed him up and down.

He glanced at his clothes and winced. Lifted a hand to his bristly chin and winced again.

He hadn't shaved since they'd arrived in town two days ago, and he'd grabbed these clothes from the hamper. Not only because he was busy trying to get Jax settled, but because he couldn't bring himself to care about laundry and shaving and most of the other tasks under the general heading of personal hygiene. A shower a day, and a bath for Jax, that was about all he could manage. His brother and sister— his *surviving* sister—had scolded him about it, back home.

He couldn't explain all of that, didn't need to. It wasn't this shivering stranger's business. "Jax is going to enroll here," he said.

"Really?" Another wave of shivers hit her, making her teeth chatter. Tony didn't know where she'd come from, but apparently her mission of mercy had compelled her to run outside without her coat.

He'd offer her his, but he had a feeling she'd turn up her nose.

"The school is closed today."

Thank you, Miss Obvious. But he guessed their presence merited a little more explanation. "I'm trying to get him used to the place before he starts school tomorrow. He has trouble with…" He glanced down at Jax, who'd leaned his head against Tony's chest, and a surge of love and frustration rose in him. "He has trouble with basically everything."

The woman frowned disapprovingly and put a finger to her lips. That was annoying. Who was she, the parenting police?

"Do *you* have a reason to be here?" he asked, hearing the truculence in his own voice and not caring.

She narrowed her eyes at him. "I work nearby," she said. "Saw you here and got concerned, because the little guy seemed to be upset. He still seems to be."

No denying that. Jax had tensed up as soon as they'd approached the preschool playground, probably because it was similar to places where he'd had other bad experiences. He rubbed circles on Jax's back. "He's been kicked out of preschool and daycare before," he explained. "This is kind of my last resort."

"You know he can hear you, right?"

He raised an eyebrow. Was she really going to go there, telling him how to raise his nephew?

Of course, probably almost anyone in the world would be better at it than he was.

"Did you let the school know the particulars of his situation?" She sat down on the end of the slide, her face concerned.

Uh-oh. She was one of those women who had nothing else to do but criticize how others handled their lives. She *was* cute, though. And it wasn't as if *he* had much else to do, either. He'd completed all the Victory Cottage paperwork, and he couldn't start dealing with the program's other requirements until the business week started tomorrow.

Jax moved restlessly and looked up at him.

Tony gestured toward the play structure. "Go ahead and climb. We'll go back to the cottage before long." He didn't know much about being a parent, but one thing he'd learned in the past three months was that tiring a kid out with outdoor play was a good idea.

Jax nodded and ran over to the playset. His tongue sticking out of one corner of his mouth, forehead wrinkled, he started to climb.

Tony watched him, marveling at how quickly his moods changed. Jax's counselor said all kids were like that, although Jax was a little more extreme than most.

He looked back at the woman, who was watching him expectantly.

"What did you ask me?" Sometimes he worried about himself. It was hard to keep track of conversations, not that he had all that many of them lately. None, since they'd arrived in Pleasant Shores two days ago.

"I asked if you let the school know about his issues," she said. "It might help them help him, if they know what they're working with."

"I didn't tell them about the other schools," he said. "I didn't want to jinx this place, make them think he's a bad kid, right from the get-go. He's not."

"I'm sure he isn't," she said. "He's a real cutie. But still, you should be up front with his teachers and the principal and such."

He started to tell her to mind her own business, but he was just too tired for a fight. "You're probably right." It was another area where he was failing Jax, he guessed. But he was doing the best he could. It wasn't as if he'd had experience with any other kids than Jax. Even overseas, when the other soldiers had given out candy and made friends, he'd tended to terrify the little ones.

"Telling the school the whole story will only help him," she said, still studying Jax, her forehead creased.

He frowned at her. "Why would you care?"

"The truth is," she said, "I'm going to be his teacher."

He felt his shoulders slump, wondering if he'd just ruined his nephew's chances at this last-resort school.

*Don't miss the next book in The Off Season series
by Lee Tobin McClain!*

ACKNOWLEDGMENTS

I've had so much help in creating *Home to the Harbor*. My agent Karen Solem, and everyone at Spencerhill Associates, provides wonderful support and cheerleading. Shana Asaro, Susan Swinwood and the fabulous art department and sales team: your hard work is so very much appreciated. Thank you!

I'm grateful to the staff of the Chesapeake Bay Maritime Museum and to Earl Swift, author of *Chesapeake Requiem*, for much of the information about boating, crabbing and oystering that appears in *Home to the Harbor*; they're the reason for what I got right, but are in no way responsible for any mistakes. The patrons, waitstaff and cooks at Old Salty's restaurant in Fishing Creek served up way too much delicious local food; if my descriptions make readers hungry, they are to blame!

When the creative life gets challenging, writer friends make all the difference. The Wednesday Morning Writers' Group, my Seton Hill colleagues and students, Sandy, Dana and Rachel: you continue to inspire me.

I couldn't write my books without the love and companionship of my closest people: Sue, Ron, Jessie, Bill and most of all, Grace. I love you all so much.

Finally, I want to thank my readers for buying and reading my books and for your kind notes, emails and reviews. I don't take any of that for granted, and it's to you that this book is dedicated.

*When a young woman is visited by a man from her past,
will her whole life change forever?*

Read on for a sneak preview of
Her Small Town Secret *by Brenda Minton*

"There's an incredibly gorgeous cowboy waiting for you in the front lobby. He might be all hat and no cattle, but I'd take him if I wasn't happily engaged," Avery Hammons's assistant, Laura, said, winking.

"Gorgeous cowboy type?" Avery asked after settling her patient's arm back on the bed.

"Avery Hammons, please come to the front desk. Avery, please come to the front desk," a male voice, not one of their staff, called over the intercom.

"Who was that?" Avery asked, leaving her patient's room, Laura hot on her heels.

"My guess is that would be our man, Mr. All Hat. Can we keep him? Please tell me we can keep him," Laura practically gushed.

Avery hurried down the hall of the long-term care facility where she worked, turning a corner and then stopping so quickly that Laura nearly ran into her. "Oh no!"

The cowboy leaned against the counter, the intercom phone in his hand. One corner of his mouth hitched up as he nudged his hat back a smidge. "Honey, I'm home."

No, no, no. Avery stood there in the center of the hall, caught in a nightmare in which Grayson Stone was the star. He was the one person who could—and would—shake up her life and ruin everything. It was what he'd always done. What he did best. He knew how to make her feel beautiful and worthless, all at the same time.

She shook her head, wanting, needing, to wake up and have him gone. She closed her eyes, said a quick prayer and opened her eyes slowly.

"I'm still here," he drawled with a slight chuckle as he set the phone on the desk.

Yes, he was still there. All six feet, lean athletic build of him. He grinned, as if this was all a big joke and he wasn't pushing her life off its foundation. Life had always been a joke to Grayson. The spoiled son of a judge and a pediatrician, he'd always been given everything he ever wanted or needed.

She'd been serious, studious, determined to change her future. She had wanted to prove that a kid from Dillon's Trailer Park could become something, someone.

Grayson was her kryptonite.

Don't miss
Her Small Town Secret *by Brenda Minton,*
available June 2021 wherever
Love Inspired books and ebooks are sold.

LoveInspired.com